THE RAGGEDY MAN

THE RAGGEDY MAN

THE RAGGEDY MAN

LILLIAN O'DONNELL

All rights reserved. This book, or parts thereof,
may not be reproduced in any form without permission.
Published simultaneously in Canada.

ISBN 0-399-

Printed in the United States of America

G. P. PUTNAM'S SONS
NEW YORK

G. P. PUTNAM'S SONS
Publishers Since 1838
200 Madison Avenue
New York, NY 10016

ISBN 0-399-14019-0

Printed in the United States of America

BOOK DESIGN BY BRIAN MULLIGAN

THE RAGGEDY MAN

THE RAGGEDY MAN

PROLOGUE

Detective Third Grade Jayne Harrow sat alone in the dusty, battered '89 Chevy parked in the turnaround at the foot of Remsen Street off the Brooklyn Heights Promenade. Despite its proximity to the water, the air was heavy, the atmosphere oppressive. The daytime high had been an unseasonable ninety degrees and evening had brought little relief. The heat made Jayne Harrow sweat and nerves made her shiver.

Since being assigned to Narcotics Division five months ago, for which she was much envied by the members of her graduating class, Detective Harrow had been riding with Sergeant Brian Ford. Ford had eleven years on the force, the last four working Narco. At this point their routine was well established: First came the tip from one of Ford's seemingly inexhaustible supply of snitches; the surveillance followed. Its duration depended on how long it took to verify the snitch's information and to establish a pattern for the movements of the suspect. Then came the raid and the bust along with the confiscation of evidence—the drugs. Ford was usually the one who went in and Harrow was backup. Occasionally, if only a small buy was planned or Ford didn't want to blow his cover, Jayne went in and Ford was backup.

Jayne had been chosen from a class of three hundred cadets at the Police Academy for training in undercover work. She had been taught to play the part of an addict, to simulate the frantic need, the mental and physical symptoms of drug dependency. She had a talent for it, and the danger was a challenge that exhilarated her. In the early months of her training, she played a major role in a couple of important busts and justified the confidence of her teachers.

Unfortunately, success and experience didn't build her confidence. Instead, it showed her how many things could go wrong. Instead of welcoming the challenge of undercover work, Jayne found herself shrinking from it. There were times when she could feel the cold breath of danger like a wind on her back, but she didn't dare turn or so much as risk a sideways glance. Either movement would have been a dead giveaway—"dead" being the operative word. She discovered that a couple of shots of vodka before going on duty would get her through her shift, and after a while, she came to rely on that extra boost. So along with the service revolver and makeup kit she carried in her big leather shoulder bag, Detective Harrow carried a couple of shot bottles of the clear, odorless liquid. She never drank in her partner's presence, but he knew what she was doing, just as she knew what he was up to. It was a standoff, but it couldn't last forever.

In the meantime, Jayne remained passive and followed Ford's orders. *If only it wasn't so damn hot!* she thought, sitting in the car waiting for Ford to return. A feeble breeze struggled up from the harbor but failed to cool her. Her bra was soaked, and sweat ran down between her legs, making dark patches on her slacks.

Jayne was twenty-four. Her face was narrow, her skin ivory in tone and without flaw, its smooth perfection accentuated by a cascade of dark curls. Her eyes were a deep, velvety brown. She was statuesque and strong, with good reflexes.

She glanced at her watch. It was just after midnight. Nothing would happen for a while. Brian always made sure to get well into overtime, despite a directive from the police commissioner which had come down hard on overtime. Uniforms, plainclothes cops, and precinct detectives had adjusted immediately, but the special squads—of which Narcotics considered itself the most elite—made it a matter of pride not to conform. As long as their arrest records and quantity of drugs confiscated supported them, they were able to get away with it. Another privilege was unrestricted jurisdiction which spread across the city. Brian Ford took advantage of that, too. By moving around the boroughs, he never became a familiar face anywhere. Jayne seldom questioned him. Tonight was one of those rare exceptions.

They were too near the Promenade, she'd pointed out. It was a hot night; the heat would drive people out of their homes to find relief. During the current heat wave four people had already been shot while sleeping on beaches and in parks.

Not here, Ford had countered. This was an affluent, upscale area. They had air conditioners here.

It appeared he was right, Jayne thought. The narrow streets were empty. There was no one on the Promenade. The windows overlooking it were closed. She reached into her bag for the vodka bottle, unscrewed the cap, and gulped greedily. She savored the liquid as it coursed through her, carrying away tension and anxiety. She relaxed, at least temporarily.

A shot broke the silence.

She stiffened and looked around, searching for the source of the sound.

She waited for a repeat, but there was none. She drew her own gun, ready to leave the car if the need arose. For several moments, she strained to hear. Nothing. Then there was a clatter like a metal trash can being knocked over and rolling on cobblestones.

A few moments after that Brian Ford came running down Remsen. He pulled open the passenger door and got in beside Jayne.

"Move it."

"What happened?"

"Nothing." He was gasping.

"I thought you were going to meet—"

Ford interrupted. "He didn't show."

"I thought he was supposed to let us know when—"

"He didn't show," Ford repeated.

"I heard a shot."

"It was a damned backfire. That's what you heard. Move it, will you? Let's get out of here. Now."

She took the Brooklyn Battery Tunnel back to Manhattan and drove directly to her own apartment on Spring Street. She got out and Ford moved into her seat.

"Good night," she said, and started up the front steps of the brownstone. By rights she should have gone back to the squad with Ford, but on their very first night Ford had absolved her of what he deemed a formality. It had been a long and eventful first tour during which she'd made an undercover buy while he observed from a distance.

"You did good," he'd said, giving her one of his most charming smiles. "I'll take care of it from here." That meant he'd see the suspect through the routine of booking and arraignment, a tedious and time-consuming process. "There's no need for you to come back to the squad."

Did that also mean he'd take credit for the bust? She didn't like to ask. "How about the report?" she asked instead.

He'd write it, he told her, and she could add her signature when she came in for the four o'clock tour.

She'd hesitated, but it was late and she was tired and so she accepted. She took it to be a onetime suspension of procedure. It turned out to be an introduction to many privileges Ford told her she was entitled to as a member of the elite force. And it was the beginning of a subtle seduction of her ethical standards.

She didn't realize what Ford was up to that first night on duty. He was young, tall, with craggy features and mild blue eyes. He had a reputation as a ladies' man, but he didn't then or ever make a play for Jayne. He let her know he thought she was attractive, but he never put any moves on her. She was on guard for that, but not for the many petty infractions of procedure that he introduced her to as a matter of course. That afternoon she arrived for work early so that she could study the report he had written regarding last night's tour and the arrest. It was waiting on her desk, accurate and concise, a model of its kind. The line that Ford had left open for her signature correctly identified her as the arresting officer. She signed and waited.

Four o'clock and the shifts changed. Ford didn't come in. Half an hour passed. Where was he? There was no formal roll call and no one seemed to notice Ford was missing. She certainly wasn't going to call attention to his absence by asking if he was on another assignment. But she was very nervous. She kept casting anxious glances toward the lieutenant's office. Suppose he came out and asked for Ford? What could she say?

Then suddenly he was there, striding toward his desk—well rested, breezy, pleased with himself and with the world. When he saw Jayne, he stopped abruptly.

"Oh damn! I forgot to tell you, didn't I?"

"Tell me what?"

"That you didn't need to come in till six-thirty. We've got a meet at Il Paradiso, a Queens social club, at seven. I'm sorry. Tell you what—we'll make it an early night. We'll use this as an opportunity to introduce you around and acquaint you with the players. We'll have a cup of coffee, take a couple of turns around the dance floor, and knock off early."

Despite her protests, he had her home by eleven.

The report she found on her desk the next morning awaiting her signature indicated they'd worked the full tour—four to midnight. Jayne timidly pointed out the discrepancy.

"Damn!" he'd said. "That means I have to type the whole thing over."

"I'll do it."

"Why should you? It's my mistake. Frankly, I don't see that it matters. I mean, nothing happened last night. Right?"

"I guess not."

"What do you mean you *guess* not?"

"Nothing happened."

"So sign."

After a while, Jayne stopped questioning the varying oversights and errors. After a while, she even stopped reading the reports she signed. She didn't check the hours, the money paid out to the snitches, the drugs confiscated. She no longer protested being dropped off at home while her partner went off to do what and where she could only guess.

But tonight as Jayne started up the steps of the brownstone, Brian called after her.

"Jayne?"

She stopped and turned. "What?"

"Nothing happened tonight. What you heard was a backfire."

It wasn't like him to offer an explanation.

"All right," she said, and put the key in the lock and let herself in.

From inside, she watched Ford drive away, then started climbing the four flights to her apartment. As she climbed, she rationalized what had happened that night. She hadn't actually *seen* anything, she told herself. Maybe what she thought was a shot had in fact been a backfire. If it was a shot, what proof did she have that Brian had fired it? She was basing her assumption on Ford's uncharacteristic agitation and on her own desire to get something on him.

As soon as she got inside her apartment, Jayne poured herself a stiff drink, knocked it off in one long swallow, and fell on the bed without even taking off her clothes. She didn't pass out. A montage of nightmare memories engulfed her. Everything was based on the early discovery that Brian Ford, her partner, was corrupt. He was not turning in all the drugs he confiscated. He kept some back and sold them sometimes to other dealers or direct to the consumer. When she'd charged him with it, he offered to cut her in, but she turned him down and in righteous indignation went directly to the lieutenant. That was two months ago, yet she remembered every word of that interview.

Lieutenant Alfonso Palma was dark and heavyset. His eyebrows were thick, with an upward slant. He had taken command of the squad shortly after the Knapp Commission investigation, and during his tenure there had not been a whisper of scandal—and given the opportunities for cheating, this was no mean achievement. He was proud of his record, and he questioned Jayne closely. In fact, he made her feel as though she was the one under investigation, as though she was trying to make trouble for her partner.

Palma glared darkly. "Sergeant Ford is a fine officer. He is experienced. He has eleven years on the force and four years on this squad. How long since you graduated from the Academy, Detective?"

"I graduated last October."

"And how long have you been with us?"

She flushed. "Three months."

"Well . . ." He raised his hands and let them drop. "You

should be glad to have someone like Brian Ford for your partner. It's an opportunity for you to learn. If you feel you're not up to the work . . ."

"I am up to it," she put in quickly, sharply.

He looked from her to the file in front of him. "You have a fine report from the Academy, but we're not playacting here. You've got to accept the realities of the street."

"I do. What I don't accept—"

"Can you attest to the precise amount of drugs Sergeant Ford confiscated on each and every arrest and can you attest to the amount he turned in on each and every occasion? Can you cite the date of each incident?"

"I saw what he took from the various pushers. I didn't count the bags, but I could tell he didn't turn in even half."

"In each instance, you make a rough estimate. Is that it?"

"Yes sir."

"A rough estimate of what he took in and what he held back for himself?"

"Yes." He had forced her to admit she couldn't document the charge. She tried something else. "He asked me to sign a false work report."

"And you did sign it," Palma reminded her. "You signed several such reports and you were paid for the overtime same as he. And you took the money."

"I went along till I could make up my mind what to do."

"Which was—to turn in your partner." Alfonso Palma scowled. "If you're not happy riding with Ford, maybe a transfer is in order. Of course, you won't get this kind of duty, maybe something in Traffic or at the precinct level. There's always an opening in Greenpoint. It's your decision, Detective."

"I don't want a transfer."

"Then don't rock the boat. Learn to be a team player."

"Yes sir." She stood up.

"Meantime, I'll have a talk with Sergeant Ford. I'll suggest he be a little more open with you. Explain things."

And Jayne waited for the results of that discussion.

Now, lying on her bed, Jayne Harrow again experienced the frustration and the anxiety the lieutenant's attitude had caused. She saw no indication in Ford's manner that Palma had in fact talked to him about the problem. She had turned him in on a very serious charge, yet Ford said nothing. Was it possible the lieutenant hadn't spoken to Ford? Maybe he'd decided Jayne's accusation had merit after all, and he was keeping an eye on Ford himself. If that was it, then he naturally wouldn't want to let Ford know he was being watched. But the time passed and nothing changed and she couldn't go on like that anymore. The tension was too much. Tonight's incident was too much. She had to know what had happened tonight between Brian Ford and the man he had gone to meet.

As she got off the bed, the room rocked. Jayne reached for the bureau to steady herself. She had to hold on to various objects on her way to the kitchen, where she put on coffee. As soon as it was ready she gulped it down, black and scalding hot. Next, she rummaged through the appliance drawer and collected a heavy-duty flashlight, an assortment of evidence envelopes, and rubber gloves, and went looking for her camera, which she found in the desk drawer. She checked to see that there was film in it and that the flash was in working order.

Jayne Harrow didn't own a car. It was too expensive to buy and to maintain. She managed very well with public transportation. The subway would get her back to where she'd parked earlier while Ford went to his meet, and do it in less time than by car. She got off at the first stop on the other side of the Brooklyn Bridge and walked along the quiet, residential streets to the Brooklyn

Heights Promenade. She took her time, peering into the neatly kept front and back yards while always heading toward the water.

Ford had a tendency to set his meets in open, public places and at a time when they were most likely to be busy. Jayne assumed that night's meeting had been somewhere along the Promenade. Ford dealt primarily with small-timers: snitches who betrayed friends, pushers who sold to children. With them he had courage. She had never seen Brian as agitated as he had been that night. More than agitated, he had been frightened.

Reaching the parking area at the foot of Remsen, Jayne set out in the direction her partner had taken. It was all so open to view from every side, she thought. The windows of the adjoining buildings were like box seats overlooking a stage. He would have wanted some cover, she reasoned. Somewhere along this path there must be a place where he could have conducted his business in private. Then she saw the trash can lying on its side, part of its contents spilled. That had to be the one she heard rolling on the pavement right after the shot and before Brian Ford returned to the car. He must have knocked it over in flight. But in flight from what?

A cool breeze was now coming off the water, but it brought Jayne no relief. From where she stood, the financial towers clustered at the tip of Manhattan were silhouetted in the moonlight, the choppy waters tipped with molten silver. The tranquil scene imparted no serenity. She checked her watch: 2:07 A.M. She took the gun out of her handbag and proceeded toward the trash can, which had come to rest amid the swings and slides of a playground. The playground also provided a comfort station of solid brick construction. The men's room was at the front facing the water; the women's room was at the back. Sheltering each entrance was a six-foot-high wall. The stench of urine was unmistakable. A thin, high-pitched squealing told Jayne she was not alone. A pair of tiny eyes glittered in the darkness. A rat. She froze in place.

Gradually, she became aware of more excited squeals coming from the men's room. A shot would scatter the rats but it would also wake the neighborhood. Maybe if she turned her flashlight on them? But the rats were about to taste flesh and could not be so easily distracted. Suppose she kicked the trash can at the same time as she shone the light into their eyes: would the combination of light and noise clear them out?

It worked, to a point. They scattered, but did not flee. Silently, they took up new positions and watched. Jayne forced herself to advance and approach the focus of their attention, which appeared to be no more than a heap of rags, an assortment of tattered garments. It turned out to be a person lying on his side, knees partially drawn up, arms crossed over his chest. His back was to Jayne.

"Hello?" she called out tentatively. "Hello?"

No response. No movement.

The bleeping of a car alarm made her heart jump but dispersed the rats. Thank God. Weak and shaking, she stuck the gun into the waistband of her slacks, and getting down on one knee, focused the flashlight while she placed the tips of her fingers just below the man's jaw to feel for a pulse. There was none. He was dead. She couldn't guess for how long. He was still warm; the cooling breeze hadn't reached in there yet.

Jayne looked at the man by the glow of her flashlight. He was young, early twenties, she thought. His face was narrow, unshaven, dirty. It was also swollen and bloodied. His hair was dark, stringy, shoulder-length.

She sat back on her heels and played the light over the rest of him.

He lay in a welter of blood. His size and weight were camouflaged by the assortment of rags in which he had wrapped himself. Nothing was identifiable as a conventional garment— trousers, shirt, or jacket. He wore a kind of tunic which was nothing more than a length of gauzy fabric with a hole cut in the middle through which he put his head, and secured at the waist with a length of rope. His legs were bare and his feet were covered by a pair of cheap-looking sandals. A multicolored scarf was wound around his head like a turban.

Careful not to change his basic position, Jayne uncrossed his arms, which were also bare, and thus discovered that the principal source of the blood was a long, uneven gash across his chest. He had been stabbed many times, but the first and most severe blow must have brought him to his knees, thus exposing his back to further attack. Nowhere did she see any indication that he had been shot. Gently, she refolded his arms. What she had heard must have been a backfire after all.

Next, she needed ID. Given what he was wearing, where would he keep a wallet? With considerable distaste, she patted him down. Nothing. If he'd ever carried any valuables, somebody had removed them. Had he been killed for money? Nowadays, the most unlikely persons carried vast sums.

Jayne got up and looked around the scene. Her light rested on a pile of cigarette butts in a far corner, some only partially smoked before being snubbed out. Marlboros. Using a small pincer, Jayne picked up three and placed them in one of the evidence envelopes she had brought with her. She examined the victim's hands and teeth but found no nicotine stains. The victim wasn't a smoker, but Brian Ford was and Marlboro was his brand. Had he been absent from the car long enough to have smoked that much?

She took pictures of the scene and of the victim, shooting from several angles. Before leaving, she made sure she had left no traces of her presence. She returned the way she had come, stopping at the first telephone to dial 911. She reported the homicide, but did not identify herself.

She hoped an RMP would get there before the rats could make significant headway.

Jayne woke with a pounding headache and a foul taste in her mouth.

Her first move was to turn on the radio, but she heard nothing about a body being found near the Brooklyn Heights Promenade. Violent death had become so commonplace, she thought, there was no guarantee it would be mentioned in the news. You had to be either famous or notorious or utterly innocent—in the wrong place at the wrong time—to be noticed, must less pitied.

She was scheduled for the four o'clock tour as usual, but she had no intention of waiting. God only knew what the situation would be by then. The body might have disappeared. She was shocked that the possibility should even occur to her, but once it did, she couldn't dismiss it. Surely Brian hadn't sunk to that?

She took a quick shower and dressed. On the way to the coffee shop where she usually breakfasted, she picked up the latest papers. She found what she was looking for deep in the Metro Section of the *Times.*

SMALL-TIME DRUG DEALER STABBED TO DEATH

On the morning of June 10, in response to an anonymous call to 911, the body of a man was found in the children's playground at the foot of Columbia Heights and Pierrepont Street off the Brooklyn Heights Promenade. He appeared to be in his mid-twenties and carried no formal identification. He was dressed in an assortment of garments, and a strip of varicolored gauze was wound around his head like a turban. Because of this, he was known to the children of the neighborhood as the Raggedy Man.

It had been late March when Jayne went to Lieutenant Palma to report her suspicions of her partner. Palma's response had stunned her and, as he had pointed out, it was only a taste of how the detectives in the squad would react if she persisted with her charges. So, she had rationalized: Ford was stealing drugs from drug dealers who deserved what they got and more. But deep down she knew that didn't excuse him. Nevertheless, she said no more. But murder was something else. What she had seen that morning was too much for her conscience to bear. She cut the *Times* piece out, folded it, and, using the machine at the local stationer, made a couple of copies.

She had no intention of appealing to Palma again. Going over his head was not wise either, but she had no choice. She called Captain Landau's office and made an appointment. On the way, she stopped at a local bar to fortify herself.

Captain Norman Landau worked in the corridors of power, but did not himself wield power. In his late fifties, silver-haired, tanned and robust, he had shaped himself in the image he intended to present when he finally did reach those upper echelons, and reach them he would. His suits were custom-made. He was active in various police benevolent associations and foundations to aid police widows and children. Crystal, his wife of twenty-four years, had recently come into a substantial inheritance and was using it to buy her way into social and artistic circles. Norman Landau was too shrewd not to listen to what Detective Harrow had to say and listen sympathetically, even to encourage her.

So Jayne recounted the raids, arrests, and drug confiscations to which she'd been a party since joining the squad. She confided her suspicions regarding discrepancies between the amount of drugs seized and the amount turned in.

Landau frowned. "You should have reported your concerns to Lieutenant Palma."

"I did back in March. He said I had no evidence."

"Did you have evidence?"

"I thought that what I saw . . . my word . . . would be enough."

Norman Landau sighed. "We've had complaints from dealers that they're getting ripped off and, to be honest with you, Detective Harrow, we don't take them too seriously. What can you expect from that scum? Charging police corruption is a good out for them. But when one of our own comes forward and accuses another officer, we must take it seriously. Unfortunately, without evidence it comes down to your word against his."

"And he's been around longer than I have."

"I'm afraid that's a large part of it. Now, if you'd worn a wire . . ." He stopped, looking her over. "Did Lieutenant Palma suggest you wear a wire?"

"No."

"Would you be willing to?"

She paled. "I don't know. Wouldn't that be entrapment?"

"Not at all."

"I just don't know."

Landau's nod indicated he sympathized. "Of course. I understand. And it would be dangerous."

"It's not that so much. It seems underhanded."

"If your partner and others with him are stealing from dealers and then themselves selling the drugs they stole, they're no longer officers of the law, they're criminals themselves. We don't need to be squeamish about the means we use to apprehend them. But if we do make the charge, we have to be damn sure it's going to stick. I point that out for your sake, Detective Harrow." His eyes fixed on hers and held.

Was it a warning, or a threat? suddenly, Jayne wasn't sure. She blinked and looked away.

"Well, you think about it," Landau said. "While you're doing that, I'll see what I can find out. Maybe I'll talk to Al Palma, without mentioning you, of course." He got up and extended his hand.

Captain Landau was giving her the brush-off just as Palma had, Jayne thought. The words and manners were different, but the result was the same. She hesitated. She hadn't even broached the real reason she'd requested the interview. She hadn't told Landau about last night, about the death of the Raggedy Man. That would be accusing her partner of murder. How would the captain have responded to that? Maybe she should be satisfied that Landau believed her about the drugs and the false work reports, and wait to see where the investigation instigated by her call to 911 would lead.

She got up and reached for the captain's hand, but he had already withdrawn it. In missing it, she lost her balance. As she flung out an arm to keep from falling, the shoulder strap of her bag slid off her arm and its contents spilled to the floor. She tried to collect the bottles and stuff them back inside before he could see them, but it was too late.

"If I were you, I'd take it easy on the booze, Detective Harrow. It won't help your credibility," Landau said.

She stood before him flooded with shame. She didn't know what to say. She wanted to deny the drinking, but it was futile with the evidence there in the bottles. There was nothing to do but leave. Her main concern was to walk steadily and get out with her head high.

In the lobby, she got an envelope from the receptionist, placed a copy of the *Times* piece on the murder inside, and addressed it to Landau. Then she left.

She headed for the nearest bar. She needed a drink to get her home. Just one, she told herself. When she reached her apartment at last, she remembered to call in sick before passing out.

CHAPTER 1

Just fifty-three miles from Mexico City lies lush, semitropical Cuernavaca. Situated in the state of Morelos, Cuernavaca is the weekend retreat for wealthy *chilangos* and foreigners. Their hillside mansions are the principal tourist attraction, but nobody gets in to see them unless invited.

Downtown Cuernavaca is compact. There are several permanent exhibits to attract the tourist—the Borda Gardens, the murals of Diego Rivera, the Palace of Cortes. At midafternoon, both the rich on their estates and the merchants and keepers of the city's historical and artistic exhibits lock their doors and rest.

Gwenn Ramadge, vacationing in her parents' house, was too active to consider a nap in the middle of the afternoon anything but a waste of time. But in this "city of flowers" everything was geared to the siesta. Business resumed at four or five in the afternoon. No one, rich or poor, sat down to dinner until nine-thirty or ten. Visitors had no choice but to adapt.

Wearing only panties, Gwenn Ramadge lay on top of the massive four-poster in the darkened guest bedroom of her parents' home while the ceiling fan whirred soothingly overhead. She looked back at the past three weeks of her stay and admitted that she liked the casual, unstructured life they led. It was completely opposite her life in New York, where every hour of her time was scheduled.

Bad investments had caused Oscar and Paula Ramadge to give up a seven-room apartment on Fifth Avenue across the street from the Metropolitan Museum, sell off their valuable furnishings, including a collection of antique silver and Oriental rugs, and move to Cuernavaca. Here they found that their dollars stretched to cover more than just basic comforts. The Ramadges rented a villa, complete with swimming pool and tennis court, that offered a panoramic view of the mountains. There was a live-in couple to cook and clean. Her parents led a wonderful life, and they urged her to share it.

Gwenn was thirty-two. A bouncy, exuberant five foot one, her energy made her seem younger. She wore her blond hair in a mop of curls that were streaked to silver by the sun. Her skin was fair and tended to burn instead of tan, so that for most of the summer she was bright red. It didn't keep her away from the beach or from the sports she loved, though now that she was running her own business there wasn't much time for either. She'd almost forgotten how much they meant to her.

In New York, the heat so welcome in early June had developed into a suffocatingly hot summer. By August, even Gwenn had had enough. She had no cases outstanding. Her last, the Trent murder, was closed. She had been instrumental in finding the killer, but worried that the evidence wouldn't be sufficient to convict. At the time, she was dating Lew Sackler, a detective on the case. She had done good work, he assured her, but she was not responsible for the conduct of the prosecution. He had told her to forget about it. Their relationship was at the point of becoming serious when Lew's father in Florida had a heart attack and Sackler relocated to be with him.

Gwenn was lonely. Her parents called routinely every week. After a casual chat they finished with the usual invitation to come and enjoy the "year-round springtime." To the surprise of both parties, Gwenn agreed at last.

Neither Oscar nor Paula Ramadge could believe that their daughter—an authentic New Yorker who'd attended the prestigious Cummings School for Girls on Madison Avenue and graduated from Barnard, who used Central Park as her playground and had the riches of museums, concert halls, and theaters spread out before her, who was accomplished in tennis, skiing, and horseback riding, who'd shared her coming-out party with a governor's daughter—could now be satisfied with running *a detective agency,* for God's sake!

How could she tolerate the company of criminals and police? Oscar and Paula asked each other. They were, after all, two sides of the same coin. The Ramadges blamed themselves for leaving Gwenn behind in New York when they moved here. It was their fault she had gotten herself into such an unsuitable milieu. So now this was their opportunity to make it right, to get her back into the style she had been raised to enjoy. It wouldn't be easy. Gwenn was a sweet child, but once she made up her mind about something, she could be very stubborn, a trait that each parent attributed to the other.

Paula Ramadge was a mature brunette version of her daughter—petite, energetic, and enthusiastic. During the auction of her most treasured possessions, she had kept her head high and not let anyone see her cry. When her society friends participated in the spirited bidding, she had been humiliated but steeled herself to hide how much it hurt.

Oscar Ramadge was a robust, outgoing man, who enjoyed the bounties he had earned. Upon declaring bankruptcy, he had turned gray almost overnight. He became uncertain where before he had charged ahead. His confident stride changed into an old man's shuffle. but when he saw how staunchly his wife and daughter stood at his side, his attitude changed. He realized that indeed he had lost material things, but these with hard work and some luck could be replaced. He adjusted his sights.

Now husband and wife discussed their daughter's situation. It couldn't be the work that was pulling Gwenn back to New York so compellingly. *Detective work, for God's sake!* It had to be a man.

Despite Gwenn's protests, they had picked up clues. There had been a past relationship that had not ended well. There was also a current somebody. When Gwenn first arrived, he'd called regularly. He'd given his name: Ray Dixon.

"He's a detective," Gwenn had told them. They'd worked on a case together. The Trent case.

Her parents had never heard of it.

"Invite him down, darling, why don't you?" Paula Ramadge chirped with enthusiasm. "We'd like to meet your young man."

"He's not my young man."

"He wants to be."

Her mother was right. Sometimes her instincts amazed Gwenn.

At the time Gwenn met Ray, she had been dating Lew Sackler, and Ray had been his partner. When Lew quit the force to be with his ailing father in Miami, Dixon had indicated he wanted to step into Lew's place. Gwenn liked him immediately. She was flattered, but she felt rushed. Ray was a one-woman man who had married his childhood sweetheart, but the marriage had failed. Without being aware that he was doing it, he had cast Gwenn as Patty's replacement. Sensing Ray's intentions, Gwenn kept him at arm's length. She had had one serious relationship that had gone bad, and she wasn't yet ready to try again.

That man's name was also Ray, an unfortunate coincidence. She'd become pregnant, and he had walked out on her. Alone in the city, without a job or friends, and reluctant to go to her parents—though she knew they would take her into their arms with love and support—Gwenn had sought some respite at the beach.

She'd gone swimming in a rough ocean, got caught by the undertow, and was dashed against the rocks of a breakwater. She shouldn't have been swimming at all under the conditions—a major storm had been forming and was already within striking distance off the Jersey coast. She knew better. She also knew that deep in her heart there was an unacknowledged, certainly unexpressed, desire to let the sea suck her down and keep her. But she was a strong swimmer and the instinct for self-preservation took over. However, she lost the baby. That was five years ago. The regret, though buried deep, would never be eradicated. She hadn't told Ray Dixon. She supposed one day she would.

"I'm not sure Ray would like it here," Gwenn replied, and she wasn't referring to the scenery or the climate. She realized it was her mother who had led her to this conclusion.

Paula Ramadge nodded sagely. "It's important to have shared interests. Particularly as your backgrounds and upbringings are very different."

"We do have shared interests."

"You mean your detective work."

"Yes."

"You won't be doing detective work for the rest of your life, I suppose."

Gwenn frowned. "I guess not." She hadn't thought that far ahead.

"You'll be wanting to raise a family."

She certainly hadn't thought that far.

"Do you have doubts as to how Detective Dixon would fit in with your friends?" Her mother was very gentle.

"Sergeant Dixon," Gwenn corrected automatically. "And I have new friends now. Ray fits in very well with them."

"Because they are in actuality his friends. Isn't that so?"

"What's wrong with that?"

"That's something you have to ask yourself, dear."

"You're way ahead of us, Mother. We're just dating, that's all."

"Good. So you won't mind if I introduce you to some really nice young men here with whom you'll find you have a lot in common?"

"Of course I don't mind, Mother."

That was all Paula Ramadge needed. She had several candidates waiting in the wings. Quickly, they narrowed down to one: Edward Cole. By then, Ray was no longer calling regularly, and after a while, he didn't call at all.

Paula Ramadge mentioned it.

"He's probably on a case," Gwenn told her. "Sometimes it's hard to get to a phone."

"Of course, dear."

The alarm was set for five in the afternoon and Gwenn was dozing when it went off. Time to get up. She had a date for tennis. With Edward, of course.

She was glad of Edward Cole's company. He was the perfect escort and companion—blond, slim, finely chiseled features, mild hazel eyes. He seemed not to have a worry in the world, a very different attitude from Ray Dixon's.

An architect, Edward Cole was currently occupied in the construction of a complex of vacation/retirement homes with extensive sport facilities, including a championship golf course, tennis courts, an artificial lake and an Olympic-sized swimming pool. Yet he seemed to have unlimited time to spend with Gwenn. In fact, the only time they were separated was during the siesta and at night. They had a lot in common—casual, superficial things perhaps, but they did form a bond. Her mother was right. Would it hold in another time and place or was it a typical vacation romance? Once she went back to New York, and she was due to go at the end of the week, it would be over. She would not be likely to see Edward Cole again. In fact, Cole did not work from a regular base. He went where the job required. Surprising, Gwenn reflected, that the man approved by her parents had shallower roots than the one of whom they disapproved.

At the sound of the door chimes below, Gwenn jumped off the bed and quickly dressed in the tennis outfit she'd already laid out. They had a date for mixed doubles at the country club. When she got downstairs, Edward was waiting, alone.

"Jill and Henry can't make it," he told her.

"Oh, that's too bad. Well, we can play singles." Actually, Edward was too strong for her, but it was too late to pick up another game.

"I thought we might take a ride up in the hills. If you'd like."

"Yes. I'd like that."

"Good. There's a little place, a *posada*, I'd like to show you."

"Shall I change?"

"You're fine as you are." He smiled with admiration.

She smiled back. "Let's go then."

"Where in the world are we going?"

They had been driving more than half an hour. As the sun sank, the hills took on a blue haze, and with the top down, the breeze made Gwenn shiver. "Where is this place of yours?"

"We're practically there. You'll love it. There's a marvelous restaurant right nearby. They serve a great arroz con pollo."

"You didn't say anything about dinner."

"It was to be a surprise."

"I don't like surprises, Edward."

"No, spontaneity isn't your forte."

"That's right. And that being so, I think you should take me home."

"Oh, come on, Gwenn. Loosen up. Relax. It'll do you good."

"Just what is it you think will do me good?"

He swept around the next turn before answering. Then he pulled over onto a ledge that offered a postcard-perfect view of the mountains and, nestled among them, the city of silver, Taxco. He held out a couple of joints. "Join me."

"Thanks. I don't do dope."

"Oh, come on. It's only pot."

"I don't care what you call it."

He shifted in the seat so that he could face her squarely. His mild eyes narrowed to slits. For a moment, Gwenn thought he was going to slap her. Then suddenly he relaxed. "Sorry. I really like you, Gwenn. I didn't mean to offend you. Of course I'll take you home, if that's what you want."

"It's what I want," she said, but he had made her feel surly and a prude. What was wrong with having standards? she asked herself.

They didn't talk and that made the ride back seem longer than it had going out. By the time they were back at her parents' house, night had fallen.

"I won't ask you to stay for dinner," Gwenn said. "In fact, I'm going back to New York on Saturday. I probably won't see you before then, so this is goodbye." She didn't thank him. There had been good times, but tonight he'd spoiled the memories.

He didn't seem to think so. "I have business in New York from time to time. May I call you?"

It was a standard ploy that didn't commit either one to anything, but Gwenn chose to be honest.

"I'm seeing someone in New York regularly."

"Oh. I didn't realize . . . I got the impression that you'd recently broken up. I'm sorry. Your parents told me . . . You know how it is." He shrugged.

"Your sources are good, but they're not up-to-date."

"I'm embarrassed, but I'm not giving up. Could be the situation will change."

Cole's reference to Ray made Gwenn realize that she had

missed him. How often in the midst of her various activities—tennis, swimming, or maybe just sitting on the terrace at the club—had she thought of Ray? How often had she wondered just what his reaction would be if he were there? She had thought that she was getting bored with the aimlessness of her days in Cuernavaca and that she needed to get back to productive work. It wasn't the only reason. She wanted to get back to Ray.

Before she knew what was happening, Edward Cole had grabbed her by the arms and roughly pulled her to him. He placed a strong, insistent kiss on her mouth. He didn't give her a chance to pull away and thus reject him; he released her first.

"You'll be hearing from me," he said, and walked out.

She heard the door close and listened for the sound of the motor as he drove off. When he was well gone, she went up to her room to change before joining her parents on the patio. Should she call Ray? She turned to the telephone, and almost as though she'd willed it, it rang. But it wasn't Ray.

"Hi. It's me. Marge."

Her assistant, Marge Pratt. Hearing her voice brought Gwenn unexpected pleasure. "How are you?"

"I'm fine. Hot. It's still hot here."

"I'll be wearing a sweater tonight," Gwenn boasted.

"Gee! I don't suppose you're in any hurry to come back."

"Well, as a matter of fact . . ."

"A couple of new clients walked in this morning." Marge Pratt talked right over her boss. "He's in real estate, she's a lawyer. They have a house on the North Shore. It's a very interesting case. I told them you'd be back on Monday."

"Well, as a matter of fact . . ."

"But they can't wait." Again the assistant overrode her boss. "They said if you could make it by Friday . . ."

"I was planning to leave Saturday."

"Could you move it up one day? It's a very interesting case."

"If I can get a seat . . ."

"I've already got you booked out of Mexico City. You need to hire a car to get you there from Cuernavaca. The Wilsons will be in your office Friday afternoon at four-thirty."

"Right." Gwenn grinned.

Marge Pratt was twenty-seven when Gwenn hired her. She was of medium height and build, with dark brown hair which she wore in a short, blunt cut, and light gray eyes. She tended to wear neutral colors which along with her low-key personality caused her to fade into the background.

Gwenn had chosen Marge from a field of applicants with better skills and more experience because Marge was in essentially the same situation she had been in when she applied to Cordelia Hart, owner of Hart Security and Investigation, for work. Gwenn had been pregnant and alone. Marge had given birth to a son and been abandoned by the father. Cordelia had extended a helping hand to Gwenn and Gwenn did the same for Marge Pratt.

What Gwenn needed was someone to type reports, keep the files, do the billing, schedule appointments—in other words, organize the small office. It shouldn't have been difficult.

Marge's idea of working in a detective agency was derived from an untold number of television shows. Each was disappointed, but each hung on: Marge Pratt because she needed the job, Gwenn Ramadge because she couldn't bring herself to fire the younger woman. Gradually, their expectations became more realistic. They learned to rely on each other. They progressed to an intuitive understanding, so that often words weren't necessary. This was such an instance.

"Four-thirty on Friday," Gwenn agreed, not asking for details, confident the matter was as urgent as Marge presented it to be. She paused. "Anything else?"

Marge hesitated. "Have you talked to Ray lately?"

"No."

"Have you seen the New York papers? How recent are the editions you get there?"

"I haven't seen the New York papers since I came. What's up? Just tell me straight out, please."

"New allegations of police corruption. Specifically in the Narcotics Division."

"So?" Ray had worked Narco for a brief period before Gwenn knew him. Now he was assigned to Queens Homicide. "A policewoman is involved. Friend of Ray's."

"Go on."

"I think you ought to hear it from him."

"You're right. Thanks, Marge. I'll see you on Friday."

After she hung up, Gwenn remained seated on the edge of the bed considering what she had just learned. It could very well be the explanation for Ray's silence, she thought, and got up to dress. Her parents made dinner a formal occasion, so she put on a long white lace shift, accenting it with gold hoop earrings and gold bracelets, and went downstairs. From the patio, their voices drifted to her on the soft evening breeze, but before joining them, she stopped in the library to look at the newspapers that were delivered every day.

She riffled through the English-language papers and found a brief reference to a commission investigating irregularities within the Narcotics Division of the NYPD. There were flurries like this periodically, she thought. The men and women who worked Narcotics were subject to stress and to heavy temptation. It wasn't surprising, or shouldn't be, that one or another succumbed. One or two gone bad were enough to discredit the rest.

Oscar Ramadge also subscribed to the *New York Times* fax, an abbreviated account of national and world events which came in daily. Everything was stripped down nowadays, Gwenn thought; strangers decided what we should know or not know; they evaluated for us. She read both accounts carefully. Ray Dixon was not mentioned in either. Gwenn wondered how Marge had made the connection. She couldn't imagine Ray had volunteered the information. Unless . . . Would he do so in the expectation that she would pass it on to Gwenn? If he'd wanted Gwenn to know, he would have called and told her himself. The national edition of today's *New York Times* would be on the stands in Cuernavaca tomorrow. But why wait?

She picked up the library telephone and dialed Ray's number. No answer.

She waited for his machine to kick in with his message; then she left hers. She told him she was going home. She gave day, time of arrival, airline and flight number.

Having passed through Customs without even unlocking a bag, Gwenn searched the faces of excited friends and relatives waiting to meet the passengers of the flight she'd just been on. She watched anticipation turn to bright fulfillment as they found each other. Ray wasn't among them.

She listened for a summons over the loudspeaker. Her name was not called out. She went over to the Air Mexico counter. There was no message for her.

CHAPTER 2

THURSDAY, AUGUST 25
MORNING

Waking with the usual splitting headache and foul taste in her mouth, Jayne Harrow made her way unsteadily to the bathroom, where she retched into the basin. Raising her head, she looked into the mirror. Bloodshot eyes stared back at her, refusing to recognize the bloated face and tangled hair, a caricature of debauchery, as herself. That creature of failure and despair was what she had become. They had done this to her and she had allowed it to happen.

The interview with Captain Landau had gone well, or so she'd thought, till his unfortunate discovery of the vodka bottles in her handbag. He'd given indication that he believed her despite that, and he would surely investigate the murder of the Raggedy Man. So, on his instructions, she continued to ride with Brian Ford and to keep a journal of events. She eased the anxiety of waiting to hear from Landau by more drinking. She started to show up for work drunk, if she showed up at all. Ford covered for her. The other cops covered for her. It was ironic, she thought, that the very men she was trying to nail and who wanted to discredit her were now protecting her. They were following the *code* and everybody on the squad knew it. By her continued drinking, she was playing into their hands, making them look compassionate. It had to stop. If she was to save herself, there was only one way to do it. She had to report to Internal Affairs.

Jayne knew her home phone was bugged. She knew that Ford or one of the others involved with him, who said hello when she came in, who smiled, who pretended to be a friend, had installed it. If she removed the bug, another would be put in. So last Tuesday she had gone outside and used a street phone to contact IA.

Since her initial complaint to Lieutenant Palma went back to March, it was difficult to convince the officer at IA that the matter was serious and urgent. The earliest appointment he could give her was for Friday. At that time it was three days off, but it seemed forever.

Wasn't there anything sooner? she'd almost pleaded.

Not unless she wanted to state her business in detail, to name names so that he could evaluate the information, the detective replied.

Jayne Harrow was not prepared to tell her story over the telephone. So again she waited.

During the ensuing period, she managed to show up for her shifts sober and to get through them without a boost. She believed she had her drinking under control. She had attended a couple of AA meetings but was not impressed. She didn't need them; she could do it on her own. As proof, she no longer carried the shot bottles in her purse; she carried a vial of Valium instead. In the morning at the first sign of the shakes she took one, and gulped more down during the day as needed. They dulled her perceptions, but nobody noticed, she thought. She was wrong.

On those three nights when she waited for her appointment with Internal Affairs, there were no stakeouts and no busts. No overtime claimed. Promptly at midnight Brian Ford dropped her in front of her house and she went upstairs, resisting the urge to go around the corner for a quick one. She took a Valium and went to bed and sank into torpid slumber.

Now, the night before her scheduled interview, she had not been sleeping more than a couple of hours when she was awakened by pounding in the hall. Loud voices called back and forth. Outside, police sirens wailed. Revolving lights on the roofs of patrol cars illumined the night. What was going on? Jayne's first reaction was that someone in the building was being raided. Who? From the nearness of the voices it had to be someone on her floor. There was only one other tenant beside herself, a young actor, Stacy Morris. Decent, hardworking, he had never been in trouble, as far as she knew. In fact, he'd helped her a couple of times when she'd come home loaded and passed out before she could get her door open. He'd taken her key out of her hand and gotten her inside and put her to bed.

More pounding. More shouting.

"Police! Open up!"

What in the world could they want from Stacy?

A heavy thud was followed by the cracking and splintering of wood as a door was kicked in. *Her* door, she realized. Men charged into her living room and into her bedroom. A portable spotlight was focused on her as she cringed against the pillows. She blinked and held up one hand to shield her eyes.

"Jayne Harrow?"

With her other hand, she clutched the bedsheet and pulled it up over her bare shoulders.

"Who are you? What do you want? What's going on?"

"Jayne Harrow?" the team leader asked again.

"Detective Harrow," she corrected. "Yes. Who are you? I don't know you. What's your name?"

"Sergeant Brendan."

"What are you doing here, Sergeant Brendan? What do you want? What right do you have to burst in here like this?"

"We've got a warrant to search the premises."

"These premises?"

"Yes ma'am."

"This is crazy. I'm a police officer too. There must be a mistake."

"No mistake."

"What are you looking for?"

He was big, overweight. His bulk filled the doorway between bedroom and living room. Through what little space was left Jayne could make out two more men in plain clothes. Then the realization hit her: they were looking for drugs.

Her stomach dropped. *Stay cool,* she told herself.

"Would you get my robe out of the closet, please?" She pointed. "It's on a wall hook to the right. Thank you. And do you have to shine that thing in my eyes? There's a light switch right beside you." She put the robe on, swung her legs over the side of the bed and felt around for her slippers. Decently covered, she stood up. "Would you tell your people not to tear my place apart? Please. It's not necessary. I don't have any drugs. If I did, I'd be crazy to keep them here, wouldn't I?"

Before he could answer, a call came from the front room.

"Sarge! Out here!"

They'd found something, Jayne Harrow thought. Of course they would. She should have known. She should have anticipated. Sighing deeply, she followed Brendan into the living room.

A pocket had been cut into the upholstery of the sofa under one of the removable seat cushions. Not very original, but then it was meant to be found, wasn't it? That was the whole idea—to catch her red-handed.

Brendan eyed the mound of packets that had been dug out and piled to one side. A sizable amount.

"You'd better get some clothes on," he told her. He let her go back to the bedroom but followed her inside. He checked the window to be sure there was no fire escape. He looked into the bathroom and then the closet. What means of escape did he expect to discover in the closet? Jayne wondered.

Apparently satisfied she couldn't get away, Brendan pulled the door shut behind him and left her alone.

Now the enormity of the situation finally hit her. She began to tremble. They had beaten her to it. Somehow, word had leaked out that she was going to talk to Internal Affairs tomorrow—no, today. Before she could accuse Ford and the others working with him, they had accused her. And they would be able to support their charge. They had evidence. She would be charged with drug possession and she couldn't deny it. Still shaking, she put on what clothes came to hand, which happened to be what she'd had on when she went to bed—slacks that were creased and a shirt with a coffee stain down the front. She wouldn't be making points on appearance, she thought. She used the precious moments allotted to her in packing an overnight bag. She hoped she wouldn't need it.

There was a sharp tap at the door.

"In a minute."

Feeling through the contents of her lingerie drawer, Jayne found a reserve. She unscrewed the cap and drank down the contents.

She took a deep breath. The shaking stopped, temporarily. The warmth spread through her body.

"How about it? You ready?" Brendan called.

She opened the door and stood stolidly, without expression, as he read her her rights.

FRIDAY, AUGUST 26
MORNING

"I think you're overreacting," Frank Wilson said as he poured himself a second cup of coffee and brought it over to the breakfast nook. He sat down opposite his wife.

"Nowadays, with the stories you hear . . . you can't be too careful," Lana Wilson replied.

"If Monique finds out we're having her investigated, she'll be very upset. She might quit. Personally, I wouldn't blame her."

"This woman we're hiring comes highly recommended," his wife pointed out. "She's a professional investigator; she's not going to give anything away."

Frank Wilson went on with his breakfast. Between bites he looked out the window towards their own private beach—the main inducement for buying the house. It was a beautiful day. The sky was without a cloud; the tide was out; sandpipers skittered in the shallow ripples. Admiring the view was an excuse for not meeting his wife's eyes.

Lana Wilson knew it. She was a lawyer in a prestigious firm, with strong hopes of becoming a partner. He was one of a coterie of vice presidents in a real estate company. Both were dedicated to their careers. They had wanted a family—later.

They worked hard and played hard. They flourished. Suddenly, they became aware that the years were slipping by. Lana noticed strands of gray in her silky sable hair and scheduled touch-ups at regular intervals. Frank was losing the battle of the bulge, which led to shortness of breath, which resulted in cutting down the length of his morning run and the intensity of his workouts. If they really wanted a family, there wasn't much time left. Lana went off the Pill and they shifted from the apartment in Manhattan to the house on Long Island. Nothing happened. They consulted doctors. Had they waited too long?

It was like a miracle when Lana came home from a routine visit to the doctor to announce she was pregnant. Their joy was unbounded. A healthy, beautiful son was born to them.

Inevitably, they came down out of the clouds and the routine of living reasserted itself, and with it their original ambitions and goals came to the fore once more. There had never been any question but that Lana would return to her job and her career after the baby came. That meant hiring a nanny. They thought that as long as they could afford to pay, there would be no problem. They had a lot to learn.

Lana's widowed mother, Thelma Selig, moved in until they could find someone.

The stress between mother and daughter was like an exposed electric wire. No matter how careful he was, Frank got in the way and suffered frequent shocks. Worst of all, the baby was affected. Bobby Wilson was turning willful. He lashed out at everyone who crossed him, including his mother and grandmother. By the time Bobby was two, the Wilsons had gone through seven nannies. The women left for a variety of reasons: Bobby was cantankerous; the grandmother interfered with their discipline; the parents expected the nanny to do housework. They were fired for one reason only—they couldn't control Bobby Wilson.

By the time Bobby was almost three, they had run out of agencies. Deciding to deal direct, the Wilsons searched the Situations Wanted column in the local paper. Monique Bruno was the first person they contacted.

She was a lovely girl with the tranquil face and soft eyes of a Raphael Madonna. In her early twenties, she looked like a high school girl, and wearing her pleated plaid skirt and knee socks, she could have passed for one. Her parents lived in Bayamón, a suburb of San Juan, Puerto Rico. She had studied to be a nurse, but didn't like the work as much as she'd thought she would. It was the sense of hopelessness pervading the hospital that she'd objected to, she told the Wilsons in the job interview. She had come to the mainland with the idea of becoming a teacher, but she had to support herself while she studied and send money home too, if at all possible. She could have gotten a job waitressing, but that would have been wasting her training. She had never been a nanny, she admitted with disarming candor, but she was the oldest in a family of six and had cared for her younger siblings, so she thought she could handle one little boy.

Lana and Frank were enchanted.

"We'll see how it works out," Lana said, trying not to sound too eager.

Monique Bruno gave her parents' address and that of the nursing supervisor in the hospital where she had taken her training.

The Wilsons exchanged glances. This girl was the answer to their prayers. "Of course, it depends on Bobby," the mother cautioned one last time as a matter of form. "He's a difficult child."

But Bobby took to Monique right away. He chortled happily whenever he was with her. He ate whatever she put in front of him. Usually he slept soundly through the night; the occasions when he woke and cried were rare and of brief duration. As was their habit, at the first sound of wailing, the whole household got up and headed for his room. They found Monique already there, holding him in her arms and crooning softly to him. Not long after that, he was asleep again. After a while, the family didn't bother to get up. After a while, he no longer cried at all.

Monique was a jewel.

At last, Lana's mother returned to her own home in San Francisco. Lana gradually took on the work load she'd carried before Bobby was born. She began to take Monique for granted. She asked her to do small additional chores—pick up the cleaning, sort the laundry, go to the post office. Monique never said no. She acquiesced cheerfully. She was becoming indispensable.

Her perfection began to grate. It seemed to Lana that her son cared more for his nanny than he did for her. Whenever she could, Lana left the office early to get home before Bobby's bedtime. Lana looked forward to gathering him into her arms, hugging him, and tucking him in. But it was Mikki he wanted.

"Mikki, Mikki," he cried, and stretched his chubby arms out to the nanny, even pushing Lana aside if she happened to stand between them.

Frank tried to console her. "He's only a baby. He doesn't know you're his mother. He thinks . . . ." Frank stopped.

"He thinks *she* is."

"Well, she's here all the time."

"And I'm not."

"That's your choice, isn't it?"

"I can't be in two places at once."

When he's a little older, he'll understand," her husband soothed. "For now, let's be grateful that we have Monique, that she's so great with Bobby, and that he likes her."

The Wilsons had this argument many times. It came to a head on Bobby's birthday, the twentieth of August.

They had planned a beach party. It rained. They moved indoors, but picnics don't work indoors. The adults drank too much. The children were restless and cranky: fights started; both winners and losers cried. Finally, the food was consumed and the guests departed. Lana collapsed into a chair. She looked over to the nanny, who had Bobby on her lap and was feeding him biscuits.

"Isn't it time for his nap?"

"Yes, it is. Actually, it's past time."

"Then take him upstairs, will you?"

Lana Wilson said no more till the nanny and the boy were gone. "Did you see that?" she asked her husband.

"What?"

"Bobby was just about out on his feet."

"As Mikki said, it's past his nap time."

"He was like that all afternoon, hardly made a sound."

"The other kids more than made up for him."

"It doesn't strike you as odd?"

"What do you mean, odd?"

"When we come home from work, he's in bed asleep. In the morning, by the time we're up, he's been fed and is napping again."

"So? You've got a schedule for him and she's following it, isn't she? What's the problem?"

The argument was raised to a new level. "I wish that once, just once, you'd take my side. You always support her."

"I don't support her. She's here doing a job you don't want to do. And she's doing it well. If you're not satisfied, then fire her. Again, it's your choice."

"You don't care if I fire her?"

"Why should I care? As long as you find somebody else . . . and we both know how hard that is. I don't think either of us wants your mother to move back in. Taking these matters into consideration, do what you want."

He hadn't expected her to hire a private investigator.

Gwenn Ramadge took a taxi from the airport. She stopped briefly at her apartment building on Seventy-second, left her baggage with the doorman, and continued downtown to her office. It was near City Hall, around the corner from the New York State Office Building. As usual, traffic was heavy. She kept looking at her watch. At the Municipal Building, she told the driver to stop, paid him, and ran the rest of the way across City Hall Park. She was out of breath when she entered the lobby of her building and saw that both elevators were on the top floor. She took the stairs one flight and stopped outside her door to catch her breath.

Marge Pratt buzzed her in. She must have seen her shadow on the frosted glass, Gwenn thought.

"They're inside, waiting." The secretary made no attempt to hide her disapproval.

"Thank you, Marge. It's good to see you too. Yes, I'm glad to be home." Seeing the younger woman flush, Gwenn eased up. "It *is* good to be back and I did miss you, believe it or not." Then Gwenn swept on past the receptionist's desk and opened the door to her own office.

"I was tied up in traffic," she apologized to the couple waiting. "My plane was on time from Mexico City, but a breakdown on the Van Wyck backed everything up for miles." She smiled ruefully and took her place at the desk. "Now, I understand from my secretary that there's some urgency here. Suppose you tell me about it."

While the Wilsons hesitated, each waiting for the other to start, Gwenn continued to observe them. They were your standard yuppie couple, she thought. She was petite, wore her dark hair sculptured to the shape of her head. Though it was the end of summer, her skin remained sunblock-pale. She wore the accepted lady lawyer's uniform: a severely tailored suit in a pastel shade—this time it happened to be pale blue. He was starting to put on weight and lose hair. He attempted to camouflage one with expensive tailoring and the other with hair bonding. They were a pair, Gwenn thought. As clients, they had dressed to impress.

It was Lana Wilson who finally explained the circumstances, and found to her dismay that she had few, if any, real complaints. She told of the difficulty of hiring a competent nanny, how happy she and her husband had been with Monique Bruno and how much their son, Bobby, liked her. Lately, however, he'd been behaving strangely.

She stopped, and Gwenn had to prompt her. "In what way?"

"He seems lethargic," the mother said.

At this point, Frank Wilson made it clear that he was not disturbed about the care his son was getting. He was here only to quiet his wife's fears, which he considered unfounded.

Therefore, Gwenn addressed herself to Mrs. Wilson. "This sounds to me like a medical problem. Have you had the boy examined by a doctor?"

"Oh yes, yes. He couldn't find anything wrong. Some children sleep more than others, he said."

"What exactly is it that you want me to do?" Gwenn asked.

"I want you to find out what she's doing to my son." She started to cry.

"Lana, for God's sake . . ."

Gwenn held up a hand to silence both. She handed Mrs. Wilson a tissue from the box on her desk, a box that was always full. "Did her references check out when you hired her?"

"She didn't have references. She had never done this kind of work before. She was very honest about admitting that."

I'll bet, Gwenn thought; that was usually the first indication there was something to hide. "But she must have told you something about herself—where she came from, what schools she attended?"

"Oh, sure. She comes from Puerto Rico. She gave us the address of her parents and also the hospital where she took nurse's training."

"And they confirmed what she told you? And the hospital vouched for her good character?"

"We didn't contact them," Frank Wilson admitted, looking sheepish. "She was everything we were looking for and we figured she wouldn't give us those names unless they would check out."

A common mistake, Gwenn thought. What was this girl up to? It could be any number of things. "Well, for starters, we'll check her identity."

"Why should she lie about who she is?" Lana Wilson wanted to know.

"First, let's find out if she did lie," Gwenn replied. "Then we'll go on from there."

Lana Wilson sighed heavily. "She was so perfect. And she was so wonderful with Bobby. I should have known she was too good to be true."

"We're getting ahead of ourselves," Gwenn cautioned. "How long has Monique been working for you?"

Again the Wilsons consulted silently and Mrs. Wilson replied.

"Just about six months. I remember it was Saint Patrick's Day when she came out for the interview. We hired her on the spot and she moved in that weekend."

"And it's only recently you've had any cause for complaint?"

"Not complaint. I don't have a specific complaint," Lana Wilson said, still obviously troubled.

It seemed to Gwenn she was more disturbed now than she had been at the start of the consultation. "Uneasiness, then. Aside from Bobby's lethargy, has anything else caused you to be uneasy?"

"I call a couple of times a day to see how everything is, if she needs anything, and to talk to Bobby. She's very slow to pick up sometimes. She's always got a good reason: she's in the basement doing laundry, out in the garden, walking with Bobby . . . something."

"But you don't believe her?"

"I want to believe her."

"Then why don't you?"

"I don't know." Lana Wilson shook her head. "When she puts Bobby on, all he does is babble."

Mr. Wilson threw up his hands. "What do you expect from a three-year-old?"

"Bobby is very articulate for his age."

Wilson just groaned.

"And she has no friends!" His wife made a charge out of it. "She gets a day off every week and when she gets back we ask her what she did and if she had a good time. All she says is that she went to New York to shop, saw a show, and like that."

"It's none of our business what she does on her time off," Frank Wilson pointed out.

"I don't care what she does," his wife retorted. "It just seems odd she doesn't have any friends."

"How can she have friends?" he demanded. "She lives in. What times does she have to meet people?"

Gwenn cut off the argument. "Who looks after Bobby on the nanny's day off?"

"One of us stays home from the office. We take turns," Mrs. Wilson explained.

"It must be good to be able to take a day off and spend it at home with your child," Gwenn commented.

"Unfortunately, I bring work home and the phone rings constantly. It's not much different than being at work."

"How does Bobby react to all this? How does he behave?"

Frank Wilson answered. "He's fine. Monique gives him breakfast before she goes. The other meals are ready in the refrigerator with instructions on how to prepare them. He sleeps most of the day. I must say he's a little cranky by suppertime, but that's all."

Gwenn looked to Lana Wilson once more. "You follow the same routine?"

"Yes."

"Most parents would consider themselves lucky. Well . . ." Gwenn leaned back in her chair. "If you want me to, I can contact Ms. Bruno's parents in Puerto Rico and also the hospital where she took her training. We'll see where that takes us."

Again the Wilsons consulted silently. Gwenn suggested no great commitment. Relieved, they nodded.

"We only want to be reassured that Bobby's safe with her," Lana Wilson told Gwenn.

"Of course." Gwenn got up, came around to shake hands, and walked the clients to the door. "You'll be hearing from me."

CHAPTER 3

Detective Sergeant Raymond Dixon had been teaching at the Police Academy for nearly two years when he was summoned by his superior and informed that one of his pupils, Jayne Harrow, had been chosen for undercover work with the Narco squad. It was a prestigious assignment. Since she had no street experience, he was to ride with her temporarily and give her a short course including an overall view of the drug scene and what her work would entail. In other words, he was to conduct a brief indoctrination.

Dixon wasn't happy. This wasn't the first time he had been called on to show a newcomer the ropes, but in the past it had always been an officer with previous experience being prepared for a special assignment, not a raw recruit—and a woman at that. The practice of throwing graduates just out of the Academy into the thick of danger was growing. The thinking was that the very lack of experience would protect the beginner and contribute to his efficacy. Until somebody on the street made him, of course.

The intent was to pull him out before that happened. That call usually came from his partner, less frequently from the officer himself.

Dixon had to admit that Detective Harrow had several points in her favor: she was attentive, compliant, and willing to learn. She gave every indication of caring about the victims of drugs and of having high moral standards. These standards, Ray thought, would be sorely tested. They would determine whether or not she survived.

At the time they rode together, Ray Dixon was in the process of getting a divorce. It wasn't only a matter of ending a marriage, but of shutting the door on a major part of his life. He was cutting ties to his wife and at the same time to a close companion. Patty Foley had been schoolmate and childhood sweetheart. He found it almost impossible to believe that during all those years each should have so completely misunderstood the other's needs and aspirations.

It was during this period that the threads of gray appeared in Ray's wavy, dark hair. A frown cut deep just above the bridge of his nose. His features appeared sharper and emphasized the fullness of his lips. He was a quiet man and he did not broadcast his sorrow and confusion. Jayne Harrow, however, sensed it and gave him what support she could.

The most important thing Dixon and Harrow learned was to trust each other.

Inevitably, the brass decided the training period had lasted long enough, and they were split up. Dixon was returned to active duty and sent to Queens Homicide. Harrow, promoted to the rank of detective, became an official member of the Narcotics squad and worked out of One Police Plaza. She was assigned a permanent partner, Sergeant Brian Ford.

They promised to keep in touch and for a while they did. There were calls back and forth. A couple of times they met for lunch, but working out of different precincts and on different shifts meant there were no points of contact. Nevertheless, they watched each other's careers. Months passed. Faced with the dilemma of her partner's behavior, Harrow wanted to go to Dixon for advice. He would support her; she was sure of it, but in doing so he would be forced to break the code of silence and would be labeled a traitor. She couldn't put him on the spot like that.

Ultimately, the word did reach Ray Dixon. He called and offered to help. She could handle it, she assured him. Now, on the very day of her scheduled appointment with Internal Affairs, the tables were turned and she was the one under arrest. She had been brought in cuffed, paraded through the building and the squad room, humiliated, charged and booked like any criminal.

Even out in Queens, Dixon heard about it. In fact, the story ran like wildfire through the entire department. He could hardly miss hearing. The media seized on it, so that the public was as familiar with the shame of it as were the cops.

Who had set her up? Who had planted the drugs? Ray had no doubt that was what had happened and he meant to get answers. Rumors abounded. The special commission would look into it, but they didn't move fast, and in the meantime Jayne Harrow was placed on indefinite suspension without pay.

Dixon telephoned his onetime pupil and partner. He insisted on a meeting. He wouldn't take no for an answer. Reluctantly, she gave in and suggested they meet at her apartment at four. Gwenn Ramadge's plane was due in from Mexico at three-thirty. Ray decided not to tell Jayne the time was inconvenient. Gwenn would understand.

Promptly at four, Sergeant Dixon rang Jayne Harrow's doorbell. There was no answer. He rang again. Nothing. She might have stepped out for cigarettes, a newspaper, groceries. She could be delayed—stuck in the subway. He waited in the hall till four-thirty. Maybe she'd left a message on his machine? He went down to the street and used the telephone on the corner to dial his own number. He heard only his own recorded announcement. He tried her number and waited till the machine clicked in with the standard message.

With a sinking sensation, Ray now did what he would routinely do in such a situation: he went looking for the building superintendent. He identified himself as a police officer and produced his ID. He also explained he was a friend of Detective Harrow's, that he was worried about her. He wanted the super, George Stavros, to get his passkey and let him in.

Sixty-two years old and a widower of two years, Stavros lived alone in the basement apartment. He was what was known as a "floating" super. He had no interest but to keep the buildings in his care clean and in working order. His only social life was in the brief encounters with the tenants. Because she was alone like himself, Stavros took particular interest in Jayne Harrow. He was familiar with her habits: what time she came in, what time she went out. He had been awakened by the raid. He looked Dixon over with considerable skepticism.

"They took her away this morning. If you're a cop, you know that. You know she's under arrest."

"She's been released."

"Well, don't you have to have some kind of search warrant?"

"I'm a friend. I had a date with her. This is not police business."

Stavros was not swayed. "I don't think she'd want me to let you in."

"Why not?"

"If you're a friend, you know why not." Stavros sighed. "Oh hell!" He hauled out a ring of keys, selected one and inserted it into the lock. Opening the door partway, he peered inside.

The shades were drawn; the apartment was in semidarkness.

"Ms. Harrow? Detective Harrow. It's George. You okay?"

While the super waited for an answer, Dixon stepped in and

located the light switch. He flicked it on. They both saw her at the same time.

She was lying on the floor in the center of the living room. Her head had just missed hitting the coffee table. Her right arm was outstretched and it looked as though it had pushed the coffee table up against the sofa and out of the way. Dixon went to her and knelt beside her. Her face was flushed, eyes closed, mouth open. She snored.

Dixon sat back on his heels. "Thank God," he murmured. "Thank God." Then he took note of the empty vodka bottle and the glass. He looked up at Stavros. "She's done this before?"

"Oh, yeah. A lot."

"Recently?"

"For the last couple of months."

Dixon frowned. "As bad as this?"

"Worse lately. She holes up with the booze for a couple of days at a time."

"Okay, thanks. I'll take care of her."

"You want some help?"

Ray started to say no; then he realized she was completely out of it. She would be dead weight. "Maybe you could give me a hand getting her on the bed."

By the time Jayne was settled and the super had left, it was nearly six. Dixon remembered Gwenn. He dialed her apartment and she picked up right away.

"Gwenn, it's me. I'm so sorry I missed your plane. Something came up and I couldn't get free. I'm sorry." He paused.

"That's okay. I understand."

He'd known she would. Gwenn was great.

"How are you?" they both asked at the same time, then began laughing.

"Did you have a wonderful vacation? How was the flight?" Ray charged ahead. "When am I going to see you?"

"Fine. I'm fine. The vacation was great. Are you all right?"

"Absolutely. Now that you're back," he added.

She glowed with pleasure. It was good to be back, good to hear his voice, to know he was close. "Have you eaten? I can fix us something. Why don't you come over?" She couldn't wait to see him.

He couldn't wait to see her. Talking to her while she was in Cuernavaca, he had sensed that more than the miles separated them. It was one of the reasons he had stopped calling—to give her a chance to find herself. Now he sensed she was indeed back.

"That would be great," he said. Then he looked over to Jayne Harrow lying in a stupor on the bed. "No, I can't. I'm sorry. Not tonight."

"Oh." She was surprised and disappointed and waited for the explanation. He didn't offer one. "Okay." It was all she could trust herself to say.

He could tell she was waiting for him to explain. Jayne would probably sleep right through the night, but she might also wake up in a few hours. If she did, it was important that he be there; otherwise she might manage to pull herself together to the point where she could go out for more booze and start the cycle all over again. He couldn't take the chance.

"You're not going to believe this, but I'm sitting up with a sick friend."

"Why shouldn't I believe it?" Gwenn asked.

"Because it's such a hoary old chestnut of an excuse."

"Isn't it true?"

"Of course it's true."

"This friend—it wouldn't be the woman cop in the narcotics scandal that's been in all the papers?"

"That's right. I trained her. I rode with her when she was fresh out of the Academy."

"I didn't know. I'm sorry."

"No need to apologize."

There was an awkward pause. Ray broke it.

"I'll call you in the morning."

"Yes, do that."

Gwenn hung up. She meant to get an early start on the Wilson case. She had a hunch that checking on the nanny was going to take more than a few telephone calls. She might have told Ray her plans, but she was hurt he hadn't been more forthcoming with her.

Let him spend a little time on catch-up, she thought.

SATURDAY, AUGUST 27
MORNING

Gwenn's instincts about the nanny proved correct. Her parents, Matilda and José Bruno, no longer lived at the address she'd given the Wilsons, and there was no forwarding address. The hospital at which she trained confirmed she had been there for less than a year, but refused to divulge the circumstances under which she'd left. Gwenn tried the local police. They had nothing on a Monique Bruno.

Using a conference hookup, Gwenn consulted her clients.

"Well, that's a relief. We can stop worrying." Frank Wilson spoke from his real estate office.

"You're satisfied?" Gwenn asked.

"Yes, why not? She didn't lie to us. Her parents have moved; there's nothing dire in that. The hospital doesn't want to say why she dropped out; it's their policy. Could be simply that her grades were no good. Who cares? We didn't hire her as a registered nurse. I'm content. Aren't you?"

"It doesn't matter whether or not I am," Gwenn replied. "If your mind is at ease about Monique Bruno and you believe she's trustworthy, then there's no need to continue."

"To continue and do what?" Wilson wanted to know.

"The next step would be for someone to go down to Bayamón, locate Monique's parents, talk to her friends, neighbors, people at the hospital."

"Who would you send?"

"I have licensed investigators on call. Actually, you could go yourself," Gwenn pointed out. "It's just a matter of asking a few questions. It shouldn't be a problem."

"It would be inappropriate." He scowled. "Also, I haven't the time." He paused. "What do you expect to learn?"

"I don't know. At this point, I can only guess."

Listening all the while on the phone in the library of their home, Lana Wilson broke in at last. "We've started this thing and I think we should see it through. We have to know, once and for all, whether we can trust Monique. If you went yourself, Ms. Ramadge, how long do you think you would need in Puerto Rico?"

"Barring unforeseen complications—two, three days at the most."

"Could you go yourself?"

"Well," Gwenn considered. "I'm just back from Mexico, as you know. The work has piled up." She knew very well it was only routine paperwork which Marge Pratt could take care of and which she would take care of whether Gwenn was there or not.

"Please, Ms. Ramadge, I'd feel so much better if you went yourself," Lana Wilson urged. "We'd be glad to pay extra for your travel time."

In fact, Gwenn shared Mrs. Wilson's qualms about the nanny, and she was reluctant to drop the case. "There'll be no extra charge."

"Thank you," Lana Wilson murmured.

"You're welcome. Now, I'll need a photo of Miss Bruno. A snapshot would do, if you have one."

"No problem," Mrs. Wilson said. "We have stacks of Bobby,

and Monique is in most of them," she observed bitterly. "I thought you might ask, so I picked out a couple of the best. I can fax them to you, if that's okay?"

"Fine," Gwenn agreed. "I'll get an early flight Monday."

"I was hoping you could leave right away."

"Tomorrow's Sunday. A lost day anyway."

"Please . . ."

"How about if I leave first thing tomorrow morning? It will save you a night's hotel charge."

"Expense is no object," Lana Wilson assured Gwenn.

"If it's difficult for Miss Ramadge to get away . . ." Frank Wilson began.

"We'd be grateful if you could go today," Lana Wilson cut her husband off.

Ray Dixon made himself comfortable on Jayne Harrow's sofa, but he spent an uneasy night conscious of her nearness and her silence. He got up several times to look in on her and found her always in the same position, sleeping soundly. At first, that reassured him; then he began to worry. Was she in too deep a slumber? Should he rouse her? Sleep was a good medicine, almost always. To rouse her would only serve to reassure him, he decided, and left her alone. Daylight came. He couldn't wait any longer. He went into her bedroom.

"Jayne?"

She didn't stir.

"Jayne?" He sat at the side of her bed, grasped her by the shoulders and shook her gently.

No response.

"Jayne. Wake up. Jayne!" He shook her harder. Her body was limp, heavy, offering no resistance. Was she in a coma? He put one arm around her to support her and with his free hand gently pried her eyes open. They stared past him unfocused. Oh God!

What should he do? Should he call 911? While he struggled to decide, Jayne Harrow suddenly shivered and with a great heave vomited all over both of them.

He wasn't angry. He wasn't repelled. He was grateful she was conscious.

He helped her clean herself up, put her in the shower, alternating hot and cold on her while she shivered and moaned. He handed her a couple of towels and went to the kitchen to put on coffee and make toast. When it was ready, he called her. She hadn't bothered to dress. She'd put on a thick terry cloth bathrobe and toweled her hair dry, and that was it. They sat across from each other at the kitchen table.

"How do you feel?"

"Not great."

"You really tied one on."

She shrugged. "I guess."

Not the regret or contrition he had looked for. "So. What are your plans?"

"I don't have any plans. I'm suspended. Haven't you heard? Suspended without pay."

"I heard. So what are you going to do?"

"What can I do? They've made their case."

"You can fight. Get a job. You need the money and you need something to occupy your time."

"What kind of a job? Who's going to hire me?" she challenged.

He wasn't stumped for long. "I know somebody."

"Yeah?" She was guardedly hopeful. "Who?"

"Get dressed. I'll set up the appointment."

He waited till she went into the bedroom and shut the door between them before dialing Gwenn's number. Her machine kicked in with the message that she could be reached at the office. He didn't wait for the number; he knew it by heart.

Marge Pratt answered. "She's on the other line with clients. Where can she reach you?"

"Ah . . . I'll call her." He started to hang up.

"Wait. Here she is."

"Gwenn? Hi. Good morning. What are you doing up and out at this hour on a Saturday? I thought you'd be sleeping late."

"I thought I would be too. I've got a new case. Very interesting."

"Oh? Congratulations. When can I see you? Can I come over?"

He didn't ask about her new case, or about her trip. Evidently he had other, more important problems on his mind. "I'm leaving for Puerto Rico as soon as I can get a flight."

"You just got back," he protested.

"This is business."

"I need to talk to you."

"I'm really sorry, Ray. As soon as I get back."

"When is that going to be?"

"A couple of days. Is that okay?"

"I suppose, if it's the best you can do."

He sounded hurt. "Want to tell me what it's about?"

He hesitated. "No. I don't think so, not on the telephone. It'll hold."

"Good. Then I'll be seeing you."

"Will you call me?"

"First thing. I promise."

He had barely hung up when Jayne came out. She was still wearing the bathrobe, but she had used a hair dryer to fluff her hair and had put on lipstick.

"So?" she asked. "No go, right? I told you. Nobody wants to hire a disgraced cop."

"Wrong. My friend wants to see you," he lied. "She's going out of town for a couple of days, but she'll see you as soon as she gets back."

"Yeah?" She looked afraid to hope. "What kind of work would it be?"

"Detective work for a private agency."

"That's terrific. Thanks, Ray. Thank you so much."

"No thanks necessary."

"Oh yes there are, and not only for the job interview. I haven't got many friends willing to go out on a limb for me. I haven't got any."

"You'd do the same for me."

"You can bet on that."

Silently, Ray Dixon prayed he'd be able to deliver. "One more thing—I want you to go to AA."

"They can't help me."

"How do you know? Have you gone to any meetings? How many?"

"Two. All the people did was sit around and talk."

"Did you talk?"

"I don't tell my troubles to strangers," she announced pridefully.

Ray was silent several moments studying Jayne. He tried to hide his pity. "You'll have to go to a lot more than two. Here's a list of the AA meetings in the neighborhood. You will go to at least one each and every day. Or else no deal. Okay?"

Jayne Harrow pursed her lips. She shrugged. "I suppose."

"I want to see a little more commitment."

"Okay. I'll do it. It's a promise."

SATURDAY, AUGUST 27
EVENING

Despite Lana Wilson's insistence that money was no object, it was clear Frank Wilson had an eye on expenses. Gwenn had certainly not intended to charge the Wilsons with the cost of a luxury hotel on San Juan's Gold Coast. However, though it wasn't the high tourist season, there were a couple of conventions in town which made it impossible to get a moderately priced room. It was either the Caribe Hilton or a night on the beach. Even at the Caribe all that was left was a cabana, but Gwenn took it gratefully.

By the time she was checked in, the soft tropical night embraced the island. The stars gleamed brightly in a deep velvet sky. The waves broke against the walls of the ancient fort of San Geronimo just off the shore from the hotel, throwing sprays of white spume that turned iridescent in the floodlights. The palm trees rustled and bowed before the trade winds. Strolling in the hotel gardens, Gwenn was reminded of Cuernavaca, which she had so recently left. The two places were different and also similar. Each was more than just a tourist resort. San Juan was a crossroads between the old world and the new. Its pulse beat to the tempo of international trade. By air and sea, it linked North and South America and Europe. It was cosmopolitan and parochial, cherishing its own culture and traditions.

As she took one last turn on the grounds before calling it a night, Gwenn thought about Ray Dixon. What had he been so anxious to see her about? She wished they had been able to get together. She wondered about his "sick friend." Maybe sometime they could come down here together, not on a case but just to enjoy the island and each other. That was what they needed—a chance to get to know each other.

Her cabana, located at the outermost end of the beach, was very much exposed to the elements and not intended for overnight accommodations, but Gwenn delighted in it for that very reason. She switched off the air-conditioning and opened the window to let in the moist, tropical air. She fell asleep to the sound of the surf slapping on the shore with hypnotic regularity.

After breakfast at poolside, Gwenn reluctantly gave up the easy ways of a tourist and got to work. She rented a Ford Escort, got a map and directions, and set out for Bayamón. She came upon it lying quietly in Sunday morning torpor. Originally a low-income development, it had grown and spread and become very much like a mainland bedroom community. The concrete houses were built low to the ground to withstand hurricanes, and close together to conserve space. Hibiscus, poinsettias, jacaranda, bougainvillea, and trumpet vine acted as gorgeous, natural dividers.

Gwenn knew, of course, that Monique's parents no longer lived there. She hoped to find out where they had gone, or at least get a sense of the kind of people they were and what was known about Monique. She knocked on a half-dozen doors without results. Reasoning that the elderly residents were most likely to have known the Brunos and would be willing to tell what they knew, Gwenn found her way to a section where the houses were older and not so well maintained, the gardens overgrown, and the carports without cars. At one of the houses, a woman sat in the shade of her porch. Her dark hair was pulled back in a knot. Her face was leathery and deeply lined, though whether by the elements or by age it was hard to tell. She wore the long black dress still traditional in some places for a married woman. She fixed her eyes on Gwenn as she approached.

Gwenn's Spanish was minimal. She was also obviously a visitor and therefore regarded with suspicion. However, Señora Josefina Alvarez's curiosity was stronger than her reticence. She peered closely at the snapshot Gwenn showed her.

"Un momento, por favor."

She handed the snapshot back and went into the house. She

was back in a few moments with a pair of eyeglasses which she put on and adjusted carefully. Then she held out her hand for the picture.

"Why are you interested in this one?" she asked.

Relieved that the woman spoke good English, Gwenn had a ready answer. "She has applied for a job with the government and we have to be sure she is of good character."

"I can tell you she is not of good character. No."

"Why do you say that?"

"I say what everybody knows. She was a wild one." Señora Alvarez's dark eyes flashed.

"What did she do?"

"She was a shame and a disgrace for her parents." The woman set her lips in a thin line.

Gwenn sensed more, a personal animosity. "She hurt you, didn't she? How? Please tell me. If there's anything I can do to help, I'll do it. I promise."

"It is too late. It was too late back then." Señora Alvarez shook her head. "My daughter, my Conchita, and María went to school together. My daughter looked up to María, admired her, wanted to be like her, and María showed her how. She taught Conchita to drink, introduced her to men, took her to parties that lasted all night. Sometimes my Conchita didn't come home till morning. One morning she didn't come home at all."

Tears filled her rheumy eyes and silently rolled down the lined cheeks.

"A week later her body washed ashore at La Parguera. They said she had been on board one of the fancy boats there, got drunk, and fell overboard. The police came to question María, but she was gone. A rich *norteamericano* took her to Miami with him."

"You keep calling her María, but you do mean the girl in the snapshot, don't you?" Gwenn asked.

But the woman wasn't listening. She was focused only on her sorrow. "My child, my Conchita . . . She was only fifteen."

Gwenn's next stop was the police station. Having shown her credentials to the desk sergeant, Gwenn explained how she had called from New York the day before and spoken to Detective Hernán Fuentes.

Fuentes, a slim, dapper man in his mid-thirties with a trim mustache, presented himself with gratifying promptness.

"Yes, Ms. Ramadge, I remember your call," he told her politely. "I also remember telling you we know nothing about the woman you are interested in. There is no entry regarding such a person in the computer."

"Do you know this girl?" Gwenn held out the snapshot she had shown Mrs. Alvarez.

Fuentes merely glanced at it. "That is *María* Bruno," he said. "The computer is a marvelous tool, señorita, but it responds precisely to precise questions. I gave it the name you gave me, Monique Bruno. It had no record of such a person."

"I understand."

"Now then, let us see." He tapped in the new name and the screen was immediately activated, producing María Bruno's file. It showed three charges of prostitution. "If you had given me the name, María Bruno, I could have saved you the journey and the inconvenience."

"I don't regret the trip to your beautiful island," Gwenn said.

Fuentes was instantly mollified. "I remember María Bruno very well. She was a wild one," he told her in an attempt to make up for his earlier reticence. "She had all the men crazy for her. From the time she was fourteen, they were after her, but she was interested only in the rich tourists. About a year ago, she met this very rich *norteamericano*."

Very rich as opposed to merely rich? Gwenn wondered rue-fully.

"He had a big yacht and he took her away with him. I don't know exactly what happened after that—whether she left him or whether he threw her out." Fuentes paused. "She had the reputation of keeping more than one lover on the string, so probably he didn't go for that and threw her out."

CHAPTER 4

Detective Hernán Fuentes supplied Gwenn with the name of Monique Bruno's lover, protector, sponsor—whatever one chose to call Ronald Bruckner—as well as the name of his yacht, *La Paloma,* registered in Nassau. It wouldn't be difficult to contact him should that be necessary. Gwenn didn't think it would be. She doubted Mr. Bruckner could tell her any more than she already knew—that the affair had come to an abrupt end. They had most likely parted with animosity on both sides and Bruckner was not likely to have any idea what Monique had done next or where she had gone. Gwenn knew more about that than he did. The rest of the story was back in New York.

She called Marge to contact the Wilsons and set up an appointment in her office for the following morning. She would have liked to spend another night of luxury at the Hilton, but her conscience sent her home on the red-eye.

"It appears she lied to you," Gwenn told the Wilsons as they sat in her office and sipped the coffee Marge Pratt had prepared. "Her real name is María Bruno and under that name she was arrested and charged for prostitution three times."

The Wilsons turned to each other in dismay.

"To be fair," Gwenn went on, "she was never convicted. In each case the charge was dropped."

The Wilsons remained speechless.

To Gwenn the story line was clear and it must have been to the Wilsons as well, but apparently they didn't want to admit it.

"The way I see it, María or Monique—let's call her Monique—was a prostitute. She left Puerto Rico with a rich man and once they reached Miami they parted company—for whatever reason. She had no other marketable skills and she wasn't the type to earn her living in an ordinary job, say as a waitress or saleswoman. She was accustomed to the high life. This job with you as a nanny wasn't exactly exciting. You agree?" Gwenn asked.

Husband and wife nodded.

"It doesn't pay the kind of money she was used to making."

"No indeed," Lana Wilson observed wryly. "Her clothes—I wish you could see her when she goes out on her day off; she's dressed to the hilt."

"Could she be making all that much extra working outside one night a week?" Gwenn wondered.

At last Frank Wilson was aroused. "What are you suggesting?"

Gwenn shrugged. She wanted them to figure it out for themselves.

"You mean she entertains her clients in our house while we're out?" Lana Wilson gasped. "In front of our child?" she added, truly appalled.

"Not in front of him, no," Gwenn assured her. "She makes sure he's asleep."

"Oh, God . . ."

"She makes sure he won't wake at an inconvenient time. Or that he doesn't see something he'll innocently tell you about later."

His mother groaned. "She's drugging him. I knew it. What are we going to do? We have to get rid of her. Right away. We can't wait another day." She sighed. "It's going to break Bobby's heart. He loves her."

"From what you tell me, Bobby loves Monique because she gives him cookies and candy and anything else he wants." Gwenn strove to console the child's mother. "She never says no to him. That's the way she got you to like her and to depend on her. How many times has she switched her day off to oblige you? Taken on extra chores?"

Lana Wilson nodded. "She runs errands, types up my letters and reports, and does it all cheerfully. She never says no to us any more than she does to Bobby." She paused. "She's too good to be true."

Lana was on the verge of tears. "We should have seen it, but we were so anxious to get somebody that we endowed her with all the qualities we were searching for."

Suddenly, Wilson changed his attitude. "You don't have proof of any of this," he charged Gwenn. "It's only a theory," he told his wife.

"Based on what Ms. Ramadge learned on her trip," she replied.

"Maybe Monique has reformed. Maybe she's straight now," Wilson argued. "Does she have a criminal record here?" he asked Gwenn.

"I don't know."

"Don't you think you should find out before making accusations?"

"I'm not making accusations, Mr. Wilson. You and Mrs. Wilson hired me to investigate your nanny. I've done so and I'm giving you my considered opinion of the results."

"It's not conclusive."

"Of course not. The only way to make sure of what Monique Bruno is up to during the hours she spends in your house alone with your son is to put her under surveillance. Depending on how long it takes to get evidence, it could run into considerable expense for you. You can go to the police, but I doubt they'll consider you have probable cause for their entering the case. Meantime, Bobby's at risk. She'll keep on sedating him. That's dangerous in itself. There's the added possibility that she might go out of the house and leave him. A fire could start; there could be a break-in; anything could happen."

"Go ahead, Ms. Ramadge. Set it up. Whatever it takes," Lana Wilson said.

"We only need to cover the house while the two of you are at work," Gwenn pointed out. "If she is entertaining, we'll tail the man when he leaves. That might be enough to appeal to the juvenile authorities to lend us a hand."

"I don't think we want to involve either the police or the juvenile authorities, do we?" Wilson asked his wife. She shook her head. "So we leave it to you, Ms. Ramadge."

"All right. I assume your house has a back door as well as a front door?"

Both Wilsons nodded.

"So that requires two operatives, myself and another."

"Whatever you say; money is no object," Lana Wilson urged.

This time her husband made no objection.

Gwenn saw the Wilsons out.

"Get me Sal Nova," she told Marge, and returned to her office.

Moments later her phone rang. She picked it up, expecting it to be Sal. It was Marge.

"Ray's here," she said. In a lower tone, she added, "With a friend."

"Oh?" Gwenn hesitated, then shrugged. "Send them in."

The door opened. The *friend* preceded Ray. She was tall, built on a large frame, and was probably attractive when at her best. She was far from that today; her skin was sallow and there were dark circles under her eyes. Her dark brown hair was lackluster. She wore a loose-fitting silk pants suit of an indeterminate color between gray and beige that didn't help her complexion. She was also ill at ease. Without Ray's urging she might not have stepped across the threshold. Was this the friend he'd been sitting up with Friday night? She did look as though she'd been sick and might still be, Gwenn thought, and looked to Ray.

He cleared his throat. "This is Jayne Harrow. Detective Harrow. I spoke to you about her before you went to Puerto Rico." His eyes were flashing signs she took to mean he wanted her to play along.

"Oh yes, of course. How are you, Detective Harrow?" She waved them to chairs while Ray continued to flash signals she still didn't understand.

"As I told you, Jayne and I worked Narco together. Then I was transferred to Homicide and Jayne got a new partner, Brian Ford. While riding with him, she uncovered strong indications of corruption. He offered her a piece of the action, but she turned it down and reported him to the lieutenant. He wanted hard evidence. She didn't have it. Meantime, word of what she'd done got out. It didn't exactly make her popular."

"No, it wouldn't." Gwenn regarded the policewoman with sympathy and respect.

"She took it as long as she could; then she contacted Internal Affairs and made a date for an interview. The night before she was due to report, a team, presumably from IA, raided her apartment and turned a cache of crack cocaine." Ray paused, then made the obvious point. "She is now in the position of having to defend herself on the very same charge she intended to bring against Ford."

"You believe the drugs were planted?" Gwenn asked Jayne Harrow.

"Yes."

"Would they really do that?" she asked Ray.

"If this thing is as big as I think, yes. IA will continue to investigate Jayne's charges against Ford, of course, but turning those drugs on her premises is pretty much damning. She's been suspended indefinitely and without pay."

"I'm sorry, Detective Harrow." Gwenn frowned at Ray, indicating he should get to the point.

"Jayne is not guilty of confiscating drugs for her own use or for resale. She's an honest and dedicated police officer. She'll be cleared, but in the meantime she needs a job."

Now she got it. Gwenn frowned. He shouldn't have sprung this on her without preparation.

"Jayne's one hell of a good investigator, Gwenn. We were partners for three months and I can vouch for her. Her brother and her fiancé were both state troopers. They died trying to stop a gang of marauders preying on campers. She joined the force to honor them. She's clean."

Gwenn looked to Jayne Harrow and waited. Now was the moment for her to make her own case, but she looked down at the tips of her shoes and remained silent.

"I'd like to help, Detective Harrow," Gwenn said, "but I don't have work to offer. As you can see, this is a very small operation. I do the investigating and all outside work. Marge,"—she indicated the outer office—"does the bookkeeping and filing and handles the correspondence. We barely keep our heads above water."

"I understand." Jayne Harrow got up.

Ray held up a hand, indicating she was to wait. "You do sometimes hire outside operators," he reminded Gwenn.

"That's true, but it's temporary. Sometimes the job is over in a couple of days."

"It's okay, Ms. Ramadge," Jayne assured her. "I'm sorry for taking your time."

At that moment, the telephone on Gwenn's desk rang. "Oh, Sal. How are you? . . . Yes, I did call." She hesitated. "I did have something, but . . ." She waved to Jayne Harrow to sit. "The situation's changed. Okay, Sal? Another time." She hung up.

"I've got a surveillance job," she told the policewoman. "I estimate it will run a week—maybe less, maybe more. We'll be watching a house on the North Shore of Long Island—doors front and rear. We're interested in what the nanny is doing while the parents of the child she's looking after are away at work."

"Physical abuse?" Harrow asked.

"No, no, nothing like that. At least, my God, I hope not. What it looks like—the nanny, Monique Bruno, was a prostitute, probably still is. The mother calls at various times during the day, so it's not likely she leaves the house. If she does, of course we tail her. The probability is that the johns come to her. Either way, she's got to be sedating the child."

"God," Harrow groaned.

"We don't need to catch them in flagrante. We'll get shots of the john going in and coming out and then tail him. Okay?"

Harrow nodded vigorously; then her face clouded. "I don't have a car."

"You can use mine," Ray was quick to offer.

"We'll rent. No problem," Gwenn countered firmly. "We start tomorrow. The clients are Frank and Lana Wilson. She's a lawyer and commutes into Manhattan every day. He's in real estate and has an office in Sands Point. They leave the house before eight each morning, so we want to be in place by seven-thirty. Since to-morrow's the first day, we'll meet at the railroad station at seven and proceed from there."

"Yes ma'am."

"Call me Gwenn."

Jayne Harrow's eyes gleamed. "You won't be sorry, Gwenn."

"I don't expect to be. Now, Marge will give you one of our standard employment forms to sign. She'll arrange for the car and give you directions on how to get out to the Island. I'll see you tomorrow."

"Yes. Thank you." She looked to Ray. "Shall I wait?"

"I'll call you later."

"I'll probably be at a meeting."

"I'll find you."

Jayne Harrow nodded and left.

Gwenn waited till she was gone and the door was firmly shut behind her. "You want to tell me why you did that?" she said, turning to Ray. "You just about forced me to hire her."

"I'm sorry. I tried to call you, but—"

"And the line was busy so you took it on yourself to come over and barge in. You could at least have let her wait outside for a few minutes and come in alone to explain what was going on."

"I'm sorry. I didn't realize the position I was putting you in. I wanted you to meet her, talk to her, see what kind of person she is before I told you her whole story."

"There's more?"

"There's more."

Gwenn threw up her hands and went around to sit at her desk again. "Let's hear it."

"Jayne's been under a lot of stress these past months."

"That's clear. Get to the point."

"There's no question that the crack found in her apartment was planted."

"By whom?" Gwenn asked.

"Probably by her partner and whoever else is involved with him. My guess is it would be guys on the squad."

"That's tough."

"She's drinking. Heavily."

"Oh, God."

"She lives alone without even a dog or a cat for company. Now she's under suspicion so she has no job. She gets up in the morning and there's no purpose to the day ahead. She has nowhere to go and nothing to do. You've given her some purpose, a reason for getting out of bed at least. She is not going to let you down, believe me."

"I don't know . . ."

"Please, if you fire her now before she even gets a chance to show what she can do . . ."

"I'm not going to fire her, but you should have told me."

"I was afraid that if you knew of her problem, she wouldn't stand a chance."

"I would have hired her on your say-so—which is what I'm doing now," she pointed out.

"And I thank you." he stopped; his eyes fixed on hers. "Welcome home, Gwenn. I've missed you. You have no idea how much."

"I've missed you too," she said.

"I had all kinds of plans for celebrating. I got sidetracked. I'm sorry."

"I understand. Jayne was counting on you. You couldn't let her down."

"If you ever suspect that she's not doing the job, that she's not one hundred percent . . ."

"I can't have her on the job if she isn't," Gwenn pointed out quietly and earnestly. "This is no routine divorce investigation. There's a child at risk."

"I know. The instant you have the vaguest notion anything is wrong, let her go. No explanation necessary." Ray moved toward her, took her hands in his. "So when are we going to get together?"

"I've got to go out to the Island this afternoon, but I should be back by . . . say, six? Is that good for you?"

He shook his head. "I'm pulling the four-to-midnight." He looked at his watch. "It's nearly lunchtime. Can we grab a sandwich?"

It wasn't what either of them had had in mind.

After an interlude that was definitely unsatisfactory for each, Gwenn and Ray parted and Gwenn drove out to survey the area where the Wilsons lived.

Finding a surveillance post in the city was relatively easy. Sitting in a parked car among other parked cars on a crowded street was not likely to attract particular attention. If anyone happened to take note, he would probably shrug it off and walk away: city people didn't get involved. In the suburbs it was different. People were curious and they were suspicious. The presence of a woman sitting in a strange car would be noted and reported. Fortunately, there was a small private beach at the end of the street, which was shared by the residents. During those last golden days of summer, it was in full use. Children, their parents, young adults, retirees, all converged on it. A beach permit was required and Frank Wilson secured one for each of the investigators, thus legitimizing their presence. If anyone wondered what they were doing sitting in the car instead of enjoying sand and water, they could go ahead and make a report. If a cruising patrol car bothered to check it out, both Gwenn and Jayne could show official ID. As long as the weather remained fair, they had no problem. If it rained, nobody was going to be out checking beach permits.

Gwenn and Jayne met the next morning, as arranged, at the local railroad station. Gwenn had a road map and they studied the positions she had marked. Before taking them up, they spent half an hour in a leisurely drive to familiarize themselves with the layout of the streets. It might be important to know which were one-way and which dead-end. They kept in touch by car phone.

The first day passed slowly and uneventfully. There was little activity either at the Wilson house or in the neighborhood. At ten-thirty, groceries were delivered to the house. A teenager came in a van and pulled into the Wilsons' driveway. He got out and rang the doorbell at the back. He made two trips, carrying a large carton and going inside each time. He was out again in less than a minute. Jayne, covering the back, reported his movements to Gwenn.

The next flurry of activity was the appearance of the man from Long Island Water to read the meters. He passed from house to house ringing doorbells, all at the rear. If no one answered, he stuck a card in the doorframe and left. He was admitted at the Wilson house and was out again minutes later.

Just before noon, the action shifted to the front, when Monique Bruno came out with her charge.

Gwenn was stunned. They hadn't made provision for this, not for her leaving the house and taking the child with her. There was a car in the garage, but apparently the nanny wasn't going to use it. Thank God for that. Gwenn's heart beat fast. If she tried to tail Monique on foot, she ran the risk of blowing the whole operation right there. Gwenn agonized and watched as the nanny took the child's hand and walked him firmly down the front path to the street and turned left—to the beach! What could be more natural and logical than taking him to the beach? Only then did

Gwenn become aware that she was sweating. Only then did she realize how concerned she was for the child.

Gwenn was wearing a bikini under her clothes. She had also prepared a beach kit containing a tube of sunblock, a collapsible beach umbrella, and a matching beach towel. She had no use for these items herself, but she knew that everybody who would be out on the beach did and she wanted to blend into the scene.

"Bruno and the boy are headed for the beach," she told Jayne over the phone. "I'm going after them."

"Right."

Harrow made no comment; no comment was called for, Gwenn thought. She reached for the canvas beach bag and got out of the car. She walked quickly so as not to lose sight of the nanny and the boy, but not so fast as to call attention to herself. At the gate entrance, she flashed her permit for the guard and passed through. She set herself up at the back on a sandy rise from which she could observe everything that was going on down below along the curving shore.

Monique and Bobby were at the water's edge. Their umbrella and chairs were already waiting for them—an indication that they were regulars. Bruno stretched out in the shade, while the boy, sun hat firmly on his head, swim trunks slipping below his belly button and in danger of going down to his ankles, toy pail and shovel in hand, joined his friends in building castles near the water.

An hour later, the nanny packed up and took Bobby back to the house. For lunch, of course, Gwenn assumed.

Harrow confirmed Gwenn's thoughts. She had binoculars and an unobstructed view into the kitchen.

Half an hour later, Harrow reported that the nanny was taking Bobby upstairs. The shades of the nursery were drawn. Would that be to help him sleep, or was it the signal that the coast was clear? This was the critical time. Gwenn and Harrow waited, fighting the drowsiness brought on by the afternoon sun and the rhythmic slap of the surf on the shore.

At four o'clock, the nursery shades went up again.

At 4:26, Monique and the boy came out. He was dressed in shorts and a T-shirt and was riding a tricycle. He seemed to be having trouble keeping it on course; Bruno had to help him. She guided him to a children's play area just inside the beach entrance. It was equipped with swings, seesaws, a jungle gym, and slides. From what Gwenn could observe, the nanny was testing his responses. Half an hour later, seemingly satisfied, she took Bobby home again.

Jayne Harrow reported the nanny was giving Bobby his dinner. At 6:18, a dark green Lexus entered the driveway, paused while the garage door went up, then parked inside.

Lana Wilson was home.

Gwenn waited till she got out of the car and entered the house.

"Time to go," she told Jayne Harrow. The first day's work was done.

They drove back to Manhattan, each in her own car, and met in Gwenn's office to discuss what they had learned. Not much. They discussed their options should Monique again come out with the child but head somewhere other than the beach. If they came out the front, Gwenn would inform Harrow what direction they were taking and Harrow would pick them up. If they went out the back, the process would be reversed. But the situation didn't arise. The second day followed the pattern of the first, except that it was less eventful, if that was possible. There were no deliveries, no metermen, no visitors except for the gardening service that came to cut the lawn and weed the flower beds.

The third day it rained.

They stayed on the job. The nanny and the child stayed home.

There was almost no communication between Gwenn and her operative, but so far Gwenn was satisfied. Detective Harrow was calm, low-key in her responses, professional in manner, and completely sober.

The fourth day, Friday, was the nanny's day off. It was decided to suspend surveillance for the day. What Monique Bruno did on her day off was her business.

"I know it's not for me to say, but I think it's a mistake," Jayne Harrow volunteered at their evening meeting. It was the first time she'd ventured a comment. "The more we know about the subject, the better chance we have of nailing her. The way she's been holed up these past days, I get the feeling she knows something's going on. She suspects she's being watched. The Wilsons could have let it slip somehow."

Marge Pratt, sitting in as usual, nodded vigorously. "The Wilsons may not care what Bruno is doing while she's away from Bobby, but Jayne's right; it could have a direct bearing."

Gwenn was surprised these two had so quickly formed an alliance. "I agree, of course. But it's the Wilsons' money and that makes it their call."

SATURDAY, SEPTEMBER 3
MORNING

On the fifth day, they resumed surveillance and continued through the weekend, and through Monday, although it was Labor Day. The Wilsons didn't go to work, but with Monique on duty they had planned to go to their club, play golf, have lunch with friends, and relax. Their friends were envious, the women in particular.

"You're so lucky," Cassie Weinstock, their nearest neighbor, already maudlin over prelunch daiquiris, told Lana. "I never did find anybody I could trust with my Jenny. I had to wait till she was in kindergarten before I could get out of the house. By then it was too late to try to resume my career. So I continued to have babies."

And using them as an excuse for dropping a career that hadn't been going anywhere anyway, Lana thought as she picked at her salad.

"Do you suppose your girl has a friend?" her neighbor asked. "Somebody like herself? I'd be glad to pay her fare from . . . wherever."

"Your kids are grown," Lana Wilson pointed out. "All four of them. Spread out through high school and college. Why do you need a nanny?"

"I'm expecting again," Cassie announced smugly. "We decided, Chuck and I, that if we wanted any more children, we'd better get to it. Time is running out. I just got the word from my doctor."

"Congratulations." *Just like that!* Lana Wilson thought, resentment behind her smile. She'd had to consult three fertility specialists and undergo two surgical procedures before she'd finally managed to conceive. "Congratulations."

"I want this baby," Cassie continued, now made garrulous by the cocktails, "but I'm remembering all the little inconveniences and I'd like to avoid them. If I could get somebody like your Monique . . . she's a jewel. But I guess you know that."

Lana Wilson bowed her head.

"Of course, Bobby is an angel. I've never heard that child cry. Every one of my four was wild. All together they were just too much for any one woman I ever brought in."

"I don't think Monique knows anybody, but I'll ask."

"Maybe the agency she came from . . . ?"

"She didn't come from an agency."

"Oh? I thought she did."

Lana Wilson wondered what her neighbor would say if she knew the jewel of a nanny had been arrested three times on charges of prostitution. What would she say if she knew they were having her investigated? That at that very moment a team of detectives was watching the house?

The only development that weekend affected Jayne Harrow. She was ordered to appear before Internal Affairs for a hearing on the Tuesday following Labor Day. Could Gwenn replace her for the one day? Jayne asked.

Gwenn assured her she could and told her not to worry and wished her good luck.

"I can't tell you how much I appreciate this," Jayne said. "So, I'll see you on Wednesday. At the station. At the usual time."

"Absolutely."

WEDNESDAY, SEPTEMBER 7 MORNING

But on Wednesday, the ninth day of the surveillance, Jayne Harrow didn't show up.

Gwenn waited in her car at the LIRR station. She waited for twenty minutes, allowing for traffic delays, then called Jayne's apartment. The machine kicked in with the routine message. Next, Gwenn tried the car phone. No response. What could have happened?

Was she drunk? Gwenn was ashamed to think that, but she couldn't help it. Was she drunk and passed out? Gwenn's immediate concern was to cover the job in hand. Sal Nova had worked in Jayne's place yesterday. Luckily, Gwenn was able to reach him before he left his house and he agreed to come out for another day. That done, she felt a bit better. Somehow, Gwenn couldn't believe that Jayne had drunk herself into a stupor. She had been attending AA meetings regularly every night after work and had been reliable on the job. The key was the Internal Affairs hearing on Tuesday. If that had gone badly, then . . .

She called Ray.

"I can't believe she'd let you down like this," he said. "She was so grateful for the work and for your trust."

"I can't believe it either," Gwenn assured him. "We've only been together these few days, but she's been stable and seemed trustworthy. How did the hearing go? Have you heard anything?"

"Not a word."

"She could have had an accident."

Ray sighed. "I'll check. What was she driving?"

"Just a second, I'll put this on the conference line." Gwenn dialed her office and Marge answered.

"Hart Security and Investigation."

"Marge, it's me. Ray needs to know the make, year, color, and license number of the car we rented for Jayne. Before we get into that, though, somebody should go to her apartment just in case . . ."

"Just in case what?" Marge wanted to know.

"Jayne didn't show up this morning. She doesn't answer her phone either at home or in the car."

"I'll go," Marge offered.

"It might be bad."

"That's okay."

"I'll start on the hospitals anyway," Ray said.

By the end of the morning neither fear had been realized. Jayne Harrow had not been in an automobile accident. She had not been admitted to any of the emergency rooms in the five boroughs or Long Island. She was not in her apartment drunk and sleeping it off.

"Did you find out what happened at the hearing yesterday?" Gwenn asked Ray.

"She never showed up," he replied.

CHAPTER 5

WEDNESDAY, SEPTEMBER 7
NIGHT

It was a fine summer night, the moon rising and a gentle breeze coming up off the Hudson. Cars were parked bumper to bumper on both sides of Riverside Drive but traffic wasn't moving. The boats moored at the Seventy-ninth Street basin bobbed gently on the calm waters. The neighborhood homeless had made their sleeping arrangements for the night.

Russ Hoffman was taking his nightly stroll with his German shepherd, Gretchen. He had turned her loose along the strip of grass bordering the river known as Riverside Park. There had been a brief shower earlier and the earth was still damp, intensifying the odors of decaying leaves. Nose to the ground, tail raised like a banner, Gretchen followed these intoxicating scents. She ran in small, excited circles. She was having a good time, Hoffman thought, taking pleasure in her freedom, while he breathed in the cool, refreshing night air.

Starting back up to the street and home, Russ Hoffman noticed a change in the dog's manner. Gretchen started to whine.

She wanted to show him something. That something was in the row of parked cars. She ran along the row, up and down, before selecting one. She barked at it, her whole sturdy body trembling.

"All right, Gretchen. All right, girl." Hoffman went to her and reached down to give her a calming pat, but Gretchen only barked with greater intensity. Her hackles rose.

Hoffman was short, chunky, and very strong. He was skilled in self-defense, being both an amateur boxer and a student of judo, yet at this moment he was uneasy. He looked around carefully before approaching the car. He called, "Gretchen, come. Heel. Sit." Though still under great stress, she obeyed the commands. "Good girl," he said, and put the leash on her. Together they moved forward.

The light was sufficient for Hoffman to make out that there was someone inside the car—slumped forward, facedown on the wheel. Was it a man or a woman? The short dark hair was no indication these days. The loose trench coat was no help. All the windows were closed. Hoffman tapped at the window on the driver's side.

No reaction. He tried again, this time pummeling on the glass with both fists.

Nothing.

Man or woman, whoever it was, was sleeping hard.

THURSDAY, SEPTEMBER 8
AFTERNOON

The news that Jayne Harrow had been found dead of carbon monoxide poisoning didn't reach Sergeant Raymond Dixon at Queens Homicide till the following afternoon. The delay was not due to uncertainty regarding the victim's identity. Because of her suspension Jayne was without her shield, but she was carrying her Detectives Endowment Association card. As soon as he saw that, Detective Charley Pulver, who had caught the squeal, was smart enough to pass the information on to his CO, who in turn made sure it reached the brass in the big building. A strategy meeting was hastily convened and it was decided to declare a news blackout. The word was to be relayed to everyone connected to Detective Harrow to keep his mouth shut.

Ray Dixon had been relentlessly checking ES and EMS units as well as the various hospital emergency rooms, all unofficially. His personal involvement was not known and so the edict was not deemed to apply to him. By the time he found out what had happened to his friend, her body had been transferred to the morgue and the car in which she had slipped from sleep to death removed to the police garage for a thorough inspection. The Riverside Drive crime scene was no longer roped off from the curious; whatever clues might have been there were there no more. There was nothing for Ray to do but go to the morgue and view the remains. He went more as a gesture of friendship than as part of an investigation. Since he was a police officer, the formalities intended to ease the shock of viewing a loved one were set aside: the drawer in which Jayne Harrow reposed was simply rolled out and the sheet covering her face raised for him to see.

She looked peaceful, he thought. It hit him hard that in death she had found rest where she had not in life. She had died alone. As far as he knew, she had no living relatives, so he claimed the body and arranged for the funeral. He could do that much for her.

The attendant told him where to go to fill out the necessary forms. When he got there, there was a message waiting for him. He was ordered to report to the chief of detectives *forthwith*.

Ray Dixon was not a frequenter of One Police Plaza. He was not accustomed to the rarefied atmosphere, and no attempt was made to put him at ease. Nor was he ushered into the presence of the chief himself. In a way, that was a relief. The chief might have taken pains to be diplomatic; Captain Landau didn't bother. He got right to the point.

"I understand you were a friend of Detective Harrow."

"Yes sir." How did he know that? Who had told him?

"You went to view her remains just now."

So that was it! "Yes sir."

Landau studied him. "And you're claiming her body."

"She has no one else, Captain." Word sure traveled fast, Ray thought.

Landau nodded a couple of times. "Well, this is a very sad thing. I'm sorry."

"Thank you."

"She was a good cop, but I think she was carrying too heavy a load. We expected too much of her."

Dixon frowned. "In what way?"

"Think about it, Sergeant." Landau leaned back in his chair. The captain presented an impressive appearance—his deep tan contrasted with his silver hair, his tweed suit was impeccably tailored. Ray felt as though he were being interviewed for a job and found himself weighing his answer. "You mean because she went straight from the Academy into undercover work?"

"Precisely."

"She was very good at it."

Landau waved that off. "Talent doesn't substitute for experience."

"No sir, I agree." Where was this leading?

"You've trained other rookies," Landau continued. "You know how much the first partner influences the beginner. Harrow looked up to you; she trusted you. Then you were transferred and she was assigned to ride with Brian Ford. They didn't get along. She didn't trust him, and he resented her, but we won't go into that. Ford insisted on making all the buys himself and relegated Harrow to backup in all but the rarest instances. She began to suspect he was hiding something. As time passed, she became convinced that he was skimming off the drugs they were supposed to turn in. He sensed her suspicions and beat her to the punch."

Dixon shook his head. "That's not the way—"

"Hear me out, Sergeant. She came to me and I told her I'd look into the matter. But before I could do anything, she went over my head to Internal Affairs. Faced with counterclaims by one officer against another, IA raided Detective Harrow's apartment and found a sizable stash."

"Planted. The drugs were planted on her. Probably by Ford."

"I have no doubt that's what she told you."

"I believe it."

"Of course you do. She was depressed and drinking heavily. Did you know that?"

"She'd stopped drinking," Dixon insisted.

"Not according to the IA panel that interrogated her."

"I heard she didn't show up for the interrogation."

"Who told you that? She showed up all right. She showed up drunk. We had a meeting and decided to keep the whole thing under wraps. But, of course, she'd ruined herself in the department and she knew it. There was nothing left for her. so she killed herself."

The circumstances dictated the conclusion and Ray had already accepted it. Now he wasn't so sure.

Landau sensed his uncertainty. "How much do you know about the manner of her death, Sergeant? Did you know the doors and windows of the car were locked? Did you know rags were stuffed in the car's exhaust pipe?"

"My God," Ray groaned.

"I don't think there can be any doubt it was suicide. We're playing it down as much as possible, keeping it out of the papers and off television and radio, for her sake as much as for that of the department. The funeral will be low-key. You understand? Private. For the family."

"There is no family," Dixon reminded him.

Landau nodded. "You did say that, didn't you?"

"I can't believe it," Gwenn said. "I don't believe it!"

"I'm surprised *you* do," Marge Pratt accused Ray.

They were in Gwenn's office. She had just come in from the day's surveillance of the Wilson house. Ray had walked over after his interview in the big building.

"I don't want to believe it," he told them both. "Jayne had no proof of her allegations against Ford. His counterallegations were proven when her apartment was raided. She appeared before IA without any defense."

Gwenn interrupted. "I thought you said she never turned up for the hearing."

"They put that out till a decision could be reached about how to handle the situation."

"They lied? Internal Affairs lied?"

"They hedged," Ray said, hedging himself.

"Call it what you want," Gwenn countered. "I don't believe Jayne committed suicide. I don't see her stuffing the tail pipe with rags, locking the doors and windows, turning on the motor and sitting there waiting to die. I don't."

"Me neither," Marge Pratt echoed.

Dixon looked from one to the other. "I swear you two are a pair. You knew Jayne Harrow for . . . nine, ten days, and it wasn't a close association. "You"—he pointed at Gwenn—"sat in a parked car while she sat in another parked car with a minimum of communication between you." He pointed to the receptionist. "You didn't even have that much contact with her, yet you're both defending her."

"You worked closely with her. You trained her. That should have forged a bond between you," Gwenn said.

"It did."

"When she was in trouble you helped her. She trusted you. Yet you're ready to believe the worst."

"I believe the evidence."

"You didn't see the evidence."

Now he was truly shocked. "Jayne never denied the presence of drugs in her apartment, only how they got there."

"I don't mean that. I mean the evidence regarding her death."

He gasped. In fact, he only knew what Captain Landau had told him. "Are you suggesting it's false?"

"Of course not," Gwenn answered promptly. "It's a matter of interpretation."

Ray thought it over—once more. "Given the circumstances and her state of mind, suicide is the logical conclusion."

"It's one. There could be others."

They looked at each other. At that moment, there was only one other interpretation and not one of the three was ready to put it forward.

"How about the autopsy?" Gwenn asked.

"Preliminary findings indicate she died of carbon monoxide poisoning. There are no apparent complications."

"How about time of death?"

"I don't know," Ray answered. The captain hadn't mentioned it—by design, or because he didn't think it was important? "Her body was found in the rental car about eleven-thirty last night."

"An estimated time of death would help."

Ray flushed. "I'll see what I can find out. As for the autopsy report, it's a little early. Since there aren't any complications . . ."

"You're satisfied there are no complications?"

"Yes, I am. I'm satisfied. Okay?"

"I'm not."

"You're going to set yourself up against the entire police department?" he asked.

"Of course not. I'm not crazy." Nevertheless, Gwenn paled at the thought. "I just need to ask a few questions. After all, Jayne Harrow worked for me. Nobody heard from her or saw her or knew where she was from Labor Day at six P.M., when she left this office, till she was found in my rental car on Riverside Drive. I assume it was my rental she was found in? Somebody did check that out?"

"Naturally. I suppose so." Ray was embarrassed.

"So why hasn't anybody come around to question me? Could it be they don't really care about the answers?"

"You've got no right to say that. They've probably contacted the rental agency direct."

"That wouldn't be the way I'd do it. Anyhow, I'd like the car back. I am paying for it. By the day," she reminded him. She turned to Marge. "Call the police garage and find out when they expect to be through with it." She flashed a look at Ray. "I'm entitled to that at least."

He had to grin. "You sure are."

"Also, I want to know what happened to Detective Harrow's reports for the last three days she worked for me. She didn't turn them in."

"She left them with me," Marge Pratt said.

Gwenn cut her off. "Those were the initial reports Tuesday through Thursday. We didn't work Friday. I need the weekend sheets, Saturday through Monday. I'm entitled to them. My clients are entitled to know what's in them. Probably they're in her apartment."

Having talked to Jayne Monday night, she already knew what was in them, Ray thought biting back a smile. What she was doing was staking her right to search Jayne's place. She didn't really care whether the report turned up or not.

CHAPTER 6

THURSDAY, SEPTEMBER 8
EVENING

Gwenn Ramadge was expert at picking locks; it was one of a variety of useful skills Cordelia Hart had taught her. On this occasion, however, Gwenn wanted to be able to show she had entered Jayne Harrow's apartment legally and in the presence of a witness. So she did the logical and natural thing—she looked up the building superintendent, George Stavros. She showed him one of her Hart S and I business cards with her name at the top left corner as proprietor.

First Stavros looked Gwenn over; then he studied the card. "Somebody from your company was here yesterday asking to get in."

"My assistant, Marge Pratt."

He shrugged. "She said Detective Harrow hadn't shown up for work and she'd been calling all morning and not getting any answer. She was worried maybe something had happened to Detective Harrow, like maybe she was sick . . . ." He let it hang.

"So you did finally open the door, but there was nobody there," Gwenn prodded.

"Right." It was a reluctant admission.

Gwenn sighed. It occurred to her that the news of Jayne's death had not yet been released, and that this reserved, colorless man had cared about her. "She won't be there now either. I'm afraid I have bad news. Detective Harrow fell asleep in her car with the motor running."

He gaped at her.

"She's dead, Mr. Stavros. I'm very sorry."

He nodded slowly several times. "It was bound to happen, drinking like she was. She was a nice woman and a good cop, too, I heard, but when the police raided her place and found the drugs she went right to pieces. Shame. Real shame." Tears shimmered along the rims of his eyes, and he made no effort to wipe them away.

"How long had she been living here?" Gwenn asked.

"About a year."

"How long had she been drinking—heavily?"

"Well, it started roughly six months ago. It kept getting worse till the raid. Then she seemed to pull herself together for a while." He shook his head. "You never know. They say you have to hit bottom before you can start up again."

"When was the last time you saw her, Mr. Stavros?"

"Oh, let's see. Today's Thursday. So, it was Monday. That's right, Monday near midnight. I was coming in from the movie and she was going out."

"Going out?"

"Right. Cops keep odd hours. She stopped me in the hall downstairs. I thought she was going to complain about the water running in the toilet tank. Actually, she thanked me for fixing it. I didn't think she'd even noticed." A tear dropped and he took a crumpled handkerchief from his back pocket and wiped his cheek.

"How about Tuesday? Did you see her at any time at all on Tuesday?"

"No ma'am."

"Was she using her apartment? I mean, was she coming home to sleep?"

He bristled. "I wouldn't know that. I can tell you she wasn't putting out her trash in the morning."

"You're very observant, Mr. Stavros."

"Got to keep your eyes open if you want to survive."

"That's true, unfortunately," Gwenn said. "Have you any idea where Detective Harrow might have been spending the nights she wasn't at home?"

"I didn't say she wasn't home, Ms . . . ." He referred to the card Gwenn had given him. "Ms. Ramadge. I only said she didn't put out the trash. That could mean either that she was drunk or didn't have any trash."

"Which do you think it was?"

"Well, she wasn't much of a housekeeper. On the other hand, she didn't have any friends, men or women. She was a loner." He paused, comparing their situations. "When did she die?" he asked abruptly.

"She was found late Wednesday night."

"There have been more people coming around and asking questions, more people concerned about her, since she died than ever came while she was alive."

"Before Wednesday night?"

"Yes. Your assistant was one. She came around noon on Wednesday."

"Who else?"

"A man came this morning. Claimed to be her brother. If I hadn't known her brother was dead, I still wouldn't have bought it. He was a Latino."

Interesting, Gwenn thought, but put it aside temporarily. "How about the police?"

"Her partner came. Sergeant Ford."

Naturally. "What did he want?"

"Same as everybody else—to get into the apartment."

"And did you let him in?"

"Yes ma'am. He had a search warrant."

Cut to the chase, Gwenn thought. "Detective Harrow was working for me these past days so I'm making the arrangements for her wake and burial. I've come to get a dress for her."

"Why didn't you say so? My God!" He was instantly stricken.

Without further ado, Stavros steered Gwenn to the stairs and they climbed up to the fifth floor. When they reached the top, he was no more winded than she. At Harrow's door he brought out a heavy ring of keys, inserted one, and stood aside for Gwenn to pass.

But she held back. "I don't like to take your time, Mr. Stavros. If you have something else to do, I can lock up after I'm through."

"That's okay. I'll wait."

"Whatever you say." It had been worth a try, Gwenn thought as she looked around. He would expect her to be curious, so she didn't try to hide her interest. Stavros had criticized Jayne's housekeeping, but Gwenn found the place orderly and reasonably clean. It was sparsely furnished in Scandinavian style. A pair of bullfight posters on the wall over the sofa provided color and energized the room. On a low chest, framed family portraits and snapshots were arranged in clusters. They were of various vintages. Two particularly attracted Gwenn.

"This must be Jayne," she said, and picking it up, brought it to the desk and turned on the lamp to get a better look.

The snapshot showed a girl and two boys. The girl was about fourteen. She had long, dark hair braided into a single thick plait that hung down her back. The boys were older, young adults actually. She wore shorts and a T-shirt and held a baseball in the act of pitching. The boys wore baseball uniforms and held bats cocked and ready to hit. All three were grinning broadly.

"Which one is her brother, do you think?"

"I don't know." Stavros was losing patience. "I'm afraid I have to ask you to get on with it."

"I'm sorry. I thought I might be able to use one of these pictures in some way in the memorial." She picked up the second that had attracted her. It showed the same three young people. By their attitude and style of dress it had been taken some years later. Jayne now wore a neat pale pink summer suit and the young men wore the uniform of the state troopers. There was definitely a resemblance between Jayne and the man at her right, so the other was the fiancé. Both gone now. Gwenn held the picture for Stavros to see.

"Which do you like?"

Before he could answer, his beeper sounded. He walked out into the hall so he could answer in private. He returned quickly.

"Ms. Ramadge, I've got to go. I have a call from a tenant. There's a water emergency downstairs. You stay and take as long as you need; just be sure to engage both locks when you leave. Okay?"

"Yes. And thank you."

As soon as he was gone, Gwenn Ramadge went back to look at the rest of the photographs. they were mostly posed portraits recording family events—graduations, weddings, christenings. Next, she sat at the policewoman's desk prepared to make a thorough search. With Marge Pratt across the street to alert her by means of the pager, Gwenn didn't have to worry about Stavros coming back and catching her prying. Even so, Gwenn was nervous in such situations. Marge on the other hand, was gaining more and more assurance. Her assistant was developing a real flair for creating diversions. However, Gwenn put certain restraints on her: no false alarms to the fire department or 911, no serious damage to property. Despite that, the young woman who appeared so plain and dull on the outside had a truly amazing capacity for invention. Gwenn had no idea what kind of emergency she had concocted this time. Water emergency, Stavros had said. That could be as simple as entering an empty apartment and jamming the toilet, or turning on a faucet in the basement. It was one of Marge's favorite ruses and guaranteed to capture and hold a super's attention.

Gwenn went through the desk quickly but found nothing. She wasn't surprised. Jayne Harrow had not produced evidence to support her charges against Brian Ford. She had been told to get evidence.

Suppose she'd succeeded? And suppose that evidence involved others besides Ford? She wouldn't have known who to turn it over to—safely. So she'd contacted Internal Affairs. That made sense. And what would she do with it while she waited for the appointment? It wasn't likely she'd left it lying around in an unlocked drawer, was it? Particularly not after the raid. It had not been turned in the raid, Gwenn decided, or Ford and the Latino man would have had no reason to come back.

She looked around for a possible hiding place. None suggested itself. Trouble was, she didn't know what she was looking for. Probably it wasn't even here. Jayne might very well have moved it. Nevertheless, Gwenn continued to search. She looked in closets and bureaus. She spent time in the kitchen probing under the sink and in the cupboards. A woman was likely to use the kitchen as a hiding pace. She went through the utility closet. On the first shelf, which was just high enough to clear the upright vacuum, she found laundry detergent, a stack of quarters for the machine, and keys on a chain. Would they be a set of extras? Gwenn went to the front door and tried them. Yes. Two standard-size keys fitted the upper and lower locks. A small key must be for the mailbox. And one other, maybe for her locker at work. She'd get Ray to check it. She put the keys in her handbag, in her elation almost forgetting the ostensible reason for coming—the dress.

From Jayne's closet, she selected a pale rose silk and found a box in which to pack it.

Before leaving, she remembered to turn off the desk lamp.

THURSDAY, SEPTEMBER 8
NIGHT

They dressed in silence. Crystal Landau, seated at her theatrically illuminated dressing table, went about the job of applying her makeup with meticulous care. The base, custom-blended to enhance her skin tone, had to be perfectly applied. Unless it was, all the other embellishments were so much wasted effort. But Crystal Landau was experienced, almost a professional. She regarded herself in the mirror with satisfaction. Yes, her complexion had just the right glow. Next came the blusher, two tones of eyeshadow, liner, mascara. Last, lipstick—only a touch: the wet look, more moisture than color.

"You look beautiful, sweetheart."

Norman Landau knew the precise moment to confirm his wife's work, but he didn't make a move to touch her. He stood back admiring as she rose from the vanity bench, dropped the filmy negligee from her shoulders, and stood before him in the wisp of bikini that was all she would wear under the gown which was spread out on the bed, a shimmer of black and silver. She walked over, picked it up, and stepped into it. She turned her back and presented herself to be zipped.

The ritual was for him to bend down and kiss her bare shoulder. Tonight, he kept his lips in the warm curve at the base of her neck longer than usual. He nuzzled. He felt his blood rising. Hands on her breasts, he pulled her to him—hard. Suddenly, she pushed him away.

"Norman, not now."

"When then?"

"Now is not the proper time to discuss our love life."

"When is the proper time? When can you fit me into your schedule?"

"Don't take that tone with me, Norman."

"I'm sorry. I'm sorry, darling, but we never have any time together."

"That's not my fault. It's your crazy hours. If you had any kind of regular schedule, we could plan."

He opened his mouth and, frustrated, closed it again. How many times had he explained that his present assignment was as close to a regular nine-to-five business job as you could get in the department, and because of it he wasn't going anywhere. She was responsible for his being mired in it. Or rather, her famous sister was responsible for getting him an appointment he hadn't wanted, that amounted to little more than being a flunky for the chief of detectives. Crystal and her family thought that putting him close to the action would get him into it, would present opportunities. The opposite had resulted. Things happened on the street, not at the computer or in the C of D's anteroom. In his time Landau had been a good street cop. His talent lay in assessing a situation, making a decision, and having the courage to carry it through. In his present position, he was denied the opportunity to use this innate talent.

He had thought of requesting a transfer, but if he ever went back to the precinct level, Crystal would leave him. He'd considered resigning, but what other kind of work could he do? Oh, Crystal's famous sister would use her influence and get him another job and he'd be even more of a figurehead than he was now.

"We've managed to have two kids and raise them pretty damn successfully I'd say, and without your sister's help. My hours couldn't have been all that bad."

Crystal was careful not to spoil her makeup by frowning. "What's that supposed to mean? Are you suggesting we should have another child? At our age? You must be crazy."

"We used to have time for each other. Now with your charity work, your committees, your fund-raisers . . ." He shrugged.

"That work you denigrate gets your name in the program right up there with the mayor and the police commissioner."

Where it doesn't belong, Landau thought. He had told her that many times. She didn't understand. The parties and the banquets were her life. She loved to make a grand entrance, to preen for the photographers, then sulk because they were seated at an ordinary table and denied places on the dais with the dignitaries. Among those dignitaries was her sister, Lady Mirabelle, former wife of the brother of a former President and currently the wife of the former Chancellor of the Exchequer, Sir Montgomery Swaze. Her generous contribution could only buy so much.

"Would you please zip me?" Crystal asked. "It's getting late. I'd like to be there before the entrée."

He did so without another word.

She returned to the dressing table for the finishing touches.

He stood in front of the bureau mirror and inserted the diamond studs into his evening shirt. They were her gift to him on the occasion of their first attendance at one of these affairs. Landau didn't know how she'd managed to pay for them, but the message was clear. It was her way of letting him know she didn't want him in uniform. His uniform would proclaim his rank, which would be the lowest in the vast ballroom. The studs in place, Captain Norman Landau returned to his wife, their eyes meeting in the vanity mirror.

"I have a surprise for you," he said. "I can't tell you what it is, not yet. But you'll be pleased."

"I will?"

"Oh yes. At least, I think so."

The light in Crystal Landau's eyes gleamed brightly. "Tell me."

"I can't."

Probably something to do with another of his sordid cases,

Crystal thought, losing interest. She adjusted the angle of a cluster of honey-colored curls over her forehead. "Suit yourself."

He was sorely tempted, but he couldn't take the risk that she might pass it on to her sister to show off. He had waited so long, so very long, for a break like this. And so had she, he thought. Poor Crystal, she was entitled to a moment of triumph. The Harrow woman's death was unforeseen and disturbing, but it presented no more than a temporary delay. At any moment he expected to get a report from Brooklyn Homicide regarding the Raggedy Man case. He'd had to exert considerable pressure. It was obvious they'd been sitting on the case and he wondered why. He wondered why the Harrow woman had left the newspaper account of the case for him, and what her connection with it had been. The phone rang and his heart jumped and he reached for the receiver.

It was only their chauffeur for the evening.

"All right, Henry, thank you. We'll be right down." He informed his wife, "The car's here."

That was another source of friction. He was not entitled to a police limo with driver. So they hired one and pulled up in front of the marquee of whatever hotel was hosting the function to emerge into the glare of the floodlights like the celebrities they were not and pass through the gawking throng. The crowd, restrained behind wooden barricades, sensed they were impostors. They conveyed it by the sudden drop in cheers and calls and applause. The level soared again as the next limo pulled up and the genuine article stepped out.

Crystal held her head high, but she knew what was going on and it hurt. Landau clenched his teeth till his jaws ached. This would be the last time they would be snubbed like that, he promised himself. Next time, they would not only be recognized, they would be cheered. The crowd would call out to them by name; they would reach out to touch them.

Friday being the nanny's day off, surveillance once again was lifted. Gwenn slept an extra hour. Upon arising, she automatically turned on the bedside radio, which was set to an all-news station, and caught the end of a bulletin regarding the discovery of the body of a policewoman in a parked car. Putting on robe and slippers, she went into the living room to try the television. Only the local station, NY1, made any mention of the occurrence. The newscaster read copy off the TelePrompTer with little interest.

Gwenn padded to her front door and brought in her copy of the *Times*. She found a brief account on a back page in the unlikely company of the financial reports. The event involved neither violence nor sex, nor did it implicate persons in high places, Gwenn thought, as she read it carefully. There was nothing in it that she had not already learned from Ray. However, she did note that the car in which Jayne died had been parked on Riverside Drive overlooking the Seventy-ninth Street boat basin.

What in the world had Jayne Harrow been doing there?

She went into the kitchen, measured out the usual three scoops of coffee and added an equal number of cups of water, and plugged in the pot. Then she sat down at the kitchen table while it perked.

The next question followed the first: If Jayne was so despondent that she not only considered suicide but went so far as to select a method and provide herself with the means, wouldn't she have chosen a better place—more peaceful and private—in which to slip into eternal sleep? Wouldn't she have chosen a place where it was less likely a casual passerby might notice her and call in the alarm? If, on the other hand, subconsciously she wanted to be rescued, couldn't she have arranged for better odds?

Now that the news was public, the police would surely be coming around to see her, Gwenn thought. She looked forward to the visit, expecting to learn as much from them as they did from her—hopefully more. They would ask about Jayne's state of mind, her job performance, and Gwenn was prepared to answer. But when the phone rang finally that morning, it was Marge Pratt reporting that the Wilsons wanted to see her. They planned to be in Manhattan and could be in her office at eleven.

Frank Wilson handled the interview.

"We've decided to call off the investigation. No offense, Ms. Ramadge, but you don't seem to be getting anywhere. And, to be honest, it's running into a lot more money than we had anticipated or can afford."

"I understand." Wilson looked tired, Gwenn thought. He had put on weight, or at least bloat, which was usually the product of worry and physical inactivity. As for Lana Wilson, she looked unhappy. "I can't encourage you to continue. I don't see a break coming."

"You did your best." Wilson got up.

He was patronizing and it irked Gwenn. "What are you going to do about Monique?"

"We're letting her go," Lana Wilson replied.

Gwenn nodded. "That's best, but how will you manage?"

"I'll work from home. Lots of people are doing that. If I need to be in court or to go to the city for a special client interview, Frank will stay home with Bobby."

"Until we find a replacement," her husband added.

"Somebody with good moral character and with references which we'll take the trouble to check before we bring her into our home."

"Knock it off, Lana. You were just as anxious to hire Monique as I was."

"That's true," his wife admitted. "So we've both learned something."

Things were not right between these two, Gwenn thought, but it was no longer her business. She did have another matter to discuss with them. "Have the police contacted you?" she asked.

Both shook their heads.

"Why would they contact us?" Frank Wilson asked.

"The investigator I hired to assist me on your case went missing for a couple of days."

Lana Wilson blanched. "You mean there hasn't been anybody covering the back? For how long?"

"No, no, I hired a replacement right away. The house has been covered front and rear from eight to six as we agreed. Detective Harrow had personal problems. She may have committed suicide." Gwenn sighed. "Her body was found in her car Wednesday night."

"That's terrible," Lana Wilson murmured.

"I'm very sorry," her husband echoed. Relief that they weren't involved overrode synthetic sympathy. "Why would the police want to talk to us? We didn't know this . . ."

"Jayne Harrow."

"We didn't know she was on the case. We never met her. What could we tell them?"

"Nothing," Gwenn agreed.

Wilson scowled. It was clear he remained uneasy.

FRIDAY, SEPTEMBER 9
LUNCHTIME

"I told you not to worry, Mr. Rossi. I told you she wouldn't be able to stand up under the pressure."

Brian Ford raised his glass and took a deep, satisfying swallow of the beer, then settled back in his chair and looked around, savoring the moment. It wasn't often he could allow himself to talk that way to the *sotto capo* of one of the major crime families in the East.

Outside, the heat rose in waves from the gray pavement. Inside the restaurant, one of the finest in the city, it was crowded but cool. The clientele consisted of the top men and women in finance, city government, the courts. Ford not only recognized faces but could put names to them. Meantime, the famous ones were looking around and identifying each other. A lowly detective sergeant was lost in such a place.

Pietro Rossi wasn't all that relaxed either. For the position he held in the family, he was relatively young. He carried a lot of responsibility but felt absolutely equal to it on his own turf. As the orphaned son of the current *capo*'s brother, who had no son of his own, benefits had been heaped on Pietro. He had received the finest education that his uncle's money and influence and his own fierce ambition, dedication, and hard work made possible. He had further ensured his place in the hierarchy by marrying the daughter of a neighboring *capo*. That Angelina was a beautiful girl and as crazy about him as he was about her, he took for granted and regarded as his due.

His father-in-law had turned over control of the local so-called adult entertainment business to him, with its attendant drug and police connections. Rossi, however, was not satisfied to delegate; he favored the hands-on style of management. So he had summoned Ford. Accustomed to conducting business in the back room of some trattoria in Little Italy, or better yet in the privacy of the back seat of his limousine, he regarded the location of the present meet as an affirmation of his status. Nevertheless, he took the usual precautions, sitting with his back to the wall and his people posted at the bar with an overview of the room.

The detective sat with his back to the window, presenting an easy target. As far as Rossi could tell, he was without backup. Was he stupid, or careless?

"So they buy the suicide theory in the big building?"

"It's not a theory," Ford reiterated. "It's what happened. Harrow couldn't stand the heat and she killed herself. The case is closed."

"Fine by me. I just don't want any surprises later," Rossi warned. "I don't want any suicide notes turning up and naming names."

"She didn't know any names. She didn't know anything. She made a couple of buys on her own at the beginning, small stuff. She never went in with me on a major bust. She was not in a position to ID anybody. I made sure of that. She was guessing all the way through."

"How much did she know about the Raggedy Man?"

"Nothing. Absolutely nothing," Ford retorted with conviction.

"Are you sure? For somebody that didn't know what was going on, she stirred up the waters."

"It never counted for anything," Ford reassured the racketeer. "She never convinced anybody. Nobody took her seriously. Now it's wrapped up nice and neat with no loose ends."

The mobster's soft, doelike eyes narrowed speculatively. "I get the feeling she meant something to you."

"She was my partner."

"Okay." Rossi dismissed it. "I sent one of my people over to her place yesterday morning. He had a nice talk with the super." The point was to show Ford there were others who could do his job.

Ford took the point. "You didn't need to bother, Mr. Rossi. I had already done that."

"How about this outfit that Harrow was working for—Hart S and I?"

Ford shrugged. "It's a hole in the wall. It's run by a woman who inherited it from another woman. Amateurs."

Rossi was not satisfied. "She hired Harrow. They spent time together. They talked. They gossiped. Women do that. She could know something. Find out."

"I don't know, Mr. Rossi. I don't know if it's such a good idea to stir up the waters. In a couple of days it will all be forgotten and we can get back to normal operation."

Rossi expected unquestioning obedience; his face darkened.

"The woman who heads the agency went over to Harrow's place last night. The super let her in and then left. She was alone inside for about twenty minutes. Doing what?"

Ford couldn't help but be impressed with the reach of the organization's intelligence network, the information they could call up and the speed with which it was done.

"I want to know why this Hart agency gave your partner a job when she was under suspension from the department. I want to know what case they had her working on. What does this woman who runs the agency think about the suicide? What's her name . . . Ramadge. Find out what Ms. Ramadge is up to. Nothing moves till you get the answer." Rossi pushed away from the table. "I'm not hungry," he announced abruptly, and started for the door.

Immediately, his bodyguards were off the barstools, one pair striding in front of him and another falling in behind.

CHAPTER 7

**FRIDAY, SEPTEMBER 9
AFTERNOON**

Gwenn Ramadge was on the verge of contacting the police herself when Brian Ford came to call on her.

He had made inquiries about her, bypassing Rossi's sources. A couple of the guys on Homicide had heard of her. She'd been in on two cases they knew about, working for the suspect, and she'd done all right. She'd not only cleared her client but turned the real perp. A sergeant from Queens was dating her, Ray Dixon, the same guy who rode with Harrow when she was fresh out of the Academy. *So watch it,* he was warned. *Don't be too quick to write her off.* Nevertheless, she didn't impress him.

To start with, her office really was as he'd characterized it—a hole in the wall. It had a window air conditioner that wheezed mightily and produced no relief. Ford wasn't there five minutes when the sweat started to pour off him. The plain woman in the outer office kept him waiting while she finished some typing. Receptionists didn't do that to Brian Ford; he was good-looking, an officer of command rank, and accustomed to making an impression. As for Ramadge herself, she was petite, full of energy, and pretty—if you liked the type. He could take it or leave it.

Gwenn could tell instantly that he felt superior. His ego filled the tiny office. He was certainly handsome and she cautioned herself not to let that affect her—one way or the other. She smiled and waved him to a chair.

"Sorry about the air conditioner. Can I get you some iced tea? Juice? Anything?"

"No, thanks."

A pause while first impressions hardened.

"What can I do for you?" Gwenn Ramadge asked.

Ford crossed his long legs, trying to adjust his angular frame to the molded plastic of the chair. "I think I may have given your secretary the wrong impression when I called."

"Oh? How's that?"

"I told Ms. . . . uh . . . Pratt that I wanted to see you with regard to Detective Harrow."

"Yes?"

"That it concerns the investigation of her death."

"Doesn't it?"

"No. That is, not officially. I don't work Homicide. I'm not on the case. I work Narcotics, and Jayne was my partner. You know that, of course."

"Yes, I do." Gwenn waited.

"Narcotics is no job for a woman. That's not to say that I don't believe women should be cops. But the drug trade? No. That should be out of bounds."

"I understand Jayne was very good at her job. She made quite a reputation early on."

"That's it! You've put your finger on it—early on. Playacting at the Academy is one thing, pretending to be an addict, fooling the dealer and making the buy in the real world . . ." He shook his head. "The strain was too much for her. She got confused. She lost track of who were the good guys and who were the bad ones."

"I saw no indication she didn't know right from wrong."

"I don't mean that. She didn't get the broad picture of the drug action in this city. She couldn't see beyond the pusher on the corner to the wholesale buy at the top of the operation."

"Didn't you explain it to her?"

"Of course. I explained that sometimes it's better to pretend to play along, to take a bribe, to let one small-timer go in order to bring down an entire ring."

"That's not an unusual concept."

"Trouble was, I couldn't be specific, I couldn't name names, so it only made her more suspicious of what I was doing."

"What *were* you doing?"

"I was making a case against one of the top Colombian drug lords. I was working on it long before Jayne was assigned to me. I couldn't bring her into it—to start with because she wasn't experienced enough and also because I was concerned for her safety."

Gwenn nodded thoughtfully. "How do you explain the drugs found in her apartment?"

He groaned. "I can't. I knew she was drinking, but I had no idea about the drugs."

"She told me they were planted there."

"Well, she would say that, wouldn't she? What else did she tell you?" Ford asked.

"Nothing. We didn't have much opportunity for conversation. We were in separate cars. We communicated only when absolutely necessary."

"Do you mind if I ask you who your client was?"

"I don't mind, but I'm not going to tell you. It's not relevant."

He smiled, but the smile was sour and gave Gwenn a glimpse of what lay beneath the charm. "When was the last time you saw Jayne?"

"You said you're not investigating her death."

"I'm not, but I heard she didn't show up for work on Wednesday morning and that you had Sergeant Dixon check the accident reports and the hospital ERs."

"I *asked* him to check. Jayne was working for me and I was anxious that something might have happened to her. As it turns out, I was right."

"Yes and no. While you and Dixon were looking for her, she was sitting in her car up on Riverside Drive very much alive. What was she doing up there?"

"I don't know."

"Is that where your client lives?"

Gwenn got up. "I'm sorry, I can't spare you any more time."

He didn't move. "Relax, Ms. Ramadge. I tried. You can't blame me for that."

"What do you want?" Gwenn asked. "Why don't you come straight out with it? Who sent you?"

"Actually, it's the guys on the squad."

"What?" It was the last answer in the world Gwenn expected.

"We feel bad for what happened to Jayne. Everybody on the squad feels bad. We took up a collection." He reached into his inside breast pocket and drew out a respectably thick envelope and thrust it at her. "For the funeral. We heard you're making the arrangements."

Gwenn made no move to take it. "Your concern comes a little late."

"I know. I'm sorry."

"She went to your commanding officer and accused you of corruption. She said you and your buddies were skimming off the drugs you confiscated and selling them yourselves. In effect, she accused you of dealing under the protection of your shield. And now you want to pay for her funeral?"

Ford waited, then seeing she had no intention of taking the envelope, placed it on her desk. "I don't know who else to give this to." He walked out.

Gwenn continued to stare at the envelope. Was that really why Brian Ford had come—to ease his conscience and that of the other corrupt cops? Or was the fat envelope an excuse to probe Gwenn's reaction to the suicide theory, to find out whether or not she bought it? Why should that matter? As long as the top brass were satisfied, who cared what she thought?

Could Ford's visit mean the brass were not satisfied that Jayne had killed herself?

Gwenn had been with Jayne Harrow the last days of her life and she could testify to the effort the policewoman was making to straighten herself out, to overcome alcoholism and to justify her charges. It was not likely that Ford had acted alone, but Jayne had not mentioned anyone else, so for now at least, Gwenn would restrict herself to his guilt or innocence. There was no question that Harrow was grateful to Gwenn for hiring her and was determined to be worthy of the trust by doing a good job on the Wilson case. What could have happened to plunge her back into despair? What could have happened to drive her to self-destruction?

What was she doing parked on Riverside Drive? Gwenn had asked herself that question. Brian Ford had asked it and pointed to an answer. Jayne was on stakeout.

Who was she watching? What building and what apartment? There were high rises and town houses, block upon block of them facing out toward the Jersey Palisades. What had drawn Jayne to that particular place? The only thing Gwenn could think of to do was to go there herself, park as close as she could to where Jayne had been, watch and wait. For what—she had no idea.

The ad appeared in the Long Island edition of *Newsday*:

Student seeks position, live in/out. Offers tender loving care for child or elderly person in exchange for room and board and nominal fee. Contact mornings only. . . .

Lana Wilson saw it, folded the paper, and handed it across the table in the breakfast nook to her husband.

"She's at it again."

"What do you mean? Who's at it again?"

"Monique Bruno, of course."

He took the paper, scanned it, and handed it back. "How do you know that's who it is? There's no name."

"I know."

"All right. She's trying to get another job. Why shouldn't she? Providing it is Monique."

"It's practically the same ad we answered, word for word. Believe me, I remember."

"So?"

"She's going to hoodwink another couple."

"She didn't hoodwink us. As long as she was in our employ she behaved herself. We don't know otherwise. And Bobby was crazy about her."

"You always were on her side."

"And you couldn't wait to get rid of her. You practically threw her out of the house."

"I gave her two weeks' pay in lieu of notice. When I found out what she was, I couldn't bear to have her around."

"You could have given her a chance to find a place to live."

"She'll find a place," Lana Wilson snapped. "You don't need to worry." Then she eased up. "I guess men react differently to that kind of thing."

"At least we don't jump to conclusions," he retorted tartly. "Oh hell! It's not worth fighting over." He got up. "I've got an early date with a possible buyer for the Spencer property. See you tonight."

Lana Wilson walked her husband to the front door, accepted his perfunctory kiss, and watched him get into his car, which was already in the drive. She waited till he backed it out, waved one last time as he turned the corner, and then waited till he was well out of sight before stepping back inside. In the kitchen, she scraped the breakfast dishes and stacked them in the dishwasher. By then the bus for the day camp had arrived to pick up Bobby. When he was gone, she was free at last to retire to the library, which she was in the process of setting up as a home office, and get to her own work—Saturdays were no longer holidays. But she couldn't concentrate. She kept thinking about that ad and about Frank's reaction. Finally, to resolve her anxieties, she picked up the phone and touched the number listed.

"Yes?"

Lana Wilson caught her breath.

"Yes?" The woman at the other end repeated. "Who is this? Hello?"

Lana Wilson recognized the voice. There couldn't be any doubt. She hung up.

Her heart was pounding. Her breath was coming in short, shallow gasps. She went to the liquor cabinet and poured out a glass of sherry, which she drank down quickly. The warmth spread through her body, calming her so that she was able to get out her household file and check the ad Monique had placed originally. She returned to her desk to make another call.

"Ms. Ramadge? This is Lana Wilson. . . . I'm fine, thanks. Actually, no, I'm not. I'm upset. Confused. I don't suppose you happened to see the Situations Wanted in today's *Newsday*. No reason why you should. I'll read it to you. 'Student seeks position, live in/out. Offers tender loving care for child or elderly person in exchange for room and board and nominal fee. Contact mornings only.' It gives a phone number."

"What about it?" Gwenn asked.

"It's her ad. Monique's. I called the number and she answered. I recognized her voice."

"She's looking for work. There's nothing wrong with that," Gwenn said. To herself, she thought: *She's looking for a new base of operations.*

Was everybody on that woman's side? Lana Wilson wondered. "You don't understand. It's the same telephone number she gave before in the ad Frank and I answered."

"Are you sure?"

"I noticed at the time that the exchange was the same as Frank and I had when we were first married and living in New York. So I was alert to it when I saw it a second time. I looked up my files. The exchange and the rest of the number matched."

"She must have moved back to the same apartment."

"It's six months since she had it."

"Apparently the space was available."

Lana Wilson would not be placated. "I want you to investigate. For me, personally. My husband would say it's none of our business. He'd say we were harassing the woman. I don't want him to know. Send your bill to me at my New York office. As I told you before, money's no object."

Lana Wilson's tone indicated she controlled expenditures and since her husband wasn't in on the conversation, she didn't have to pretend otherwise. Interesting, Gwenn thought.

"Whatever you say, Mrs. Wilson. Do you happen to know Ms. Bruno's present address?"

"That's what I want you to find out. You can do that, can't you?"

"No problem, Mrs. Wilson. No problem at all."

Gwenn decided to ask Ray to get it for her.

His pleasure at hearing from her turned to wariness. "Why do you want to know?"

"I have a client who wants to know."

"Why?"

"It's a simple request," Gwenn countered. "Why are you making so much of it?"

"You can get the information easily enough on your own. Why are you calling me?"

"Maybe it's an excuse. I haven't heard from you. Is it because you don't want to talk about Jayne?"

"There's nothing to talk about. The case is closed."

"It looks more and more like Jayne was an embarrassment to the department and they're all glad to be rid of her. Now you've joined them."

"That's not true!" he retorted indignantly.

"Sergeant Ford was here yesterday. He left a wad of cash to help defray the funeral expenses. Considering she was trying to get him and his buddies thrown off the force, I'd say it's conscience money."

"I tried to help Jayne," Ray insisted. "You, more than anyone, know that."

"Why were you so quick to buy the suicide theory?"

"I didn't want you to get in over your head."

"You did it for me? Thank you. I appreciate your concern."

"Ah, Gwenn. Don't be like that."

"If you didn't want to involve me, why did you bring her to me in the first place?"

"I wish I hadn't."

"I'm glad you did. She was working herself back to health, mentally and physically. I could see it. I could feel it. What reason could there have been for a relapse?"

"The IA hearing."

"We don't even know there was one. Don't you think we should find out? Don't you think we owe her that much? Why do you persist in refusing to look beyond suicide?"

Ray was slow in replying. "I'm not ready to consider the alternative," he admitted.

"Ah . . ." Gwenn sighed. "We're going to have to. Sooner or later, we're going to have to."

The word "murder" remained unspoken by either Gwenn or Ray, but it was at last tacitly accepted. It led to a trail both were reluctant to start out on, a journey that required more than a telephone call to organize. They made a date for seven that night at Gwenn's place. She would provide her standard fare: pasta and a sauce made from a special recipe of Cordelia Hart's which Gwenn cooked up in quantity and stored in jars. Her culinary skills extended to a salad with an olive oil and vinegar dressing. Ray would provide the Chianti.

Gwenn left the office early under the approving eye of Marge Pratt.

"Have a nice evening," she said to her boss.

"It's business."

"Sure it is." Marge Pratt grinned. "That doesn't mean you can't enjoy."

Gwenn didn't argue.

SATURDAY, SEPTEMBER 10
EVENING

Gwenn had inherited more than a recipe for pasta sauce from Cordelia Hart. Her friend had left her the agency, of course, and the co-op. It was in a solid prewar building and had two bedrooms and two baths. The location on Seventy-second Street between Lexington and Third was considered prime. The furnishings dated back to Cordelia's parents and were dark, gloomy, and massive. Bit by bit, Gwenn replaced them with some of the pieces she'd managed to save when her parents had to give up their place on Fifth, pieces she had particularly loved and kept in storage while she moved from one temporary rental to another. She introduced modern pieces that blended with both. After four years she was still in transition. Probably the job would never be complete, she thought, and she didn't mind one bit.

At seven precisely, the doorbell rang and Gwenn Ramadge answered. Raymond Dixon, bottle of wine in one hand and flowers in the other, dark eyes alight, stood on the threshold. He was tall, she was short. While he bent down, she reached up and tilted her head for his kiss. It was firm and sweet as she remembered. And all too brief. She came down off her toes, led him inside, where he put the bottle and the bouquet down on the hall console. They came together in an embrace that grew more urgent as it lasted.

It was interrupted by the ringing of the telephone.

They stopped and after a few seconds separated. Gwenn crossed the long, narrow living room to her desk, which was set in an alcove at the front of the building.

"Hello?"

"Ms. Ramadge? This is Frank Wilson."

"Oh yes. Hello." She looked to Ray and mouthed silently, "Sorry". He picked up the bottle and the flowers and headed for the kitchen. He was careful to close the door behind him. "Yes, Mr. Wilson. What can I do for you?" Gwenn asked.

"I just wanted to let you know the police have been here as you anticipated."

"About Detective Harrow? What did you tell them?"

"Nothing. We don't know anything."

"Exactly. What were the names of the officers? What division were they from? Do you recall?"

"There was only one, Sergeant Ford. He didn't mention a division."

"He should have. Probably you missed it. Doesn't matter. Did he indicate what he expected to learn from you?"

"He said it was an informal visit to clear up a couple of details. I guess that's what they always say."

"More or less," Gwenn agreed.

"He asked about you."

"Did he?" She hadn't expected that.

"Wanted to know how we came to hire you and how you happened to bring in Detective Harrow. I told him you were recommended by a friend, highly recommended. As for Detective Harrow, we had no idea. That's what you told us to say."

"It's the truth, isn't it?"

"Yes."

"Well then, you have nothing to be concerned about."

"I guess not. Well . . . you told us to let you know . . ."

"Yes, and I appreciate it. Thank you."

But Wilson was reluctant to hang up. "I hope that's the end of it."

"I hope so too." It wasn't the answer he wanted, of course. "I see no reason why it shouldn't be," she added. "Call me if it isn't." She hung up with an audible click as the receiver settled in its cradle. She went into the kitchen.

Ray had uncorked the wine and was arranging the flowers.

"Sergeant Ford turned up at the Wilsons'."

"How did he find out they're your clients?"

She shrugged. "It seems the Harrow case isn't closed after all. Somebody besides us is having doubt. Doubts about suicide usually indicate murder."

The word spoken at last. They looked at each other. Gwenn now plunged ahead.

"The motive is obvious: Jayne's charges of corruption. Somebody killed her to silence her."

"Ford?" Ray suggested.

"Everything points to him," Gwenn agreed. "But I don't know. Whatever Ford might have been doing—skimming, taking bribes, tipping the dealers in advance of a raid—he wasn't in it alone."

"Has it occurred to you that the murder was committed by somebody other than a cop? Corrupt as these men may be, I don't think they would kill one of their own."

"Who then?"

"Could it have something to do with the case the two of you were on?"

"Jayne never had contact either with the clients or the subject of the investigation."

"Are you sure?"

"As sure as I can reasonably be."

"That's not good enough."

"You're right." She shook her worry aside. "Let's eat."

Everything she needed to prepare the simple meal was laid out on the kitchen counter. She lit the gas to bring the water for the pasta to a boil. While waiting, she tore the lettuce for the salad. Ray poured each of them a glass of wine. Together they pulled out the drop leaf table in the living room and set it. In twenty-five minutes they sat down.

It was tacitly understood they were not to discuss the case while eating. They talked in short, unsatisfactory bursts, mostly about Gwenn's trip to Mexico—what she had seen, how she had passed the time, about her parents. Ray contributed little. It struck Gwenn that what her mother had said was true; aside from their work they had few shared interests. It saddened her. She refused to accept it and kept trying different topics: the U.S. Open currently being played at Flushing Meadows, the coming political battles—matters about which neither much cared.

After they had eaten and cleared the table and stacked the dishes in the dishwasher, they took their demitasse out to the small balcony that faced toward the East River. The twilight deepened into night. The lights of the city came on all around them. It was sultry and they would have been more comfortable inside with the air-conditioning, but they both found the view romantic and glamorous and challenging. Gwenn reopened the subject that was on both their minds.

"Why is Brian Ford running around asking questions about Jayne? Shouldn't whoever's carrying the case be doing that?"

"Charley Pulver was carrying. The case is closed," Ray reminded her.

He still refused to admit a department cover-up, Gwenn thought with a flare of impatience. Maybe his loyalty was justified, maybe not. He chose to turn his back on the question. She didn't, couldn't.

They slipped into another long silence, sipped the bittersweet coffee, and watched as night took over the city.

"Why don't we treat this like two separate cases?" Gwenn suggested. "One: murder linked to police corruption. There's no way I can handle that. What cop is going to talk to me? What cop is going to answer my questions? But they'll talk to you. It's your right and your responsibility to find out what happened."

He nodded.

"You and Jayne were close," she continued. "She called on you for support and you responded. She must have given you some hint of what Ford was involved with, of what she had on him and the others, if there were others."

"She said it was better for me not to know."

"You accepted that?"

"What choice did I have?"

"None." She reached for his hand and clasped it.

"Jayne told me she'd promised Captain Landau not to discuss her suspicions with anyone. He was going to make inquiries on his own."

"So he believed her. Or, at least, she thought so," Gwenn reasoned.

"He believed her right to the point of her suicide. That's what he told me."

Under the guise of sympathy the captain had tried to convert Ray to the official line, Gwenn thought. Had he succeeded? "Did you ask him whether Jayne ever did produce evidence to support her charges?"

"*He* asked *me.*"

"And you told him you didn't know."

"Naturally."

"And he was satisfied with that."

"Of course. Why shouldn't he be?"

They were back at the beginning, she thought. "That's what we, what you," she corrected herself, "need to find out." Also, it would be helpful to know why Ford came to see me. It wasn't to contribute to Jayne's funeral expenses, that's for sure. Meantime, I'll try to find out what he wanted from the Wilsons. I think I'll go out there tomorrow and get acquainted with the neighbors."

Back inside they lingered over the goodnight kiss. Their emotion was nearing a point that demanded resolution. They both knew it, but this was not the time.

CHAPTER 8

Nothing like a little friendly gossip, or unfriendly as the case might be, Gwenn thought as she set out that crisp, sunny Sunday. Traffic was light and she estimated she should reach the Wilsons' place by ten, but she was in no hurry. She hadn't quite made up her mind how to present herself to the Wilsons' neighbors. Introducing herself as a private investigator sometimes elicited eager cooperation, but could also result in resistance. Everybody had something to hide, to a lesser or greater degree. In protecting some small and innocuous secret, a critical clue might be dismissed or purposely hidden. She decided to present herself as *Mrs.* Ramadge, married, with a young child, and interested in buying a house in the neighborhood. If pressed, she would say it was the Wilson house. Why not? It might lead to interesting bypaths.

The first doorbell she rang was that of the Wilsons' nearest neighbor. It took a while for someone to respond.

A middle-aged woman with a beehive of gray hair scrutinized

Gwenn through a glass panel in the door. Satisfied that Gwenn was no threat, she opened the door—on a chain.

Even out here, Gwenn thought. She shuffled her feet, smiled, and managed to look embarrassed. "My name is Gwenn Ramadge. My husband and I are thinking of moving out here. Buying a house." She paused, took a breath. "I feel so foolish, and I know it's an imposition, but before we pull up stakes and move, I'd like to know what we're getting into."

"Excuse me?" The woman's disapproval was obvious.

Time to be ingenuous, Gwenn thought.

"Real estate agents tell you what you want to hear, naturally. And there are certain questions they can't answer. Are the people friendly? Would we be accepted by the community? Are there children in the neighborhood? My boy is three years old—would he find playmates his own age? How about help? I expect to commute to my job in the city, so how about a day-care center?" The light came from behind the woman, so her face was in shadow and Gwenn couldn't read her expression. "Please, may I come in for a few moments?"

"I'm not the lady of the house."

"Oh." Gwenn was flustered. "I'm sorry."

"I'm the housekeeper, Mrs. Serena Browning."

"I'm very sorry to have taken your time, Mrs. Browning. Is the lady of the house in?"

"No. Mrs. Dailey is not at home."

"When do you expect her?"

"Not till five at the earliest."

She should have presented herself as conducting a survey, Gwenn thought; then she could have come back. She had not chosen her role well. "I see. In that case, perhaps . . . would you mind helping me out? You could answer my questions, I'm sure. I'd be so grateful."

"Well . . ."

"It would be just between us . . ."

"You're sure you're not a reporter or a police officer or anyone like that?"

"A police officer? What in the world makes you think I might be a police officer?"

The housekeeper shrugged. "There have been rumors."

"What kind of rumors?"

Peering through the glass, Mrs. Browning checked the street in both directions. "You'd better come in," she said. She pushed the door closed to release the chain and then opened it just enough for Gwenn to sidle inside.

Gwenn was not permitted to linger in the vestibule long enough to form more than an impression about the place. The interior was gloomy, in keeping with the exterior, which was half-timbered Tudor in style. The long, narrow hall ran the length of the house. It was paneled in some dark wood; it didn't matter what kind because so many photographs covered it. They were all photographs of horses or of persons in settings related to horses: stables, racecourses, paddocks. Gwenn would have liked to examine them at length, but the housekeeper hurried her along.

"This way."

She led Gwenn all the way to the rear of the house into an old-fashioned pantry, which opened into a huge, very modern, very well-equipped kitchen that was flooded with sunshine. The window that admitted all this light gave on part of the cove shared with the Wilsons, but the Wilson house was well screened by a stand of black Japanese pines and a thicket of bayberry bushes. Both were prime property, Gwenn thought.

The housekeeper waved Gwenn to a chair at the butcher block table and sat opposite her, taking the time to look her over. For her role as a young mother, Gwenn had chosen to wear a long flowered skirt topped by an oversize linen blazer. Her mop of blond curls and sun-reddened complexion fit perfectly.

"You said you're interested in buying a house. Nothing around here is for sale."

"The agent showed us a really lovely place in this area, right nearby, in fact," Gwenn told her. "Maybe the owners don't want it known they're selling. They might be financially embarrassed. These are not good times for people living on a fixed income."

Mrs. Browning nodded sagely. She was in her late fifties, Gwenn judged. Though her hair had faded into gray, her skin was fresh and clear. She wore steel-rimmed bifocals. Her slacks were well tailored and sharply creased. Her long-sleeved shirt was starched and blindingly white. She was stolid and appeared secure in her position. She must have been with the Daileys for a long time.

"These old places are expensive to maintain. You want to be careful not to get in over your head," she warned.

Gwenn smiled. "Thanks, but that's no problem." She didn't know why she was moved to add, "I've just come into a very large inheritance."

"I see. Congratulations." The housekeeper became friendly. "I always think it's better if the woman controls the purse strings." She paused, but it was evident she had more to say. "You mentioned the real estate agent showed you a house nearby. Could it have been the one adjacent?"

Gwenn shrugged, playing the game with her. "I suppose the word will get out sooner or later."

Mrs. Browning seized on what she considered an admission. Her eyes glittered behind the thick lenses. "So she's finally throwing him out."

"Who's throwing who out?"

"Mrs. Wilson. The house is hers. She paid for it with her money. So, if it's on the market . . ."

Gwenn backed off. "I only know it's for sale; I don't know why."

"Poor Lana, she's put up with so much from that man. She'll be better off without him."

"Sounds like you've known the Wilsons a long time," Gwenn observed.

"It's a typical situation around here," Serena Browning explained. "The girl, plain but with plenty of money. The man, with no assets but his own charm. It didn't take long after the wedding for Frank Wilson to start cheating on his wife. At least in the beginning he had the decency to get a room outside, to dirty somebody else's sheets. This girl he brought right into the house, ostensibly to take care of his son, but actually to be his mistress. Lana works in the city. He has an office here in the town near enough to come home for lunch, which he did every day, except weekends, of course. His wife is home weekends. He'd park down the road and sneak in the back thinking nobody noticed, or if anyone did, that we're all too dumb to figure out what he was up to. Disgusting."

It really was, Gwenn thought. And with the child upstairs in the nursery under sedation, it could have been disastrous.

"Then, all of a sudden, it stopped. He stayed away. Meantime, cars took up positions at the front and rear of the house."

"You noticed."

"As I said, *Mrs.* Ramadge, we're not dumb out here and we keep our eyes open."

"We?"

"The whole neighborhood is talking about it. We figure you and the other woman are private investigators getting evidence for the divorce. We figure Frank Wilson caught on that he was being watched and lay low for a couple of weeks. Then the girl, Monique, left, bag and baggage. And now you appear."

Gwenn flushed. "You recognized me?"

"Actually, no, but your performance wasn't totally convincing. Who else could you be? Why would you be asking such inane questions?" As Gwenn's color deepened, the housekeeper added, "Don't feed bad, Ms. Ramadge, private detectives are no novelty around here."

Nevertheless, her performance, as Serena Browning called it, had elicited new and interesting information, Gwenn thought. She wondered just how much Lana Wilson knew about her husband's dalliance with the nanny. Should she talk to Monique next? Maybe it would be better to go back to Jayne Harrow's place and see if she could discover any indication that Jayne had learned of the affair. Gwenn recalled Jayne's eagerness to continue the surveillance on Friday, Monique's day off, despite the Wilsons' order to suspend it. She might well have stayed on the job on her own time and in tailing Monique discovered the illicit affair. Then what?

Gwenn still had the extra set of keys she had found in Jayne's apartment. Strictly speaking they belonged to Ray's part of the case. She'd meant to turn them over but forgot. There was no reason why she couldn't go back and take another look before doing so. She could even call and suggest they go together. But she didn't.

SUNDAY, SEPTEMBER 11
AFTERNOON

Gwenn Ramadge remained on the FDR Drive, not exiting until she reached lower Manhattan. After a frustrating search of the Village streets, she finally found a parking place. She was hot, tired, and annoyed with herself for wasting time by not putting the car in a garage. She decided she wanted, and deserved, a nice cool drink and a good dinner; she hadn't eaten since breakfast. There were plenty of good restaurants in the area, but since she wasn't familiar with any, she based her selection on ambience rather than cuisine and selected one that displayed the sign *Gar-*

den in the Rear. She was delighted to find a small, tinkling fountain and umbrella-shaded tables. The menu consisted mainly of northern Italian dishes. Gwenn ordered a draft beer and relaxed.

For the hour or so she spent there, Gwenn put the Wilsons, Jayne Harrow, and even Ray out of her mind. At last it was time to go, but she was still resolute in keeping her mind clear of past assumptions and free to absorb whatever new evidence she might discover. On her way to the car, Gwenn decided not to use it. Jayne's place wasn't far. Walking would work off the meal and be a lot easier than finding another place to park.

A lot of people were out enjoying the mid-September evening; none had any interest in Gwenn as she climbed the stoop to Jayne's front door and put a key in the lock. Inside, it was dark and quiet. Gwenn remembered there was no elevator. She groaned at the thought of climbing four flights.

Once she'd made the climb and was inside the apartment, she was glad she'd gone to the trouble. She had a hunch there was something waiting to be found and at last she could take the time to look for it. As was her habit, Gwenn started by going through the desk. Jayne had kept her documents neatly ordered, but there was nothing pertaining to police business, nothing with regard to her work with Brian Ford, nothing to do with the Wilson case. But she must have kept records of some sort. Methodically, Gwenn went through the less likely places.

Her heart jumped when she came on an appointment diary in the drawer of the nightstand, but from the day of Jayne's suspension to the day Gwenn hired her, the pages were blank. After that, the hours on the job for Hart S and I were noted without comment. The back pages listed the telephone numbers for the cleaner, the supermarket, the stationer's, the liquor store. Ray's number at home and at the office were there, but not other name that might indicate a personal relationship. Gwenn felt a twinge of pity. She was surprised not to find her own address and telephone noted. Maybe Jayne had that and everything pertaining to the Wilson case in the rental car. It would explain how Ford had found out about them.

When Gwenn left Jayne Harrow's apartment the sky was dark, with only a narrow luminous streak at the western horizon. By the time she picked up her car and drove uptown to her place on East Seventy-second, it was totally night. After unlocking the front door, she reached inside for the light switch.

From pitch-black, the room jumped into light.

A shambles.

Gwenn gasped and stood where she was, unable to believe what she saw. It looked as though a giant hand had picked up the room and shaken it, or as though an earthquake had struck. The pictures were off the walls and on the floor amid shattered glass. A small bookcase had been tipped over, and books and mementos, including Gwenn's swimming and track trophies, were tumbled on the floor. They were dented but not beyond repair. The Waterford crystal plaque she'd won when representing her school in the Eastern Field and Track competition prior to the Olympics, however, was shattered. That brought tears welling up, but Gwenn sternly forced them back while she completed the inspection. The upholstery was slashed, apparently at random. No earthquake could do that. The drawers of her desk were open; the papers that had been inside were stacked on top of the desk. Only a human hand could have done that.

In a daze, Gwenn went into her bedroom. More of the same. The bureau drawers had been rifled through and her underthings dumped out. Her vanity table had been swept clear of makeup and perfume. The bed had been stripped and the mattress cut in shallow thrusts as though the perp already knew the search was futile. So much of this was unnecessary, Gwenn thought, whatever the perp was looking for. Trembling, fearful of what else was in store for her, Gwenn took a deep breath and opened the closet door. She pulled the chain for the overhead light.

Everything seemed normal. Her clothes hung in the accustomed orderly row, her special dresses each in its separate plastic cover. Gwenn took pleasure and pride in the decoration of her closet, and she was relieved to see that on the shelves above the rod the various containers—hatboxes, shoeboxes, boxes for sweaters, all coordinated in a rosebud design—were stacked and appeared undisturbed. But that didn't fit the pattern. Trembling, she reached out to separate the dresses and make a closer inspection.

Under its cover, her favorite aqua silk cocktail dress was cut to rags. On the next hanger, a bright red suit was in shreds. One by one, she went through every outfit she owned. Not one would ever be wearable again.

Hate. Vicious hate. A chill traveled through her whole body. She couldn't bear to look anymore. Later. For now, she shut the closet door and went into the kitchen. All her dishes were on the floor, swept off the counter and shelves. The same with the contents of the refrigerator.

This was finally too much. Great, dry, racking sobs shook her. She stood in the midst of the wreckage of her home, heaving out the pain.

Why? Why would anyone do this?

She waited for the flow of tears that would bring relief, but they didn't come. Now was not the time for crying anyway, she thought. Straightening up, she strode over to the nightstand to the telephone. She intended to call 911, but held off. What could she tell them? She would report a break-in, but nothing had been taken. She hadn't walked in on the intruder, hadn't been injured or threatened. Actually, she *had* been threatened, Gwenn thought, and in a most insidious and effective way. Would whoever responded to her complaint understand that? If he did, he would ask who she suspected, and she wasn't ready to make a specific accusation.

So she called Ray and sat down amid the destruction to wait.

He came quickly. At his ring, she ran to let him in.

"My God!" he exclaimed at the sight of her, and took her into his arms. Looking over her shoulder at the damage, he repeated, "My God! Are you all right?"

She nodded.

"You need a drink."

"Maybe a glass of sherry."

"I'll get it." Before going for it, he took a look around. "There's a lot of anger here. And frustration. Somebody wanted something and didn't find it."

"Wanted what?" Gwenn asked.

"You know what. You must know. Come on, sweetheart. I'm on your side."

"Are you sure?"

He winced. "You didn't mean that. You're upset, understandably. I'll get the sherry."

He knew where she kept it—in the bottom section of one of the kitchen cabinets—and was pleased to find that it had been overlooked by the intruder. However, it took him a while to find a couple of glasses to serve it in. Having poured, he handed her one, cleared a place beside her, and sat waiting for her to speak in her own time.

"If you're referring to evidence to support Jayne's charges, you're wasting time. If she had any documentation, she didn't entrust it to me. If she'd turned it over to anyone, it would have been you."

He shook his head. "We've been over that. She didn't want to involve me."

"She was secretive by nature," Gwenn mused aloud. "The last time we talked was in my office the night before she was due to appear before the IA board. I got the feeling she was onto something relating to Monique Bruno, the woman we were investigating for the Wilsons, but she wasn't ready to say more. I thought I might find reference to it in her apartment. That's what I was looking for earlier, but I wasn't successful."

"Somebody thinks you were."

"Somebody," Gwenn repeated. "Let's be up front about this. It was Brian Ford or one of his buddies did this. Cops. A bunch of cops did this. They came in here like goons and vandalized my home. This is their message, loud and clear."

"All right, maybe Ford is responsible," Ray admitted. "This damage is part frustration at not finding what he's after and part intent to terrorize you into giving it up if you've got it stashed somewhere."

"I don't. I swear. Look, Ray." Gwenn took a deep breath. "Right after you told me Jayne was dead, I went over to her place and got the super to let me in. I didn't have time for more than a quick look around, but I did find a spare set of keys and used them to go in earlier tonight. This"—she indicated the shambles—"must already have been done."

"So Ford thought you got the evidence the first time."

"But he had already been there ahead of me. There was also another man, a Latino. The super told me."

"Then he thinks Jayne gave it to you, or told you where to find it."

"She didn't. How many times do I have to say it?"

"I believe you, but how are we going to convince Ford and the others? Because you're right; there are others." He took her hands in his. "I don't know how to handle this and it's driving me crazy," he blurted out. "But I intend to make sure you're safe. Nobody is going to do anything like this to you again."

"Oh, Ray . . ." The tears trembled in her eyes and finally spilled over.

He took her into his arms and they held each other. After a

while, she stopped crying, took the handkerchief he offered, and wiped her eyes.

"Time to clean house," she said.

"I'll do it."

"We'll do it together."

They started in the kitchen. She handed him a broom and he swept from the corners to the center, making a pile of the broken crockery and glassware. She scooped up the shards and dumped them into the trash container. There wasn't much that could be salvaged. They worked in silence for over an hour but the job was far from done when they decided to stop.

"Tomorrow I'm going to have a Fox lock installed, the kind with the bar set into the floor," Gwenn told Ray.

"Why don't I sleep over? On the sofa, of course," Ray gallantly offered, while eyeing the protruding tufts of stuffing askance.

CHAPTER 9

Gwenn Ramadge awoke abruptly with that sense of disorienta-
tion she sometimes experienced upon oversleeping. As she lay in
the gloom of early morning, the events of the night flooded over
her, bringing a return of the dismay and helplessness she had felt
then. She turned over and buried her face in the pillow; she was
not ready to deal with them. She realized at that point that she
had not overslept, and that it was the ringing of the telephone
that had awakened her. It continued to ring relentlessly. *Let the
machine take the message,* she thought. She listened to her own
voice make the announcement; then the caller was on the line.

"Gwenn? I'm sorry to disturb you . . ."

Gwenn rolled over. She opened her eyes. She checked the
clock.

"Gwenn, it's Marge. I'm at the office."

She checked the clock. Seven-thirty! Marge Pratt was no more
an early bird than Gwenn. Occasionally she might go in at eight
if there was a backlog of work, but this was unprecedented.

"I'm sorry to disturb you."

Her secretary's voice quavered, Gwenn noted as she sat up, reached for the receiver, and turned off the machine. "What's happened?"

"The super called me. He noticed our door was ajar. We've been broken into."

Gwenn's stomach dropped. She waited for a moment till she could get hold of herself. Then she thought of how Marge must feel. "Are you all right?"

"I am now. I must admit that when I first walked in, it was a shock. But I'm okay now."

"Are you sure? Maybe you should go home. I'll come over and get you."

"I don't want to go home. I can't leave the place like this. Wait till you see it."

The complaint meant more than any number of reassurances. "If you say so."

"I do."

"Is there much damage?"

"More of a mess than damage," Marge replied. "They went through your desk, and the files were dumped out. I don't know why they had to do that." Marge was fussy about the files. She had her own private system and got cranky if anybody, even Gwenn, went into them.

"Anything missing?"

"Can't tell till I get them back in order. That's going to be a day at least."

"They take anything?"

"What's to take?"

True, Gwenn thought. They kept only petty cash on hand. They used only standard office equipment which had been bought secondhand. "Right. I'm on my way."

But Marge didn't hang up. "Gwenn? Should I call nine-one-one?"

Gwenn hesitated. Reasoning along the same lines she had the night before, she came to the same decision. "What can they do at this point?" She hung up. She put on her robe and slippers and went out to the living room to tell Ray.

He was gone.

She had made up the sofa for him. It was stripped, the bedclothes neatly folded and stacked, pillow on the top and a note on top of that.

You were sleeping so peacefully I didn't want to disturb you. I fixed coffee; just plug in the pot. I went down and got milk, o.j., and eggs. They're in the fridge. Also, bread for toast. Call you later.

Gwenn smiled and surveyed her home anew. In the morning's optimism, she saw it differently. The broken glass was just that—broken glass which could easily be replaced. So could the dishes. The furniture could be reupholstered, and she'd been meaning to get a new mattress anyway. The valuable carpets her mother had managed to set aside when their possessions were put up for auction had not been damaged. Her precious Chippendale desk wasn't even scratched. She was lucky. Actually, cleared of debris, the place didn't look all that bad. Ray's note and his thoughtfulness in providing for breakfast warmed her spirit. She went into the kitchen and found the percolator with a cup and saucer ready beside it. He hadn't forgotten a thing.

When she was in a hurry to get downtown, Gwenn left the car and took the subway. She was certainly in a hurry this morning.

At her office door, Gwenn automatically reached for the knob and then stopped. There might be prints. Probably not; the perp appeared to be experienced and would take elementary precautions. However, both the lock and the frame showed nicks and scratches where it had been forced, probably with a crowbar. Nothing subtle, Gwenn thought, steeling herself. She took a deep breath, grasped the knob firmly, and walked in.

Marge Pratt was sitting on the floor, legs crossed, sorting through mounds of loose papers. At her boss's entrance she looked up.

"Hi, you're fast."

Gwenn smiled and asked again, "Are you all right?"

"I'm mad, that's all."

"It could have been worse," Gwenn told her. "You should see my apartment."

"They broke into your apartment?" Marge asked, wide-eyed.

Gwenn nodded. "Some time yesterday, probably late morning or early afternoon. From the damage, I figure there had to be at least two of them. They probably saw me leave in the car and figured they could take their time. They trashed everything. They even cut up my clothes."

"No!"

"Fortunately, not everything—only my good clothes, the things I really liked."

"Why?" Marge asked.

"To scare me."

Marge Pratt wanted to offer comfort to her boss, to put her arms around Gwenn, but she was embarrassed and instead just touched her lightly on the shoulder. "You could come and stay with me and Bruce for a while." Bruce was Marge's son. "Or we'll come and stay with you for a few days, if that's better. As for clothes, you can take anything of mine."

"That's nice of you, but I'm okay, honestly. I'm not going to cry over a few dresses. And I'm not going to let these people scare me either."

Gwenn passed on into her private office, examining the things that were a part of her professional life—the simple furnishings, the business machines. Her desk was as she'd left it—a stack of mail to be answered at the left, daily calendar to the right. She opened one drawer after another, looked inside, and then shut it. "Nothing appears to have been touched."

"The files," Marge reminded her.

"Oh, sure."

They went back to the reception room.

"I got the handyman to help me stand them up again. Everything was scattered all over the floor. He helped me pick them up and put them back, but not in any kind of order. It looks like Harrow's employment file is missing. I don't know what else, if anything."

"I don't think the same perp was responsible for both jobs," Gwenn told the secretary. "The search of my apartment was violent and destructive; the perp was as interested in venting his rage and terrorizing me as in whatever he was looking for. Here, the search was impersonal. He was actually neat. It seems to me that he tipped over the file cases with the intent to hide what he was after, not for emotional catharsis."

"You don't think it was the cops?" Marge asked straight out.

Gwenn met her gaze. She wanted to be as honest with Marge as Marge was with her, but she had to consider Ray.

"I don't know what to think."

Marge nodded; she understood. "Should we dust for prints?"

"I don't think there are any."

"I guess not, but just in case . . ." Marge trailed off. "What are you going to do?"

Gwenn broke into a sudden smile. "I'm going shopping."

She'd never have a better excuse to buy herself a whole new wardrobe, Gwenn thought, and headed for Bloomingdale's. She was so bemused that she rode past the stop. She decided not to go back but to let fate guide her. She got out at Sixty-eighth and walked over to where she'd left her car. Once in it, she called Ray.

"Gwenn! How are you? Are you all right?"

"I'm fine. Thanks for the supplies you put in for me. That was thoughtful."

"You're welcome. Listen, if you have any more cleaning up to do, I'm off at four."

"That's nice of you, but first, did you ever get that address I asked you for?"

"Where are you now? Are you home? I'll look up the address and get back to you."

"I'll hold."

"You're not home, are you? Ah, Gwenn, you promised to take it easy."

"I didn't promise to cower behind closed doors or to give up my job. So you can help me or not, as you want. I still haven't heard anything about the autopsy. Don't tell me it's too soon."

"No, it's not too soon," he admitted. "I'm sorry, I've had a lot on my mind." He was silent for a long moment. "Jayne died between six and eight Wednesday night, the same night her body was found."

"In the rental car?"

"Yes."

"Parked on Riverside Drive?"

"Given the MO, moving her would have been awkward. I think we can rule it out."

"How about her date with IA Tuesday morning?"

"Apparently she did show up. We don't know what she did in the interval."

Gwenn digested all this. "She was working on the Wilson case for me. I think she was onto something. The car with her body in it was parked on Riverside Drive. The ad placed by Mrs. Wilson's ex-nanny listed the Riverside Drive exchange. Coincidence?"

"Who can say?"

"I can find out," Gwenn replied. "I can answer the ad. I can say

I'm looking for a nanny for my son. I'll see where that takes me. At least I'll be out of your hair for a while."

"Honey, you're not in my hair."

"You are getting flak about me, aren't you?"

"I've had a couple of calls from the big building," he admitted.

"This morning?"

"Yes. But I don't give that any significance."

"I think you should."

"They want to know how you're doing with the case. I tried to tell them you don't confide in me. They don't believe it, of course."

"I'm sorry," Gwenn said.

"They want me to get you to lay off."

"What did you say?"

"That I have no influence."

"Right."

Ray chose to ignore the edge in her response. "I also told them you don't know anything."

"That's nice."

"You know what I mean. I was trying to get you off the hook."

"Next time they ask, you can tell them I'm following a new line of investigation. That should please them."

"I'm only trying to help."

"Who? Me or your buddies downtown?"

"Both."

"You can't."

As soon as she'd said it Gwenn stopped, aghast. She'd stumbled on the truth. It was no longer possible for them to act independently, to run separate investigations. He was a police officer; she was a civilian. A private investigator had certain privileges but was a civilian nonetheless. As a police officer, Ray was bound to reveal any information he might acquire, in whatever manner. She couldn't ask him to withhold anything. Even if he were willing to remain silent about any aspect of the case, he might in some offhand moment unintentionally let something slip.

"It isn't going to work."

"I know," he agreed. "What are we going to do?"

"We could make a pact not to discuss the case." Gwenn sighed. "That wouldn't last long."

"You wouldn't consider dropping it?"

"Are you asking me to drop it?"

"You know what's involved. We've discussed it."

"And my answer is the same as before; I feel an obligation to see it through."

"Right. I'll miss you."

"I'll miss you." She started to hang up.

"Hey," Ray stopped her. "Before it becomes official, don't you want that address?"

The house was one in a row of small Georgian mansions on the crest of Riverside Drive looking out across the Hudson to the Jersey Palisades. Twin pillars flanked the entrance and supported a small balcony. It had recently been sandblasted to a wedding cake white and gleamed in the sun. Driving slowly, Gwenn headed around the block, paying particular attention to the rear of the houses. *Always know the way out before going in,* Cordelia Hart had taught, and the lesson proved valuable more than once. So now Gwenn noted that the rear of each of the buildings gave out on a common alley. It was clean, well swept, without a scrap of litter. Trash cans were tightly covered and lined up beside each door, in keeping with the character of the neighborhood.

It was quiet, residential, conservative. There were no shops, no commercial establishments. Residents were probably served by the shops on Broadway. Not particularly handy, Gwenn thought, but the clarity of the air, the view, and the tranquillity in the midst of a teeming city more than made up for it. As for parking, the situation was just as tight here as anywhere else. Having completed a three-block-grid search, Gwenn was just about ready to go into a garage when she spotted somebody pulling out just down the block. She made an illegal U-turn to beat a car coming around the corner from Seventy-third, which prompted the driver of the other car to lean on his horn. She ignored him and pulled into the space. She got out, closed the door, and walked away while he was still shouting words she chose not to understand.

Dodging traffic, she crossed the street and entered the building's vestibule. The building was five stories high and on the wall to Gwenn's right were five mailboxes, as well as five bells. Gwenn rang the one marked *M. Bruno,* and waited until she heard a scratchy sound indicating the speaker phone had been activated.

"Yes?"

"Ms. Bruno?" Up to that moment, Gwenn had not figured out what her approach would be. "I'm a neighbor of the Wilsons. Out on the Island?"

There was a long pause. "Yes?"

"I understand you no longer work for them."

"No, I don't." Her voice was low, husky.

"I'd like to talk to you. May I come up?"

"Well . . ."

"I realize I should have called first. I apologize. I was in the neighborhood and I thought, why not? But if it's a bad time . . ."

"How did you find me? The Wilsons don't have this address."

"You had an ad in the paper."

"It gave a telephone number, not an address."

"Well." Gwenn was used to thinking fast. "I called the paper. I got it from them."

"They're not supposed to give out that information."

"I have a friend who works in the classified." Sensing continued resistance, Gwenn rushed ahead. "Actually, Ms. Bruno, I'm a private investigator and I'm looking for information about the Wilsons. I'm willing to pay generously if you have what I need. How about it? As long as I'm here, why don't you let me come up? It might be to both our advantages."

"Well, I guess it's okay. But just for a few minutes."

The connection was broken and almost immediately the buzzer sounded, unlocking the front door. Gwenn turned the knob and entered. She found herself in an elegant lobby with a floor of black and white marble and mirrored walls in which an Austrian crystal chandelier was reflected. The tiny elevator was done in red lacquer and gilt.

The person who admitted Gwenn was barely recognizable as the woman she'd had under surveillance for ten days. Gone was the fresh, scrubbed schoolgirl. As a nanny, she had worn her long, thick dark hair in a single braid down her back. The short kilt and plain white blouse had suggested a uniform. In her present persona, Monique Bruno appeared to be in her late twenties, and a heavy scent of decadence enveloped her. Last night's makeup was smudged around her eyes. Her hair was loose, a dark cloud framing her pale face. She wore a long satin robe tied at her waist with a wide sash. She was barefoot, and Gwenn suspected that under the robe she was naked.

She looked around. The room's interior was consistent with the rococo ornamentation of the rest of the building. It was an oversize boudoir.

Monique Bruno sensed Gwenn's reaction.

"This is my cousin's place. She's letting me use it till I get an apartment of my own, or a job that would be live-in. Whichever comes first."

"I see."

Nevertheless, Bruno felt the need to go on explaining. "I apologize for the way I look. I just got up. I have that awful flu that's going around. I'm all stuffy." She gestured to her nose.

"That's too bad. I won't keep you long. The Wilsons say you're a wonderful nanny. Their son, Bobby, was crazy about you. You were happy there. With all that happiness, I don't quite understand why you left."

"I don't want to be a nanny all the rest of my life."

"Then why the ad?"

"I plan to go to night school here in New York. So I need to go on being a nanny for a while, but I have to stay here in New York."

"That's reasonable. Still, no offense, Ms. Bruno, but you don't look like a nanny."

"And you didn't come here to hire one," she countered.

"I never said I did," Gwenn parried. Delving into her handbag, she brought out one of her business cards and handed it over.

Monique Bruno took it and squinted as though she had difficulty reading.

"I'm investigating a murder," Gwenn told her.

"A murder?" Bruno almost seemed relieved. "I don't know anything about any murder."

Actually, Gwenn was trying to shock her into an admission of the affair. "Let's start over again and this time we'll be honest with each other. What do you say?"

Monique didn't say anything.

"For starters, you didn't quit the job with the Wilsons. You were fired. Isn't that true?"

The former nanny shrugged. "Lana never liked me. She would have fired me early on, but she desperately needed somebody to look after Bobby and both Bobby and her husband were strong on my side."

Gwenn was surprised at the quick admission. That was where Monique should have dropped it, but she went on.

"Lana is going to have trouble whoever she brings into the house. She's a very jealous woman."

"And Frank Wilson has a roving eye."

The response to that was another shrug.

"Did it rove in your direction?" Gwenn asked.

"What do you think?"

"I think, Ms. Bruno, that you were having an affair with your employer's husband."

"So we had an affair. That happens. Nobody got murdered over it."

"I hope not."

At that point, the former nanny realized she wasn't doing herself any good. "I'm not answering any more questions. I don't have to and you can't make me. You're not a police officer." She thrust Gwenn's card back at her. "You're nobody."

The first time a suspect had said that to her, Gwenn felt as though she'd been slapped. It still hurt each time it happened, but she refuse to let it diminish her. Certainly she didn't let it stop her.

"You're still seeing Frank Wilson, aren't you?"

Monique kept her lips compressed as though to prevent any word from slipping through, but her eyes flickered.

"Mrs. Wilson was suspicious of what was going on while you were alone with the boy. It was her idea to hire my agency to find out. Her husband had no choice but to go along. Naturally, he alerted you and the lunchtime dates were temporarily suspended, yet you continued to sedate Bobby."

"No, I didn't."

Gwenn recalled the child's lethargy and lack of balance when he emerged from the house after his nap. Maybe it was a holdover of the earlier dosing suggesting permanent damage, and that was even more disturbing. For the moment, Gwenn dropped it.

"But you and Frank Wilson did arrange to see each other on your day off."

"What I did on my day off is my own business."

"Frank Wilson convinced his wife that it was, but Detective Harrow, who was sharing the surveillance with me, didn't think so. She chose to continue on her own time. She was at the Wilson house on the Friday morning when you left in the car the Wilsons made available. She followed you here."

"So?"

"So she parked and waited and watched who came in after you."

"Other people live here. They have visitors."

"Detective Harrow watched and waited for many long hours in the hope that she would recognize someone she could link to you. And she did."

"Who?" Bruno challenged, eyes flashing, color rising.

"Frank Wilson, of course. He couldn't keep away from you even for a few days."

A smiled played mischievously at the corners of the ex-nanny's mouth. "He's crazy for me."

Another fluctuation of the young woman's emotional barometer, Gwenn thought. "And you?"

"I'm crazy for him too, you bet."

"Then you don't care whether or not Lana finds out?"

"She'll find out soon enough."

"Why do you say that?" Gwenn asked, but got no answer. "I suggest you were making every effort to keep her from finding out and that Detective Harrow's discovery of the affair was a severe blow to your plans. She tried to blackmail you."

Gwenn didn't believe that for a moment. It was possible, however, that Jayne had set a trap for the pair, intending to hand them over either to Ray or to her.

"One of you killed her to keep her quiet. Or maybe you did it together."

The soft and voluptuous young woman aged and hardened before Gwenn's eyes as she considered her options. Finally, Monique strode to the house phone on the wall beside the front door.

"This is Ms. Bruno in five D. There's a woman here who refuses to leave. Will you please come and show her out?"

"That's not necessary, Ms. Bruno. I'm going." Gwenn opened the door and paused on the threshold. "Think about what I've said."

Leaving the building, Gwenn crossed the street and got into her car. What would the woman do next? she wondered. Contact Wilson, of course. And what would he do? Gwenn had no idea, but she was prepared to sit and wait for as long as it took to find out.

Not ten minutes later Monique Bruno came out. She was dressed in a summer suit of a beige so pale it was almost white; the jacket and miniskirt were set off by dark hose and white shoes with pointed toes and stiletto heels. Her long hair was brushed up into a soft French knot. This was a meld of the woman's two personalities, Gwenn thought as she watched Bruno teeter to the curb to hail a passing cab. She had no trouble getting it to stop.

Gwenn turned on her ignition. Traffic was light, so she could afford to let a couple of cars in between before following. The taxi cruised to the first eastbound street, circumvented the Museum of Natural History, and cut across Central Park to Fifth Avenue and then on to Madison and turned uptown on Park Avenue. The buildings on each side lined the elegant thoroughfare like sentinels, each with its staff of doormen, porters, and maintenance people dedicated to the service and protection of the tenants. Just before reaching Eighty-fourth, the cabdriver obligingly used his right-turn indicator so that Gwenn had ample warning to make the turn behind him and avoid getting trapped by the light. He went on to the end of the block and stopped at a building on the corner of Lexington. Gwenn pulled in behind a UPS truck double-parked for deliveries.

Meanwhile, a doorman ran out from the lobby to open the cab door for Monique Bruno. He touched his cap and as soon as she was out ran ahead to open the building door for her. She thanked him. She nodded to the deskman as she passed on her way to the elevators. It was evident she knew them and they knew her. She knew where she was going and nobody challenged her right to go there.

As the light turned green, Gwenn maneuvered back into the traffic flow. She continued past the building Monique Bruno had entered, turned on Lexington and circled the block, this time looking for a place to park, but quickly abandoned the idea. There wasn't enough space between bumpers to squeeze in a bicycle. Besides, just any space wouldn't do. She had to be able to keep an eye on the building entrance. There was a spot in front of a fire hydrant, but a meter maid could come by at any time and not just write a ticket but order her to move on. She pulled up in front of the building and waited. It wasn't long till the doorman emerged, approached her window, and tapped on it officiously. She rolled it down.

"There's no parking here, miss."

"I see that, but I need a place for maybe an hour or so. I thought you might know if somebody along here"—she gestured at the parked cars, which looked as though they hadn't been moved in days—"is about to come out." She had a twenty-dollar bill in her hand and she let him see it.

The name tag affixed to his jacket pocket identified him as Fred. He was slight in build, sandy-haired and fair-skinned. It took only one darting glance of his small gray eyes to see what was being offered. He palmed the money with the smoothness of long practice.

"I'll take care of it." He gestured for her to get out.

"I want to stay with the car."

He nodded. "Give me five minutes."

He went back inside, said something to the deskman, and came out again. Without so much as a glance in her direction, he strode to the end of the block and expertly jockeyed a couple of cars around. He waved Gwenn forward. Suddenly there was space where none had been before.

After that flurry of activity things settled down. People came and went in and out of the building. Any one of them might have had a connection with Monique Bruno; Gwenn had no way of knowing, but she continued to sit there. At 2:05 P.M., Frank Wilson, striding briskly, turned the near corner and entered the building.

He was greeted with the same familiar deference Monique Bruno had been shown, and his actions indicated he knew his way around. At 3:10, Wilson came out. He left as he had come, on foot.

Twenty minutes after that, Monique emerged. The doorman got her a cab. Gwenn watched her get in and watched the cab pull away.

After that flurry of activity things settled down. People came and went in and out of the building. Any one of them might have had a connection with Monique Bright. Gwenn had no way of knowing, but she continued to sit there. At 2:05 P.M., Frank Wilson, striding briskly, turned the near corner and entered the building.

pull away.

CHAPTER 10

Obviously, Wilson had an assignation with his son's ex-nanny, Gwenn thought, but what was all this shifting of locations about? If she went to Fred the doorman again, she ran the risk that he would report to Wilson and to Monique that a woman had been asking questions about them. Undoubtedly, Monique had already told Wilson that Gwenn had traced her and knew about their relationship. Whether that had precipitated this recent meeting, or whether it had been scheduled, didn't seem important. Talking to Fred again, couldn't do much harm, she decided. She got out of the car and walked across the street.

"I'll be going now," she told him. "By the way, I thought I saw Frank Wilson leaving the building."

"Yes."

"I thought he lived on the Island."

"That's right. He's the building rental agent. Comes in a couple of times a week."

"Ah." She nodded. "You have apartments available?"

"A couple of subleases."

That hardly required two visits a week to administer, Gwenn thought. How venal was Fred? She pulled another twenty out of her wallet. "How long has Ms. Bruno been occupying her present apartment?"

Fred pursed his thin lips, considering. Then he shrugged, deciding the information could be easily obtained elsewhere. "She moved in a couple of weeks ago."

About the time the surveillance of the Wilson home had begun, Gwenn thought, holding back the twenty.

It was an indication she wasn't getting her money's worth, Fred realized, and threw in an extra. "But she hasn't been here much, at least up to now. She has a place on the Island."

Gwenn released the money. "Thanks."

"Anytime." The doorman cracked a thin smile.

MONDAY, SEPTEMBER 12
AFTERNOON

At last Ray Dixon admitted to himself that he was trying to construct a building without digging a foundation. Gwenn was right, Jayne Harrow had not committed suicide; she had been murdered. So the first question was: Why had everyone in the department been so willing to settle for a verdict of suicide?

Because it was the easy way out?

Because murder would raise more questions embarrassing to the department?

Jayne had already brought charges of corruption against Brian Ford, which had been turned against her. She had been shown to be an alcoholic. The raid on her apartment and the discovery of a cache of drugs indicated she was at least as corrupt as the cops she was accusing. What else could they fear from her? They must think she had finally found hard evidence to support her hitherto vague allegations. Carrying that a step farther, they must think

Jayne had entrusted that evidence to Gwenn. The unnecessary vandalism in Gwenn's apartment spoke the message loud and clear: Turn it over or suffer the consequences.

His recent visit to the big building had been in response to an official summons, Ray thought as he crossed the red-tiled court fronting One Police Plaza. Now he was coming on his own initiative. Then, he had been told what his attitude with regard to Jayne's death should be. Now, he had a message of his own to deliver. The trouble was, he wasn't sure precisely whom he should deliver it to. There were three possibilities; the first and most likely was Brian Ford.

Most squad rooms are alike. Whether in antiquated structures or in ultramodern renovations, they are all cluttered, crowded, and noisy. This one at the nerve center of command might have been expected to intimidate a mere sergeant from a borough, but Dixon was too charged up to be affected. Although he had met Ford before at certain police functions, he asked to have the man who had been Jayne's partner pointed out to him, to be sure of his identity. Then he made his way to Ford's desk and stood there.

Ford looked up. "Yes?"

"I'm Sergeant Dixon."

It took Ford a moment to place him. "Oh, sure. How are you?" He extended his hand.

Ray hesitated just long enough for Ford to drop it, creating an embarrassing moment for both.

The two men continued to take each other's measure. Standing while the narcotics cop sat, Ray had the advantage of looking down on Ford. On the other hand, Ford was on his home turf.

"Jayne told me a lot about you," Ford said. "You taught her the ropes. She thought the world of you. I feel real bad about what happened." He waved Ray to a chair, but Ray continued to stand. "Truth is, she was too fragile for this kind of work. Maybe sensitive is a better description. You must have spotted that."

"No, I didn't. In fact, I thought the opposite. So did her teachers at the Academy."

"They saw her in a controlled setting. It's different in the real world. We both know that. It turns out I was right, unfortunately. So what can I do for you, Sergeant?"

Now Dixon took the chair he had been offered, pulled it close to the desk, and sat. He spoke confidentially. "Maybe we can do something for each other."

"What would that be?"

"You're interested in the evidence Jayne had to support the charges against you."

Ford leaned back. "There is no evidence. There never was. If there had been she would have put it on the table at the start. I don't know where these rumors come from."

A complete reversal, Ray thought. The man had gall. "If you didn't believe such evidence existed, what were you doing in Jayne's apartment? What were you doing in Gwenn Ramadge's place?" Before Ford could speak, Dixon held up one hand. "Don't ask me who Gwenn Ramadge is. You know that she runs Hart S and I. You went to see her. You know she hired Jayne Harrow."

"I also know she's your girlfriend."

"Good. I'm glad you know that. So you understand that I don't like what you did. She told you she doesn't know what you're looking for, that Jayne Harrow didn't tell her. I don't like it that you didn't believe her. I like it even less that you trashed her place. Don't do anything like that again. If you do, or if you touch her or upset her in any way, I'll see to it that you regret it."

"Take it easy, Sergeant. I don't know what you're talking about."

"You can pass it on to your buddies or whoever else might be interested that Gwenn Ramadge is not involved. If she had evidence, Detective Harrow did not pass it on to Miss Ramadge and Miss Ramadge did not come across it when she was in Harrow's apartment. So leave her alone." Dixon's eyes glittered. "Got that?"

"I've got it, Sergeant."

Dixon went on. "As far as you are personally concerned, I'll make you a deal. If I happen to come across anything that might interest you, I'll let you know. We can take it from there."

Ford's smile was a smirk of satisfaction. "It'll be a pleasure, Sergeant."

We'll see about that, Dixon thought as he walked out.

That interview had been easy because Ray and Ford were of equal rank. The next would involve confronting a superior—Lieutenant Alfonso Palma. It was reasonable to assume that Palma, as Jayne's CO, was aware of the turbulence in his command even before she reported it to him. Whether or not he took part, encouraged, or ignored it, the knowledge made him morally responsible and he could be counted on to transmit Ray's message. Ray sent his name in and awaited the lieutenant's pleasure.

In the meantime, he reviewed the points he intended to make. There would be no overt physical threat. Palma, with his big, beefy build—barrel chest and gut spilling over his belt—was himself physically intimidating. As to the hint that Dixon might be bought with a share of the profits from the sale of stolen drugs, it might work with Ford, but Palma was not likely to fall for it. Palma was likely to turn the offer against Ray.

When the lieutenant received Dixon at last, he tilted back in his swivel chair and bestowed a broad but insincere smile on him.

"What are you doing in our neck of the woods this time, Sergeant?"

The question appeared simple, but was actually calculatedly intricate. It indicated that Alfonso Palma remembered Dixon had been there before and why. Also, he knew where he came from. It implied, subtly, that Dixon was out of his league.

"I've done a lot of thinking about Detective Harrow's death since then," Ray replied. "I've decided it's my duty to inform you that I no longer think it was suicide. I think Jayne was murdered."

Palma, florid face expressionless, studied him. "When did you change your mind?"

Dixon took note that he didn't ask *why* but *when.* "When my girlfriend's apartment was broken into and trashed last night."

"Who do you think was responsible?"

"Somebody from this squad."

"That's a serious accusation."

"That's not a formal accusation, but I thought you should know."

"And you think that whoever trashed your girlfriend's apartment was the one who murdered Detective Harrow." It was a statement.

Dixon nodded.

"And do you have a particular member of this squad in mind?"

"I don't—yet."

"Who assigned you to the case, Sergeant?"

"Nobody, Lieutenant. I'm working on my own time."

Palma raised both hands and dropped them in an exaggerated gesture of resignation. "I don't suppose I can stop you."

"No, Lieutenant, you can't."

"However, let me give you a friendly warning: Be damn sure of your facts before making an accusation, that is if you expect to continue your career in the department. As for your girlfriend, remind her that interfering in police business could cause her to lose her license."

"She would respond with a reminder to us all that police intimidation is illegal."

Palma held the winning hand, Ray thought as he left the lieutenant's office. The interview had not turned out as he'd planned, but at least the message had been delivered: *Stay away from Gwenn Ramadge.*

So that was two down and one to go, the one being Captain Norman Landau.

Jayne had spoken highly of him. Landau had listened to what she had to say, had promised to look into her charges. But nothing came of it. Jayne was a rookie who had gotten a bad report from her partner and her CO. The charges could be viewed as her attempt to retaliate. Add to that the general knowledge that she was drinking heavily, and it certainly didn't make her particularly credible. You couldn't blame Captain Landau for not sticking his neck out for her, Ray thought. The suicide verdict closed the case. Calling it murder would reopen it and renew the charges of corruption. Landau would be questioned about his failure to act. Through his wife and her socially prominent sister, Norman Landau had connections that went to the very top. Once turned on him, the spotlight would reach them and fix them in its merciless glare. They would not forgive or forget.

Norman Landau regarded Dixon gravely.

"I just had a call from Lieutenant Palma about you, Sergeant," he said. "I don't like what I hear. I thought we understood each other. Has anything changed since our last talk?"

Things moved fast in the big building, Ray thought. They took the offensive instantly. He had to hold firm under Landau's scrutiny. "My friend's apartment and office were broken into and vandalized."

Though mild, the captain's tone was fraught with disappointment. "I can understand you're upset over what happened to Miss Ramadge, but that doesn't warrant unsubstantiated accusations. Have you proof that it was in fact police officers who broke into her place and caused the damage and distress?"

"Who else could have done it?"

"Well, that's the question, isn't it? It seems to me you're jumping to a dangerous conclusion. I expected better from you."

He was so reasonable—on the surface, Ray thought.

"On the other hand, if your suspicions are correct, I want to know about it. I want to find out who the men involved were so they can be punished. They should be punished. This is a matter for Internal Affairs. You agree?"

Dixon nodded. "I wouldn't want anything like this to happen to Ms. Ramadge again."

Landau was openly shocked. "Insofar as my people are concerned, I can assure you it won't."

"Thank you, Captain." The interview was over, but Ray Dixon continued to stand there.

"Something else, Sergeant?"

"I've been working on the case on my own time and I intend to continue."

"Ah yes, I assumed you would." Landau was thoughtful. The more he mulled it over, the more convinced he became that the murder of the Raggedy Man was at the core of the case, that it was woven into the spider's web of corruption. As far as he could see, neither Sergeant Dixon nor his private-eye girlfriend knew anything at all about it.

"You would like to work on it full-time, right?" Landau didn't wait for an answer. "In view of your close familiarity with the background, I think you should."

Dixon gasped. He hadn't expected this, certainly not so easily.

"Who's your CO over there in Queens? I'll arrange for a temporary transfer . . . not to us, here . . . No, that's not a good idea. How about to Homicide up there where she was found? That would be the Fourth, right?"

"Yes, Captain." Dixon could hardly get it out.

"You can work with whoever's carrying."

"That would be Pulver. Charley Pulver."

"Oh yes, I know him. Good man. Well then, that's it. Good luck and keep me informed."

"Thank you, Captain."

Landau smiled and waved him off.

Ray Dixon came out of the big building dazed. Three interviews had resulted in three different reactions and now he was officially assigned to investigate Jayne's murder. He could hardly believe it. The best part was that Gwenn would be safe. Nobody would dare harass her now. He couldn't wait to get to a phone and tell her.

He tried the office and got the answering machine. He wondered why Marge Pratt wasn't there, but let it pass. He tried Gwenn's home and got the machine again. He left identical messages:

Gwenn, it's me, Ray. I've got news, big news. Call me. Whenever you get home.

He remembered to try the car phone. No reponse. Where could she be?

After talking to Fred, the doorman, Gwenn drove back to Monique Bruno's place on Riverside Drive. She arrived at the time of the changeover for alternate-side-of-the-street parking and was able to find a spot on her first tour. She walked into the small mansion without any attempt at subterfuge and rang Monique Bruno's bell.

"Who is this?"

The voice was low, seductive.

"This is Gwenn Ramadge, Miss Bruno."

"What do you want?" The tone changed to harsh and annoyed.

"We need to talk," Gwenn told her. "It's important for both of us."

"I haven't got time," Monique said, and hung up.

Gwenn buzzed again. No reply. She pressed the button and held it.

There was finally a crackle that indicated the receiver had been picked up and the line was open. "Go away. Go away or I'll call security and have you forcibly removed."

"And I'll be back. Talk to me now and you'll be rid of me for good," Gwenn reasoned. Sensing uncertainty, she added, "Otherwise, I'll have to go to Frank Wilson."

"All right, all right. You can come up for five minutes, that's all. Five minutes and you're out of here."

"Deal."

The buzzer releasing the lock sounded so quickly Gwenn had to run for the knob to get it in time.

Upon entering the apartment, Gwenn found Bruno between personas: not the schoolgirl nanny, not the morning's seductress, not the sexy and elegant kept woman. The robe she wore was old and stained, short enough to reveal that her legs were covered with a dark fuzz and needed shaving. Her hair tumbled loose on her shoulders and appeared to be in need of a good brushing. Which was the real Monique?

"What are you doing with two apartments?"

"What are you talking about?"

"If you want me to leave in five minutes, you're going to have to cooperate, Miss Bruno."

"I said you could come up. I didn't promise to answer questions."

"Right," Gwenn acknowledged. "So, let me tell you how I see the situation. You have a history of success in—let's call it the escort business. It makes sense that when you came to the mainland you continued in that kind of work. So I assume that one apartment, this one, is for the business of entertaining your clients, and the other, the one on the East Side, is provided for you by your lover."

She paused, but Monique remained silent.

"Let's go back to how you met Frank Wilson."

"The Wilsons answered my ad."

"Come on, Ms. Bruno. Do you expect me to believe that hiring out as a live-in nanny was your idea? That you were honestly interested in that kind of work? A woman with your endowments?"

"I did that kind of work in my hometown."

"I know that and I get the impression from talking to those who knew you back then that you came to the mainland to get away from babysitting and nursing. You were a party girl. You met Frank Wilson at a party. He fell for you, hard, and offered you a permanent arrangement. Thinking he meant marriage, you accepted. But it turned out he already had a wife and child. Getting free wasn't that easy. So he worked out a scheme to have you with him. He wrote a Situations Wanted ad, put it in the paper, and made sure his wife saw it. He coached you for the interview and made sure you were hired.

"At first it went well. Everybody was satisfied: the child enjoyed the attention you gave him; Mrs. Wilson was pleased by your willingness to do extra chores; Frank Wilson, well served on two counts, was ecstatic. Imagining yourself to actually be the lady of the house, the role you were merely playing, gave you a taste of the life you expected to lead when Wilson got his divorce. After a while, though, the novelty began to wear off. You became bored. You couldn't be bothered to play with Bobby as you had in the beginning. He turned irritable and had trouble falling asleep when you put him to bed for his afternoon nap, so you started sedating him. After a while, his mother became anxious about his extended periods of lethargy. She was afraid you were in some way responsible and talked about getting rid of you. Frank did everything he could to dissuade her. Finally, he agreed to hiring a private detective to find out what was going on."

"You."

Gwenn nodded.

"Well, what have you found out?" Monique challenged.

"Enough for Lana Wilson to want you out of her house. So

Frank Wilson set you up in one of the sublease apartments handled by his agency. He didn't know you had already made your own arrangements."

The part-time prostitute and part-time nanny scowled. From an assortment of manicure tools spread out on the coffee table in front of her, she selected an emery board and began to file her long nails.

"I assume he doesn't know that you're shuttling between that place and this and that you're using your old skills."

Monique Bruno glared. "Are you going to tell him?"

"It depends."

"How much?"

"I don't want money. I want some straight, honest answers."

"That's what she said, your partner. Frankly, I don't see that there's anything to get so hot about. It's nobody's business but mine and Frank's."

"How about Lana?"

"Well, her too. Sure. Frank and I intend to get married, but we have to wait on some kind of prenuptial agreement he has with Lana. He has to stay married to her for a certain length of time and then he gets a settlement. There's a lot of money involved, so we have to be patient."

Gwenn's sweeping gesture took in the room and its appointments. "You consider this being patient?"

"I spent over six months out there on Long Island with only a three-year-old kid for company," Bruno flared. "I'm only human. Bobby's a great kid and all that, but he's not even mine."

"True." Gwenn nodded. "So on your day off you've been coming here for a little change of pace."

"Right."

"And to make a little extra cash."

"That too. The job didn't pay that much."

"This has been going on for a considerable time."

"Well, yes." She tossed her head.

"While you continued your affair with Wilson on a daily basis—in his own home."

"It was his idea."

"And Detective Harrow found all this out. You were afraid she'd tell Wilson and you'd lose him."

"Listen, I wasn't going to lose him, believe me. He might not like what I was doing, but he was hot for me." She preened. "No way I was going to lose him."

"You killed Detective Harrow to keep her quiet."

"I'm telling you—no. Frank didn't know about this setup and I didn't want him to find out, but I didn't kill anybody over it."

Gwenn took a deep breath. "You were afraid Detective Harrow would report to me, then I would tell Mrs. Wilson and she would throw Frank out without a cent. You wanted to get married but not to a pauper."

The downstairs buzzer sounded, harsh and peremptory. Monique jumped as though an electric charge had gone through her. "You asked for the truth and now I've told you. Go away."

"Frank Wilson is your chance for a normal life. He offers you social status and the comforts of money. Without them, he's no good to you."

The buzzer sounded a second time. Monique frowned and nervously gathered up her manicure equipment.

"I assume that's a client," Gwenn said. "By the way, who pays the rent for this apartment? Who do you work for?"

"Get out. Now. Oh, please . . ."

"I'll go, but let me ask you one more question: Do you really believe Frank Wilson intends to marry you? Do you think he ever intended to marry you?"

Monique flushed. "Please," she entreated as the buzzer sounded for the third time.

"Don't answer now. Think about it, then call me," Gwenn said. "We'll talk some more."

CHAPTER 11

MONDAY, SEPTEMBER 12
LATE AFTERNOON

At Monique Bruno's urgent entreaty, Gwenn took the back stairs instead of waiting for the elevator, so she wouldn't run into the client on his way up. She would wait and get a look at him on his way out, she thought. Meantime, as she settled herself in the car, Gwenn was confronted with an ethical dilemma: Just how much of what she had learned in the past few hours was she obliged to turn over to her client? Lana Wilson had hired her to locate Monique Bruno. Gwenn had done that. She should turn over the subject's address, but she was not required to give her deductions and inferences. Those were links to Jayne Harrow's murder and it would be wrong to involve Lana with that. That in turn brought Gwenn to another problem: Which of the two addresses should she give Mrs. Wilson? Both, she decided, since both had been turned while Mrs. Wilson was paying for her time. She would turn them both over, and then give up the case.

Using the car telephone, Gwenn tapped out the client's number.

"Mrs. Wilson? I have news for you."

In the course of the night, Monique Bruno came to the window three times and looked down toward where Gwenn was parked. She might have looked out like that on Wednesday and spotted Jayne. Would she have known who Jayne was and what she was doing?

Gwenn imagined Jayne on stakeout, watching, taking photographs, keeping a time log. Then shortly before two A.M., Monique's lights went out. Gwenn turned on the ignition and headed for home.

Before turning on the lights in her apartment, Gwenn looked to the answering machine. Its red message light blinked brightly in the dark. She turned on the nearest lamp and tapped the message button.

Gwenn, it's me, Ray. I've got news, big news. Call me. Whenever you get home. The machine whirred and buzzed, indicating the end of the message.

The next message was Ray again. *I forgot to tell you, I'm working out of the Two-Oh. Here's my new number. Take it down.*

He sounded excited, so it must be good news. But it was too late to call now, she decided, and she was very tired. She was so tired that after undressing she didn't even hang up her clothes but just dropped them on a chair. She crawled into bed and immediately fell asleep.

It was still dark when the telephone woke her. She felt as though she'd slept for hours, but according to the digital display of her bedside clock, it was only 4:32. She groped for the receiver.

"Hello?"

"Miss Ramadge? This is Monique Bruno. I'm sorry to disturb you, but I need to talk to you as soon as possible. Could you come over in the morning?"

"Certainly. Anytime," Gwenn murmured, still not completely awake.

"Eight o'clock. Is that too early?"

"No, that's fine. I can come sooner if you like."

Monique Bruno didn't answer right away.

"Miss Bruno? Are you all right?"

"Yes, I'm fine. I'll see you at eight."

"Ah . . . Miss Bruno? Would you like to give me an idea of what this is about?"

"When I see you." She started to hang up and then added, "You know where I am?"

"At the Riverside address?"

"Right."

After that they both hung up.

Gwenn settled back into the warm bed and pulled up the covers. No need to turn out the light, she hadn't turned it on. But now sleep eluded her. She shifted from side to side, but couldn't get comfortable. Her mind churned. What did Monique want? She should have insisted on an indication. The minutes dragged. By the time the first pale light appeared along the horizon, Gwenn was wide awake and possessed by a sense of urgency she couldn't explain but which was focused on Monique Bruno. She got out of bed, reached for the clothes she'd left on the chair a few hours earlier, and put them on. She stopped only long enough for a cup of instant coffee and then went down to her car. It was 6:32 on the morning of Tuesday, September 13, when Gwenn Ramadge stood at the front door of Monique Bruno's building and rang her bell.

No answer.

It didn't worry Gwenn. Actually, now that she was there an hour and a half early, she felt foolish, but not so foolish as to go away.

She rang again, hard. She paused and tried again, keeping her finger pressed to the button for a good long time. When there was still no answer, all the earlier vague anxieties returned. She had to get in. She couldn't leave without making sure that Monique was all right. So, one after the other she pressed all the buttons on the panel. And she got a response. People yelled at her to go away, to get lost. Lights came on, not only in Monique's building but in others on both sides of the street. However, nobody buzzed her in. She pounded on the door.

"Let me in! If somebody doesn't let me in, I'm calling the police!"

"What's going on here?" The voice was that of a man with an accent she couldn't place. She turned.

He stood behind her—thin, shoulders hunched forward, chest concave. A sudden dry cough and nicotine-stained fingers apparent when he put his handkerchief up to his mouth suggested he was a heavy smoker. He was very pale, lips moist and full, eyelids heavy. An aura of decadence hung about him, the sickly sweetness of corruption.

"Who are you?"

He made her a slight bow. "Laszlo Darvas. I manage this building and others on this street. What is the commotion?"

She listened intently, trying to home in on the accent: Middle-European maybe? "I'm afraid something's happened to Miss Bruno."

"Such as?"

"I don't know. I talked to her on the phone about half an hour ago. She asked me to come right over. Now she doesn't answer her bell." Gwenn purposely shaded the time in order to underscore the urgency.

He shrugged. "She must have fallen asleep while waiting."

"You think she's sleeping through all this?" Even as Gwenn asked, the shouting subsided and the lights went out window by window. "I demand you let me into her apartment so that I can make sure she's all right."

But the manager wasn't impressed. "Who are you?"

Gwenn was asked that question many times while on a case. If she told the truth, that she was a private investigator, what would the manager's reaction be? Whoever ran this operation couldn't appreciate his letting her in to snoop. Laszlo Darvas was nominally manager for the row of elegant buildings, but she suspected he was actually spy, security guard, and enforcer—for the brothel.

"I'm a friend of Monique. We went to school together and we worked for the same escort service in San Juan. She was going to help me get work here."

The manager glanced at his watch, a Patek-Philippe. "At seven in the morning?"

"I know it's strange, but she sounded upset; that's why I came straight over. That's why it worries me that she doesn't answer."

"Well . . ."

"I don't want to call the police, but I'm very concerned. I don't want to make trouble for you, Mr. Darvas, but if she's sick . . ."

"All right. I shouldn't, but . . . come on." He unlocked the entrance door and stood aside to let Gwenn pass.

Once inside she was careful not to let him see she was familiar with the layout, and deferred to him. They took the elevator and rode up in silence. He tapped lightly on Monique's door, then with increasing urgency. Finally, he took a ring of keys from his back pocket, selected one, and inserted it in the lock. With a click, the door opened.

The room was empty. The silk-shaded lamps were still lit, but their rosy glow was washed out by the gray dawn that seeped in between the partially drawn drapes. A bottle of champagne in a cooler floated on melted ice. The acrid smell of cigarettes was too strong for the air-conditioning to dispel.

"Miss Bruno?" Gwenn called. "Monique?" Instinct drew her to the bedroom.

The girl lay on the bed on her back, arms and legs outflung. Her hair, washed and styled, was a glorious dark cloud around her pale face. The rose satin robe she'd worn on Gwenn's first visit was half open, revealing her luscious nakedness.

Quietly, as though afraid to disturb her, Gwenn went to her, bent over her and placed two fingers at the base of her jaw, feeling for the carotid pulse. After several moments she straightened up and shook her head. "She's dead."

"What happened?" Darvas asked, but he didn't step forward to look himself.

"I don't know," Gwenn replied. Monique had given no indication of being addicted, but maybe . . . in the early stages . . . "Did she do drugs?"

Darvas shrugged. "Probably. In the end, they all do. I mean . . . Oh hell! This is bad, very bad. I'll have to make a call."

"I'll do it if you want," Gwenn offered.

"You?"

"We're talking about calling nine-one-one, aren't we?"

"Oh yes, certainly. Nine-one-one."

"For your own protection you should call nine-one-one first. Afterwards, you can call anybody you want."

"Who would that be?"

"The landlord, I suppose. Whoever you work for. How would I know?" Gwenn brushed it aside. "You'll want to notify your boss, give him time to prepare before the police ring his bell and start asking awkward questions."

"You're too smart for your own good, young lady," Darvas warned. "You better be careful where you stick your nose."

For answer, Gwenn walked around the bed to the telephone

and pressed the three numerals and waited for the ring. As the operator came on the line, Darvas came around and snatched the phone out of Gwenn's hand.

"I want to report a sudden death," he said.

As usual, an RMP team was the first to respond and it arrived within minutes. Brief as it was, the interval hung heavy for Gwenn Ramadge and Laszlo Darvas. After contacting 911, the manager made no calls. Probably because he didn't want to do so in her presence, Gwenn thought, nor did he want to go out and leave her alone to do—God only knew what he thought she might do. Remove evidence? Plant evidence? So they sat and watched each other till the buzzer from downstairs signaled the arrival of the first police contingent.

Patrol officers Reilly and Jackson took a quick look around and then got down to confirming the facts the 911 operator had given them. At that point, Gwenn revealed she was a private investigator. She handed the officers her card.

Darvas was outraged. "Why didn't you tell me who you were?"

"If I had, would you have let me into the apartment?"

"You lied. You said you were a friend of Miss Bruno's from Puerto Rico," he charged.

"If I hadn't, you wouldn't have let me in here and she might have lain like this for days."

"Okay, cool it," Officer Reilly broke in. "Save it for the detectives." His voice cracked nervously. He was young and a rookie and had never responded to a homicide complaint. He didn't want to make any mistakes. "You, miss, you sit over there." He pointed to the sofa. "You," he told Darvas, "over there." That was the far side of the room so they couldn't communicate. He'd forgotten they'd had plenty of time to communicate and concoct a story before he and his partner arrived. Where were those detectives anyway?

Meanwhile the rest of the investigation team were trickling in—crime scene experts, forensic detectives, photographers. They barely glanced at Gwenn Ramadge and Darvas as they passed through to the bedroom. Last to arrive was the detective who, by virtue of having picked up the phone on 911's relay of the complaint, was carrying the case. Kevin Derr's first order of business was to confer with the two uniforms. After that, he too went into the bedroom and joined an assistant medical examiner, Hamilton Smith, who was already on the job.

"So what do you think, Doc?"

Smith was a sportsman. His years in the sun had dried him out to a nutlike brown. His hair and eyebrows were a thick white. It was difficult to tell his age, but he was not too old for the job. By no means. With the years he had accumulated knowledge and experience and skill, for which he was respected by his peers.

Smith frowned. "Pity," he commented to Kevin Derr. "Young, beautiful woman like this self-destructing. I hate to see it."

"Drugs?" Derr asked, himself feeling little sympathy.

"Sure. Notice her pupils. Also . . ." Smith reached for the wide kimono sleeve of the robe and folded it back to point to the needle mark.

"But no tracks," Derr observed.

"So she OD'd the first time. Happens."

"I guess. How about time of death?"

"I can help there," Gwenn said. She had gotten up, walked to the door, and now joined them.

Derr consulted his notes. "I'll get to you shortly, Ms. . . . Ramadge. Please wait in the other room."

"I spoke with Miss Bruno at precisely four thirty-two this morning. She called me. She—"

Kevin Derr was a creature of habit and order. He didn't appreciate being interrupted, particularly by a civilian. "According to the statement you gave"—once again he leafed through his notebook—"to Officer . . ."

"Reilly." Gwenn provided the name.

"Thank you. I know his name. According to what you told Officer Reilly, you spoke to Miss Bruno half an hour before you turned up on the doorstep demanding to get into her apartment. According to the manager, that was seven A.M. So that would make it six-thirty when you spoke to her."

"No. It was four thirty-two by the digital readout of my bedside clock. Miss Bruno said she needed to see me first thing in the morning and we agreed I would come over at eight. She was very nervous. Stressed out. I didn't like it. I couldn't get back to sleep for worrying. Finally, I decided to come over and make sure she was all right. I told Mr. Darvas I'd just talked to her because I didn't think he'd buy my waiting two hours if I was really concerned."

"I'm not sure I do," Derr said. "We'll get into that. Meantime . . ."

Gwenn would not be dismissed. She appealed to the ME. "I'm sorry, Dr. Smith, I don't mean to intrude, but I thought it would be helpful for you to know she was alive at four thirty-two."

Hamilton Smith frowned. "Don't I know you? Yes! You're the PI who was involved in the Brides' case a couple of years ago. Ramadge, isn't it? Hart S and I. Well, well. What's your interest in this?"

"I was interviewing Miss Bruno in connection with the death of Detective Jayne Harrow."

"As I recall, you were determined not to get involved with any more homicide assignments. Very determined."

"And I meant it, but—"

"Harrow!" Kevin Derr recognized the name. Everybody in the division knew it. It meant trouble. He found the card Gwenn had handed him and really looked at it. "This is you?"

"Right."

"And you were interviewing this victim, Monique Bruno, with regard to the suicide of Jayne Harrow?"

"Homicide," she corrected. "I believe Jayne Harrow was murdered."

"It's been marked a suicide and cleared. The case is cleared."

"I'm treating it as a homicide."

"You can treat it any way you like, Ms. Ramadge, the fact remains that officially——"

"Argue it out between yourselves," Hamilton Smith interrupted. "I've got other calls. So, unless there's something else, we'll transport." He signaled the orderlies. "Here's a quick rundown," he told Derr. "Probable cause of death: drug overdose administered by injection. Time of death: dependent on amount and purity of agent but not sooner than four-thirty A.M. and not later than seven A.M. Okay, Ms. Ramadge?"

He waited till the zipper on the body bag was closed before addressing Derr.

"She's okay, Detective. You can relax. You might even listen to what she has to say."

Derr managed a sour smile.

CHAPTER 12

Detective Kevin Derr was not pleased. The last thing he needed at that point was a big case. He was due to go on vacation the following week and this investigation gave every indication of dragging on for God only knew how long. Close to sixty and looking toward retirement, he aimed to stay out of trouble. Monique Bruno, the victim, was evidently connected to Detective Harrow in some way, and Harrow had been trouble for everybody while she was alive. Her suicide had put paid to all her accusations, and now here was this other woman, Gwenn Ramadge, stirring it all up again.

Derr sighed lugubriously. "Let me get this straight," he said to Gwenn after Hamilton Smith was gone and the body had been removed. "Miss Bruno called you at four-thirty A.M. How did she come to do that? What did she want?"

"I don't know. She didn't say. She indicated it was urgent, that's all."

"It must have been for her to call at that hour."

"I thought so."

"But you weren't close friends. This was a lie you told Mr. Darvas."

"I explained . . ."

"What was your relationship with the victim?"

"I'd been investigating Miss Bruno on behalf of a client."

Damn! Derr thought. On his arrival and first view of the victim he had pigeonholed the death as a routine drug OD. With Ramadge's appearance and statement, it showed signs of turning into one of those convoluted *mysteries* detectives hated. However, if a link could be established between Bruno and Harrow, then he might be able to pass the case off to Charley Pulver, who was running the Harrow case. "That's very interesting," he encouraged Gwenn.

"I took Detective Harrow on a temporary basis for the express purpose of helping me watch Miss Bruno."

He would definitely be able to pass this on to Pulver, Derr thought, and his spirits lifted.

"Who's the client?"

That was a question Gwenn was always cautious about answering, but in this instance it had already been both asked and answered. "Mr. and Mrs. Frank Wilson. Detective Ford has already interviewed them."

Watch it! Derr thought. With one bad move he could make trouble not only for himself but for a lot of others. "What is Detective Ford's interest?"

"You'll have to ask him."

"I'm asking you."

"I can't speak for Detective Ford."

"I want straight answers, Ms. Ramadge."

"I'm doing my best."

"You're evasive."

The exchange was rapid.

"I'm trying to cooperate," she insisted. In fact, she felt as though she were picking her way through a minefield. "Jayne was Detective Ford's partner. He's naturally concerned about clearing up the circumstances surrounding her death."

"Let's see if I've got this straight." Derr paused to sort out the facts. "Some people called Wilson hired you to investigate Monique Bruno and you hired Harrow to assist you. Okay. What were the Wilsons looking for?"

"They'd hired her as a nanny to look after their son. They were interested in her moral character."

"And?"

"I suspect Mr. Darvas, the manager, is the one we should be asking. He might even be able to tell us who her last visitor was. He knows what's going on in the building and, I suspect, in the adjoining buildings."

Derr studied Gwenn through narrowed eyes. "When was the last time you spoke to the victim—in person?"

"About five yesterday afternoon."

"Where?"

"Here."

Derr made no attempt to hide his surprise. "What was the subject of your conversation?"

"I can't tell you that."

"Sooner or later you'll have to. Why not get it over? Look, Ms. Ramadge, I'm not anxious to take you in and put you through the rigors of an official interrogation." Since Derr intended to get rid of the case, he was speaking the truth.

Gwenn didn't know that. The Wilsons were her clients. As such she owed them the protection of confidentiality.

"Well." Derr sighed. "Let's not be precipitous. Why don't you go on downstairs and sit for a while and think it over. I need to get a statement from the manager and there are a couple of other things I need to clear up. It shouldn't take long. Then we'll talk again."

"I won't change my mind."

"We'll see." He summoned one of the uniforms. "Take Ms. Ramadge down to the lobby. Get her coffee and a Danish or something. Coffee okay, Ms. Ramadge? Would you prefer something else?"

"Coffee would be good, thank you."

Why the sudden courtesy? Gwenn wondered. It put her in mind of a classical quotation: *Timeo Danaos et dona ferentes*, from Virgil's *Aeneid*. Roughly translated, it meant, "I fear the Greeks even though they bear gifts," and referred to the Trojan horse. It was obvious that Kevin Derr had been around a long time and had a reason for everything he did, so she'd better not let her guard down. She could, however, accept the coffee and pastry.

Gwenn waited, but it was taking longer than anticipated.

She sat on a small, satin-covered settee amid the marble pilasters, enjoying the snack provided on Derr's order. She watched as the various experts who had converged in response to the complaint straggled out of the tiny elevator and passed her on the way to the front door and out to the street. Their number and the diversity of their expertise impressed her, as it had on previous occasions when she'd been present at a murder scene. On this morning, however, she was very concerned about her own part in the situation. Under Officer Reilly's eye, she had time to ponder. There were questions that needed to be asked and answered.

Q: Why had Monique Bruno called her with such urgency?

A: To tell her something.

Q: What?

A: Gwenn already knew about Monique's past. She knew about her affair with Frank Wilson, the steamy trysts conducted in Lana Wilson's own house—in her face, you might say. Gwenn knew that Monique had been cheating on Wilson by reverting to her trade, which she had never completely abandoned. She also knew this was where she operated.

Q: What else was there to tell?

A: Plenty. For instance—for whom was she working? Who

paid the rent for the elaborate apartment? To put it bluntly, who ran the brothel? Who was her pimp?

Q: Why was Monique killed?

A: Obviously, to stop her from revealing his identity.

Q: How did the killer know Monique was getting ready to talk?

A: He was there when she made the call to Gwenn. Or the phone was bugged. Gwenn liked that answer better. Much better.

Q: Who bugged the phone?

A: It was ordered by the head of the operation. Probably, it was standard procedure. The actual installation would be by whoever kept an eye on the ladies in the buildings—Mr. Darvas in all likelihood.

Q: Why did Monique decide to talk?

A: Monique, being sensitive to her situation, had surely sensed she was in danger. By sharing what she knew with Jayne, she had thought to protect herself. Instead she had speeded up her own demise.

A pair of RMPs coming out of the elevator broke Gwenn's concentration. Among the first to arrive, they were always close to the last to leave. *Where was Derr,* she wondered. How much longer did he expect her to wait? Was this some kind of ploy to make her lose her composure?

"Officer," she called to Reilly. "Would you check with Detective Derr and find out how much longer he expects to be?"

At that moment, Derr himself emerged from the elevator. "Sorry, Ms. Ramadge. Sorry to have kept you waiting so long. Something's come up and we'll have to postpone our talk. I tell you what, why don't I give you a call? I have your number." He held her business card in his hand, palm out.

Gwenn was taken aback. "Fine." It was all she could say. As Derr motioned to Reilly and they both got back into the elevator, she spoke up. "When the manager and I entered the apartment and found Miss Bruno, Mr. Darvas was very anxious to make a phone call of his own before notifying nine-one-one. I suspect he wanted to—"

Derr cut her off. "Thank you for the information. However, allow me to draw my own conclusions."

"I only wanted to point out that whoever he intended to notify, he's probably done it by now."

"So noted, Ms. Ramadge, so noted." He pressed the button and the elevator door closed.

The encounter had been brief. If all he'd wanted to do was tell her that she was free to go and that he would contact her later, why hadn't Derr simply sent somebody with the message? Why had he come himself?

Another small mystery to add to the puzzle.

Emerging at last from the dark lobby into the midmorning sunshine was blinding. Gwenn blinked several times while she stood on the portico overlooking Riverside Drive, the shimmering waters of the Hudson, and the Palisades. Her vision adjusted, she walked down to the curb seeking a break in the traffic so she could cross over to her car. The light changed. She made sure to look both ways before starting across. When she was in the middle of the street, she heard the unmistakable roar of an accelerating motor behind her and turned to see a blue pickup truck pull away from the curb and head straight for her. For a split second she froze where she was; then instinct took over.

She ran as she had never in her life run before, but she was trapped. Cars parked bumper to bumper were a barrier blocking escape to the sidewalk. She was athletic, trained in horseback riding, swimming, tennis. She'd loved team sports: basketball, track. She had narrowly missed qualifying for the Olympic broad jump. That was years ago, but the body remembered. Adjusting her stride, Gwenn hurtled over the hood of a pearl-gray Mercedes; using her right hand and arm as a fulcrum, she pivoted and rolled over to the other side. A hiss of hot air scalded her as the truck roared past.

Shaking, Gwenn stayed down behind the Mercedes in case of gunfire. Thank God there wasn't any.

Tires squealing, the truck made a sharp turn around the corner and disappeared as quickly as it had appeared. The light turned green and after a barely perceptible pause during which the various drivers wondered what had happened, what they had actually seen, traffic returned to normal.

Slowly, Gwenn emerged from cover. She hadn't seen the driver, couldn't even tell whether there had been one or two persons in the cab, much less attempt identification. She hadn't even thought of the license number. The whole thing had happened too fast. Even if she could locate a witness who had been quick-witted enough to get the license number, how could she prove the intent had been to run her down? She couldn't. Yet Gwenn was convinced the truck had been lying in wait for her.

She considered going back to Monique Bruno's apartment to tell Detective Derr what had happened. He'd think she was overreacting. He'd probably tell her it was her own fault for not being more careful. Even if he believed her, what could he do about it? She looked up to the fifth-floor windows of Monique's building and thought she saw movement, a curtain raised at the corner and dropped again. Was it possible somebody up there had seen the whole thing? She was getting neurotic, Gwenn thought. *Get hold of yourself. Go home. Take an aspirin. Lie down.*

Within a few feet of her car, Gwenn felt around in her handbag for her keys. She was about to unlock the door at the driver's side, of course, when she pulled back as though she'd had an electric shock. *The driver's seat was set back in line with the passenger seat.* Gwenn was only five foot one. She couldn't comfortably reach the gas pedal unless the seat was well forward. Since she was the only one who ever drove the car, there was no reason for the seat to be in any other position. She stood where she was, key in hand, staring as though doing so would make the seat return to its normal position.

Somebody had tampered with the car. Somebody had unlocked the door and gotten in. Finding the lack of legroom awkward, he had adjusted the seat while he worked and then forgotten to put it back as it had been.

Gwenn shivered in the hot sun. Was this the second line of attack in case the first, the rundown attempt, failed? No way she was going to get in the car to find out. Let Derr call the bomb squad. Let them come and find the device and dismantle it. They might even be able to trace the components and discover who was responsible. She felt a surge of optimism, but it didn't last. She acknowledged that she didn't want to appeal to Kevin Derr, not for help and most certainly not for sympathy. She headed for the corner telephone and called Ray at the new number he had given her.

"Homicide. Detective Morrissey."

"Sergeant Dixon, please."

"He's not at his desk. Can I help you?"

"Ah, no . . . this is a personal call. Do you know where I can reach him?"

"Sorry. Would you like to leave a message?"

She hesitated. "I'll call later."

"Okay."

He hung up, leaving Gwenn disappointed, feeling as though the ground had been cut out from under her. She realized suddenly how much she depended on Ray, how accustomed she was to his being there. It was his emotional support she wanted; the details of reporting to the bomb squad she was certainly capable of handling herself. The easiest way was through 911, she decided. Having set the process in motion, Gwenn found an empty bench overlooking the park and the river and sat down to wait.

As usual an RMP team arrived first. Both officers were young and overweight, and set in the rut of routine. Before any examination of the complaint, they verified Gwenn's ID. Gwenn was reminded of the admissions clerk in the emergency room taking down name and address and insurance number while the patient bled. When she managed to introduce her status as a private investigator and showed her card, they were grudgingly attentive to her story and, of course, wrote it all down. They walked over to her car with her, and, of course, peered in through the window. They agreed the seats were in alignment when they should not have been so. The older of the two, Prescott, according to his name tag, asked a sensible question.

"Why would anyone want to blow up your car?"

To Gwenn the answer was simple: somebody thought she knew too much. She didn't, but that was beside the point. To explain it to the two officers, she would have to give an account of the Harrow and Bruno homicides. It would confuse them. What could she say that was direct and credible?

"I've been getting death threats."

Both cops gaped at her.

As soon as she'd said it, she was sorry. She didn't like lying. "Hate calls and death threats," she enlarged, and made it worse.

They were impressed.

"Why?" Prescott asked, concerned.

"I'm investigating a homicide and somebody's trying to scare me off." That was getting back to the truth, she thought. The trashing of her apartment and the attempt to run her down were certainly intended to be threats and to frighten her.

If Prescott had at that point asked what case she was working on, Gwenn would have refused to answer, but he didn't ask. He motioned to his partner and they stepped aside to consult.

"We'll contact the bomb squad," Prescott informed her. "They'll send a team to check your car. The squad is based at Rodman's Neck, so it'll take a while."

It took a very long while.

Meantime, the street was cleared. More blue-and-whites arrived, roof lights flashing, sirens wailing. Detectives came in unmarked vehicles. Traffic was diverted. Cars parked anywhere near

Gwenn's Volvo were towed out of what was deemed the danger zone. It was nearly two when the bomb removal van arrived. In instances where the bomb could not be disarmed at the site, the van was equipped to carry it to the firing range, where it could be safely detonated.

The two men who got out wore protective suits. They conferred with detectives and patrol cops, then made a slow and deliberate inspection of the vehicle—from the outside. Having done that, they approached Gwenn with the same deliberate movements they'd used in inspecting the car.

"Ma'am? I'm Sergeant Wesley. This is Sergeant Kelleher."

The two were very much alike, Gwenn thought—lean, tanned, their faces bearing deep creases put there by the danger of the job.

The speaker's manner indicated he had seniority.

"What makes you think somebody's planted a bomb in your car?"

Gwenn didn't want to mislead these men—they would after all be risking their lives—but she had to stick to her story. She tried to phrase it so that it was the truth. "There has been a previous attempt on my life. And there have been threats."

"Was bombing specifically mentioned?"

"No."

"Well, we'll take a look."

They went inside the van and when they came out again they had added headpieces to their gear. They looked like astronauts getting out for a walk on the moon, Gwenn thought, stepping out of range as she'd been ordered to do.

The two sergeants worked slowly, very slowly. Most likely, the device would be connected to the wiring of the ignition or else to the trunk lock. Another possibility was a bomb connected to a timer or one that could be triggered by remote control. They found none of these. They checked the doors and looked under the hood. When they removed their head coverings, an indication they were through, they were smiling.

The crowd behind the barricades broke into applause.

"Thank you." Gwenn was relieved and embarrassed at the same time. "I'm sorry for the trouble."

"It's our job, ma'am." Sergeant Wesley hesitated. "About those threats—you ought to report them. You don't want to have to call us again."

She flushed. "No, I don't."

"Here." He held out her car keys. "Go ahead. Get in. It's safe."

"Thank you again." Nevertheless, Gwenn waited till they were gone, the crowd dispersed, and the police had removed the barricades before approaching her car. She had been assured it was safe, so she got in. She put the key in the ignition and turned it. The motor caught and purred. Would it be safe the next time she turned the key? She couldn't call the bomb squad every time. Using the car phone, she called her office.

"Marge? It's me. Are you all right? Is everything all right?"

"Yeah, sure," her secretary replied. "How about you? Are you okay?"

"I'm fine. Now listen. I want you to close the office right away."

"But it's only—"

"I know what time it is. Just do it. And cancel any new appointments. That's important. No new clients."

"Okay." Marge knew it was useless to argue or try to find out what was behind all this. "Have you talked to Ray?"

"I got his message and his new number. I'll get in touch with him when I can. I don't want you contacting him. I mean that, Marge."

She hung up in the midst of Marge's anxious admonitions.

TUESDAY, SEPTEMBER 13
LATE AFTERNOON

Whoever the perp was, he was not working alone, Gwenn thought. He had a sizable organization and a good information network. Nevertheless, Gwenn believed she had a grace period before his next move.

The attempt to run her down might very well have been a scare tactic to make her vulnerable to the next ploy, which was the bomb threat. Was that also intended merely to make her more nervous and unstable? What would it lead to? She had called the police on what amounted to a false alarm. Next time they might not be so ready to respond, and she might be reluctant to call. Either way, the car had become a source of danger. She had to get rid of the car.

She was afraid to use it, so she had to find a place to put it. She couldn't afford to abandon it on the street and she couldn't afford expensive garage space. There were, however, many small garages on the Upper East Side that catered to long-term clients, regulars as opposed to transients. One such garage was run by a man who had been a client and became a friend. Walter Neufeld.

Neufeld had a ten-year-old son, Walter junior. Junior was shy and didn't make friends easily. He was constantly ridiculed, used as a butt for jokes and pranks. His parents decided to transfer him to a private school. Things didn't go well there, either. The boys came from rich families. They got lavish allowances, wore expensive clothes—things Walter could have, though with effort, given his son, but didn't because he considered having them wouldn't be good for him. He was shocked when the headmaster called and told him his son had been caught stealing. Junior tearfully denied it. And despite the fact that the missing items were found in his locker, Walter believed the boy and hired Gwenn Ramadge to clear him.

Gwenn found it significant that the stolen items had belonged to teachers rather than schoolmates. She was intrigued that Junior, who was usually the last one to be picked when sides were chosen up for games, should have been sought out and invited to join the school's most prestigious secret society. She learned that in order to qualify, he was to take certain items from specific members of the faculty—teachers who were not popular, who were strict disciplinarians. If caught, he was on no account to reveal why he had stolen what he had stolen or that he had been ordered to do it as part of the initiation. Gwenn also learned that it was intended he should be caught and the real test was keeping silent, which Junior grimly set himself to do.

By talking to the teachers whose possessions had been taken and to the boys whom they had most penalized, Gwenn got the answers she needed. As a result of her investigation, the society was disbanded and its leader expelled. Walter junior was admired by the students for having honored the code. He was presently in therapy and gaining confidence as well as physical and mental health. Walter Neufeld credited it all to Gwenn.

"Hi!" he called when he saw her coming down the ramp. He approached the window, but his smile disappeared when he got close enough to read her expression. "What happened? Did you have an accident? Are you all right?"

"Somebody tried to plant a bomb on me."

"What?"

"No, that's not right. I thought someone might have planted a bomb in my car. I called the police; they checked the car and say it's clean."

"Thank God." Neufeld scrutinized her. "You want to tell me why anybody would want to plant a bomb on you?"

The question couldn't be avoided. She sighed. "It's better for you not to know."

"If you say so."

"I need a favor."

"You've got it."

"You haven't heard what it is."

"Doesn't matter."

"Oh, Walter, I'm so grateful." She had to swallow a couple of times to clear the lump in her throat. "I'd like to leave the car here with you for a couple of days. But it could be dangerous for you. I don't think I was followed and if I was, I don't think they'd tamper with the car while it's in the garage where the wrong person could trigger the device. These people have no conscience, but they are practical. Just the same, it's a risk for you and everybody in and around the building."

"I'm not worried," Walter Neufeld assured her. "Tell you what, we'll give it a quick new paint job and put on new plates just to make sure. Okay? What color would you like?"

Gwenn didn't like the turn the case had taken. It was all starting to come together, but not in the way she had hoped for. Instead of being elated, she was depressed. Through Monique, Jayne Harrow had uncovered a link to further police corruption. However, it still lacked hard evidence, Gwenn reminded herself. She could be inferring too much from the situation. But in her heart, she knew she was not.

Leaving Walter Neufeld's garage, she started for home. She could walk it easily and had done so many times. On this mild afternoon, her pace lagged and she acknowledged that she was not only afraid to use her car, she was afraid to go home. She was afraid of what might be lying in wait for her.

On impulse, she stepped to the edge of the curb and flagged a passing taxi.

She gave the driver the first destination that popped into her head: the Waldorf. It was big, impersonal, anonymous. She would be lost in it, for a while anyway.

She checked in. Once in the room, she hung out the *Do Not Disturb* sign, locked and bolted the door. She took off her shoes, folded back the coverlet of the bed, and lay down. She immediately fell into a deep sleep.

CHAPTER 13

**WEDNESDAY, SEPTEMBER 14
MORNING**

Science tells us there is no such thing as a dreamless sleep, but
whatever dreams, or nightmares, she may have had, Gwenn was
mercifully spared remembrance. She awakened naturally at her
accustomed time and was instantly alert and aware of where she
was and why. She also knew she couldn't stay there long, the reason being that in order to get the room yesterday, she'd had to
use her credit card with her real name. So whoever might be
looking for her wouldn't have much trouble tracing her. Gwenn
had no idea what the day would bring or where she would lay her
head that night—maybe home; probably not. In the meantime,
she availed herself of the present comforts, including a scalding-
hot shower in the luxurious bathroom. She ordered from room
service—eggs sunny side up, bacon, whole wheat toast, coffee—
and requested the *Times* and the *Post* to be sent with it. By the
time the order arrived, she was dressed.

She drank the coffee first, then ate the eggs and bacon even before unfolding the newspapers. She wanted to be fortified to deal with whatever might confront her.

There was nothing in the newspapers about Monique Bruno's death. Gwenn turned on the radio and searched the dial. Nothing. It was almost twenty-four hours since she had demanded entrance to the prostitute's apartment, plenty of time for the police to dig up Bruno's history and present occupation. The press would seize on it; it was the kind of story the tabloids loved. So it must be that the police were sitting on it. That didn't come as a big surprise, but how long would they be able to keep it quiet? Another day or two, not much more. It was up to her to make good use of the time. She had come to certain conclusions, but she was still reluctant to accept them. Before doing so, she had to eliminate all possible alternatives no matter how farfetched they might seem.

She paid her bill and checked out. She took a cab to Penn Station and caught the 9:22 to Sands Point. From there she took another cab to Frank Wilson's office.

He got up to greet her, shook her hand, and led her to the client's chair. He returned to his own place at his desk, giving Gwenn plenty of time to look around and be impressed.

Actually, Gwenn thought the flowered chintz and reproduction furniture and paintings were more suitable to a village tearoom, but she said what she knew he wanted to hear. "Delightful office."

"Thank you. Lana thinks it's overdone."

Gwenn let that pass.

"So, Miss Ramadge. What are you doing in these parts? How can I help you? Are you in the market for a house?" he joked.

She took the opening. "How is the market these days? How's business?"

"Business?" He was surprised at the turn, but went along. "Not too bad for this time of year."

"How are rentals?"

"Rentals are as usual. What's this about, Miss Ramadge?"

"It's about Miss Bruno."

He frowned, annoyed. "What about her?"

"You haven't heard?"

"Heard what?"

Gwenn hesitated. How to put it? He had, after all, cared for her. "She's dead."

The color drained from his face. "Dead?" he repeated as though to make sure he'd heard right. "How? What happened? Was it an accident?"

"Apparently, it was a drug overdose."

"No. She didn't do drugs," he countered quickly and positively.

"Were you close enough to her to know?" Gwenn asked gently.

He looked away. "I thought I was."

Gwenn almost felt sorry for him. "I understand that when Mrs. Wilson fired Monique, you installed her in one of your rental apartments in Manhattan."

He shrugged, struggling to recover. "The poor girl didn't have anyplace to go. Lana wouldn't wait till she found a place. Sometimes Lana is . . . relentless. So I let Monique have the place temporarily."

"No charge?"

He shrugged again. "She wouldn't have been able to afford it."

"She paid you in other ways."

"What?"

"That was crude. I'm sorry. I apologize—though you're not in a position to be sensitive. Your actions have been anything but honorable."

He flushed a deep, unhealthy scarlet. "I don't know what you're talking about."

"Of course you do. You cheated on your wife and actually conducted the affair in her home. Ugly, Mr. Wilson. Very ugly. Your wife found out and threw your girlfriend out. Monique then went back to her old trade."

"No."

"You were obsessed with Monique. The thought that she was selling herself to other men was more than you could bear. You were consumed by jealousy. You killed her."

"No. You're wrong."

"Did she tell you what she was doing? Did she taunt you with it?"

"You're wrong. You're way off. You don't know what you're talking about." He was fighting his sorrow and also fear of the trap Gwenn was weaving.

"Where were you yesterday morning between four-thirty and seven A.M.?"

"Home. In my bed, asleep. Is that when it happened?"

"You tell me."

"I don't know. I was at home in my bed . . . wait a minute. I wasn't asleep."

"You weren't?"

"Bobby woke me. He was sick. He had an upset stomach and had thrown up all over himself. He knocked on my door and woke me."

"I take it you and your wife have separate rooms. Why didn't Bobby wake her?"

Wilson hesitated. "Lana wasn't in her room. I looked."

"Where was she?"

"I don't know."

"Out of the house?"

"Yes."

"And when did she get back?"

"I don't know. I was too concerned with Bobby. You can talk to the boy if you don't believe me."

"You're basing your alibi on the evidence of your three-year-old son?"

Frank Wilson smiled wryly. "No. I know you have a low opinion of me, Miss Ramadge, but I don't go down that far. I'm basing it on my Aunt Rita, who is staying with us, and on the doctor, of course, Dr. Emerson Conklin. I called him. He wanted to give me instructions over the phone, but I insisted he come over. I told him Lana was spending the night at the house of a college friend, and I didn't consider myself competent to give Bobby the medication. He came. I don't know what time he arrived or when he left, but I'm sure he does. It will show in his bill." He paused. "Is that good enough, Ms. Ramadge?"

"Why didn't you tell me this in the first place?"

"It concerns our personal and private life."

"I still need to know what time Mrs. Wilson got home."

"And I still don't know. I sat up with Bobby till I was sure he was sleeping soundly. Then I went back to my own room. I didn't see Lana till breakfast."

"You didn't try to contact her?"

"Why? The crisis was over."

"You did tell her that Bobby had been sick?"

"Of course, and she was very upset. A friend of hers is running for country supervisor in Suffolk County and Lana is active in the campaign. The meeting she'd attended ran late. The car broke down on the way home. It took an hour before AAA responded; then she had to be towed. It took more time for repairs."

"You told the doctor she was staying overnight with a college friend," Gwenn reminded him.

"Why complicate matters?"

"At the time, you didn't really know where your wife was."

"No."

"She didn't call to tell you?"

"No."

"You didn't find out till yesterday morning."

"That's right."

"Then did you call the garage? Or AAA?"

"You mean did I check up on her? No, I did not. I had no reason."

Maybe he had no reason, Gwenn thought, but she did. It involved a couple of phone calls, which she made from a public phone down the street from the real estate office. The results did not support what Wilson had told her. There was no record of Lana Wilson's call to AAA in the middle of the night, nor any record of a tow. The question now was: Who was lying, Frank or Lana?

At this point it would have been useful to have a car. It occurred to Gwenn that she could have safely rented. It was too late now, so she called the local taxi service again.

It was just after one P.M. when Gwenn's taxi pulled up in front of the Wilson house. She paid off the driver and took a few moments to collect herself as he sped away.

Silence enveloped her. At first it seemed deep and complete; then gradually she became aware of its components—the soft hiss of a light breeze off the water, a scampering of squirrels through the pine trees, a dog barking in the distance, and finally, most pervasively and characteristically, in the background the steady slap of surf on the shore. Long Island Sound was a sheltered body of water, rarely agitated, so despite the clear sky there were indications that a storm was forming. Gwenn walked up the path to the Wilsons' front door and rang the bell.

In due course, a woman with snow-white hair fluffed high on top of her head, and wearing white sweats embossed with gold in a pattern of vines and leaves, appeared. She squinted through dark glasses that covered most of her face.

"Yes?"

"Is Mrs. Wilson at home?"

"Who wants her?"

"Toot! Toot!"

Gwenn rose on tiptoe to look over the woman's shoulder. She saw a towheaded, blue-eyed boy of about three energetically pedaling a tricycle down a long corridor.

"Toot! Toot!" He raised his right arm and made a pumping motion, as though he were pulling the cord of a train whistle.

Bobby, Gwenn thought, recognizing him from the surveillance.

The child increased speed, emerged into the wider section of the hall, and headed straight for where Gwenn and the older woman were standing.

"Bobby! Look out!"

The child swerved just as the two of them jumped back. He laughed gleefully at their discomfiture.

Nothing wrong with him, Gwenn thought. This was not the sluggish, apathetic child Lana Wilson had described and she had observed.

The woman shook her head as Bobby pedaled away furiously. "He's a handful. At this age they're never still. What did you say your name was?"

"Gwenn Ramadge." She proffered one of her cards.

She looked it over. "I'm Frank's aunt, Rita Clement. Mrs. Wilson's in the shower. Do you want to give me a message?"

"I'll wait, if you don't mind."

Mrs. Clement wasn't pleased. She was uncertain as to how to treat Gwenn—reluctant to admit her into the house, but uncomfortable about shutting the door in her face and leaving her to stand on the porch. Gwenn solved the problem for her by stepping forward firmly and forcing Mrs. Clement to give way.

She looked around curiously. Despite the long hours she'd spent watching the house, she'd never been inside.

They were in a circular hall facing a curving staircase. A formal living room opened off to the right, the dining room to the left. Straight ahead, the narrow corridor Bobby Wilson was using as a racecourse led to the back. A pair of chairs flanked the standard console against the stair well. Gwenn went over and sat. "I'll wait," she repeated.

"I'll tell her you're here." Mrs. Clement started for the stairs. As she did, Bobby emerged from the dark end of the corridor in another rush of speed and stopped in front of Gwenn.

"Mama's not taking a shower. She's in her office." He indicated a closed door at the far side of the living room. "Are you going to be my new nanny?"

"No."

"That's good because I don't want another nanny."

"Why not?" Gwenn asked. "I thought you liked your last nanny. You did like Monique, didn't you?"

"She was okay in the beginning. She was nice. She gave me cookies and took me to the beach. Then she got cranky and fussy and made me take naps in the afternoon. When I didn't sleep she gave me medicine. Nasty medicine. It made me sick."

"Did you tell your parents?"

"I told my daddy. He said I should do what Mikki told me. He liked her. He liked her better than me. Better than Mama. He came to see her when Mama wasn't home."

Children were observant, Gwenn thought, and intuitive. "Did you tell your mama?"

He shook his head. "I didn't want to hurt her feelings."

Gwenn's heart went out to him. She wanted to take him into her arms and hug him. "Have you been sick lately, since Monique went away?"

"I threw up last night."

It was possible that the drugs Monique had been administering to make the boy sleep during her assignations with his father had a residual effect. Reactions were individualistic and unpredictable, particularly in the case of a very young child.

"What's going on?"

The door Bobby Wilson had indicated as leading to his mother's office opened and Lana Wilson came out.

"Miss Ramadge! Well, this is a surprise." She waited for Gwenn to say something. When she didn't, Mrs. Wilson herself filled the awkward void. "Have you met Frank's aunt, Mrs. Clement? Aunt Rita, this is the investigator I told you about."

At last Mrs. Clement bestowed a smile of approval on Gwenn.

"What can I do for you, Miss Ramadge?" Lana Wilson asked.

"I need to talk to you. Privately."

"Well, I was just about to drive Bobby to the pool for swimming class. Would you take him over there for me, Aunt Rita? Miss Ramadge, this way."

She led Gwenn across the living room to what must have originally been an open porch and was now Lana Wilson's home office. It was spacious enough to provide an informal conversation area and a well-equipped work space with desk, filing cabinets, and word processor. She had moved fast in setting it up, Gwenn thought, and it was obvious she was proud of the room and what it represented. She glowed. In fact, her whole aspect was changed from what it had been when Monique Bruno was under her roof; the perpetual frown was gone; her shoulders no longer slumped.

"You've done a fine job here," Gwenn complimented, and they both understood she referred not just to the room but to her own regeneration. Lana gestured toward the sofa, and Gwenn settled herself informally on the end cushion.

"I have disturbing news. Monique Bruno is dead."

Lana Wilson gasped. Her glow turned sallow. Bright eyes became opaque and guarded. "Was she in an accident? What happened?"

"She died of a drug overdose. It might or might not have been self-administered."

"I didn't know she took drugs."

"I'm not sure that she did," Gwenn replied.

Lana Wilson stared. "I don't understand. Then how did she die?"

"She could have been knocked unconscious and the drug administered while she was helpless."

"You mean she was murdered?"

"Monique died between the hours of four-thirty and seven yesterday morning. Where were you at that time?"

"Me? I was here, home, in bed and asleep. Where else should I have been?" she answered promptly.

"And Mr. Wilson? Where was he?"

"In his bed." Then she added, "I assume."

"You have separate rooms?"

"Lots of couples do. For a variety of reasons, not necessarily to do with sex."

"How about Mrs. Clement? Can she confirm you were at home?"

"Aunt Rita went to a ladies' bridge party. Where is all this leading, Miss Ramadge? What is your interest? You don't work for me anymore, by your own choice. So this is none of your business."

"I resigned so that I could make it my business," Gwenn told her. "The police will certainly make it theirs. They'll be coming around again and this time they won't be easily satisfied." She looked hard at the woman who had been her client. "Monique Bruno worked for you and lived in your home for over six months. She was like one of the family. They'll want to know why, all of a sudden, you fired her."

"It wasn't all of a sudden. I fired her on information you provided. Actually, on your recommendation. Are you going to deny that?"

Gwenn shook her head. "What matters at this point is that you weren't satisfied you'd got rid of her once and for all. You called and asked me to find out where she'd gone. What you really wanted to know was whether the affair between her and your husband was still on."

"What do you mean—still?"

"You used to commute to Manhattan every day. Your husband has a local office here, not fifteen minutes from the house. He came home on his lunch hour and had sex with your son's nanny. Monique used drugs to make sure the boy would sleep. Despite that, Bobby sensed there was something going on between his dad and his nanny. Your neighbors knew what was going on. Are you going to claim you didn't?" It was a hard thing to say to Lana Wilson and Gwenn was as gentle as she could be. "It isn't as though you had illusions about why Frank married you."

"He loves me—in his way."

Probably, Gwenn thought. "There must have been other women before Monique and you must have known about them, too. You tolerated them—to a point. He seemed to have known when this point was reached, and to have gotten rid of them.

"This time it was different." Gwenn watched Lana's reactions as she constructed her version of the emotional triangle. "He was crazy about Monique. Obsessed with her. You were afraid he might actually accept the meager provisions of the prenuptial agreement for her sake and leave you." And she in turn was as obsessed with her philandering husband, Gwenn thought. Passion distorted natural emotions.

"In addition, Monique was caring for your child. Bobby was as crazy about her as your husband was, or so you thought. She was stealing both of them. You had to get rid of her. If you fired her out of hand, Frank might go with her. So you hired me in the hope that I'd find something in her background that would give you an excuse to fire her and make him break off with her as he had with the others. Unfortunately, it didn't work out that way. I did give you reasons you could use, and you did get rid of her, but that didn't end the affair. You could sense that if anything it was more intense, so you hired me once again to find out where

Monique Bruno had gone. I gave you two addresses." Gwenn paused. By doing so, had she facilitated the crime? Doggedly, she continued.

"You recognized one address as being that of a building managed by your husband's company. You went there, but you didn't find Monique so you went to the other. You realized then that your husband had known Monique before she came to work for you. When or how he met her wasn't important. She was his mistress and he introduced her into your home. You were stunned at the extent of the betrayal."

Lana Wilson said nothing, showed no expression.

"You made up your mind to kill Monique Bruno and you didn't waste any time. Your aunt was to attend a bridge party on Monday and you were going to a political meeting in Suffolk County. Getting the drug was no problem; drugs are available on every street corner. Administering it was another matter; she wouldn't willingly hold still. You had to get her to turn her back on you long enough so you could hit her and render her unconscious. Was it as simple as asking her to bring you a glass of water?"

"No, it wasn't like that." Lana Wilson shook herself. "I did go to my friend's campaign meeting. It ran late. Then my car broke down. I had to call AAA, get towed, wait for the mechanic . . ."

"Your meeting ended early. You didn't have a breakdown; you didn't get towed; you didn't need repairs. Those things are so easy to check, Mrs. Wilson. I'll ask you once more: Where were you yesterday morning between four-thirty and seven? Don't say you were home because I know you weren't. Your son was sick in the night and your husband called the doctor. He can testify you weren't there."

"All right," Lana Wilson admitted. "I did go up to the apartment on Eighty-fourth, but she wasn't there."

She was doing business at the other location, Gwenn thought. "What did you do then?"

"I waited in my car across the street for a while, but she didn't come out."

"So?"

"I came home."

"What time was that?"

"I don't know. It was getting light. I wasn't thinking about the time."

But Gwenn was. It was of the utmost importance. She had contacted Lana Wilson from her car late Monday afternoon and given her the two addresses. Within the following twelve hours, approximately, Lana made the decision to kill her husband's mistress and devised the plan. She got hold of the drug. She went first to one residence and then the other. There she gained admittance and committed the deed. Possible, yes. Over a period of days rather than hours, Gwenn wouldn't have questioned it. Within the constricted time frame and taking into account the sloppy alibi, she had to reject it. Yet she continued to probe.

"You gave up just like that?" Gwenn demanded. "This woman seduced your husband and administered drugs to your child and you gave up? You didn't go to the other address?"

"No, and I'm glad I didn't. I was prepared to kill her, that's true. If I'd found her I would have done it. Thank God it didn't work out. Frank isn't worth it."

And now, at last, Gwenn believed her.

CHAPTER 14

While she waited for the taxi to pick her up and take her to the station, Gwenn Ramadge was struck by the irony of events. Jayne Harrow and Monique Bruno had not known each other in life, had not even met, but in death they were inextricably entwined.

The train was on time, uncrowded, the air-conditioning in full operation. Gratefully, Gwenn took a window seat but saw nothing of the passing scenery.

Ray had introduced Harrow to her and prevailed on Gwenn to give her a job. Jayne had been grateful and eager to repay them both for their confidence. Gwenn recalled how reluctant the detective had been to suspend surveillance of the nanny even for a day when ordered by the clients. It was not only likely but probable that she had decided to continue the tail on her own. That much could be taken as fact. When she didn't show up for work on Wednesday morning and they searched for her, while Ray called the hospitals and Marge went to her apartment, Harrow could very well have been sitting in the rental car outside the mansion on Riverside Drive. She could have been watching the clients come and go, taking pictures, keeping a log. Suddenly, she could have recognized somebody.

The train stopped with a jolt that coincided with Gwenn's mental jolt.

But it was not Frank Wilson Jayne recognized! It couldn't have been. Jayne had never met Wilson. She didn't know what he looked like. Who then?

The train gathered speed as it pulled out of the Woodside station. As it plunged into the tunnel to Manhattan, Gwenn felt as though she were at the center of a kaleidoscope, lights flashing all around, the clanging of wheels reverberating in her head.

Jayne Harrow's field of acquaintances was limited to small-time hoods—and the men she worked with. If the man she recognized was a cop, his presence indicated that the corruption on the squad had spread from drugs to prostitution and at last she had the evidence to prove it. Now suppose that as Jayne made him, he also made her. It must have been a shock to both of them, Gwenn thought, and shuddered. What would he have done? Nothing, she decided, not right then. He hadn't come prepared for murder.

He went away, but came back later.

Gwenn visualized the scene.

Jayne sat in the car as the cop approached. It was a hot night, so the windows were closed and the air conditioner was running. He tapped on the window. Maybe she thought he wanted to make a deal for her silence. He had a lot to lose. She lowered the window. Seizing the moment, he reached in and . . . what? Pushing her head down smartly against the wheel wouldn't hurt her—both wheel and dashboard were padded. So how did he knock her out? What did he use? Not a nightstick; that would indicate he was in uniform. He was not likely to come on such an errand in uniform. So what did he hit her with? Suddenly, she had it: he hit her with the butt end of his gun.

Such a blow should have left a mark which the ME performing the autopsy could identify, but Jayne's thick, dark hair might well have hidden it, Gwenn thought. Since the police had already pronounced that the death was due to a drug overdose, the ME had little incentive to look for it.

"Last stop!" the conductor sang out. "Last stop. Everybody out!"

Gwenn didn't hear him; she was still reconstructing. Having knocked out the victim, all the perp had to do was make sure all the windows and doors were closed, turn off the air conditioner—if it was in fact on—stuff the rags into the tail pipe, and walk away. Simple.

"Miss? Miss? You can't stay on the train."

The rags, Gwenn thought. He couldn't have counted on there being rags available, so he must have brought them. The rags indicated premeditation and a connection to the Raggedy Man, but what could it be?

"Miss? Are you all right? Miss?" The conductor's irritation changed to concern.

Gwenn looked up at him and then around at the empty car. "Are we here? I'm sorry. I didn't realize . . . I must have fallen asleep."

The conductor pressed his thin lips together in disapproval. "This car is going into the barn, miss."

"Yes, yes. I'm sorry."

She got up and headed down the aisle to the exit with the conductor close behind to make sure she got off. By that time, the platform was empty of passengers. She looked back to ask directions, but the conductor was gone and the train was starting to move out, so she took the nearest stair. It brought her to the main waiting room, where she found a place to sit while she tried to sort out the thoughts that tumbled in her head.

It was logical to assume that Jayne had a camera and that the perp had taken it and whatever film was in it. He also took the record she'd been keeping of those who went in and out of the building across the street. He was still looking for evidence she had regarding his drug connections. Obviously, he hadn't found it or he wouldn't have needed to go through Jayne's apartment and afterwards Gwenn's home and office. Where was it? It did exist. Everything that happened after Jayne's death testified to that.

That evidence was the most valuable thing Jayne Harrow possessed. Where did one usually keep valuables? Not lying around in the house. Not hidden in a lingerie drawer, or under the mattress, or carried in a boodle bag. Not in some airport or bus-terminal locker either. No, it would be in a safe-deposit box in a bank. Of course. Of course, Gwenn thought. It seemed so obvious she wondered that she hadn't thought of it before, but then neither had anybody else.

Drawing a deep breath, Gwenn delved into her handbag. Wedged in a deep corner were her friend's keys on a plain metal ring. Examining them, she selected a distinctive small, flat key. This had to be the one, she thought, but there was no marking to indicate the name of the bank.

No problem, Gwenn thought. It was logical for Jayne to have done her banking in the neighborhood where she lived and that she would have a checkbook or a passbook with the name and address of the bank prominently displayed. She took a deep breath and relaxed. After a few moments, she got up and, following the appropriate signs, made her way to the subway and headed downtown, once again to Jayne Harrow's apartment. She let herself in with another of the keys on the ring.

Finding what she was looking for in the center drawer of the desk, she broke out in goose bumps.

Get out! she thought. *Fast.* At the door, she stopped and went back to take both the check and pass books with her in case someone else turned up with the same idea.

Now what?

She wasn't ready to go home yet, nor to turn up on Marge's doorstep. For one thing, she'd be too easy to locate, and for another, she'd bring trouble to Marge and the boy. If she was going to be on the run for a couple more days, she'd need money. Cash would make it possible to use a name other than her own. She located a cash machine and withdrew five hundred dollars. That was the ATM limit and left all of five dollars on deposit to keep the account open. If she should run out of cash . . . well, no use worrying about that now.

Her next move was to get a room, and she decided to go back up to the Thirty-fourth Street area where she felt more comfortable. There was a hotel up the street from the station that catered to business people, conventions, groups of all kinds. She would be swallowed into anonymity there just as she had been at the Waldorf. Before checking in, however, Gwenn went to a lobby phone and contacted Marge Pratt.

"Gwenn! Oh, Gwenn, thank God! Where have you been! We've been so worried about you."

"Who's we?"

"Ray and me."

"I thought I told you not to contact him."

"I couldn't help it. He called me. What was I going to do, hang up on him?"

"No, I suppose you couldn't. What did he want?"

"Wanted to know where you were, of course. Were you all right. I told him I didn't know. He was very upset. Naturally. He also—"

"Hold it. Not now. I want you to go down and call this number from the booth on the corner." Gwenn gave the number of the phone she was using. "Don't waste any time."

Marge Pratt sucked in her breath. She loved this kind of thing, this intrigue. It made up for all the dreary hours. "I'm on my way."

Gwenn smiled to herself and hung up. Marge never questioned or argued. She would carry out the instructions with military precision. Gwenn waited in the booth. The phone rang as quickly as Gwenn had expected it would. Good for Marge.

"Yes."

"It's me."

"Right. Now, I want you to go to the office and look up the employment contract Jayne Harrow signed with us. Messenger it to Grace Russell at the Stamford. Mark it: *Due to arrive.* Do it right away and be careful. Don't stay in the office any longer than you have to."

"Right." She was very excited. "Who's Grace Russell?"

"Me. You said Ray left a message?"

"Yes, yes, he did. He said to tell you that he's been officially assigned to the Harrow–Bruno case. He wanted to make sure you knew. He left you his new number."

"I have it."

Marge Pratt waited, but Gwenn didn't add anything. "So what should I tell him when he calls again? He's bound to call again."

"Tell him I'll be in touch."

"Uh . . . one more thing—when should I open the office?"

"I'll let you know." She hung up before Marge could ask any more questions she wasn't prepared to answer. That done, she headed for the beauty parlor she'd noticed on the mezzanine.

In an hour and a quarter, Gwenn Ramadge emerged a brunette. Her new dark hair was styled in soft waves that framed her face, like Jayne Harrow's. She wouldn't fool anyone who had actually known the policewoman, but a casual acquaintance wouldn't question her identity. Now she was ready to register.

Confidently, she stepped up to the desk and checked in under the name she'd given Marge—Grace Russell. Asking if there was any mail for her, she was handed the envelope Marge Pratt had messengered over. In her room, Gwenn opened the envelope and withdrew the contract between Jayne Harrow and Hart S and I. She sat down at the small writing desk in front of the window to practice copying the signature over and over and over.

It didn't take long before the copies began to resemble the original. Resembling wasn't good enough, however. In the bank, Gwenn would be handed a card that showed the authentic signature and she would be required to sign underneath, so a direct comparison was unavoidable. Banks did not take lightly to forgery. Gwenn considered putting her right arm in a sling and claiming she'd had an accident. Actually, that would call attention to the disparities. She could also say she was a sister or other relative acting as executrix of the estate. That required all kinds of documentation, and there was a waiting period. Gwenn couldn't provide the first or afford the latter, so passing herself off as Jayne was the best bet. If, God forbid, they knew at the bank that Jayne Harrow was dead . . . *Don't think about it!* She resumed practicing the signature.

In another hour, she was satisfied it would do, but by then the banks were long since closed.

Feeling at least temporarily secure in her new identity as Grace Russell, Gwenn left the shelter of her room and passed through the crowded lobby to the street. Shopping had become a necessity and Macy's was only a block away.

There was more to being on the run than people realized, Gwenn thought. She'd had a good shower at the Waldorf that morning, but then she'd had to put on the same underwear. She also desperately needed to brush her teeth. She slid her tongue over them and felt a furlike coating. Entering the huge store, Gwenn headed first for the lingerie department. There she bought two changes—bikini panties and bras—and two pairs of panty hose as well as a short, loose nightie and matching robe. In the sportswear department, she selected a basic outfit of beige slacks and blazer with T-shirts in yellow, red, and a beige with white stripes. She tried them on and got a small shock when she looked in the mirror. Who was that brunette? And why was she wearing an outfit that might suit Gwenn Ramadge but made Grace Russell look drab and washed out? She returned them to the racks and changed colors—red, for the slacks and jacket, solid white and black shells, and a flowered pullover. When she looked in the mirror again, she smiled. Much better.

Gwenn hadn't spent money on herself so freely for a long time. In spite of the situation, she was enjoying it. She bought a long skirt of a sheer, floating material in tawny golds and oranges; either the white or the black shell would go with it. A floppy hat with poppies around the crown finished off the costume. Now she needed a small suitcase in which to pack her acquisitions. No problem; the store carried just about everything.

In her handbag Gwenn routinely kept lipstick, a pressed-powder compact, and a pocket-sized combination comb and brush. She went across the street to Woolworth's and bought a toothbrush and toothpaste. Thus equipped, she went back to her room. She stripped and got under the shower. She lathered and let the soapy water cascade over her. At last, reluctantly, she turned the water off and stepped out. She dried herself and put on the new nightie. She brushed her teeth, devoting time and attention that would have pleased her dentist enormously. Finally, she turned down the bed and crawled between the sheets and fell promptly asleep.

She woke at nine P.M. Sending down for a club sandwich and a beer, she turned on the television and watched the news on CNN; at that hour the networks were into prime-time programming. She tried NY1, but there was nothing on the police corruption story or the Bruno case. She finished her snack, turned off the set, and went back to bed.

The next time she woke it was seven A.M. The day was overcast. She put on her red slacks and black shirt and packed the rest of her new things in the suitcase she'd bought, then left it in the hotel checkroom. After that, she turned in her key and paid her bill. Then she fortified herself with a hearty breakfast in the hotel coffee shop. By eight, she was ready for action. Her idea was that Jayne Harrow had rented a safe-deposit box and that it would be in the same bank in which she maintained a checking or savings account. In fact, many banks made such an account a condition for renting out a safe-deposit box. That bank, Gwenn now knew, was near where Jayne lived. So Gwenn headed for the subway and by eight-fifty that morning stood at the door of the Village Trust.

Before entering, she looked through the plate-glass windows that fronted the street. It was a standard layout; nevertheless, she wanted to make sure that she knew where the regular tellers sat and what section was set aside for the officers, and whether the vault was located in the basement or upstairs. It turned out that it was on the main floor at the back, separated merely by a low railing. From where she stood she could actually see it, massive door ajar.

She entered the bank finally with a confident step, knowing where she was headed and letting everyone who saw her know it too.

"Hello," Gwenn greeted the woman who sat at the desk just inside the railing, between it and the partially open vault. "I'd like to get into my box, please."

The woman returned Gwenn's smile. She was about forty, dressed not expensively but with care. Her hair was what the stylists called "sunstreaked" and it became her. A plaque on the desk bore the name Enid Masters. "Have you got your key?" Ms. Masters asked.

"Of course."

"You'd be surprised how many people come in without it."

"Really?" Gwenn delved into her handbag, felt around for a few moments, then pulled out her wallet. From a zippered compartment she produced a small key holder in dark green, unbuttoned the flap, and handed over the flat key. She held her breath. If it was refused, Gwenn was prepared to be flustered, disbelieving, upset. None of that was necessary.

"Thank you." Ms. Masters pulled out a file drawer and fingered through it. She removed a card. "Thank you, Miss Harrow."

Bingo! Pay dirt. The first time. Gwenn was elated, but of course didn't allow herself to show it. At this point a bank guard approached and Gwenn's stomach fell.

"I'm going out for coffee, Enid. You want your usual?"

Enid Masters was in the act of pulling out a chair for Gwenn at the desk. "I'll skip the Danish today, George. Just coffee." She put the card down and handed Gwenn one of the bank's pens. "Putting on weight again," she confided. "It's a constant battle. Sign on the next line please, Miss Harrow."

Gwenn sat and as she took the pen, she noted there was only one signature on the card, that of the original entry. Fighting to keep her hand from shaking, she signed directly underneath. "Don't I know it." She picked up the card and handed it over.

Enid Masters barely glanced at it before disappearing into the vault. Moments later she was back with a long, flat metal box. "This way." She indicated one of a row of private cubicles and went in. She placed the box on the counter and pointed to the call button. "Ring when you're through," she said, and closed the door behind her.

She'd done it! Alone with the box, Gwenn gloated. Now she could allow herself to tremble as she loosed the catch at the front of the box and lifted the lid. The contents were few and not impressive. A standard police evidence envelope contained three cigarette butts. A lab analysis report indicated the saliva secretion marked the smoker as having O-negative blood. A manila envelope contained three strips of film negatives, each strip consisting of four frames. Gwenn held each up to the light but couldn't make out what any of them represented. She'd have to get prints made. Looking into the envelope once more, she discovered a slip of paper caught in the corner. It read, in Jayne's writing, "Evidence collected June 10th, 2:07 A.M. Children's Playground, Brooklyn Heights." There was also a newspaper clipping:

SMALL-TIME DRUG DEALER STABBED TO DEATH

On the morning of June 10, in response to an anonymous call to 911, the body of a man was found in the children's playground at the foot of Columbia Heights and Pierrepont Street off the Brooklyn Heights Promenade. He appeared to be in his mid-twenties and carried no formal identification. He was dressed in an assortment of garments, and a strip of varicolored gauze was wound around his head like a turban. Because of this, he was known to the children of the neighborhood as the Raggedy Man.

Gwenn put everything in her handbag, closed the box, which was now empty, rang the bell, and stepped out of the cubicle.

"I'm finished," she told Enid Masters, and handed her the closed box.

Another customer was waiting.

"I'll be right with you," Enid Masters said as she gestured to Gwenn to precede her, expecting she would want to see her property securely returned and locked up.

All Gwenn wanted to do was to get out of there. It occurred to her, however, that she should show interest. "Thank you," she said, and went ahead obediently. She watched as Enid Masters returned the box into its slot, closed the individual door, and locked it first with the bank's key and then with the one Gwenn handed her. That done, she returned Gwenn's key and together they stepped outside. Hugging her handbag close, Gwenn left the vault area. Behind her, she heard Ms. Masters greet the next customer.

"Good to see you, Mrs. Hoyt. Will you be requiring envelopes for your coupons today?"

Somehow Gwenn managed to saunter on her way out of the bank. Having reached the relative safety of the street, she still expected that at any moment someone would come up behind her, put a hand on her shoulder, and challenge her identity, but it didn't happen. Her heart still pounding, she ducked into a coffee shop and hurried to a rear booth. A waitress came promptly and Gwenn ordered coffee.

Gwenn had recently converted a small utility room in her apartment into a darkroom, and any photographs she took on the job she developed herself. But she wasn't ready to go home yet and she was reluctant to turn Jayne Harrow's film over to a stranger. Film went astray more often than people realized, got lost or mixed up. A one-hour processing place should be safe enough, she thought. There was one on Madison in the Fifties that she'd used before learning to do it herself. Worth the trip uptown.

The waitress brought the coffee.

Gwenn got up. "Cancel it. I've changed my mind."

"But . . ."

"I'll pay for it. Here." She put a dollar bill on the table.

"Coffee's a dollar fifty."

"What?"

"It's a dollar fifty if that's all you're having. People come in and sit here for an hour over a single cup of coffee . . ."

"I'm not sitting here, I'm going," Gwenn retorted. "Oh, never mind." She put down another dollar. "Keep the change." Even as she stalked out she wondered what she was so hot about.

She took the E train to the Fifth Avenue stop and exited on Madison. The place she remembered was still there on the second floor of a tired brownstone wedged between two high-rise office buildings. She climbed the crooked stairs. *Fast Photos* had become *Kwik Kopies.* In a corner a cardboard sign promised: *Photos Processed While You Wait.* She opened the door and went in. A young man in jeans and a crisp white shirt was running a copying machine. He was the only one working; she was the only customer.

"Yes?" he asked, not pausing.

"I'd like to have these developed." She handed over the envelope with the film. "Your one-hour service, please. I'll wait."

"That won't make it any quicker."

"I have nowhere to go."

He shrugged. "Suit yourself."

What could happen in an hour? Gwenn asked herself. Nevertheless, she stayed, went to the far end of the room, and sat on the wooden bench.

After about twenty minutes, an elderly man came in. He wore a helmet and ankle clips around his frayed trouser cuffs. He turned over several envelopes. Obviously a messenger, Gwenn thought. After that there was a steady stream of customers, but the place was never crowded. Gwenn began to wish she had the coffee she'd spurned earlier. She was watching the hands of the clock when her name was called.

"Miss Ramadge? Your order is ready."

"It is?" She sat where she was. "It is?" She jumped to her feet and hurried to the counter. "Thank you. I really appreciate this. Thank you."

"Well, things are slow, so why not?" The young man handed her the envelope and watched as she fumbled for her money and paid.

"Thanks again," Gwenn said, and turned so abruptly she nearly ran into the customer behind her. She couldn't wait to see the pictures, but as she started back to the bench where she'd been sitting she could feel the clerk's eyes still on her. She'd find another place. She walked out, ran down the stairs and out into the street. There was nothing on the block. As she walked along Madison toward Fifty-third, she was attracted by the sound of running water. Paley Park!

It was dubbed a "vest pocket" park. Originally an unsightly empty lot, it had been donated to the city by William Paley as a place for the refreshment and relaxation of its people. There were trees in tubs, tables and chairs, and deep at the rear, stretching from one building wall to the other, a waterfall. It was no longer the novelty it had been—mid-Manhattan now boasted several even larger and more dramatic cascades—but to the New Yorkers who came here, this remained the sentimental favorite. At this hour it was uncrowded. Gwenn sat at a rear table and opened the envelope that held the prints.

At first, she couldn't make out what they represented. The lighting was poor, casting eerie shadows and causing distortion. After considerable study she identified a body. There were several shots of the body taken from different angles. She was both dismayed and puzzled. Who was the dead person? Why had Jayne Harrow rented a safe-deposit box to preserve pictures of him? Studying them further, Gwenn made out a washbasin. The body was lying on the floor, partially underneath it. Was the place a public washroom? Over to one side was a pile of what looked like cigarette butts. The next photo was a close-up of the cigarette butts. Probably the cigarette butts in the evidence envelope came from that pile. These had to be shots of a crime scene and the victim. No wonder the clerk at Kwik Kopies had looked at her so strangely.

Gwenn went through them once again. They had been taken by someone who was familiar with the requirements of evidence, but was not a professional photographer. Jayne herself? That seemed reasonable. The various angles indicated the photographer wanted to document certain details. In the first shot, the victim was lying on his side, knees partially drawn up, arms crossed. In the next, the arms had been opened out—by the photographer?—and the camera focused on the wound, a long, ragged slash in the middle of his chest. Gwenn now saw that he had been stabbed many times. The next photograph showed wounds in his back. She theorized that he was attacked from the front and cut first in the chest, then in trying to get away presented his back to the assailant, who continued to hack at him relentlessly. She couldn't tell what he looked like. He was a bundle of rags soaked in blood.

"The Raggedy Man," the *Times* had called him.

Gwenn put everything back into her handbag and left the park to look for a telephone. She was lucky that the first one she found was not only free but in working order. She dialed Ray's new number. He picked up promptly.

"Homicide. Sergeant Dixon."

"Ray, it's me."

"Gwenn! Thank God. I've been trying to get you. I've been worried sick. Where have you been? Where are you? Are you okay?"

"I'm fine. I need to talk to you, but not on the phone. I need to see you."

"Sure. Come on over. I'm at the Two-Oh."

"No, not there."

"Why not?"

She couldn't find the words. Jayne had cast the police in the role of villains and she'd had good reason. Gwenn didn't. Certainly she had no reason to mistrust Ray.

He sighed. "All right. I'll come to you. Your office? The apartment?"

"You know the little park between Fifth and Madison on Fifty-third?"

"Paley Park. Sure."

"Meet me in half an hour."

"Why there, for God's sake? What's going on?"

"Don't bring anybody with you. And make sure you're not followed."

"Who's going to follow me? And why should I—"

But Gwenn Ramadge had already hung up.

Ray Dixon held the receiver in his hand for several moments before slowly hanging up too. He rose, reached for his jacket, which was draped over the back of his chair, and put it on, making sure it covered his shoulder harness. Glancing around, he caught Charley Pulver, his partner on the Harrow case, watching him.

"One of my snitches," he felt constrained to explain.

Pulver nodded. "Want me to come with you?"

"No, thanks. He's the nervous type. Clams up in the presence of a third party."

"Right."

After that, Dixon got out fast. He felt the blood surging and hoped Pulver hadn't noticed his agitation. He wouldn't have mentioned the call from Gwenn even without her caution. On the other hand, without it he might not have considered Pulver's curiosity out of the ordinary. It wasn't like Gwenn, he thought. She didn't go for the cloak-and-dagger stuff. She didn't panic easily either. She had said not to bring anybody. Dixon took that to mean another cop.

Ray took a taxi, but the shortest route is not always the quickest. At Fifty-seventh and Fifth, he was caught in the gridlock that had become ordinary in certain parts of the city. He abandoned the cab and ran the rest of the way. He arrived gasping—from the exertion and the anxiety.

The park was crowded and more office workers from the

nearby buildings were trying to shoulder their way in. Where was Gwenn? He had expected her to be waiting at the front, but she was nowhere to be seen. He felt his heart thud in his chest.

"Gwenn?"

He could barely hear himself over the roar of the cascading water.

"Gwenn?"

He spotted someone waving from the rear and began to push his way through till they were face-to-face. "Gwenn? Is it you?" He stared openmouthed. "What have you done to yourself?"

She had to smile. "You don't like me as a brunette?"

"I like you no matter what color your hair is, but . . . I don't understand what's going on. Why have you changed your hair and why are we meeting like this?"

She stood on tiptoe and spoke into his ear. "I've got Jayne's evidence." Before he could comment, she took his hand and led him to the edge of the pool into which the water splashed, and they sat together on the rim of the retaining wall. She opened her handbag and gave him the two envelopes and waited for him to examine the contents.

He took his time. "What do you make of these?" he asked at last, pitching his voice low and speaking directly into her ear as she had spoken in his.

"They document a homicide," she answered. "The pictures show the victim and the scene. Jayne's notes give the time and place."

"But not the identity of the victim."

"The newspaper calls him the Raggedy Man."

"Why didn't she give his real name?"

"She didn't know it. She must have thought the time and place of the murder would be sufficient to get that information." She looked earnestly at Ray. "From the police case file."

"She had access. Why didn't she get it?"

"Being under a cloud as she was?"

"She could have come to me. I would have helped her. I always helped her," Ray pointed out.

"Exactly. She didn't want to put you on the spot where your loyalty was tested, where you were forced to make a choice between her and the department."

"Is that why you've been running away from me? Don't you trust me?"

"I trust you." They looked into each other's eyes. "It's the others I don't trust."

"What others?"

"You agreed it was cops who planted the drugs on Jayne. You agreed it was cops who searched my place. You worried that there would be more violence and you wouldn't be able to protect me—again, from cops. Have you changed your mind?"

"God, no! It's tearing me apart. Look, Gwenn, I've shown you in every way I can that I care about you. If you don't know it now, I don't know how to convince you. I love you." His dark eyes burned with the intensity of frustration. "Damn it, I love you. Why won't you believe it?"

Her hands trembled and her heart pounded. This was the moment Gwenn had been anticipating, both wanting it and fearing the commitment that would be required. Now that it was here and Ray had declared himself, she was surprised by her own reaction. Her past reservations were swept away and she was elated in an exultation she couldn't ever remember. "I do believe you, but you never came out and said so." Which was unfair, she thought, since whenever he seemed on the verge of speaking out, she'd taken care to divert him.

"I thought you knew."

"Every woman likes to be told."

Pressed close by people on either side, Ray Dixon put his hands on Gwenn's shoulders and murmured, "I love you, Gwenn Ramadge."

"What did you say?"

He raised his voice over the sound of the water. "I love you!"

She heard him and so did some others, who looked in their direction and smiled broadly. As acknowledgment of their approval Ray leaned forward and kissed her gently on the lips.

"Well?"

"I don't know what to say."

"Then why did you encourage me to declare myself? Did you enjoy seeing me humble myself?"

"No, never. Believe me, Ray. I only needed to know where your loyalties lie."

He frowned; it was becoming habitual. "How do you mean—my loyalties?"

"It doesn't strike you as odd that you're suddenly assigned to the investigation of the Harrow–Bruno murders, the outcome of which is critical to the entire department?"

"I have personal knowledge of one of the victims, Jayne Harrow."

"You're satisfied that's the reason?"

"Yes."

"My connection to both victims and you and I being friends doesn't enter into it?"

"To some extent, yes, but I've made it clear . . ."

Gwenn sighed. So they'd already tried to pump him.

"Now I get it," Ray said. "That's what all this hide-and-seek, using street phones, dyeing your hair black . . ."

"Brown."

"Whatever. You should have called me."

"I tried. I did. You weren't there."

"You couldn't have tried very hard." He groaned. "You don't trust me. You were afraid to turn over evidence that Jayne's murder and Monique Bruno's murder were linked to police corruption. You thought if I was forced to choose between you and them . . ."

"No. I was afraid you might let something slip, inadvertently."

"You think I'm that dumb?"

"I'm sorry."

"And this setup here." He indicated the crowded park and the waterfall. "This was to interfere with reception in case I was wired. You think I would come to you wearing a wire?"

"I'm sorry." She looked down. "I did show you Jayne's evidence though."

"Because you didn't know what else to do."

"No, because you've been on Jayne's side from the very beginning! You believed her charges were real and honest. You brought her to me. Up to now we've not only been working separately but in essence against each other. Isn't it time for us to work together?"

Dixon's frown eased. "Partners at last?" He grinned. "Okay. The first thing we've got to do is find a place for us to work and for you to stay."

"Not my apartment or my office."

"No. And no hotels either. How about moving in with me for a few days?"

"That's the first place they'll look."

"Let them!" Ray Dixon exclaimed. "I'll tell them we've gotten together. I'll tell them you've turned some evidence and I intend to keep them informed of our progress—in return for a piece of the action, of course."

"Will they buy it?"

"The guilty party will," Ray assured her. "Being corrupt himself, he'll readily accept corruption in somebody else."

CHAPTER 15

Dixon was determined not to let Gwenn out of his sight. He went with her to the hotel checkroom to pick up her suitcase. He got his car and drove her out to his place in Queens. The building was small and had no doorman. As Ray carried the valise and ushered her through the lobby, one of his neighbors came out of the elevator. With one all-encompassing glance, she assessed the situation.

"Hello, Mrs. McPherson," Ray greeted her as usual. "Nice day."

Mrs. McPherson nodded, gray eyes gleaming, smiled and waited for the introduction. When it was evident there wasn't going to be any, she pursed her lips and tossed her head and swept past the two of them and out the front door.

Ray chuckled. "It'll be all over the building that you've moved in with me. I figured anything I said would only stimulate speculation. Do you mind?"

"Not if you don't."

His apartment was on the sixth floor at the front. He had his key ready, opened the door, and stood aside for Gwenn to enter. There was no foyer; one stepped directly into the living room—a large room facing west that was bathed in the rays of the midafternoon sun. A picture window, uncurtained, venetian blinds adjusted to give a clear view, overlooked a small traffic island with benches set under trees. Young children played and senior citizens dozed. Turning away from that, Gwenn looked around at the place Ray lived. The furnishings were sparse but the pieces substantial, in the style of the American West.

"This is nice, Ray."

"Thanks. A couple of years ago I took a trip to New Mexico and I liked the style. It's cumbersome for an apartment, but as long as you don't clutter it, it works."

"It looks great."

They stood there grinning at each other.

"Is there somewhere I can hang my clothes?" Gwenn asked, in part to dispel the awkwardness.

"Oh sure. This way." Ray led her into the bedroom. He put the suitcase on the bed, opened the closet, and shoved his things to one side. "Will this be enough? And how about drawer space?" He walked over to the bureau. "I can consolidate my stuff so that we each have two drawers. Will that be okay?"

"It's fine. Thank you."

"Good. Well. Oh, fresh towels . . . I'll get them. If you want anything to eat, the kitchen's over there." He pointed to the other side of the living room. "Just help yourself. I thought we'd eat in tonight. If that's all right?"

"Sure. I'll cook."

"Uh . . . no offense, but do you know how to make anything other than pasta?"

"Actually, no."

"I do."

They both laughed.

"So. You get settled and I'll fix us something light for an early dinner. A cheese omelet? Then we'll get to work. Okay?" For a moment he let his anxiety show.

Nodding, Gwenn acknowledged it. "Make my omelet real dry."

"Ah, ah . . . ." He waggled a finger. "Taste first, criticize after."

While Ray set places at the table in a small alcove off the kitchen, Gwenn unpacked her recent purchases and hung them in the part of the closet Ray had cleared for her. She washed her face, changed from the black shirt to the white, refreshed her lipstick, and gave her dark hair a vigorous brushing. Finally, she presented herself.

"Can I help?"

Ray was mincing green peppers. He looked up. "It's going to take some getting used to."

"My hair? Is it that bad?"

"It's not bad, just . . . different."

"Hopefully, it won't be for long." He didn't comment, so she went on. "I've been thinking."

"I wish you wouldn't, not till after dinner anyway. Here." He handed her a pair of stemmed glasses filled with a pale amber liquid. "Put these on the table, please."

"I thought we were going to work."

"We are. This is our ration."

In a few more minutes everything was ready and they sat down to eat. The omelet was light and fluffy, a bit more liquid than she was accustomed to, but Gwenn had to admit it was delicious; the consistency allowed her to savor a variety of flavors she might not have been aware of otherwise. With it, Ray served a salad with balsamic vinegar dressing. The wine enhanced rather than dulled the taste buds. She was disappointed there was no dessert—she had room for it. In fact, she didn't feel at all full. The meal probably had more staying power than she realized.

"Perfect. Hit the spot," she pronounced, wiping her lips and putting down the napkin. "I'll do the dishes."

"Nobody does the dishes; there's a dishwasher," Ray announced complacently.

The table was cleared and in place of the meal Jayne Harrow's file was emptied and the contents spread out: the photographs, the cigarette butts and lab report, the *Times* clipping, Jayne's brief notation.

Ray began. "Several questions come to mind: Why did Jayne go to so much trouble to hang on to this stuff? Why did she care about the murder of a small-time drug dealer?"

"She thought Brian Ford had killed him. He was one of the dealers Ford regularly did business with. She couldn't prove the corruption charges, but she thought she might be able to prove he had committed murder."

Gwenn warmed to the idea. "The Raggedy Man could have been one of the dealers Ford was ripping off. He got tired of paying. He threatened to turn Ford in and Ford killed him." Then she paused and shook her head. "If Jayne suspected Ford had committed murder and had proof way back in June, why didn't she produce it?"

Ray had his own misgivings. "Why did Ford walk away? Wouldn't it have been easier to report the killing? The victim was a known criminal. Ford could have claimed he was attacked by the Raggedy Man. Struggling to defend himself, he turned the knife against his own assailant. He would have got away with it."

Gwenn frowned. "I'm not so sure. Look at those wounds." She pointed to the close-ups of the victim—the battered, mauled, disfigured face. "That goes beyond self-defense."

Ray got up, poured a cup of coffee for each of them, and came back. "What we need is to see the official case file. That means contacting the guys in Brooklyn Homicide to make sure the time, place, and evidence they have matches what's in Jayne's packet."

"They'll match." Gwenn was confident.

"I think so, but we can't take it for granted. We've got to be sure we're dealing with the same case. After that, we'll check Ford's alibi."

"Right." Gwenn took one last swallow of the coffee, pushed away from the table, and got up. "I won't be a minute."

"What's the rush?"

"Well, don't you think we should get going? We've wasted enough time already."

"I agree; I'm going. But you're staying."

"Why?"

He looked straight at her. "I'll do better without you."

She flushed.

"If there is a cover-up, they're going to play their cards close to the vest. The presence of a civilian isn't going to help."

"I guess not."

"You stay here and take it easy. Relax. You'll be perfectly safe. Don't open the door and don't answer the telephone. Let the machine . . . No, I'll turn the machine off. If I should need to get in touch I'll let the phone ring three times, hang up, and call again. God! You've got me doing it." He started to put the manila envelope in the inner pocket of his jacket, then changed his mind and placed it in the top desk drawer.

Watching him make preparations, Gwenn could tell he was nervous. "Take care of yourself."

"Don't worry." He kissed her on the lips, a long, soft, sweet kiss.

The sun set early at that time of year, Gwenn thought as she turned on a lamp and lay down on the sofa to rest. It was seductively comfortable, but she didn't fall asleep. Her mind kept churning, going over the same ground again and again. Why hadn't Brian Ford admitted the murder? If he had killed the

Raggedy Man, wouldn't it have been easier to say so? She kept coming back to that. It was an obstacle she couldn't get around.

The ringing of the telephone made her jump. She reached for it and then remembered the arrangement: if it was Ray, he would ring three times, hang up, and call again. She counted five rings and still going. Wouldn't it ever stop? And just then it did. According to her watch, it was now ten P.M. She must have dozed. Ray should be back soon. She got up and went to the kitchen to make fresh coffee. While she waited for the percolator to go through its cycle, the phone rang again. The ringing continued for fifteen times precisely. Who could it be? Whoever it was had to know somebody was there or he'd give up sooner. It was for Ray, of course, and it could be urgent. She stared at the phone, itching to answer. Finally, she couldn't bear it any longer.

"Hello?"

"You must be a sound sleeper, Ms. Ramadge."

"Who's this?"

There was a pause. The caller spoke to someone in the room with him. "Say hello to your girlfriend, Ray."

Gwenn waited, but nothing happened.

"Come on, Ray, talk to her," the caller urged. Then he spoke into the mouthpiece again. "Looks like he wants to die a hero. So it's up to you, Ms. Ramadge. You'll have to save him in spite of himself."

"Who is this? What do you want?"

"I want all the material you took from Jayne Harrow's safe-deposit box. All of it and not copies—the originals."

"I don't know what you're talking about."

"Get dressed and be downstairs in front of the building in ten minutes precisely. A car will be waiting to bring you here. If your story and Sergeant Dixon's match and you turn over the evidence, I'm sure we can reach some agreement."

"What story?" she asked, but he had already hung up.

After a couple of moments she hung up too.

He'd given her ten minutes to dress, but she was already dressed, so she had time to call 911 and report that Ray was being held . . . somewhere and that she was about to be kidnapped. Not very convincing, but she had to try. She picked up the receiver. No dial tone. The line was now dead. Whoever was running this operation was smart enough to take elementary precautions, so she could forget about trying to sneak out the back door; it would be covered. If she wanted to help Ray, her best bet was to follow instructions.

Heart pounding, Gwenn got her jacket. Then she opened the drawer in which Ray had placed Jayne's envelope. Where could she hide it? They would tear the place apart to find it, and ultimately find it they would, no matter where she put it. So she might as well bring it and try to use it as a bargaining tool. She put it in her handbag, fixed the door catch so it would lock behind her, and took the elevator down to the ground floor.

The lobby was brightly lit but empty. With as firm a step as she could manage, Gwenn crossed to the door, pulled it open, and stepped out into the street.

It was a cool, dark night, refreshing after the day's heat, but Gwenn had little chance to savor it as she noted a long, sleek limousine at the end of the block pull out and glide toward her. It stopped in front of the building canopy. The driver got out. He was dressed in a well-tailored dark business suit and wore dark glasses.

"Ms. Ramadge?"

"Yes."

He opened the rear door and courteously handed her in. Wasting no time, he got back behind the wheel. Gwenn was intent on determining where they were going, and the driver had no reason to be suspicious, so neither noticed the car parked across the street as it pulled out and followed without turning on any lights.

It was immediately clear to Gwenn that they were headed toward Manhattan. They came off the Queensboro Bridge and headed west, crossing through Central Park; that indicated to her that their ultimate destination was the elegant mansion on Riverside Drive where Monique Bruno had plied her trade and where she died. Gwenn allowed herself to be led inside to the red lacquer elevator and then to the door of the hooker's apartment without comment. Brian Ford opened the door. He stared.

"Ms. Ramadge? Is it you?" He stepped to one side. "Come in. Have a seat. You know, I think I like you better as a blonde."

Gwenn looked around and saw that he was alone. "Where's Ray? What have you done with him?"

"Let's not stand in the hall, shall we?" As Gwenn swept past, Ford dismissed the driver with a nod. "We haven't done anything with him. That's so melodramatic. We had a talk, Ray and I. I convinced him as to his best interests and we made a deal."

"Who's *we*?" Gwenn pounced on what she considered a slip.

Evidently Ford did too, because he flushed and evaded the question. "Sit down, Ms. Ramadge. We have a lot of ground to cover."

"Where's Ray Dixon? I'm not going to say another word till I see him."

"At this moment, that's somewhat difficult," Ford replied. Automatically, he fell into a soothing, sensuous mode. His blue eyes looked deeply into hers; his voice caressed her. "He's a lucky man to have a beautiful woman like you care for him."

Pulling back, Gwenn broke the spell. "I demand to know where he is."

Ford shrugged. "All right. At this moment he's en route to Kennedy Airport. He'll be on the first flight out to Buenos Aires. Later on, you could join him. Who knows?"

The color drained from Gwenn's face. "I don't believe it."

"As I said, you could join him." He held out his hand. "You did bring it, didn't you?"

Gwenn hesitated. Resistance was useless. She'd end up battered and bruised for nothing, beaten up for no purpose. She opened her handbag and gave him Jayne's envelope. Watching Ford go through the items one by one made her sick. Finally, he was through.

"Something's missing."

"No. It's all there."

"Ah, Ms. Ramadge, I'm disappointed in you. I thought we understood each other." He almost purred. "You're not being straight with me and unless you are, I can't let you leave. Do you understand what I'm saying?"

"You think I'm holding something back."

"Very good." He was sarcastic.

Gwenn frowned. "You and Jayne Harrow were partners. She believed you were stealing drugs from the dealers you arrested. While trying to compile evidence to support these charges, she stumbled on proof that you had committed murder."

He sat down and crossed his legs. Despite the casual attitude, he was sharply focused on her every word and look. "Go on."

"On the night of June ninth, you had a date with one of your regulars, a dealer known as the Raggedy Man. That's what the children of the neighborhood called him. You drove over with Detective Harrow, but she remained in the car while you went to the meet, which, appropriately enough, was in the children's playground off the Brooklyn Heights Promenade. She says so in her notes relating to that particular tour."

"So?"

"The Raggedy Man was late. While you waited, you smoked. You can make out a pile of butts in two of the photographs. See?" She pointed. "I think we can safely assume Detective Harrow returned to the scene later and took these pictures. She also sent some of the butts to an independent lab for analysis of the saliva." She paused for emphasis. "What's your blood type, Sergeant?"

He shrugged. "I'm a nonsecretor. You can't get my blood type by saliva testing."

Gwenn froze. So that was why Jayne Harrow was in possession of the evidence for approximately three months but did not present it. When she sent the evidence she'd collected at the crime scene, she must also have sent stubs from Ford's desk ashtray along with it in a separate envelope. The results dubbing him a nonsecretor exonerated him. She must have been as shocked as Gwenn was now.

"You didn't do it," Gwenn said with awe. "You didn't kill either the Raggedy Man or Jayne Harrow. You're innocent."

"You've got that right."

She struggled to adjust to the discovery. "Since the evidence doesn't incriminate you, why are you so anxious to get hold of it?" He didn't answer, so she went on, letting her instincts guide her. "You were there. You must have been there. You saw the crime committed. You know who did it."

The bedroom door was flung open.

"No more questions. No more talk," Alfonso Palma ordered.

Gwenn had never seen him before and had no idea who he was. She didn't know anything except that he intended to kill her. It was in his eyes as he raised the gun and took deliberate aim. At point-blank range, she didn't have a chance in the world.

There was a sharp explosion. The sound reverberated in her ears. When it faded, Gwenn was still standing.

She felt no pain. Still rooted in place, she watched this man whose name she didn't know, whom she had never seen, raise his gun a second time, slowly, very slowly, almost as though it were too heavy for him. She cringed in expectation of the second shot. When it came, the stranger was the one who went down.

She heard shouts in the hall outside and wood splintering. She realized then that both shots had come from behind her. Brian Ford had fired both times. He had shot the stranger and saved her life. The men who had forced the door and tumbled into the room would have been too late.

"You okay?" Captain Landau asked Gwenn.

Her knees were weak, her stomach heaving; she was afraid she would be sick right there in front of everybody, but she managed to nod.

"You don't look so good," Landau said. "If you're not a hundred percent, I'm going to hear it from Dixon."

"Ray knew about this?"

"Are you kidding? He'd never let us use you in any kind of sting. When he finds out what we did and how long we let it go, he'll be mad as hell."

"Where is he?"

"We put in a call to Brooklyn Homicide for him."

"He's not at the airport? He's not going to Buenos Aires?"

"He ought to be coming through that door at any minute."

"Who's not going to Buenos Aires?" Ray Dixon asked.

Gwenn's answer was to fling herself into his arms.

With a smile twitching at the corners of his mouth, Landau turned discreetly away. While the EMS team worked to stabilize Alfonso Palma and ready him for transport, Landau addressed himself to Brian Ford.

"You want to make a deal? Now's the time."

CHAPTER 16

Gwenn turned down Ray's offer to go back to his place. She wanted finally to go home, no matter how much of the damage from the break-in still remained. She wanted to have her own things around her, sleep in her own bed, however lumpy and bumpy it might be.

She slept till eleven. Waking, the first thing she did was turn on the radio. She was still in robe and slippers, eyes puffy, hair tousled, yawning, when the downstairs bell rang and the doorman announced Ray. She padded to the door to let him in.

He held up a brown paper bag with two containers of coffee and her favorite cheese Danish. "Breakfast," he announced.

"Great." She led the way to the kitchen.

"Did I get you out of bed?"

"Just about. I was listening to the news."

"So you know."

"Only that Lieutenant Palma was DOA at St. Luke's–Roosevelt. So I assume he died without talking."

Ray handed her the morning paper. "It's all there."

SHAKEUP IN NYPD
Over forty cops to be booted

CAPTAIN WORKING UNDERCOVER FOR IA
BREAKS CASE
New Corruption Scandal
Captain Norman Landau promoted,
leapfrogs to top job in Detective Division

"Ford is spitting it all out," Ray told her. "I doubt he'd be talking so freely if Palma were around. According to Ford, the corruption was spread through the entire division. The guys were stealing from the dealers and Palma was raking in a percentage of their take."

Gwenn gasped.

"Palma was the spider in the center of the web. He was the organizer, the troubleshooter, the enforcer. Knowing that the criminal was in no position to appeal to a higher authority, Alfonso Palma could vent his frustrations. He could beat, kick, slash, and maul anybody who stepped out of line. The lieutenant didn't do drugs—that was the way he got his high."

Gwenn shuddered.

"So when the Raggedy Man balked and threatened to go to IA and blow the whistle on everybody top to bottom, Ford told Palma and Palma, as usual, was ready to take care of it. He instructed Ford to proceed as always. So Ford set up the meet, but when he got there, the Raggedy Man was already dead."

Gwenn sighed. It kept getting uglier and uglier.

"The way Ford figured, Palma got to the meet first. He smoked while he waited. "We've checked Palma's blood type and it's consistent with the saliva secretions on the cigarettes. Ford is not—"

"He isn't a secretor. I found that out last night," Gwenn put in.

"Right. On his way to the meet, Ford heard a backfire. He got there in time to see Palma drive away. He didn't know what to do. He didn't dare report the crime—not for fear of implicating himself but for fear of implicating Palma and with him the whole division. There was nothing for Ford to do but turn his back and keep his mouth shut—which was exactly as Palma had planned."

Gwenn nodded. It fit, it made sense, but . . . she wasn't comfortable with it.

Ray continued. "Shortly after starting to ride with Ford, Jayne spotted signs of corruption involving her partner. She went to the lieutenant and charged Ford with falsifying reports and stealing drugs. As she was new on the squad and couldn't offer proof, Palma brushed aside her accusations. But she persisted. She refused to give up. He had no choice but to take her seriously.

"So he started a campaign to discredit her and besmirch her reputation. When he learned she intended to appeal to IA, he set up the raid on her apartment and planted the crack. That should have destroyed her."

Ray paused.

Gwenn set aside the coffee and pastry and listened with her full concentration.

"Ford can't attest to the rest from his own knowledge and observation, but it follows logically. While working for you, Jayne began to rehabilitate herself. She discovered that the subject of your investigation, Monique Bruno, was a hooker plying her trade out of a mansion on Riverside Drive. On stakeout, Jayne made Alfonso Palma as he entered the building. She was smart. She figured he had business there. At the very least he was the bagman collecting protection money. She continued to watch and I'll bet any amount you want that she recognized other men going in and out—cops. This time she got them on film and she was ready to lift the lid on the whole steamy mess.

"Jayne had made Palma, but, unfortunately, he had also made her."

Gwenn felt a surge of excitement. That was the way she had reasoned.

Ray went on. "Jayne had become more than an irritation; she was a serious threat. He determined to get rid of her once and for all—along with any evidence she might have. Palma was arrogant, but he was no fool," Ray pointed out. "He decided to make Jayne's death look like a suicide. She had been suspended from her job, was under investigation by IA, and was drinking heavily. Her depressed state was well known. He didn't think anybody would question that she had killed herself." Ray took a deep breath. "He didn't know *you*.

"When he found out later that you had also been in contact with Monique Bruno, he worried about how much she had passed on to you, or might pass on later. He decided he had to plug that leak, too."

"I suppose Laszlo Darvas, the manager, told him I'd visited Monique."

"I think we can safely assume Darvas reported to Palma," Ray agreed.

"And Palma, following the same pattern he'd used in killing Jayne, rendered Monique unconscious and then injected her to make it look like either suicide or an accident."

"And then you turned up again," Ray said.

"Yes. I can see that might have been annoying."

"At the least."

"So he decided to throw a scare into me," Gwenn mused aloud, "first by trying to run me down and then by making it look like a bomb had been planted in my car. That's why Detective Derr kept me waiting in the lobby so long. Darvas had notified Palma and he needed time to organize." She sighed. "I refused to believe the police were responsible."

"I didn't want to believe it," Ray said. "If it had been anyone but you, I don't think I would have."

She reached out a hand to him. "I'm sorry."

"Don't be. I would have had to face it sometime. Anyway, it's my fault. I'm the one who introduced Jayne and got you involved."

Gwenn brushed it aside. "We each did what we had to do. The trouble is—a couple of things don't fit."

"What do you mean they don't fit?"

"They don't fit," She reiterated. "For starters, how come Captain Landau and his people just happened to be outside the door of Monique's place at the critical moment? Not that I'm not grateful, you understand."

"They didn't just *happen* to be there. I figured you might get the urge to wander, so I asked Captain Landau to assign a man to keep an eye on you."

"The phone kept ringing," Gwenn explained. "I couldn't help answering."

"Sure."

"Ford made me think they had you."

"You didn't actually believe I'd made a deal with them?"

"Of course not, but it would have been comforting to know there was help close by. It would have been comforting to know I wasn't alone."

"We felt it might be better if you didn't know."

"Thanks a lot. Well, maybe you were right, maybe I would have given it away. So, I assume that when I came out of your apartment, the detective followed, called for backup, and everybody assembled at Monique's place and waited for the opportune moment to break in. How could they know when that occurred?"

"I put a miniature transmitter in your handbag."

"I wish I'd known *that!*" Gwenn took a deep breath and then had to smile ruefully. "What else did you plant on me?" She raised both hands. "Never mind. Just tell me one more thing: Why did you go to IA? I thought you didn't trust them."

"I work for IA."

It took Gwenn a while to make that fit. "You've been working for Internal Affairs right along?"

"No. I went to them after your apartment was trashed. You remember I told you at the time that I didn't know how to protect you? That's when I volunteered. I was referred to Captain Landau. He was getting ready to break the corruption scandal wide open. Jayne was to have been a principal witness."

"Oh, Ray," Gwenn sighed. "I don't know what to say except thank you. I wish Jayne had known Landau was on her side."

"So do I, but she had reached the point where she didn't trust anybody but you and me."

"Are you going to stay with Internal Affairs?" Gwenn asked.

"No. Captain Landau is staying. He's moving up and wants to take me with him. He's made me an offer, but I'm turning it down. I'm resigning."

"You don't mean from the force?"

"That's what I do mean. It's changed. Everything's changed. There have been police scandals before, but this . . . these men . . . They're not cops tempted beyond their ability to resist; they're crooks out looking for ways to score. They're rotten inside. They lust after evil."

Gwenn was shocked. "You're condemning the whole department because of a few bad cops."

"More than a few."

"You'd be helping to get rid of a lot of them."

"The cancer goes too deep."

Gwenn sighed. "So what do you plan to do with yourself?"

"Get a job in the private sector."

"Doing what?"

"Investigating. I'm an investigator, right? I'm trained for it and I'm good at it. Don't you think I'm good at it? I have experience. The security and investigation business is thriving. I shouldn't have any trouble finding work."

"No, probably not," Gwenn admitted, but she was having difficulty separating Ray from his badge.

"Actually, I thought you might give me a job."

"Me?"

"You need somebody. You're always calling for outside ops at the last minute and paying top dollar. You'd be better off having an extra hand on the payroll. I work cheap."

Oh my! Gwenn thought. "You'd be an asset, no doubt about that." What else could she say? And it was true, but . . . "You wouldn't be happy here, Ray. Not for long. You're a cop and you always will be."

"Being a cop is okay. I don't want to be a spy."

"That's an outmoded attitude," Gwenn told him. "What you would be doing in IA is separating out the bad from the good, restoring the honor of the department."

"You don't think we can work together. That's it, isn't it?" Ray challenged.

"It wouldn't be easy," she admitted. "I suppose we could learn. But there's no rush. Let's wait awhile. Let's at least wait till this thing is over."

"It is over. What are you talking about?"

"Are you sure?"

"Of course," Ray answered, but suddenly he wasn't so sure.

"Ford shot Palma before Palma could shoot me and we took it for granted that Ford's purpose was to save me," Gwenn said. "But suppose it wasn't? Suppose I was an excuse for Ford to shoot Palma and silence him?"

"You're reaching."

"I don't think so. You said yourself Ford wouldn't be talking so freely if Palma were alive," Gwenn countered. "Palma would certainly put a different spin on this whole story."

"Well, sure."

"With Palma eliminated, Ford gets to tell it his way. He puts the blame on Palma and saves his own neck and plenty of others. He can name anybody he wants as having been part of the racket and that person is as good as convicted, and anybody he says is clean—walks."

"All right, but how about the cigarette butts found at the scene? You're the one who made a big deal out of the saliva secretions indicating a blood type that matched Palma's. How are you going to get around that?"

"I don't have to. The blood type only tells us who smoked the cigarettes. It doesn't tell us who committed the murder."

Ray groaned.

"So why don't we wait till the case is officially cleared? By then you may change your mind about resigning." Gwenn thought about what her mother had said. "We should get to know each other better."

"Absolutely." He grinned. "I'm all for that."

"There's more to a relationship than working at the same job and being sexually attracted."

"Those aren't bad for starters," Ray suggested.

Even her mother would agree with that, Gwenn thought.

6

Religion in the Year 2000

Religion in the Year 2000 ★ ★ ★

by ANDREW M. GREELEY

SHEED AND WARD : *NEW YORK*

*For the Vaneckos—Jim, Pat
and, of course, Seamus*

The author wishes to thank the editors of *The Critic* for their kind permission to reprint material in chapter 6 which first appeared in their pages. My thanks are also due Mrs. Nella V. Siefert for her typing and supervision of the manuscript.

Contents

Contents

List of Tables

Religion in the Year 2000

1 ★ ★ ★

Introduction

The study of the future is a relatively new development in Western culture. In the stable world that persisted into early modern times, there was generally not enough change to persuade people that the chronological future—that is to say, the next fifty or hundred years—would be any different from the present. Mythological futures may have existed, but they were generally in a different order of reality from the real world in which people lived. Thomas More's Utopia was quite literally "no place" that was expected actually to exist. With the industrial and scientific revolution of the late eighteenth and nineteenth centuries, it became possible to dream of future worlds which were something more than mythological but which, in fact, represented real possibilities if scientific development were to continue. The tremendous intellectual breakthrough that

3

the evolutionary theories of the nineteenth century represented made it possible for man to grasp conceptually the idea of a world very much different from his own and yet the result of logical development of realities already at hand.

However, it was well into the twentieth century, and indeed toward the middle of the twentieth century, that the study of (to use Robert Heilbroner's phrase) "the future as history" became common; at the present time there exists a large and rapidly expanding literature on the future. While some of this still smacks of science fiction or the philosophical dreams which mark such radical theorists as Ignatius Donnelly, most of it is soberly realistic. The literature is sober because the concept of long-range planning demands that those responsible for the future of society take into account both the resources and the demands that the next generation or the next century or the next five centuries are likely to generate; and it is realistic (at least reasonably realistic) because the art of projecting from present trends—particularly in the economic disciplines—is quite well-developed. The projections that planners of the future make are internally consistent and precise if one is willing to accept, at least for the sake of argument, their assumptions. The most sophisticated projectors of the future will give one a whole series of assumptions from which one can choose and describe what the future will look like from any given set of assumptions.

As Peter Berger has pointed out, there is very little in the current literature of the future about religion, mostly because the futurists assume that religion either will not play much part in the future, or is irrelevant to human behavior (an assumption which, by the way, is implicit, so that no data are advanced to establish it).

But if the futurists have been silent about religion in the year 2000, theologians and journalists have not. It is curious that the scholarly trend projectors do not seem to think that religion is important, but that those who write magazine and newspaper articles think it is important enough to large numbers of people to deserve a considerable amount of typeface.

The journalists—and the theologians who learn about sociological trends from the journalists—see changes in religious behavior in terms of dramatic trends. There was a religious revival, we are told, after the Second World War, and more recently we are going through a period of religious decline. For those theologians who are particularly crisis-oriented, the present alleged decline is seen as the last gasp of Western Christianity. God, we are told, is dead. In the stirring words of Thomas J. J. Altizer:[1] "We must realize that the death of God is an historical event, that God has died in our cosmos, in our history, in our *existenz*."

In addition, the feeling is widespread in the collective semiconsciousness of academe that religion is a thing of the past. Professor J. D. Watson pointed out in his book *The Double Helix*[2] that no intelligent man could possibly believe in the existence of God. So if the historians of the future are uninterested in religion, and if the theologians of the present are terrified about the prospects of religion, it may well be that religion has no future. The replacement of religious superstition by enlightened science predicted since the time of Voltaire may at last be taking place.

It well may be; though it should be remembered that the prediction has generally been wrong every time it has been made. The wise man is permitted to remain skeptical until he sees more conclusive evidence. He will also be aware that there is a very substantial difference between the history of the future as written by sober men who carefully project trends into the future, and the strongly value-laden, philosophical statements that religion cannot survive in the age of science. To the latter statement, the response must be made that it has, so far.

What is somewhat disturbing to the professional sociologist is that his discipline is frequently cited both by theologians and by journalists as providing evidence for the demise of religion. He may even be more dismayed by the fact that the word most frequently used to describe the progressive decline of religion, "secularization," has been introduced into the contemporary consciousness perhaps more by Max Weber, one of the Holy Father Founders of contemporary sociology, than by any other man. Yet Weber could not conceive of a world without some sort of religion, and the most prominent of the Weberian disciples of contemporary sociology cannot either.

Later on in this volume I will devote some attention to the evidence from certain public opinion polls produced to support that version of the secularization hypothesis which is adduced as evidence of the progressive decline of religion.

Suffice it to say at the present time that those sociologists (some believers and some agnostics) who specialize in the sociology of religion are not altogether favorably impressed by the persuasive power of the data that the theologians and the journalists most frequently cite.

This volume, then, is an attempt, within the framework of sociological discipline, to write responsibly about the future of religion. It will project present trends into the future, with the future herein defined as the next century, more or less; these projections will be rooted in a critical examination of the popular version of the secularization hypothesis. The author is convinced that there is very little in the way of either sociological theory or empirical data to confirm that hypothesis; quite the contrary. Both the data and the theory of sociology would suggest that by the latter third of the twenty-first century, religion, as well as God, will be alive and well.

It is important to emphasize that this conviction was arrived at independently of the author's personal commitment to a religious faith. It is possible, for example, to be an unbeliever, as were both Durkheim and Weber, and yet be convinced, as Durkheim was, that "there will always be religion." Similarly, it is possible to a believer, as is Peter Berger, and still be far more prepared than I am to accept the secularization hypothesis. Berger is ready to say that indeed the modern consciousness cannot conceive of the transcendent, but this does not mean that there is not a transcendent—it simply means that in the present state of historical development the consciousness of educated man cannot conceive of it. He then goes on, as we shall mention later, to cite some "signals" of a transcendence which fly in the face of the assumptions of modern consciousness. I am not as ready as Professor Berger to agree that the modern consciousness—at least outside certain segments of academia—is all that unreligious, though I do think that Professor Berger's writing on the signals of the transcendent is remarkably stimulating and provocative.

In other words, a man's commitment to a given religious tradition is not such as to be arrived at by taking a public opinion poll and cannot be revoked by a change in public opinion. My commitment to the Catholic tradition of Christianity was not arrived at or sustained by counting noses. But even if the secularization hypothesis—at least in its popular version—were established both theoretically and empirically to be incontrovertible, the convinced Christian (and I am a convinced Christian) would simply say, "It's going to be tough without the rest of you guys."

My contention is that the theory and the data are not such as to force me to any such belligerent act of faith. Insofar as it is possible in any intellectual activity—and it is perhaps never completely possible—my argument in this volume will be made independently of my own Catholic Christian commitment.

But it will not be made independently of a sociological commitment, for as a sociologist it seems to me that I am committed to a profound skepticism about societal generalizations. The hard-nosed skepticism of the sociologist asks for evidence and wants to have that evidence fit into a coherent theoretical framework before he is convinced. Furthermore, he is also profoundly skeptical about dramatic social changes. Thus, in the recent election when commentators and analysts were announcing that there was a basic change going on in the political patterns of the Republic, the sociologist was just as skeptical as he is forced to be when he is told that a dramatic change is going on in religious behavior. He knows that there is a built-in trend toward consistency, stability, and permanence in human behavior and the patterns of human relationships. He also knows that certain social institutions, such as the family and religion, have marked every human society that the world has ever known. While he does not reject on a priori grounds the possibility that man has evolved to a stage where family and religion can be dispensed with, neither is he prepared to accept the fact of such evolution until he is faced with overwhelming evidence.

Indeed, given the many similarities between religion in the year 2000 B.C., religion in the year 1000 A.D., and religion today, the sociologist will assert that until he sees powerful evidence to the contrary, he is not going to be prepared to believe that religion will be all that much different one hundred years from now. It will change. It may even change substantially from its present manifestations; yet unless he sees dramatic evidence, the sociologist will be unwilling to concede that someone who could live in a state of suspended animation for a century would have much difficulty in identifying religious institutions and behavior in the year 2070.

It might be argued, then, that this is a doggedly conservative volume; but it is conservative only in the sense that every scientific work must be conservative. One accepts hypotheses as being substantiated only when one has collected evidence to support such hypotheses. Many Christians might even rejoice if the secularization hypotheses were true, because as Harvey Cox, in his popular work *The Secular City*, contended:[3] "Then authentic Christianity could begin, being finally divested of the superstitious relics of the past." It does seem to me, however, that on the basis of the data and the theorizing currently taking place in the sociology of religion, the sociologist is forced to conclude, for weal or woe, that the secular city is not only not yet upon us, but shows no signs of coming into existence.

It is perhaps appropriate at this point to establish some definitions. We have already said that the future we are concerned with certainly means no more than a century, and for all practical purposes no more than the next half a century. The definition of religion must be more precise. The one I find most satisfactory is Professor Clifford Geertz's:[4] "Religion is a system of symbols which acts to establish powerful, pervasive and long-lasting moods and motivations in men by formulating conceptions of a general order of existence and clothing these conceptions with such an aura of factuality that the moods and motivations seem uniquely realistic." Geertz's definition is very carefully and precisely worded (as we shall see in a later chapter) to be elastic enough to include a number of kinds of "symbols" which might not, in the ordinary use of the word, be considered religious.

A related concept is the concept of the "sacred"; and here I use the word in the more or less ordinary sense, a sense which, I take it, has been shaped considerably by Durkheim and by Rudolf Otto. The sacred is that which is not ordinary or profane. It is, in Otto's words, "the totally Other," that which transcends the ordinary, everyday experience, and which puts man in contact with another and very different order of reality.

One of the very tricky issues in the sociology of religion is whether you can have a religion without the sacred. It must be noted that Geertz's definition, at least on the face of it, tends to leave that question somewhat open; and as we shall see later, some theorists conceptualize religion in such a way that it need not include symbols which allegedly represent "transcendent" objects. One could, therefore, have a "profane religion" or a "secular religion." It could in turn be argued that religion has a future but that the sacred does not. We shall note the importance of this distinction in a later chapter. Suffice it to assert at the present time that the argument of this volume is that the empirical data available to us do not indicate a demise of "sacred religion." My own personal theoretical inclination, as I shall note later on, is to suspect that there is a "sacralizing tendency" in the human condition by which the symbols even of a secular faith are so set apart from the profane, and eventually so cloaked with ritual and tradition, that they become in fact "functionally sacred."

It might also be well here to preview one of the major arguments that will be used. I will express profound skepticism as to whether the combination of belief and unbelief which characterizes the present religious condition represents a substantial deterioration of religious commitments of the past. Those early researchers engaged in the presumably scientific study of religion who argue (as Charles Glock, Rodney Stark, and John Thomas have) that their findings represent a change from some previous condition of religious faith are engaging in what those sociologists who permit themselves to be witty call "the good old days" fallacy. In the absence of survey data from the past, we cannot say with any pretense at science that there has been a change. On the contrary, what we know from the anthropological literature leads us to believe that doubt, uncertainty, agnosticism, and even atheism, were not at all unknown in man's past. Clifford Geertz has remarked that someone could readily write a book called Belief and Unbelief in Primitive Societies, and that the subtitle could be Faith and Hypocrisy in Primitive Man.

To the sociologist, then, who says that opinions must have been different in the past from what they are in his data, we are forced to respond: "How do you know? You weren't there, and neither were any other collectors of opinions." Furthermore, when he points to a decline in church attendance as evidence of the deterioration of religion, we will respond that in some countries such devotion has declined and in others it has not, and that the latter category includes both the most industrial and the most agricultural of Western countries. In addition, the factors making for modification of church attendance rates seem to be quite independent of scientific and industrial revolu-

tions. We observe that the careful study done by Gabrielle
LeBras and his disciples in France indicates that traditions
of religiousness and irreligiousness are deeply rooted in the
historical past; certain regions of France which are irreligious today were irreligious three or four centuries ago, presumably long before technology and science produced secular man.

Finally, when a proponent of the secularization hypothesis points his finger at the religious masses as being apathetic
and "unauthentic" in their religiousness, we can only reply
that there is no evidence to suggest that the saving remnant
—that is to say, those who were authentically religious—
has ever been very large.

In any of its forms, then, we will not be persuaded by
the "good old days" fallacy; on the contrary, we will insist
that the only time series study of the sociology of religion
of which we are aware shows little, if any, signs of the
erosion of religious commitment.

In the next chapter we will attempt to describe the
secularization model, and then, in the two following chapters, consider both the empirical data and the theoretical
formulations of the sociology of religion which bear on this
model. In further chapters we will consider what sociology
might project for the future of theology, liturgy, the clergy,
and organized religion.

NOTES

[1] Thomas J. J. Altizer and William Hamilton, *Radical Theology and the Death of God* (Indianapolis: Bobbs-Merrill, 1966), 11.

[2] J. D. Watson, *The Double Helix* (New York: Atheneum, 1958).

[3] Harvey Cox, *The Secular City* (New York: Macmillan, 1965).

[4] Clifford Geertz, "Religion as a Cultural System," in Donald R. Cutler (ed.), *The Religious Situation* (Boston: Beacon Press, 1968), 643.

2 ★ ★ ★

The Secularization Model

David Martin[1] tells an interesting parable. He describes a time and a place where the elite of a society have become agnostic and skeptical. The masses are superstitious; the young either do not care about religion or are experimenting with strange oriental sects; political leadership pretends to be religious for its own purposes. Religious organizations continue to exist, but there is little of the prophetic about them in their ministry to the cultural and psychological needs of their members.

Is this the decline of organized religion pictured in Harvey Cox's *The Secular City*? Is this the beginning of religionless Christianity prophesied by Dietrich Bonhoeffer? Not exactly, for what Martin is talking about is the city of Rome in the year 30 A.D.

First, we must establish what we do *not* mean by secu-

larization. We do not mean a concern with the problems
and responsibilities and challenges of this world. When
Max Weber said that ancient Judaism was more secular
than the classic religions of India, and when he further
declared that Protestantism represented an even more secularized religion, he very clearly was not saying that either
Judaism or Protestantism was not religious or did not concern itself with the sacred. As Professor Guy Swanson[2]
phrases it:

Judaism and Protestantism incorporated a greater secularization
than did other religions in just one specific sense: in them it
was the general orientation and meaning of human behavior,
not its detailed contents, which had sacred significance. Thus
God desired not burnt offerings for the following of a particular
formula in prayer, but a spirit attentive to him and a contrite
heart; not intellectual assent to some list of his attributes but a
commitment to his service wherever it might lead.

Thus, for both the Jews and the Protestants, there is a
great deal more concern about this world and this world's
activities than there was in either China or India, and the
individual believer also is given a great deal more room for
decision-making as to how he should serve the demands of
the sacred than was conceded either in the primitive nature
religions or in the ancient Chinese and Indian religions.
Swanson compares this development with the emergence
of rational and bureaucratic organizations:[3]

Rather than employing rules that govern the exact procedures
by which work is carried out, the complex organization specifies

the work to be accomplished, leaving to employees many decisions about how best to obtain objectives. . . . What in the religious sphere we call secularization seems to be of the same order as professionalization and bureaucratization, and to have similar roots and consequences.

Talcott Parsons and other disciples of Weber see the great religious changes of history as precisely this kind of secularization: A greater freedom of movement for the individual believer involving almost necessarily a greater concern for this-worldly activity, but not in any sense the exclusion of the value of the otherworldly. I have no quarrel with this definition of secularization, but the secularization model that I wish to examine in greater detail in this chapter is a different one. Swanson, following Thomas O'Dea, calls it "secularism":[4]

Secularism is the denial that a sacred order exists, the conviction that the universe is in no meaningful sense an expression or embodiment of purpose, the belief that it is unreasonable, other than anthropomorphically, to have toward the universe or its "ground" a relationship mediated by communication or by any other interchange of meanings—to have toward it a relationship in any sense interpersonal. The clearest example is atheism. The more common approximation to secularism is intellectual agnosticism.

Peter Berger describes the same notion somewhat more simply: "Secularization means that religion doesn't have as much influence as it used to on human life and its influence

is waning." In his book *A Rumor of Angels*, Berger sum-
marizes and accepts (more or less) the factors involved in
this decline in religion's importance:[5]

1. . . . religiosity (that is, religious belief and practice within the
traditions of the principal Christian churches) has been on the
decline in modern society. In Europe this has generally taken the
form of a progressive decline in institutional participation (attendance at worship, use of the sacraments, and the like), though
there are important class differences in this. In America, on the
contrary, there has been an increase in participation (as measured by church membership figures), though there are good
reasons to think that the motives for participation have changed
greatly from the traditional ones. It is safe to say that, compared
to earlier historical periods, fewer Americans today adhere to
the churches out of a burning desire for salvation from sin and
hellfire, while many do so out of a desire to provide moral instruction for their children and direction for their family life, or
just because it is part of the life style of their particular neighborhood.

2. . . . Whatever the situation may have been in the past, *today*
the supernatural as a meaningful reality is absent or remote from
the horizons of everyday life of large numbers, very probably
of the majority, of people in modern societies, who seem to
manage to get along without it quite well.

Professor Huston Smith gives a slightly different definition. For him "secular" means "those regions of life that
man understands and controls, not necessarily completely,
but (as the saying goes, and here it is precisely accurate)
for all practical purposes."[6]

Thus defined, secularization has increased steadily with the advance of civilization. Primitive man obviously managed or we wouldn't be around, but there was little in his life that he understood sufficiently to effect clean control over it. As a consequence his society was whole, compacted in the sense—among others—that the sacred encompassed almost everything; economics and medicine, for example. Among tribal peoples hunting and husbandry have sacred sides to them: Today priests are occupied with their sacred buffalos, and totemic rites bind Arunta hunters to their prey in ties that both expedite and legitimize their kills. Likewise with healing: medicine men are simultaneously physicians and priests.

In *civilizations* the situation is, as we know, otherwise. Whether we read "In God We Trust" on our currency as vestigial or as a precise index of the degree to which the almighty dollar has become in fact our god, western economies have become completely secular. This is not to claim that we understand or control the economic order completely, but it does say that we believe that what happens in the economic order is due either to planned human intervention or to chance and that what we don't understand of it is due to our (provisional) ignorance rather than to its (in-built) mystery. Similarly with modern medicine. Priests now enter the picture with the approach of the inexorable—death. Healing itself, even psychiatric healing, has become a secular art.

Politics is a third sphere of civilized activity that has become secularized. In China the process is currently passing through a decisive phase as Mao's theologically oriented cultural revolution goes to the mat against the practical pragmatisms of nation building. But in the West the battle is over. The splice between politics and religion (the priest-king) has gone the way of the splice between medicine and religion (the medicine man). To see Lyndon Baines Johnson as having been even once upon a time a holy man requires the spiritual clairvoyance of a Hindu. (The reference is to Goswamy's surprising astrological discovery during the heat of the 1964 presidential campaign that the Democratic candidate had spent his preceding incarnation as a sannyasin practicing austerities along the banks of the Ganges [7:191].)

However, Smith is somewhat less convinced that secularization has occurred in as pervasive a fashion as Peter Berger would think:[7]

It might seem natural to suppose that with man's progressive mastery of domains of his existence and the attendant fissiparous emancipation of these from the custody of religion, the sacred is shrinking, becoming residual. We shall do well, however, to resist jumping to this conclusion hastily. The family, too, once held sway over activities that have progressively moved away from it—activities like manufacturing, education, entertainment, and religious instruction—but it doesn't necessarily follow that the family dimension has declined in importance. It could continue to be important but in different ways; as the locus of intimacy, for example, which in our impersonal society has become more problematically important than ever before.

Berger, Swanson, Smith—none of whom, by the way, are terribly pessimistic about the future of religion, as we shall see later—present a precise and sophisticated set of definitions of what secularization means. In the more popular discussion the word is used much more imprecisely.

There are, it seems to me, at least six different meanings that it seems to have in popular literature.

In the more popular writings on the subject, secularization, it seems to me, can be any one of the following six things:

1. Modern science makes it impossible for the educated man to believe.

2. Modern man is not motivated by religion in his daily life.

3. There is a drift away from religious faith and commitment.

4. Religion and society are not in close contact with each other, and there are vast areas of human behavior on which religion has no direct influence.

5. Religion is more and more relegated to the private sphere of man's activity and has no influence on the public sphere.

6. The sacred, that is to say the transcendent totally Other, has little or no influence on human behavior, and little or no role to play in human life.

In the popular writings there is some difficulty in distinguishing between long-range and short-range terms, with one group of authors arguing apparently that secularization, or at least dramatic secularization, is a relatively recent event. The death of God, then, has happened since the end of the Second World War, or perhaps even since 1960. Other writers, however, would see a much longer trend and in this respect, I think, would be closer to men like Berger. But most of the popular and serious writers are saying much the same thing: The spirit of the contemporary world is hostile to traditional religion and particularly to the sense of the sacred, and both religion and the sacred are declining in influence both in society as a whole and in the lives of individual members.

The first argument for this stand is on the level of common sense. Everybody knows, we are told, that religion has less influence than it used to; it is evident that men are more secular than they used to be and that the mystical and the sacred have less impact on human behavior than they used to have. To some extent I think this is the kind of argument that Peter Berger uses, even though he admits that since "sociologists and their like have been around for only a rather short time, it is not clear to what extent their findings can be rigorously compared with the situations in previous periods for which different and only imperfectly comparable data are available." He nonetheless asserts that "Today the supernatural and the meaningful reality is absent or remote from the horizons of everyday life of large numbers, very probably of the majority of people in modern societies." I find this form of argumentation in an otherwise excellent book to be somewhat peculiar, since Professor Berger does not tell us what his evidence for this is, and since most of the empirical data which he does cite in the book seem rather to indicate the contrary. My own impression is that Berger's arguments are more theoretical than empirical, and that he is inclined to argue to the fact of secularization from a priori theories which make secularization inevitable. We will turn to these theories—and they are quite intellectually respectable ones—in subsequent paragraphs; but as far as empirical data are concerned, Professor Berger does not adduce any and is content with the simple assertion that "everyone knows" that there has been secularization.[8]

The second line of argumentation is based on the collection of empirical data, however, and normally takes two forms, both of which are exemplified in the work of Charles Y. Glock and Rodney Stark, although Father John Thomas anticipated these argumentations more than a decade before either of these two writers. Glock and Stark discovered that most of their respondents, whatever their religious faith, were committed to the basic tenets of traditional religion. But their questionnaires, like most survey research questionnaires, permitted the respondents gradations in their agreement or disagreement; one could therefore agree strongly, agree somewhat, or say that an assertion was certainly true or probably true. The two authors then discovered that in many of the more liberally inclined Protestant denominations there were substantial numbers of respondents who were willing to say only that the existence of God was probably true, and even more would qualify their confidence with the word "probably" on a number of other propositions of doctrinal orthodoxy. Glock and Stark conclude, therefore, in a jump of logic that is completely unjustified, that those who say that something is probably true are doubters. They thereupon permit themselves a certain amount of surprise at the very large numbers of doubters within the traditional religion and suggest that this may, indeed, be evidence that traditional religious orthodoxy is losing its grip on large bodies of those who still are willing to affirm membership in religious denominations.

Glock and Stark are far too competent as sociologists to affirm with absolute confidence that there is proof of secularization, because they do not have data from the past. They turn to other evidence, however, to substantiate somewhat the conclusion that there probably has been a deterioration of religious commitment. They focus on the fact that when asked to describe how they thought of God, many respondents were not inclined to say He was a person; since a personal God is part of the Christian tradition, this is presumed to indicate that the tradition is weakening. A number of other poll takers and authors of quasi-sociological articles rely very heavily on ambiguity about the personhood of God as a sign of the deterioration of religious faith.

A third argument is willing to concede, in the face of the data that we introduce in the next chapter, that religious participation and commitment are apparently still quite high in American society, but contends that the United States is the only nation in the Western industrial world of which this is true. In this country, it is said, special social reasons have contributed to the survival of religious commitment, and hence the slowing down of the secularization process. Some who favor this argument will add, as has Professor Berger, that the secularization is going on from within the American churches as they become less and less religious in their goals. The argument concludes by pointing out that one need only visit European countries or look at the European survey data to realize that church membership and church attendance are very low in these countries and that in some of them, such as England, comparative figures from the preceding century indicate the extent of the decline in religious practices.

I must say that this argument is the one I have always found the most persuasive, though a reading of Professor Martin's book on the sociology of religion in England has caused me to have serious doubts about the force of the argument.

Another form of argumentation consists of pointing out how many institutions in society used to be influenced by religion and how few of them still are. Science, education, politics, law, medicine, social welfare—all of these used to be, if not completely under the control of the churches or of religion, at least heavily influenced by them. But in the modern world these institutions are quite independent of the churches. Church doctrine and church membership seem to have little or no impact on what occurs in the institutional structure outside the church boundaries. It is frequently asserted that the evidence for this evaluation is so obvious as to be beyond question. That the social process described in the argument has happened must readily be admitted, but as we shall see in the next chapter, this does not necessarily substantiate the idea that the influence of religion is deteriorating. Religion may have less direct extensive influence, but this does not mean that the intensity of its impact and its potential for indirect influence on

much of the rest of society is in the process of being eliminated.

Yet another argument tends to be somewhat a priori.
Those who support it analyze either urban industrialism or
scientific technology and point out how the rational, empirical, pragmatic implications of these two phenomena
leave no room for the mythical, sacral, and otherworldly
concerns of traditional religion. Thus, Rudolf Bultmann's
whole approach to "demythologizing" the Scriptures is
based on the assumption that modern scientific man simply
cannot accept myths. That Bultmann could live in Germany in the 1930's and not realize the power of myths on
modern scientific man seems well-nigh incredible to the
present writer.

A more sophisticated and social psychological form of
this argument is presented by Peter Berger and is based on
an analysis from the point of view of the sociology of knowledge—of what he calls the probability structure. He says:[9]

Each plausibility structure can be further analyzed in terms of
its constituent elements—the specific human beings that "in-
habit" it, the conversational network by which these "inhabitants" keep the reality in question going, the therapeutic practices and rituals, and the legitimations that go with them. For
example, the maintenance of the Catholic faith in the consciousness of the individual requires that he maintain his relationship
to the plausibility structure of Catholicism. This is, above all, a
community of Catholics in his social milieu who continually
support this faith. It will be useful if those who are of the greatest emotional significance to the individual (the ones whom
George Herbert Mead called significant others) belong to this

supportive community—it does not matter much if, say, the individual's dentist is a non-Catholic, but his wife and his closest personal friends had better be. Within this supportive community there will then be an ongoing conversation that, explicitly and implicitly, keeps a Catholic world going.

But according to Berger, the modern world no longer has one such plausibility structure:[10]

This pluralization of socially available worlds has been of particular importance for religion, again for far from mysterious reasons, the most decisive being the Protestant Reformation and its subsidiary schisms. It is this pluralization, rather than some mysterious intellectual fall from grace, that I see as the most important cause of the diminishing plausibility of religious traditions. It is relatively easy, sociologically speaking, to be a Catholic in a social situation where one can readily limit one's significant others to fellow Catholics, where indeed one has little choice in the matter, and where all the major institutional forces are geared to support and confirm a Catholic world. The story is quite different in a situation where one is compelled to rub shoulders day by day with every conceivable variety of "those others," is bombarded with communications that deny or ignore one's Catholic ideas, and where one has a terrible time even finding some quiet Catholic corners to withdraw into. It is very, very difficult to be cognitively *entre nous* in modern society, especially in the area of religion. This simple sociological fact, and not some magical inexorability of a "scientific" world outlook, is at the basis of the religious plausibility crisis.

It is, therefore, from Berger's point of view, the very plurality of the marketplace of ideas (a marketplace which, as Berger's friend Thomas Luckmann points out, turns us all into consumers of ideology) that is at the root of the religious crisis and the spread of secularization. It is a very persuasive argument, although I was a bit surprised to see Professor Berger using it after he had taken Bultmann to task for presuming that "no one who uses electricity and listens to the radio can any longer believe in the miracle world of the New Testament." It is also worth noting that Professor Berger has apparently overlooked the fact that it is precisely in those countries where the religious pluralism is most likely to be found that organized religion is also able to count on the strongest commitments. Thus, for example, in thoroughly pluralistic societies like the United States and Holland, where the Protestant and Catholic "plausibility structures" are apparently in competition with one another, both religions seem to have far more vigor than they do in those nations where the competition of religious plausibility structures is less of a factor. Unquestionably the open marketplace of ideas has turned into a deluxe supermarket in recent times. One can purchase almost any commodity one wants, yet it remains to be proven that when shopping for ideology modern man is necessarily an impulsive buyer. Quite the contrary; he seems very skillful at blocking out of his perceptions a good many products that are at variance with the commitments he has already made—which is simply another way of saying that one can create a psychological world in which one's plausibility structure is quite intact. This is especially easy if, as in the United States and Holland, religion and membership in religious denominations become highly important means of social location and self-definition.

As far as I am aware, these are the major arguments advanced in favor of the secularization hypothesis, and they are all rooted in the assumption that scientific, rational, technological man cannot really accept the mythological and the sacred. Some, like Professor Berger, may lament this; others may rejoice in it; some may see it as a long-range trend; others as a trend which has only recently begun to have its full impact. Some may argue for it in terms of common sense; others may adduce elaborate intellectual argumentations for it; but no matter which way the cake is cut, it comes to the same thing: There is no room for religion in a scientific, technological world. One concludes, therefore, that either religion is finished, or religion must reform itself, or, as I think Professor Berger concludes, religion will probably have to wait until a more sympathetic plausibility structure develops.

But, as the man says in *Porgy and Bess*, "It ain't necessarily so."

NOTES

[1] David Martin, "Towards Eliminating the Concept of Secularization," in Julius Gould (ed.), *Penguin Survey of the Social Sciences* (Baltimore, Md.: Penguin, 1965).

[2] Guy A. Swanson, "Modern Secularity," in Donald R. Cutler (ed.), *The Religious Situation* (Boston: Beacon Press, 1968), 802.

Reprinted by permission of the Beacon Press, copyright © 1968 by Beacon Press.

³ *Ibid.*, 803.

⁴ *Ibid.*, 803-04.

⁵ Peter L. Berger, A *Rumor of Angels* (New York: Doubleday, 1969), 5-7.

⁶ Huston Smith, "Secularization and the Sacred: The Contemporary Scene," in *The Religious Situation*, 583-84. Reprinted by permission of the Beacon Press, copyright © 1968 by Beacon Press.

⁷ *Ibid.*, 584.

⁸ I remember, in the early stages of *The Secular City* controversy, how utterly astonished Professor Harvey Cox was at my insistence, in a rather fierce article in *Commonweal*, that he was gratuitously assuming the existence of a secular city in the face of considerable sociological evidence to the contrary. Professor Cox seemed astonished that a sociologist would deny the obvious fact of secularization and suggested that it might conceivably be my religious commitments which prevented me from seeing it. Unlike Professor Cox, I am a sociologist, and hence must look for evidence; and unlike Professor Berger, I am far more of a data collector than I am a theoretician. While I am impressed mightily by abstract sociological theorizing, I still want to see the evidence. I am not persuaded, and I do not think any sociologist should be persuaded, merely by the assertion that "everyone knows" that secularization has occurred.

⁹ Berger, *op. cit.*, 45.

¹⁰ *Ibid.*, 55.

3 ★ ★ ★

The Data

A great deal is probably revealed about my own sociological biases by the fact that I present a chapter on data before a chapter on theory. Surely the University of Chicago tradition of sociology has never been accused of being too theoretical, and during my years as a student there, it would have been almost impossible for anyone aspiring to the role of creator of "general theory" to find a faculty member who was not quite sure what he was talking about. I must confess, however, that for me the University of Chicago was a case of coming to my own and my own receiving me. I am quite prepared to take any number of things on faith, either religious faith or human faith, or even on the faith that the statisticians are not lying to me when they assure me that a given sampling system is, indeed, a valid one. But I will not accept anything as massive in its implications as the secularization hypothesis until I see convincing empirical data. In some sense this may be a weakness, because I may miss the opportunity of gaining tremendous insight from a handful of cases. My passion for evidence (be it in statistical tables or elsewhere) may blind me to some things which are so immense that one does not need evidence. Nevertheless, as I have said before, the sociologist is, or at least should be, in the evidence-gathering business, and therefore he must take a close look at the empirical data available to him before he willingly assents to the validity of a hypothesis. For others, other methods may be available —poetry, metaphysical insight, divine revelation—but the sociologist *qua* sociologist must look at the data.

Perhaps the most striking way of beginning to present the data is to cite Professor Swanson's consideration of the question of whether "religious institutions or interactions with the sacred order are on the wane." Swanson's method is a clever one; he admits that no comparisons can be made with religious behavior of the past, so therefore he argues that what we might well do is compare religious behavior in the present with political behavior in the present. He points out that "Almost every informed student of the subject seems to believe that the American political system is vital and effective." Does religion, then, fall below politics in its vitality and effectiveness? Here I quote a "sample" of his comparisons:[1]

Item: Approximately 60% of the American electorate votes in national elections. Approximately 68% of the adult population attends religious services in any given four-week period and 79% claims church membership. [36:181; 32: chap 4; 23: 671–679].

Item: 76% believes that the churches are doing a good or excellent job in its area of the country; 80% believes that national or state governments are doing that well [25: 326–337; 32: chap 11, 12, 18].

Item: 27% of the electorate reports it discussed politics with others prior to an election; 90% of the people in the Detroit area, the only geographic source of data on this point, reports discussing religion with others during the month just past [18 and 32:53].

Item: Fourteen out of every hundred Americans have written or wired a congressman or senator, 7 out of a 100 have done so more than once. 24% of the population has called on someone to invite his membership in a church. 88% of the population prays frequently or every day; 40% read from the Bible in the month just past and between 60% and 65% read from it during the past year. In metropolitan Detroit, 65% of all adults is self-exposed to religious programs on radio or television and 75% to reports of religion in the newspapers [32:68–69; 24:145–157; 25: 326–337; 19: card 9 col 14, 15].

Item: Approximately 5 families in every 100 made a financial contribution to a political party or candidate in 1956. At least 40 in every 100 made a financial contribution to a religious body; 3 in every 100 tithe [32:60; 25:326–337; 5].

Item: The major Protestant denominations once again have an ample supply of ministers in service and also of candidates for the ministry, despite growth of church membership (and of numbers of local churches) far in excess of the rate of growth of the national population and despite sharply higher standards of training and ability required of students entering ministerial curricula. Positions in state and federal governmental service are going begging for lack of suitable applicants.

Item: Only 7% of all respondents says it has no strong feelings about its religious beliefs. Although there seem to be no dependable national estimates, the proportion of the electorate that declares itself indifferent to political positions and issues is always greater than 7% [24:149].

Item: 51% of the American people correctly name the first book of the Bible. That is about the proportion that knows the number of Senators from its own state—and that can spell "cauliflower" [22].

Item: 95% does not know what the initials IHS represent, just about the number which does not know that all members of the House of Representatives are elected every two years [22].

Item: 95% knows the name of the mother of Jesus. That is the proportion that can state the term of office of the President of the United States and correctly locate Texas or California on a blank map [22].

Item: Only 34% can correctly identify the Sermon on the Mount or can give the names of the current United States Senators from its state [22].

Item: About the same percentage of the population knows that there are new editions of the Bible as knows that the President can override a Congressional veto. The respective figures are 64% and 67% [22].

As Swanson concludes:

There is no point in continuing; the comparison can be multiplied at great length and with the same result. In the absence of good, longitudinal information, we cannot be certain of the meaning of the statistics on religion, but in the presence of comparable information from contemporary politics, I believe that the religious data require our being cautious indeed concerning assertions of the present irrelevance of religion for the personal lives and the institutional commitments of most Americans.

Professor Swanson is quite correct when he says that there is little in the way of good, longitudinal data available on religious practice and beliefs. There were no survey researchers in the nineteenth century, for weal or woe. But there does exist one relatively short-term longitudinal study. In 1965 the Gallup organization replicated for *The Catholic Digest* an earlier study done by Ben Gaffin and Associates in 1952. Exactly the same questions were asked in '65 as in '52. While the wording of the questionnaire left considerable room for improvement, the quality of the data is generally excellent—at least as far as survey research in the sociology of religion goes. Thirteen years is not a very long period. Yet, given the tremendous change in the world from the early fifties to the mid-sixties, and given the fact that the religious revival is alleged to have ended in the fifties and a period of religious decline set in in the early sixties, one would expect that in that thirteen-year period there would be some change in religious belief and practice in the American population. As a matter of fact, Professor

Martin Marty, in his essay on the data, makes a very strong case for expecting that there should be measurable influences of the secularization phenomenon.

However, as Table 1 shows, there is almost no change either in basic doctrinal commitments or toward membership and church attendance for American Gentiles. As far as the Gentiles are concerned, then, secularization, if it is occurring at all, is occurring at so slow a rate that no measure of it could be found in the thirteen years covered by the two studies.

But it might be argued that quite clearly something is happening in the Jewish population, and obviously something is, but the picture here is very ambiguous. Propositional orthodoxy—never as important for Jews as for Gentiles—seems to be declining, while at the same time synagogue attendance is going up, as is affiliation with congregations. Furthermore, as Marshall Sklare has pointed out

TABLE 1[2]

CONTINUITIES AND CHANGES IN
RELIGIOUS BELIEFS AND BEHAVIOR

(Percent)

Religious Beliefs and Behavior	1965			Change from 1952		
	Protestant	Catholic	Jewish	Protestant	Catholic	Jewish
Continuities: Believing in God	99	100	77	0	0	−21
Believing Christ is God	73	88	—	−1	−1	—

TABLE 1[2] (*Continued*)

Religious Beliefs and Behavior	1965			Change from 1952		
	Protestant	Catholic	Jewish	Protestant	Catholic	Jewish
Believing in Trinity ...	96	86	—	−2	− 1	—
Believing in prayer	94	99	70	0	0	−19
Praying three times a day or more ..	23	25	5	+2	− 3	− 4
Believing in life after death	78	83	17	−2	− 2	−18
Believing in heaven ...	71	80	6	−4	− 3	−15
Active church member ..	75	80	62	0	+ 3	+12
Changes:						
Believing religion important in own life ..	74	76	30	−2	− 7	−17
Attending church weekly ...	67	33	4	+5	+ 8	− 8
Attending church at all	67	87	61	—	—	+17
Believing Bible inspired	85	82	17	0	− 6	−28
Reading Bible at least once weekly ...	47	37	31	+7	+15	+17
N	(3,088)	(1,162)	(128)			

in his Highland Park studies, there seems to be a U-curve in religious behavior for American Jews, with it declining in the second and third generations and then beginning to move up in the fourth generation. The complex question for the relationship between religious ceremonial and ethnic identity among American Jews is beyond the scope of this volume, and probably beyond the scope of any sociologist who is not able to operate as part of the Jewish tradition. But if the Jews are being secularized, it certainly must be noted that it is a strange form of secularization which involves more frequent attendance at synagogues and more formal affiliations with religious groups.

But at least religion is declining among young people. Everyone knows this—everyone, in fact, has known it for a long time—and one needs only to talk to the regulars on the Catholic lecture circuit to realize that there are many problems to be faced even on the campuses of religious colleges. (Of course those who are regulars of the lecture circuit have been saying this for the last quarter of a century, but this may be another matter.) What, then, can be said about the faith of the young?

In Table 2 we present data on the religious attitudes and behavior of those who were under twenty-five at the time of the 1965 survey compared with those who were over twenty-five. (Jews are excluded because of the very small sample of Jews which makes it impossible to find enough under twenty-five for serious analysis.)

Catholic young people are, if anything, more orthodox than their predecessors. There are some minor signs of a

TABLE 2

TABLE 2

RELIGIOUS ATTITUDES OF RESPONDENTS UNDER
TWENTY-FIVE AND OVER TWENTY-FIVE IN
RESPECTIVE GROUPS (IN 1965)

(Percent)

Religious Attitudes	Catholic		Protestant	
	18-25	Over 25	18-25	Over 25
There is a God	100	99	100	97
Bible is inspired	76	83	74	86
Pray	99	99	90	94
Life after death	85	81	72	77
Heaven	84	79	68	70
Hell	76	70	57	54
Against mixed marriage	62	62	65	74
Birth control	21	38	17	18
Divorce wrong	37	36	12	10
Church member	87	90	62	76
Clergy not very understanding	59	43	58	50
Sermons not "excellent"	93	70	76	68
Church too concerned about money	23	16	12	15
N	(135)	(1,027)	(259)	(2,829)

downward trend in orthodoxy among young Protestant respondents, but certainly not of such a magnitude as to allow
us to believe the newspaper accounts of the vast apostasy
among the young. Once again we must assert that while
the measures which survey research is able to use are at
best only indicators, and sketchy indicators at that, they
still should be sensitive enough to pick up any massive
changes in religious attitudes and behavior, and as far as
the last thirteen years are concerned, or as far as the dif-

ference between those under twenty-five and those over twenty-five is concerned, the changes are just about invisible.

But surely those who are involved in scientific and academic careers are not able to stand the strain of the tension between science and religion. While the typical young person may not be feeling the impact of secularization, we can reasonably expect the young person who is, let us say, a graduate student in the arts and sciences in one of the great American universities to be seriously caught in the religious conflict. Fortunately, the National Opinion Research Center from its study of the June 1961 graduates in graduate school in the middle 1960's is able to test this hypothesis.

It was assumed that the group most likely to be affected by a secularization trend would be those who were in the Ph.D. programs in the top twelve graduate schools in the country,[3] for in these graduate schools the strongest conflict between religion and academic secularism presumably would be encountered. Table 3 shows, first of all, that there is some erosion of church affiliation among the arts and science graduate students in these top twelve universities but that the erosion is something less than a massive apostasy. Ninety-five percent of the students were raised in affiliation with organized religion, but only 75 percent still maintained a religious affiliation. This, of course, is a considerable loss for the organized church, but it must be remembered that this loss occurs among those young people where presumably the loss will be most massive and that even here, the loss still constitutes only a fifth of the population. The most notable losses are among American Protestants, who suffer a decline of 16 percentage points between the original religion and the current religion of the graduate students. The Catholic loss is only 1 percentage point and the Jewish loss, at least as far as religious affiliation goes, is 4 percentage points.

TABLE 3[4]

RELIGIOUS AFFILIATION OF ARTS AND
SCIENCES GRADUATE STUDENTS IN
TOP TWELVE UNIVERSITIES

(Percent)

Religious Affiliation	Original Religion	Current Religion
Protestant	54	38
Catholic	17	16
Jewish	19	15
Other	5	6
None	5	25
Total	100	100
N 908		

Table 4 turns to the question of church attendance of graduate students. Quite astonishingly, the Catholic graduate student at the top twelve universities is considerably more likely to go to Mass every week than would the typical Catholic in the general population. Protestant church attendance is substantially under the average of the general population of Protestants, though one-fifth of the Protestant students attend church every week in the top twelve graduate schools and almost half attend at least once a month. Interestingly enough, the percentage of Jews attending the synagogue at least once a year is only 1 percentage point different in the graduate school population (62 percent) and in the general population. Thus one can say in summary that while there is some erosion in weekly church attendance among Protestants studying for Ph.D.'s at the top twelve graduate schools, there is no evidence of a notable secularization of either the Catholic or Jewish respondents and that the general picture of church attendance and affiliation among the graduate students is one that indicates an astonishingly high percentage of religious behavior.

TABLE 4

CHURCH ATTENDANCE OF GRADUATE STUDENTS
BY RELIGION (ORIGINAL RELIGION)
(Percent)

Church Attendance	Protestant	Catholic	Jewish
Weekly	21	78	1
2 or 3 times a month .	14	4	3
Monthly	12	5	7
2 or 3 times a year ...	26	9	38
Yearly	12	0	14
Never	15	4	38
Total	100	100	101
N	(510)	(158)	(180)

One might suspect that the graduate students in the "hard" sciences would be the most likely to have problems between their religion and their science. Table 5 indicates that no such close relationship exists across the three major religious groups. The Catholics in the "hard" sciences (physical sciences and biological science) are more likely to be weekly churchgoers than Catholics in the arts and letters, while the reverse is true for Protestants. The Jews in the "hard" sciences are also the most likely to be among those who never attend religious services. The reason for the differences among Catholics may simply be sampling variation or may have to do with the fact that Catholicism has made its peace with Galileo and Darwin but not yet with Kant, Freud, and Comte.

TABLE 5

CHURCH ATTENDANCE BY RELIGION BY FIELD
(Percent)

Church Attendance	Protestant		Catholic		Jewish	
	Sciences	Arts and Letters	Sciences	Arts and Letters	Sciences	Arts and Letters
Weekly ...	16	24	89	68	1	1
2 or 3 times a month..	17	13	—	7	4	3
Monthly ...	14	11	2	7	7	8
2 or 3 times a year ..	26	25	5	13	30	41
Yearly	16	10	—	—	12	17
Never	11	17	5	4	45	31
Total	100	100	101	99	99	101
N	(198)	(310)	(64)	(94)	(73)	(107)

The picture that emerges, therefore, from Tables 3, 4, and 5 is that of a graduate student population of which one-fourth belongs to no denomination and one-fourth goes to church every week. If there is conflict in the minds of these young people between their scholarship and religion, it would be presumed that those who are religious would be the most likely to have problems with the academic environment in which they are studying and that therefore they would score lower on academic values, lower on plans for academic careers, lower on self-rating as intellectuals, and higher on dissatisfaction with the schools they attend, which, by hypothesis, should stand for values that cannot be reconciled with religious faith.

Table 6 shows that while there is some slight support for such expectations, the religious students (Catholics who go to church every week, Protestants who go two or three times a month, and Jews who go once a month) are less likely to have an academic career (73 percent versus 79 percent), and less likely to choose "working in the world of ideas" as a career value (78 to 89 percent). However, there is no difference in the choice of "opportunity to be original and creative" and in self-definition as "intellectual," nor is there any difference in their evaluation of the schools they have attended. Furthermore, the religious students show no particular signs of emotional strain in their position. They are more likely to describe themselves as happy and have fewer worries than their nonreligious counterparts. There was only a slight difference in the proportion reporting an "A" average.

TABLE 6

RELIGION AND ATTITUDES TOWARD ACADEMIA
(Percent)

Attitudes toward Academia	Religious* (320)	Non-Religious (564)
Occupational values:		
Original and creative	85	86
World of ideas	78	89
College or university as career employer ..	73	79
Rating school as "excellent" in:		
Research facilities	72	63
Curriculum	43	43
Students	38	38
Faculty	77	78
Self-description:		
"Intellectual"	45	47
"Happy"	24	17
"Liberal"	32	37
Average number of worries	3.0	3.5
Percent GAP "A"	10	8

* Catholics going to church weekly, Protestants two or three times a month, Jews once a month. (Those whose original religion was "other" are excluded.) N=24.

On two of the items, therefore, there is a negative correlation between religion and academia. But the strength of the correlation is rather weak and does not establish any major conflict apparently for the vast majority of religious students.

While NORC's promises to the schools that participated in the study make it impossible for us to review data for individual institutions, we can say that the patterns reported in these paragraphs persist through all of the twelve graduate schools and that no particular school seems to be more irreligious than any of the others.

To some extent, the rather striking religiousness exhibited by these graduate students in the early 1960's may be related to the appearance on the campus of large numbers of Catholic graduate students, apparently for the first time in the history of American higher education. This is not to argue that Catholics have increased the level of church attendance among other students. It is quite possible, however, that the religious participation levels for Jews and Gentiles are about what they always were but that the inclusion of many Catholics has substantially affected the proportion of the future academicians who are also churchgoers. It may well represent a beginning of a major change in the composition of American academia if churchgoing Catholics in the future hold as many major university appointments as Jews.

Table 7 indicates that the churchgoing Catholics are not very different from other graduate students in their values and career plans. They are more likely to consider themselves intellectuals than the nonreligious of all faiths, more likely to describe themselves as politically liberal, just as likely to plan academic careers, just as likely to value originality and creativity, and less likely to value working in the world of ideas. The last fact is the only evidence that there is any conflict between the ideals of secular academia and fervent Roman Catholicism, and it is slender evidence with which to substantiate the secularization theory.

TABLE 7

RELIGIOUS CATHOLICS AND ATTITUDES TOWARD ACADEMIA

Attitudes toward Academia	Percent
Values:	
Original and creative	86
World of ideas	68
College or university career	79
Self-description:	
"Intellectual"	54
"Happy"	24
"Liberal"	47
Percent GPA "A"	8
N	(121)

How can one reconcile the apparent diversity between the statistical data reported in this section and popular impressions? These impressions are summed up by the editorial writer of the *Christian Century* who said that one needed only to talk to young people for five minutes to be aware that something important was going on.

First of all, it might be remarked that the five-minute conversation was not exactly a sustained interview. Be that as it may, it might be that the measures available in the surveys we relied upon do not tap the dimensions of religious restlessness and revolution that actually exist. Secondly, it could well be that the revolutionary elites are so small that they do not turn up in a national sample. Those who have been seriously influenced by "atheistic" or "secular" theology may be too small a proportion of the national population of young people to effect any change in average figures of religious attitude and behavior. Thirdly, it may be that our impressions are based on the "dog bites man" approach to reality. That most young people differ very little in their religious attitudes from their parents is not news and we do not notice it. But that some think very differently from their parents is news, and we do notice it, though the group that represents disagreement and change may be a very minute part of the total population. It is also possible, of course, that there may be dramatic changes between 1964 and 1965, when the data in this section were collected, and 1967, when the data were published. But as we have noted before, the sociologist is always skeptical of dramatic changes, because the general behavior of large populations tends to be relatively stable. When someone says to a sociologist that things have changed since the data were collected, he is forced to reply that they may have, but that there was no indication in his data that such a change was impending, and that he will be skeptical of it until he sees data as strong as his indicating that a change has occurred. It is also possible that considerable numbers of young people go through agonies over their religious faith but somehow manage to survive the agony without very much change in their basic orientation concerning religious doctrine and practice. Our data may indicate that while the crises of faith are more serious and more frequent than they were in the past, they are not yet necessarily the beginning of a loss of faith or departure from organized religion.

Nevertheless we are forced to assert, on the basis of our data, that while the problem of growing up religiously may be more acute in contemporary American society—or it may be simply more explicit—its ultimate resolution seems not to differ very much from that arrived at by the generations over twenty-five.

There unquestionably are changes in patterns of religious behavior. There may have been, in the late 1950's and early 1960's, something of a downswing in religious activities— at least if we are to use the annual Gallup poll data on church attendance as an indicator. In 1955 the percentage attending church on the Sunday before the poll was taken was 49 and in 1966 it was 44. On the other hand, the data we cited earlier show that between 1952 and 1965 there was an increase of eight percentage points in Catholics' weekly church attendance and five percentage points for Protestants, with a decline of eight percentage points for Jews. It is a mistake, however, to make too much of either set of figures. For reasons we do not understand, there are cyclical patterns in religious behavior, with upswings and downswings apparently following each other at intervals of from five to ten years. In any event, church attendance in the middle 1960's is higher than it was in the middle 1930's, and one would be as ill-advised to argue for a religious revival on the basis of those statistics as one would be to argue for a religious decline on the basis of shorter-range statistics.

It may be conceded, then, that the evidence available to us gives little or no sign of secularization taking place at a rapid pace in American society. But what about European societies? In Professor Swanson's words: "Surveys in Scandinavia, Italy, the Low Countries, Czechoslovakia, and Great Britain report that between 80% and 85% of adults are believers,"[5] a proportion somewhat lower than the United States, but not as overwhelmingly lower as one might expect. Professor Berger somewhat ruefully notes that in one poll in West Germany only 68 percent said they were certain there was a God, but 86 percent admitted to praying.[6]

Professor David Martin's summary of the religious situation in England provides some fascinating data.[7] In one study it was found that

Of the doubters and agnostics and atheists, over a quarter say they pray on occasion to the God whose existence they doubt; one in twelve went to church within the past six months compared with one in three of those who say they believe in God. Over half the nonbelievers consider that there should be religious education in schools. Of those who say they believe in a deity, one in five are definite in their assertion that they do not believe in life after death; one-half say they never go to church, and a quarter never pray, or pray only in church. Of those who don't believe in a deity or are agnostics, nearly a quarter tend to think that Christ was something more than man. Of those who say he was only a man, one in five also say that he was born of a virgin. Nearly nine out of ten believe in God, while two-thirds believe that in some way Jesus was the immediate representative of God. One person in three says daily prayers, 60 per cent have some belief in prayer, and 50 per cent of those who do not go to church still believe in prayer. Only one in fifteen wants to abolish religious education.

In the course of a year, nearly one out of every two Britons will have entered a church, "not for an event in the life cycle or for a special personal or civic occasion, but for a service within the ordinary pattern of institutional religion." Seventeen percent of the population went to church on the Sunday previous to the survey; 20 percent goes every other Sunday; 25 percent every month; and 40 percent every three months.

The British data, when amassed in the rather striking fashion with which Professor Martin presents them, are quite surprising, at least for an American who is inclined to think of England as being a far less religious society than his own. Church membership and church affiliation in England may be less striking than in the United States, but basic religious convictions still seem to persist in great masses of the population. Professor Martin suggests that in England social class differences have a great deal to do with the lower levels of church attendance, particularly among the working class, who, as Martin wryly observes, are inclined with some reason to view the Anglican parson not merely as a squire, but as a squire from the seventeenth century. Father Emile Pin makes a similar suggestion about the religious situation in France. One could conclude, therefore, that in the United States and Holland, for example, social forces have combined to reinforce the high level of church attendance because religious observation and participation are important means of social location and self-definition; while on the other hand, in France and England, social forces have produced exactly the opposite behavior, and one would lose both social location and self-definition if one crossed class lines and attended church too frequently. But religious faith of some sort, however vague, seems to persist despite these problems.

Nor is nonaffiliation all that new. Historians of earlier religion in America point out that the overwhelming majority of the population did not belong to or attend church until the time of the Wesleyan revival. In the year 1760 there were allegedly thirty thousand atheists in the city of Paris. Professor Martin notes that London was a hotbed of religious indifference and nonobservance, even in the midst of the so-called "religious" seventeenth century. "We need only look at Hogarth to appreciate both the brutalized life of the London slums and the literally somnolent piety of the churches. The picture here is a long way from the orderly rural world of a squire like Sir Roger de Coverley presiding over a rural congregation." Martin also cites the case of a village in the eighteenth century which had 401 citizens but only 125 Easter communicants.

Data out of the past are spotty and the data for the present are thin and sometimes contradictory. But it is difficult, in the face of it, to conclude either (a) that religious nonobservance is something new, or (b) that current non-observance in European countries is a sign that the vast majority of men are loosening their hold on religion, or at least on some of the essential religious beliefs. One may write this off as a residue of the past or as a persistent superstition, but the important fact to remember is that the residue persists and so does the superstition, and persists in large segments of the population.

At the beginning of my career as a sociologist, one Catholic colleague dismissed me as a naive empiricist, as I remember it, because I argued that Catholics from Catholic colleges were just as likely to go to graduate schools as Catholics from non-Catholic colleges. I suppose every survey researcher trotting out his tables filled with his beloved statistics is open to the same charge. Do we really believe that tables present "reality"? Do I really believe that the fairly substantial mass of data which I have gathered in this chapter really adequately analyze the nature of modern man's religious problems and dilemmas?

The only answer I can give is that of course I don't, but when someone asserts that he knows many people who don't believe in God, or that a far higher proportion of his friends don't believe in God than are to be found in my national samples, I must respond that my national samples are representative and his samples are not. But the data presented in this chapter do not prove that religion is "healthy" today, nor do they prove that there is no crisis nor hypocrisy nor unbelief nor doubt nor anxiety. They really don't prove much of anything, I suppose, but what they don't prove in a great big spectacular way is the secularization hypothesis, for the data have been considered as a test of the hypothesis and they do not support it.

Man may have been more religious in the past—this we

do not know—more people than the 80 to 85 percent in the Western world who believe in God at present may have believed 150 or 200 years ago, but one wonders how many more. It is also possible that the first real impact of secularization is only now being felt, but it apparently has not been notably felt between 1952 and 1965 in the United States. Nor does the conflict between science and religion seem to be nearly as powerful on the campuses of the great multiversities as it should seem for the secularization hypothesis to receive any substantial confirmation.

To put the matter somewhat differently: I am unaware of any existing empirical evidence collected by sociologists to provide anything but the most tenuous and marginal support for the secularization hypothesis. It has not been proven. And if it were such an overwhelming social development in the contemporary world, one would have thought that there would be at least some impact on the indicators of survey research, no matter how crude these indicators are. Therefore, if one is to project into the future on the basis of the only empirical indicators available to the sociologist, then one would be very hard put to it to project a decline in religion. If the trend, for example, in the 1952 and 1965 studies were to continue for the next fifty years, American Catholicism would be, at least in its essentials, little different from what it is today (though Heaven knows how it might change organizationally). American Protestantism might be faced with some long-run erosion; American Jews might not believe very much formally, but would be flocking to the synagogues with remarkable frequency.

The secularization hypothesis, then, when examined in the light of survey research data, must be judged with Sportin' Life's searching evaluation: "It ain't necessarily so."

Or, in the somewhat more scholarly terms of Professor Huston Smith:[8]

How does it stand with the sacred? . . . (1) More of the sacred persists than meets the eye. (2) What remains of the sacred is durable, sufficiently so that it is not likely to decline much further. (3) On the contrary, the sacred is likely to make a comeback; there are already signs of it. Thus the current low water mark of the sacred represents not so much a transition point in a long-range, irreversible trend as a temporary dip caused by a spiritual drought that another century could easily reverse.

Professor Smith, then, is willing to go far beyond the evidence of the survey data and suggest that religion may be about to enter a much brighter era.

Another indication of the persistence of the sacred can be found in the psychedelic revolution. When Tom Wolfe argues in *The Electric Cool-Aid Acid Test* that Ken Kesey and his Merry Pranksters are, in fact, a total religious community, he is not engaging in mere rhetoric. Kesey and his disciples were engaging in behavior on their trips (whether in a bus or on drugs) that anthropologists of another planet would almost automatically categorize as religious.

At the root of the emergence of the psychedelic is the end of scientific, democratic, secular rationalism and a return to the primordial, instinctual, ecstatic irrationalism that was permitted and even encouraged in most preindustrial societies—the culture and the social organization which has made our economic abundance possible was designed basically to meet the emotional and spiritual needs of Adam Smith's Economic Man. It has not succeeded in its goals and, at least by the inhabitants of psychedelia, it has been found wanting for the service of other goals. Its rational, civil, optimistic, individualistic citizen is, from the viewpoint of psychedelia, only half a man, a man caught in the "work-war-wed bag"; man who, as the Beatles put it, lives a dull, routine life.

I'm not suggesting that the society of bourgeois economic rationalism is about to collapse, but I am suggesting that it is in serious trouble; an increasing number of its more sensitive younger members want to have no part of it, and see the madcap irrationalities of psychedelia as a highly desirable alternative.

Let me quote a wide variety of very different observers to sustain this thesis of mine. In reviewing *The Academic Revolution* by Christopher Jencks and David Riesman, in the June 22, 1968, issue of *The New Republic*, Martin Duberman comments:

Today's student radicals are far more disenchanted than Jencks and Riesman. Their disgust with traditional procedures is grounded in a growing distrust of rationality itself, of the importance of gathering and transmitting factual information and technical expertise. They are angry because they know that their growth depends on more than the accumulation of information. The kind of growth they value—increased openness to a range of experience, emotional honesty, personal interaction—seems actually threatened and compromised by additional proficiency in the manipulation of ideas and things. In a brilliant article in *The Nation,* Michael Crozier, professor of sociology at the University of Paris, has recently put his finger on the source of current student unrest in this country: it is a rebellion against the new hyper-rationalist world, where the capacity for abstract reasoning is considered the gauge of human worth and the precondition for human happiness. Or, as Berger, one of the hippie heroes of "Hair" succinctly puts it to his teachers: "Screw your logic and reason." The rationalist tradition, as the student rebels see it, has produced a race of deformed human beings, or rather, a race of thinking machines; heads (the old-fashioned kind) without bodies or feelings. The new generation does not wish men to become mindless; they wish them to become something more than minds. Unlike Robespierre, who enthroned reason, these revolutionaries search for a way to topple it.[9]

The most self-consciously esoteric of the rock and roll groups (and to date, probably the wildest of them, The Doors) are described by Jim Morrison, their vocalist, in *Life.*

The sound of The Doors is primitive and mystical, the erotic rushes of the organ, the pirouetting of the guitar, the compulsive hide-and-seek of the drums, the dark green lyrics. The music has no meaning, just mood. "Rather than start from the inside," says Morrison, "I start on the outside and reach the mental through the physical." He seeks an unlicensed freedom "to try everything," his mind playing host to angels and devils. He tries to share a catharsis with his audience. . . . He suddenly quotes William Blake: "If the doors of perception were cleansed, man would see things as they are, infinite." Then adds, "We are The Doors, because you go into a strange town, you check into a hotel. Then after you've played your gig, you go back to your room down an endless corridor lined with doors until you get to your own. But when you open the door, you find people inside and you wonder: Am I in the wrong room? Or is this some kind of party?"[10]

A much more rational and empirical description of things is given by Professor Huston Smith:[11]

Item: Lest the preceding episode be discounted on grounds that it is precisely what one might expect from Southern California, I choose my next one from more staid New England. Two years ago a group of eight MIT upperclassmen formed a preceptoral group and asked me to be their instructor. It was to be an independent study project which the students were to conduct themselves; my role was to be that of adviser and consultant. Ostensibly on Asian thought, it began respectably enough with standard texts from the Chinese and Indian traditions, but, as the weeks moved on and the students' true interests surfaced, the original syllabus began to lurch and reel until I found myself holding onto my mortar board wondering whether to continue the role of sober professor or turn anthropologist, sit back, and observe the ways of the natives. For natives in thought-patterns they were; far closer to Hottentots than to positivists. In the end the anthropologist in me triumphed over the academician, for I found the window to this strange and (in the technical, anthropological sense) quite archaic and primitive mentality irresistible. I cannot recall the exact progression of topics, but it went something like this: Beginning with Asian philosophy, it moved on to meditation, then yoga, then Zen, then Tibet, then successively to the *Bardo Thodol*, tantra, the kundalini, the chakras, the *I Ching*, karati and aikido, the yang-yin macrobiotic (brown rice) diet, Gurdjieff, Maher Baba, astrology, astral bodies, auras, UFO's, Torot cards, parapsychology, witchcraft, and magic. And, underlying everything, of course, the psychedelic drugs. Nor were the students dallying with these subjects. They were *on* the drugs, they were eating brown rice; they were meditating hours on end; they were making their decisions by *I Ching* divination, which one student designated the most important discovery of his life; they were constructing complicated electronic experiments to prove that their thoughts, via psychokinesis, could affect matter directly.

And they weren't plebeians. Intellectually they were aristocrats with the highest average math scores in the land, Ivy League verbal scores, and two-to-three years of saturation in MIT science. What *they* learned in the course of the semester I don't know. What I learned was that the human mind stands ready to believe anything—absolutely anything—as long as it provides an alternative to the totally desacralized mechanomorphic outlook of objective science. Some may see the lesson as teaching no more than the extent of human credulity. I read it otherwise. If mechanomorphism is the truth, then indeed the students' behavior reveals no more than man's unwillingness to accept it. But if being *is* sacred, or potentially sacred, the students' phrenetic thrusts suggest something different. In things of the spirit, subject and object mesh exceptionally. No faith, no God; without response, revelation doesn't exist. It follows that the sacred depends, not entirely but in part, on man's nose for it. Given noses as keen for the chase as were those students', if the sacred lurks anywhere in the marshes of contemporary life, it is going to be flushed out. Or better—because it goes further in bridging the subject-object dichotomy—drives which are this strong help to *generate* the sacred.

Smith goes beyond Duberman, beyond Berger, the hero of *Hair*, and beyond Morrison of The Doors, and explicitly suggests that the psychedelic phenomena are a search for the sacred. He is by no means the only one who makes this suggestion. Professor Albert Goldman of Columbia observes that the Beatles are gurus because they "confront their audience with the most basic unbearable truth," and The Doors are shamans, and that The Doors' leader, Morrison, is being particularly shamanistic in the most famous of The Doors' recordings, a Thing called "The End"—a "happening" which concludes in a wild, oedipal fantasy as the singer kills his father and rapes his mother. Goldman also sees The Electric Circus phenomenon as a religious rite in his chapter "The Emergence of Rock," in *New American Review*:[12]

... For all of its futuristic magic, the dance hall brings to mind those great painted caves such as Altamira in Spain where prehistoric man practiced his religious rites by dancing before the glowing images of his animal gods.

Magnetized by the crowd, impelled by the relentless pounding beat of the music, one is then drawn out on the floor. Here there is a feeling of total immersion: one is inside the mob, inside the skull, inside the music, which comes from all sides, buffeting the dancers like a powerful surf. Strangest of all, in the midst of this frantic activity, one soon feels supremely alone; and this aloneness produces a giddy sense of freedom, even of exultation. At last one is free to move and act and mime the secret motions of his mind. Everywhere about him are people focused deep within themselves, working to bring to the surface of their bodies their deep-seated erotic fantasies. Their faces are drugged, their heads thrown back, their limbs extended, their bodies dissolving into the arcs of the dance. The erotic intensity becomes so great that one wonders what sustains the frail partition of reserve that prevents the final spilling of this endlessly incited energy.

Goldman may seem to be exaggerating, as may Professor Richard Poirier of Rutgers University, in the August 25, 1968, *New York Times Magazine,* when he says of the Beatles:

"And the time will come," it is promised in one of [the Beatles'] songs, "when you will see we're all one, and life flows on within you and without you." As an apprehension of artistic, and perhaps of any other kind of placement within living endeavor, this idea is allowable only to the very great.

But it seems safe to assume that such a respectable journal as the *New York Times Magazine* did not think Professor Benjamin DeMott of Amherst exaggerating in his analysis of rock music:[13]

But the chief need, perhaps, and there is no sense, incidentally, in pretending that only rock types share it, is relief from significant life-quandaries and guilt. And chief among the quandaries is one that comes down roughly to this: I, an educated man (or adolescent), thoughtful, concerned, liberal, informed, have a fair and rational grasp of the realities of my age—domestic and international problems, public injustices, inward strains that give birth to acts of human meanness. But although I know the problems, and even perhaps the "correct" solutions, I also know that this knowledge of mine lacks potency. My stored head, this kingdom—my pride, my liberalism, my feeling for human complexity—none of this alters the world; it only exhausts me with constant naggings about powerlessness. What can I do?

.   .   .   .

"Bring along your views," says the rock invitation "Your liberal opinions. Your knowledge of atrocities committed by numberless power structures of the past. Your analyst's ideas about today's Oedipal hangup. Your own manipulative, categorizing, classifying, S.A.T. braininess. You can not only cross the rock threshold bearing this paraphernalia, you can retreat to it, consult it, any time you want—by tuning back into the lyrics. No obligation, in this pop world, to mindlessness. . . .

"But now if you'd like something *else*—if you want your freedom, if you'd care to blow your mind, shed those opinions, plunge into selflessness, into a liberating perception of the uselessness, the unavailingness, the futility of the very notion of opinionated personhood, well, it so happens to happen there's something, dig, real helpful here. . . ."

What is being said is that the rock invitation offers the audience a momentary chance to have it both ways: If I accept the invitation, I can simultaneously be political and beyond politics, intellectual and beyond intellectuality, independent and beyond personal independence.

So psychedelia takes man away from the ordinary into the *really real* which, as any reader of Mircea Eliade knows, is precisely what religions have always attempted to do— to transcend the finite, ordinary, and confused of their everyday life and bring man into touch with the basic realities of the universe. Whatever else it may be, psychedelia is a *religious* movement.

I am not, mind you, saying that it is merely a religious movement—it is certainly influenced by the "camp" of homosexuals, by many self-conscious and explicit psychoanalytic concepts, by a certain amount of psychotherapy, and also, like everything else in the United States, it is to be feared, by pure economic greed. But after the layers of greed, madness, psychoanalysis, and homosexuality are peeled away, there still is in psychedelia something profoundly religious, and it is, in its own way, a judgment on the failures of the Christian religions of Western society.

Even Professor Berger seems at times to be not all that sure that secularization has carried the day:

. . . a little caution is in order. There is scattered evidence that secularization may not be as all-embracing as some have thought, that the supernatural, banished from cognitive respectability by the intellectual authorities, may survive in hidden nooks and crannies of the culture. Some, for that matter, are not all that hidden. There continue to be quite massive manifestations of that sense of the uncanny that modern rationalism calls "superstition"—last but not least in the continuing and apparently flourishing existence of astrological subculture! For whatever reasons, sizable numbers of the specimen "modern man" have not lost a propensity for awe, for the uncanny, for all those possibilities that are legislated against by the canons of secularized rationality. These subterranean rumblings of supernaturalism can, it seems, coexist with all sorts of upstairs rationalism.[14]

Why this survival? Berger tips his hand, I suspect, to what he really believes when he says:

. . . it is not unthinkable, after all, that in a world as poorly arranged as this one, we may be afflicted with "needs" that are doomed to frustration except in illusion (which, of course, is what Freud thought). . . . [But] it is possible to argue that the human condition, fraught as it is with suffering and with the finality of death, demands interpretations that not only satisfy theoretically, but give inner sustenance in meeting the crises of suffering and death.[15]

Whatever the reason, the religious aura and the religious terminology utilized in many of the movements that are in revolt against the scientific, rational, optimistic society would at least give pause to those who are predicting the demise of man's religious inclinations.

We are therefore permitted on both quantitative and qualitative grounds to be skeptical about the secularization hypothesis. Indeed, one might even go further and say that we are obliged to be skeptical about it. But what can we say of the arguments in favor of the secularization theory that were advanced in the preceding chapter?

First of all, it is easy enough to respond to Glock and Stark and the others who think that a "probably true" response means doubt. It may, but then again it may not, and for example when one says "probably true" to a proposition that the Bible is a literal word of God, one may be a doubter or simply be rather more theologically sophisticated. And when one says that he is not "absolutely certain" about the existence of God, he may simply be indicating enough sophistication to know that the existence of God cannot be sustained with the certainty of a mathematical theorem. Thus, the Glock and Stark data may indicate doubt or they may indicate a greater religious and theological sophistication. In the absence of comparative data from the past, we simply do not know, but it is naive to assume that there was not doubt, uncertainty, or hesitation in the past, and it is equally naive to assume that skepticism, uncertainty, and ambiguity became widespread only in the middle of the twentieth century—or for that matter, only in the middle of the nineteenth century.

Similarly, one would be very wise to refrain from arguing to any conclusion from uncertainty about a "personal" God, because "person" does not mean quite the same thing now as it did at the Council of Chalcedon. To say that God is not a person can easily mean, and probably does mean for most people, that He is not a person as I am a person, for in modern parlance, "person" and "human being" mean practically the same thing. He who rejects a "personal"

God may simply be rejecting a highly anthropomorphic notion of God, a rejection which shows not doubt but theological sophistication. Sociologists and journalists who argue that the description of the Deity in abstract terms indicates a decline of faith would do well to consult the *Summa Theologica* of Thomas Aquinas, or the writings of St. John the Evangelist, for if *ipsum, esse,* and *logos* are not abstract terms, then nothing is.

Furthermore, the Bultmannian notion that anyone who turns on the electricity or listens to the radio cannot believe in the mythical assumes that everyone who takes advantage of electronic progress is necessarily committed to the world view of a rather limited number of men who made the breakthroughs in basic research from which the radio and other electronic wizardry proceeded. One can use the radio, turn on an electric light, and be wildly, manically mythological and superstitious. The scientific, rationalistic world view has by no means permeated the general population—not even the well-educated population. And indeed, it would seem from the current psychedelic revolution that the ones most likely "to cut out" on the scientific, rationalistic world view are those who have been exposed to it in its most sophisticated version—that is to say, the version to be found at Harvard, M.I.T., Columbia University, the University of Chicago, and the University of California at Berkeley.

One may also grant that social institutions are not as overtly and obviously religious as they used to be. Robert Bellah, in a masterful essay, has pointed out that while the

United States is religiously neutral officially, we have never-theless evolved a civil religion built around the Constitu-tion, the Declaration of Independence, and in particular the Office of the Presidency, with its great mythic events, such as the Revolutionary War and the Civil War; its heroes and martyrs—Washington, Lincoln and, more re-cently, John F. Kennedy; its ceremonials, most impressively the inauguration of the President or his burial; and its religious vision, most particularly America as the New Eden, the New Canaan, the New Exodus People. So at least in the political sphere, if we do not have an established religion, then we have established a civil religion. Similarly, it is not clear (as we shall discuss in the next chapter when considering the controversy between Talcott Parsons and Thomas Luckmann) that religion does not still have a powerful influence in other areas of life indirectly through the conscience of its members. The involvement of the churches, for example, in both the civil rights and the peace movements would indicate that religion and religious ideals can still have a tremendous impact in areas of society which are officially and formally nonreligious.

Finally, it seems to me that Professor Berger's "sociology of knowledge" approach to secularization might helpfully be balanced by some social psychology. Man's selective ability not to perceive, or to misperceive, things that he does not want to perceive is immense. The vast majority of human beings, even those who are allegedly well-educated, it is to be feared, have no particular desire to expose their religious convictions or their plausibility structures to the threat that confrontation with a different set of convictions or a different plausibility structure might engender. Among those who are willing to take the risk of looking doubt and infidelity square in the face, there are many for whom the risk is not very great, either because the psychological needs that religions serve in their lives are so powerful that they are not inclined to give up their plausibility structure, or because their antagonisms toward their parents are so powerful that they are almost passionately eager to find a new plausibility structure. I would not be in any position to estimate what proportion of the adolescent or early adult population actually takes a critical yet balanced approach to the question of science versus religion, or even admits that there is a possibility of a confrontation between the two, and approaches this confrontation in a curious and unthreatened fashion. Even if we could find a sample of such young people (for I believe if the confrontation occurs anywhere, it will be during youth), we will then have to determine whether in fact the conflict of plausibility structures is as unfavorable to religion as Professor Berger seems to think it will be. Until then, I trust he will forgive me if I am politely skeptical of his plausibility-structure conflict and of his theoretical argument which compels us to accept secularization as a fact—particularly in the face of overwhelming statistical data which does *not* support its factuality.

If, then, there is no definitive evidence to support the secularization hypothesis, why is it so popular? It seems to me that there are any number of reasons for this; all kinds of people—journalists (particularly those writing for religious journals), religious leaders, professional viewers-with-alarm, and other insecure types—have a considerable amount of emotion invested in the proposition that the world is going to hell in the proverbial hand basket. Secondly, theologians feeling very much in the backwaters of the university world are frequently almost pathetically eager to prove that they are as enlightened as are their colleagues in the "real" sciences, who apparently are the people they have in mind when they speak of modern man. Exactly how many such "modern men" are going to be won over by such watered-down versions of traditional Christianity as, for example, Paul Van Buren or the Bishop of Woolwich present may be an open question. But theologians and divinity school students frequently seem even more eager to profess their commitment to secularization than do their colleagues in other departments—a strange sort of envy, to say the least.

I think there is also, among certain religious writers, a rather snobbish contempt for the religion of the masses. Such religion—frequently called "culture religion" or "folk religion"—is "unenlightened," "superstitious," "conservative," and "fundamentalist," all of which may simply be another way of saying that a typical Sunday morning congregation has yet to read Paul Tillich, much less Dietrich Bonhoeffer. The typical elite religionist is horrified by what he considers the "sluggishness" of the religious masses and will be very happy to see their form of religion rapidly vanish from the scene. It is not quite clear, however, who would provide the funds for the religionist's tenured appointment if there weren't religious masses.

But the most important reason for the secularization hypothesis being popular is the persistent belief in certain areas of the scholarly world that religion and science are incompatible. Here, at least, Professor Berger is right. In some parts of academia the plausibility structure is such that religion cannot even be considered, but is dismissed with the facile agnostic answer that one can neither prove nor disprove the existence of God or of the Transcendent. My own impression is that this plausibility structure is more widespread among the social scientists and the humanists than it is in the physical or biological sciences, although interestingly enough, the social scientists and the humanists are likely to fall back on arguments from what they take to be physics or biology to support their position. Perhaps the physical scientists and the biologists are less likely to be so certain about incompatibility because they realize what a chancy, uncertain, unpredictable thing the scientific quest really is.

In addition, there is the fact that contemporary philosophy of language can make a very strong case for the invalidity of "God talk," and that this allegedly "scientific" approach to the use of language seems to provide some kind of reassurance that there is a conflict between science and religion. In other philosophical eras such a jump from logic to reality would leave philosophical heads spinning, but this is a subject beyond the scope of the present volume.

The relationship between religion and society has indeed

dramatically changed—not since the nineteenth century, nor since the fifteenth century, but at least as far back as the emergence of the world religions several centuries before the coming of Christ. As Talcott Parsons (whom we will listen to very carefully in the next chapter) points out, there is an evolutionary process at work in these changes. But it would be far more appropriate to attempt to sort out the highly complex relationships between religion and society, instead of spending our time predicting the demise of religion, a demise which, as we said previously, has been predicted many times in the past, always, at least to date, inaccurately.

The tension between science and religion can hardly be denied, but it is beyond the scope of this volume and the competencies of this writer to suggest when or whether there can be a resolution of this tension. If the impressionistic evidence of Huston Smith is to be believed, there are signs, indeed, that the nonrational may be in the process of overcoming the rational, a prospect which Catholic Christianity at least cannot rejoice over. But the obvious conclusion that one must draw in this chapter is that whether or not there is a necessary, built-in conflict between science and religion, the overwhelming majority of people have not yet felt the tension to be so unbearable that they have been forced to reject the core concepts of religion. It is beyond the province of the sociologist to say whether some day they might. We can say that there is precious little evidence in the available situation to force us to conclude that they will. But of course if one wants to make an act of faith in such an eventuality, one may. Such an act of faith is hardly scientific.

NOTES

[1] Guy A. Swanson, "Modern Secularity," in Donald R. Cutler (ed.), *The Religious Situation* (Boston: Beacon Press, 1968), 811-813. Reprinted by permission of the Beacon Press, copyright © 1968 by Beacon Press.

[2] Tables 1 and 2 are from, "The Religious Behavior of Graduate Students," *Journal for the Scientific Study of Religion*, Vol. V, No. 1 (1965), 34-40.

[3] The top twelve schools were Harvard, Chicago, Columbia, California (Berkeley), Yale, Princeton, Cornell, Michigan, Illinois, Wisconsin, California Institute of Technology, and Massachusetts Institute of Technology.

[4] Tables 3, 4, 5, 6 and 7 are from Martin Marty, Andrew M. Greeley and Stuart Rosenberg, *What Do We Believe* (New York: Meredith Press, 1968), 101-102.

[5] Swanson, *op. cit.*, 804.

[6] I am reminded of the now legendary comment of Peter H. Rossi that he wasn't sure he believed in God, but he certainly believed in evil spirits, because after all, his house was haunted.

[7] David Martin, "Towards Eliminating the Concept of Secularization," in Julius Gould (ed.), *Penguin Survey of the Social Sciences* (Baltimore, Md.: Penguin, 1965).

[8] Huston Smith, "Secularization and the Sacred: The Contemporary Scene," in *The Religious Situation*, 585.

[9] Copyright © 1968 by *The New Republic*. Reprinted by permission of The Sterling Lord Agency.

[10] Robin Richman, "The New Rock: The Most Popular Music," *Life* (June 28, 1968), 59. © 1968 Time Inc.

[11] Smith, *op. cit.*, 594-95.

[12] Albert Goldman, "The Emergence of Rock," in Theodore Solotaroff (ed.), *The New American Review* (New York: New American Library, 1968). Copyright © 1968 by Albert Goldman. Reprinted by permission of The Sterling Lord Agency.

[13] Benjamin DeMott, "Rock as Salvation," *The New York Times Magazine* (August 25, 1968). © 1968 by The New York Times Company. Reprinted by permission.

[14] Peter Berger, *A Rumor of Angels* (New York: Doubleday, 1969) 30.

[15] *Ibid.*, 31.

4 ★ ★ ★

The Theories

Most of the sociological theorists who manifest their on-going interest in the sociology of religion are not directly concerned with the secularization hypothesis but are rather intrigued by the complex and fascinating nature of the relationships between religion and society. Nevertheless, they are doing their work in a world where the hypothesis in one form or another is fairly popular. They are surely conscious of the nineteenth-century prediction that science would replace religion, so there is an implicit dialogue between the theorists and the supporters of the secularization hypothesis. The theorists are, by and large, not convinced. Thomas Luckmann and Peter Berger are the only two prominent writers of whom I am aware who would subscribe to the secularization hypothesis as it was outlined in previous chapters. Luckmann's concept of secularization is an extremely sophisticated one, and coexists consistently with his assertion that religion is built into the human condition. So, while he may take a somewhat dim view of the future of the organized traditional churches, he is by no means willing to predict the decline of religion in the future, but rather suggests the emergence of a new social form of religion. His friend and co-worker, Peter Berger, on the other hand, admits that the secularization mentality is widespread, but Christian that he is,[1] he sums up his reaction by suggesting that while secularization is a fact, its factuality does not mean that it is a true response to reality, and then proceeds to suggest certain "signals" of transcendence which prove that secularization is "wrong." So Luckmann and Berger, each in his own way, end up by defining secularization in a fashion that means anything but the end of religion.

Other theorists are apparently willing to grant much less to those who propound the theory of secularization. There are two main streams in contemporary sociology, running back to the two founders of the discipline, Max Weber and Emile Durkheim, both of whom were immensely interested in religion. The perspectives of these men are not opposed, necessarily, and the most recent writers, such as Luckmann and Berger, attempt to integrate the two. But it is difficult to affirm simultaneously Weber's insights and Durkheim's, and there is some justification for considering the two traditions separately, particularly because they each emphasize a somewhat different social function of religion.

Durkheim was primarily interested in the "function" of

religion. Religion for him was the cement that held society together. It was man's consciousness of the social forces which society brought to bear on his life; it was especially communal awareness of the "effervescence" which societal religious rituals produced. Religion was society's consciousness of itself. The disciples of Durkheim, the most famous of whom was probably the Anglo-Polish anthropologist Bronislaw Malinowski, developed this insight somewhat further and argued that religion was a set of common convictions, commitments, and rituals around which a society could organize itself and without which societal unity was not possible. Religion "integrated" society and preserved it from "disintegration" in times of stress and trouble. Malinowski, for example, was particularly expert in describing how religious ritual prevented society and its individual members from "disintegrating" when faced with the phenomenon of death.

I would place in the Durkheim tradition the very influential American writer on religion, Will Herberg, and the vast mass of imitators and disciples that his famous book *Protestant-Catholic-Jew* has produced. For Herberg there were really two kinds of religion in the United States: first, the "overarching religion of Americanism,"[2] which provides the values and rituals that cement together American society—values and rituals which Herberg thinks are empty of any meaningful Judaeo-Christian religious content; second, the denominational religion which operates within the context of the religion of Americanism. This "denominational" religion makes an American either a Protestant or a Catho-

lic or a Jew, and gives him a means of both self-definition
and social location within the larger and more amorphous
American social structure. One form of religion then provides social integration and another form provides personal
integration within the larger society. In both instances,
however, religion is essentially a society-building apparatus
which helps to create the framework within which men
cooperate with their fellowmen. Herberg and most of his
followers are highly critical of this American "culture" religion because it does not seem to be "prophetic" enough.
This issue is not relevant to the present volume, however,
save indirectly. Herberg and his followers may not like
American religion, but they don't doubt its existence or
staying power.

It can be seen that within their tradition it is difficult to
argue against the continuation of religion. A society cannot be held together without religion. There will always
be a society, and Durkheim concludes, therefore, that there
will always be a religion. Durkheim could have gone further
and argued that religion will always generate a sense of the
"sacred," for the effervescence of the collective ritual action
does bring man into contact with something he perceives
as the "totally other," even though in fact it is nothing
more than the social pressures which society itself generates.
Some more recent disciples of Durkheim would probably
be inclined to say that society can be held together by a
set of conventions, convictions, and rituals that do not
partake of the nature of the sacred. In other words, there
may be a view of the ultimate nature of things common to

societies which deny its transcendence, or at least ignore it. I am unaware, however, of any theorist of this tradition who asserts that such a society has yet come to be.

Max Weber, on the other hand, engaged as he was in a lifelong dialogue with Marxism, stressed the importance of religion as a "meaning" phenomenon. Weber did not want to disagree with Marx about the tremendous influence that the economic structure had on the rest of society. But he also was convinced that economics wasn't everything and that the other structures, including "meaning" structures, influenced society and indeed influenced the economic order. His famous essay *The Protestant Ethic and the Spirit of Capitalism* was designed essentially to show that the "meaning" system which was a Protestant ethic had at least as much influence on religions of the capitalist economic system as capitalism had on the development of the Protestant meaning system. His later works on the religions of the Orient and on Judaism, as well as on American Puritanism, were really part of the same basic intellectual concern. So the Weberian tradition in the sociology of religion focuses more on the meaning function of religion. If one turns back to Professor Geertz's definition of religion as cited in the introductory chapter of the present volume, one can see that Geertz's definition makes little reference to the role of religion in holding society together and emphasizes much more the role of religion in "formulating conceptions of a general order of existence."

Obviously, the meaning and belonging functions of religion cannot be separated. We learn a particular system of religious meaning from the society to which we belong, and the set of convictions which enables us to interpret the general order of existence also facilitates our participation in the society with others who hold the same broad conceptions. Religion as a social meaning is obtained from and reinforced with belonging, and religion as belonging generates social meaning which enables us to cope with events that threaten either the structure of our own personalities or the structure of society.

While in my judgment Geertz has given by far the clearest presentation of the social role of religion, Parsons is the most influential of the present-day interpreters of Weber and also has directly addressed himself to the question of religious evolution and secularization.

In a long essay in a volume honoring the work of sociologist Pitirim Sorokin, Parsons[3] takes sharp issue with Sorokin's notion that "Religiousness *ipso facto* implies otherworldliness, supplemented only by spontaneous altruism." Parsons responds that "The predominantly this-worldly orientation to be found in medieval Christianity and in the 'aesthetic Calvinism' as studied by Max Weber can just as validly be described as religious." He then applies his more general theory of action through the question of religious development and develops what I find to be the most useful theoretical perspective on the sociology of religion yet produced.

Like all other aspects in the course of social, cultural and personality development, it (religion) undergoes a process of differentiation in a double sense. The first of these concerns differentiation within religious systems themselves; the second, the differentiation of the religious elements from the non-religious elements in the more general system of action. In the latter context the general developmental trend may be said to be from diffusions of religious and non-religious components in the same action structures to increasingly clearer differentiations between multiple spheres of action.

To translate the Parsonian prose somewhat, he is saying that in earlier times when societies were still quite simple, elements of belief and behavior that were directly religious and others that were not were fused together in undifferentiated structures; but as society became more complex these simple structures became differentiated into a complex of related but independent structures. Thus, in the primitive society there was no distinction between religion and the society; in the city states of the Mediterranean, religion was not distinct from the political structure, but the two of them were a least in part distinct from the rest of society. And as time went on, Church and state differentiated themselves, each assuming responsibilities appropriate to itself and operating with relative independence of the other. Thus as society becomes more and more complex, and as religion itself also becomes more complex and diversified, the religious components both of society and of the individual personality became more and more differentiated from the rest of society. The process that others might call secularization, therefore, Parsons calls differentiation, and views it as not so much conflict between science and reli-

gion as the inevitable result of an increasingly more complex and specialized society.

A critical religious event which ushered in the modern
world, in Parsons' view, occurred when:[4]

Luther broke through. . . . to make the individual a *religiously*
autonomous entity responsible for his own religious concerns,
not only in the sense of accepting the ministrations and disciplines of the Church, but also through making his own fundamental religious commitments.

But this "individuation" of religion does not, in Parsons'
frame of reference, make religion any less important. On
the contrary, one's choice of a religious "meaning system,"
or at least one's application of this meaning system to concrete situations, is now more important because it has become a matter for conscious choice.

Parsons has applied the theory of differentiation to the
family, arguing against those who saw the importance of
the family declining in modern society. But in Parsons'
scheme of differentiation the family does not so much decline in importance as slough off responsibilities it previously had in the more simple society, responsibilities which
were not primarily familial. But the family itself survives,
and survives with immense importance—perhaps even
greater importance—because it is now free to play its principal role without having to assume responsibilities that
are not properly its own; and its principal role is the social-
izing of children and the facilitation of interpersonal behavior between husband and wife. Similarly, religion has

not lost any importance because it has been stripped of what were, in effect, accidental functions. It is now able to concentrate directly on its essential function of providing a value system of ultimate answers and basic moral postures.

Thus Parsons would argue that while many of the institutions of modern society are not directly under the influence of religion, and may not even acknowledge explicitly the ethical values of the Judaeo-Christian tradition, nonetheless these institutions have, by the very fact that they have evolved from the process of differentiation in the society where the Christian ethic was strong, assumed into their structure many Christian ethical values. This is all the more true since those who operate in these non-ecclesiastical corporate structures do have an ultimate system of meaning and value according to which they will make many, if not most, of their decisions as members of the other corporate structures.

Note well that Parsons is not saying that all businessmen, social workers, lawyers, and doctors are always moral or Christian in their decisions; what he is saying is that to a considerable extent the structures in which they work took their origins from a more simple structure which was Christian in shape, and that those who currently operate in these structures still, to a very considerable extent, operate with a world-view, a system of meaning and of moral value, which was shaped by the Christian and Jewish religions. Men may commit aggressive war, for example, but so they did in the ages of faith; but men also seek peace, and they seek peace on grounds that are implicitly, if not explicitly, religious. Men may cheat and lie and steal, but they also condemn cheating and lying and stealing and strive with a greater or lesser degree of success to curtail these activities in the various structures of society, and they attempt to control them from motivations that are implicitly religious —at least to the extent that the motivations have been shaped by overarching religious value systems. Men, more or less successfully and more or less sincerely, try to help their fellowmen, and while they do so in the name of fear or of economic necessity or political opportunity, they also do so, at least in part, because of ethical considerations which are rooted in the Judaeo-Christian ethical traditions. The fact that they do so as the result of individual initiative rather than ecclesiastical decree seems to Parsons to represent gain rather than loss.

Thomas Luckmann's position is similar to Parsons', yet different in an extremely important respect. Instead of describing separation of religion from other structures of society as a differentiation, Luckmann sees it rather as the result of the inability of religious institutions to generate value schemes which were meaningful or relevant to those other institutions; hence, organized religion is now merely one of the competing value schemes that are operative in modern society. The "new social form" of religion, in Luckmann's viewpoint, is a combination, or perhaps a mixture, of elements from a number of different interpretive schemes —political democracy, Freudianism, familialism, and traditional religion. These value schemes, in his judgment, are still very important because they do provide the interpretive map which man needs to explain himself with reference to the rest of society. But such an ultimate explanation is necessary only in the familial and other interstitial areas of society which are not co-opted by the large corporate structures such as occupation, profession, education, and government. Traditional religion, then, has influence for Luckmann only as part, and perhaps not always the most important part, of the new social form of religion, which includes many other interpretive schemes, and the whole new social form of religion operates only in areas of human life where the new corporate structures have not generated their own self-sufficient value systems.

As I read Luckmann and Parsons, there are two basic differences between them. Both agree that religion is primarily a meaning-giving system, an interpretive scheme. But Luckmann does not see traditional religion as any longer possessing a monopoly on ultimate interpretation, nor as having much influence on man's activity in the large corporate structures. Parsons, on the other hand, as we have noted, thinks that religion does, at least indirectly, affect much of what goes on in the other corporate structures, and I think would also be inclined to give far more importance to the remaining influence of the Judaeo-Christian tradition than Luckmann would.

The question is, to a very considerable extent, one of fact, and the data are not available for us to judge the fact. My own hunch is that the truth probably lies somewhere in between the two positions, leaning more heavily toward Parsons than toward Luckmann. The big American business

corporation, for example, engages in all sorts of socially enlightened behavior, both inside itself and in relationship to
the larger society. Such behavior can even be justified to
some extent in terms of profit motivation, which is presumably the basic principle of productive economy (the
value system which in Luckmann's framework the business
corporation has generated for itself).

This socially enlightened behavior can be justified to
trustees and stockholders as redounding to the long-range
financial benefit of the corporation. Furthermore, corporate
survival is more important than maximizing profits, and
socially enlightened attitudes and behavior are functional
for survival. Yet the Parsonians here could make a response
with telling effectiveness and demand of Luckmann's disciples why the corporation must be socially enlightened to
survive. They could respond by saying that activities such as
donations for higher educational institutions are functions
of the corporation because they supply a steady stream of
skilled personnel. One would not want to deny this, yet
most large corporate grants to education do not automatically guarantee future personnel. On the contrary, many of
the social activities of the corporation seem to be dedicated
to enhancing the corporation's public image rather than
serving any immediate short-run purpose. The critical point
for Parsonians, then, is that they are able to ask why it is
necessary for a corporation to have a public image of being
socially conscious or charitable. And the only reply one
could make is that social conscience and charity have been,
however imperfectly, institutionalized in the value system of

both the larger society and the nonreligious organizations. I think that this is precisely Parsons' point: Modern man working in a large corporate structure which is infused to some extent with Christian values, and himself directed to some extent by the same values, may be behaving religiously a good deal of the time, though it is not always immediately clear to him that it is religious behavior, both because the influence is indirect and because it is implicit.

I am not particularly satisfied with the reply that there is a good deal of hypocrisy in the large modern corporate bodies, be they political, economic, or educational. There was also a good deal of hypocrisy in any age or faith that one might choose to name. The medieval barons, for example, were presumably Christians and devout members of their church, but their behavior was motivated by a combination of Christian values and the functional requisites of economic and military survival with a good deal of rationalization mixed in.

The final point of Professor Parsons' theory should be noted at least in passing, since it is something of a response to Luckmann, although it was written before Luckmann's book. To those who argue that the Christian ethical system has not been able to keep up with the demands of the modern world, Parsons replies with characteristic precision by saying that in fact there has been tremendous ethical progress within the Christian denominations in the past several centuries. The problem is not that there has not been ethical progress, but that the problems have become far more complicated; hence while Christian ethics are superior to what they were, the problems with which they must cope have grown more difficult at a more rapid rate than the ethical systems have advanced.

The dialogue between Parsons and Luckmann which we have outlined here is a fascinating one, and not at all unrelated to the question of the future of religion. For if one sides with Parsons, one would be inclined to say that the Christian religions may have more *actual* influence on social behavior than they had in the past, for now religion exercises influence through the free choice of individual human beings rather than through an elaborate system of external social pressures. If, on the other hand, one sides with Luckmann, one is ready to say (at least up to a point) that the actual influence of organized religion on human behavior has declined somewhat.

Luckmann does not see religion vanishing from the scene, of course; quite the contrary. So depending on which viewpoint we take, we project into the future not the absence of religion, but rather, on the Parsonian side, a continuation of the Christian denominations, with perhaps an increase in their ethical influence; and on the Luckmann side, a continuation of the denominations as part of a new social form of religion, with little influence of religious values beyond the ecclesiastical structure, the family, and interstitial areas of society.

While the data are conflicting, my own inclination, as indicated previously, is to side with Parsons, and hence the projections I will make in the chapters to come will assume, at least minimally, the continuation of the present level of influence of Christian values on the world beyond the religious sphere. For those who would be more inclined to follow Luckmann, let me conclude this argumentation by asking two questions: When, in the whole history of the human race, have religious bodies been as free to disagree with national policies as the American denominations were to oppose the Vietnamese war? and whatever the extent of their impact on the change of national policy, has there ever been a time when the churches have had even as much influence as they had in helping to shape the change in national policy? These may be the good old days.

Perhaps the differences between Parsons and Luckmann are not, in the final analysis, very great. Both agree on several points:

(1) Religion has no, or very little, direct influence on the nonreligious corporate structures of contemporary society.

(2) Religion does have considerable influence, however, and that direct, on man's more intimate relationships, because there is a close link between the primordial ties of family and man's ultimate interpretive scheme.

(3) Organized religion does continue to be important to man, though it must compete with other ideologies in the marketplace of interpretive schemes.

(4) Man makes his own choice in his interpretive schemes, at least within the constraints imposed by his culture and his personality, and is not *ipso facto* by birth handed a ready-made interpretive scheme.

(5) Despite this fact, however, organized religion does

make a major contribution to the formation of the interpretive schemes of a good many, if not most, people.

Both Parsons and Luckmann, then, do not see a future in
which there will be no religion, or even one in which there
will be no organized religion. Parsons is somewhat more inclined than Luckman to see the traditional churches having
considerable influence in contemporary society. Furthermore, whereas Luckmann could grasp the interpretive as
suggesting that the religious voluntaryism of the contemporary scene actually represents a deterioration of the Judaeo-
Christian tradition, Parsons actually sees it as religious
progress. While neither author addresses himself directly to
the question of the sacred or the transcendent, one could
surmise from their work that Parsons would be more inclined to argue that the sacred will continue to be a meaningful category of human existence, while Luckmann would
see other non-sacral interpretive schemes not exactly re-
placing the sacred entirely, but at least winning some believers away from sacral interpretations. Thus if we rephrase
the theoretical question to say: "Is religion becoming unimportant?" both Parsons and Luckmann would say "No."
If we rephrase it to say: "Is the sacred becoming unimportant?" Parsons again would say, in all probability, "No,"
and Luckmann would say "Somewhat."

Both the theories we have discussed are intellectually impressive, and neither has yet been adequately tested against
the available empirical data, although one can perhaps say
in all fairness that, on the basis of the data available, points
must be scored on Parsons' side. But to some extent there

may be an element of "much ado about nothing" in the debate (a debate which, incidentally, the two authors have not carried on between themselves, as far as I know—I am not only the referee of this "debate" but also its promoter). Parsons' brilliant student Clifford Geertz seems to imply that man's ultimate interpretive scheme, willy-nilly, becomes something pretty close to the sacred. According to Geertz,[5] it is the purpose of "religious symbols" *to "establish powerful, pervasive, and long-lasting moods and motivations in men"* which formulate "conceptions of a general order of existence." According to Geertz, man is "least able to tolerate a threat to our powers of conception, a suggestion that our ability to create, grasp, and use symbols may fail us." In other words, man must be able to interpret disorganized and chaotic phenomena that impinge on his consciousness. He must have a system of meaning which can serve as a road map through his life. There are three points where chaos threatens to deprive man not merely of interpretations, but indeed of interpretability. Meaning is required in times of bafflement, pain, and moral paradox —when man's analytic capacities or his powers of endurance or his moral insights are pushed to their limits. The strange, the painful, the unjust, all have to be explained, or the world stops being interpretable.

But these conceptions of the general order of existence are, in Geertz's definition, clothed "with such an aura of factuality that the modes and motivations seem uniquely realistic." In Geertz's theory there are other forms of meaning systems—common sense, science, ideology, aesthetics.

But religion has a different aura from all of these. In his words:[6]

The religious perspective differs from the commonsensical in that, . . . it moves beyond the realities of everyday life to wider ones which correct and complete them. Its defining concern, moreover, is not action upon those wider realities but acceptance of them, faith in them. It differs from the scientific perspective in that it questions the realities of everyday life, not out of an institutionalized scepticism which dissolves the world's givenness into a swirl of probabilist hypotheses, but in terms of what it considers wider, nonhypothetical truths.

Rather than detachment, its watchword is commitment; rather than analysis, encounter. And it differs from art in that, instead of effecting a disengagement from the whole question of factuality, deliberately manufacturing an air of semblance and illusion, it deepens the concern with fact and seeks to create an aura of utter actuality.

Religion, then, represents the "really real." Its meaning system is imbued with "persuasive authority" and is rendered "inviolable by the discordant revelations of secular experience." Ritual is the core of the religious symbol system because "In a ritual, the world as lived and the world as imagined, fused under the agency of a single set of symbolic forms, turn out to be the same world. . . ."[7]

So then religious moods and motivations are "uniquely realistic":[8]

But religious belief in the midst of ritual, where it engulfs the total person, transporting him, so far as he is concerned, into another mode of existence, and religious belief as the pale, remembered reflection of that experience in the midst of everyday life are not precisely the same thing, and the failure to realize this has led to some confusion, especially in connection with the so-called "primitive mentality" problem.

Geertz is asserting, therefore, that in the religions anthropologists know, the meaning systems which cope with those questions which cluster at the outer limits of interpretability are sacred—that is to say, they are linked inevitably with something transcendent, really real, which takes man out of his ordinary life experience and which, in ritual or out of ritual, could frequently even be called ecstatic. While Geertz does not make the leap, it seems to me that one might suggest that any meaning system which attempts to cope with the problems of interpretability has a built-in strain toward the transcendent—even if the system does not address itself to the issue of the transcendent, or even quite explicitly denies the transcendent. I am not suggesting that everyone who professes one form or another of agnostic humanism has necessarily turned his own system of coping with the question of interpretability into something that is transcendent—for something less ecstatic— but it does seem to me not implausible to suggest that in the ideology of the liberal humanist there are certain beliefs and certain symbols which are inviolable, and his reaction when these beliefs and symbols are questioned is out of all proportion to the manifest content of the symbols. It has frequently seemed to me, as one who has for some time worked with the American Civil Liberties Union, that some of the most ardent civil liberties enthusiasts are indeed highly religious people, and that the ACLU is their church. They have cloaked the principles and propositions and beliefs of this organization with, to use Geertz's words, "an aura of factuality that makes the moods and motivations seem uniquely realistic." The fervent "psychoanalyst" or the fervent "scientist" or the fervent political radical can, almost without any advance warning, become quite literally "ecstatic" about their own convictions. To argue that their faith in science or psychoanalysis or political revolution has become "really real" is merely, it seems to me, to state the obvious. When man pushes to the outer limits of interpretability, he also pushes toward the transcendent—or, to put the matter somewhat differently, from the ultimate interpretive scheme to the Ultimate.

From the viewpoint of functional sociology, the distinction between ultimate and Ultimate may be somewhat unimportant. Whether one's means of coping with the final problems of interpretability involves the sacralizing tendency or not, it is still true that the meaning system plays a relatively similar function in man's social behavior. And even if it is neither explicitly nor implicitly sacral, it is still very likely to be something over which man is ready to fight, and if need be, even die. Psychoanalysis, science, liberalism —all have their saints and their devils, their canonical revelation, their mythical events in the past, their unquestioned propositions, and their unassailable ethical beliefs. One need not, it is to be supposed, call them "sacred," but can be content with saying, with Geertz, that they have "a

unique factuality." So be it, then. The sacred or the transcendent, if it is declining at all (as we noted previously, the
psychedelic explosion suggests that it may not be), is being
replaced by new symbols that are clothed with "an aura of
factuality that . . . makes them seem uniquely realistic."
The new religions, then, which claim to be non-sacral have
rather few adherents and seem remarkably similar to the
older sacral religions from the point of view of human behavior, and seem to suggest not that the sacred has vanished,
but rather that even in those who reject it, it survives in
somewhat new forms.

Modern man does not attribute many things to direct
divine intervention, while his ancestors apparently did,
though to what extent even the ancients really believed that
lightning was Thor up in the heavens striking down his
enemies may be problematic; but the "mysterious," the
"awesome," the "totally Other," or, to use Geertz's somewhat more neutral words, "that which challenges interpretability," still remains very much a part of the human condition. Man is still capable of ecstasy when he is wrestling,
particularly in ritualistic fashion, with such dimensions of
his life, and there is no evidence in the empirical data and
no compelling reason from the best theorizing to say that
the mysterious, the awesome, the uninterpretable are any
less present in the human condition than they were in the
past. Religious beliefs of some sort continue at high levels,
and the growing revolt against rationalism in Western
society suggests the appearance of new and perhaps deviant
forms of the sacred. The boundaries between the sacred

and the profane, while they may be more precisely drawn than they were in the past when even distinction was not thought of, but it does not seem accurate to say that the sacred is unimportant because its function is now limited to coping with questions of ultimate interpretability (just as Talcott Parsons argues that it is not fair to say that the family is unimportant simply because it does fewer extraneous things than it did in the past).

So far in this chapter we have discussed the two major traditions of the sociology of religion, the second at somewhat greater length than the first. As it was said at the beginning of the chapter, there is an obvious overlap in the two traditions, for the belonging function of religion and the meaning function overlap. We receive our meaning systems because we belong to human communities, and the human communities are held together, at least in part, because they share common meaning systems. In addition, religion is able to provide us with a form of belonging precisely because it is belonging which enables us to share meaning with others and the meaning in itself is reinforced because it is a communal and not an individual meaning system. Yet the two functions are somewhat separate. I have argued elsewhere that an excellent predictor of the strength of organized religion in a given nation is the relationship between the meaning and the belonging function—that is to say, if, in a given country, one's belief also confers upon one social- and self-definition over against others, then the belief is likely to be more elaborate and the organizational commitment flowing from the belief more vigorous. In religiously pluralistic societies, therefore, orthodoxy rates, as well as church membership and church attendance rates, will be higher than they are in societies where there tends to be either officially or unofficially a single religion, or where the identification of religion and social class makes social class available as an alternative means of self-definition.

The United States, Canada, Ireland, parts of Germany, then, are societies where the measures of orthodoxy and organizational commitment will be higher than they would be in countries like Spain, France, England, and Scandinavia. The level of orthodoxy and of religious involvement is to some extent determined not by how scientific or industrial a country is, but rather by the social and historical experience that it has had, and particularly by whether it is religiously pluralistic or not. The paradox is a powerful one. Religious pluralism, so feared by the ardent defenders of orthodoxy, turns out to be its best guarantee.

Furthermore, in precisely those societies where, because of religious pluralism, there is somewhat higher explicit orthodoxy and more organizational involvement, religious groups are also most likely to produce an elaborate institutional structure, including not only schools and hospitals but also publishing firms, universities, magazines, newspapers, and bureaucracy. While it is fashionable to criticize such institutional manifestations, it also should be realized that in their absence a critical and sophisticated religious elite will also be absent. It is in the religiously pluralistic countries, therefore, that one can expect religion to have its greatest intellectual and social vitality, self-criticism to be the most active, and motivation to adjust to the changing social reality the strongest. Something of a multiplier effect is at work: it is precisely in those countries where religion is most vigorous that the organizational mechanisms appear which tend to maintain and reinforce the vigor; while it is precisely in those countries which lack vigor to begin with that one fails to find the institutional structures to stir up any sort of prophetic restlessness. One need only compare, let us say, Scandinavian Lutherans in the United States and Scandinavian Lutherans in Scandinavia to note the difference.

My own somewhat minor contribution, then, to the theory of the sociology of religion is to argue that the shape of organized religion in modern Western society is, to a considerable extent, determined by the relationship between the meaning and belonging functions of a specific religious tradition in a specific social context.[9] I further suggest that, paradoxically, it will turn out to be precisely in those countries where religion is most likely to play a self-defining role (Herberg's much abused "Culture of Religion") that religion will be most likely to generate a critical, prophetic, and progressive elite.

The first three chapters of this volume about the future of religion have been explicitly negative in their intent. The secularization hypothesis was examined as a possible basis for projection into the future and found unsatisfactory, at least in its more simple forms, for both empirical and theoretical reasons. However, in our consideration of the secularization hypothesis, I believe we have also outlined enough information about the present state of religion to enable us to make a positive description from which we can project into the future.

Religion is man's attempt to provide ultimate explanations of life; in most instances it is a communal explanation, although he also makes it uniquely his own. In this ultimate explanation there is a strain toward the ecstatic and the transcendent. In addition to providing him with an explanation—or more precisely, in the very act of providing an explanation—of the ultimate, religion also furnishes man with a primordial criterion for identifying with others and for defining himself over against others. In earlier and more simple societies religion as a meaning system and religion as a social organization were only vaguely distinct from other culture systems and social organizations. Religion, mysticism, science, art, and polity were all very closely identified with one another; but as society grew more elaborate and complex, differentiated social institutions emerged which specialized in one or the other dimensions and refused to belong to the total conglomerate. Religion then became a specialized institution and a specialized meaning system distinct from and sometimes in conflict with other institutions and other value systems. Its conflicts both with the state and with science have been particularly marked. Nevertheless, religion continues to influence the other structures of society both because most social agents still have their ultimate value systems shaped more or less by the traditional religion and because most social institutions are

rooted in a culture which was more or less formed by traditional religion. As religion has become distinct from other
social institutions and other cultural systems, the individual
religionist has become more of an independent consumer
of religious ideologies and also an independent moral agent
which, as Talcott Parsons points out, is the important contribution of Protestantism for the development of the
Western religious tradition. The individual chooses his own
church more or less freely and determines the extent to
which he will accept the church's teachings and the church's
religious obligations. He determines also to what extent he
will honor his religious ideals in life outside the religious
structure, since the religious organizations can no longer
exercise compulsion to obtain his compliance. If the values
of the larger society are the same as those of a religious
organization (against defrauding the poor or the widows,
for example), then society is as likely to impose religion's
ethical demands on him as it was in the past, and perhaps
more so.

But the differentiation of structures and the religious
liberation of the individual have not meant a decline in the
importance of religion. Men are still in awe of the mysterious, the uninterpretable; while the mysterious may not be
coterminous with life any more, it is still at the core of life.
Faith, superstition, magic, ritual, often in strangely trans-
muted forms, persist in society, and there is no empirical
evidence to indicate that they influence appreciably fewer
people than they did in the past. Whatever empirical data
are available suggest the persistence of both faith and super-

stition, and also, in some countries, very high levels of religious practice, with little change in the time periods for which empirical data are available.

The prosperity of religious organizations seems generally to be independent of scientific and technological advancement (at least in the North Atlantic nations); it seems to be related rather to social and historical circumstances. The religious organization prospers in those countries where it has become effective as a means of self-definition, and particularly in those countries where it has managed to become identified with ethnic background. It is less prosperous in countries where there is an established church or where religious organizations in general have become identified with the middle and upper class.

New humanistic religious forms are evolving. Some of them have merged with traditional religions (for example, the strange love affair between religion and psychiatry) and others have remained more independent (though even religion and science have carried on a long flirtation). But even these new religious forms have a strong tension toward sacralizing themselves. Furthermore, where they attempt to maintain a distinction betweeen themselves and traditional religion, they appeal to very small minorities. Hypocrisy, unbelief, agnosticism, atheism and indifference are not rare in modern society and they *may* be even more common than they were in other eras, but the available anthropological evidence suggests that they were not so very uncommon in other eras either.

If we focus on the United States, we must also note that

American religion, as Seymour Martin Lipset and others have said, has shown a remarkable ability for combining the secular with the sacred for the whole history of the nation. Given the size of American society and its complexity, it is possible for American religion to contain within itself a vast number of seeming contradictions. There is a general religion of Americanism, or a civil religion, to use Robert Bellah's phrase, which ties together the social structure around the office of the presidency and the revealed wisdom of the Constitution. But this established religion has within it values that can be used—as they have been both by the civil rights and the peace movements—to severely criticize the failings of American society. There is furthermore a vast amount of superstition, magic, and folk religion in the United States, but also, in the divinity schools and seminaries, an extremely sophisticated and modernistic version of religion. There is religious conservatism in many grass roots congregations, but also religious radicalism in areas of social conflict and disorder. Radical fundamentalism is in open conflict with liberalism that is at times almost undistinguishable from secular humanism.

American religion is basically activist, yet the majority of the Trappists in the whole world are American, and one must not forget the utopian community tradition in American Protestantism. American religion is very much a part of the Establishment (to use a term that sociologists know corresponds to no existing reality) but is also severely critical of the Establishment. It is institutional, but at present it is producing its own underground.

In conclusion, I would like to suggest that the secularization hypothesis so beloved by graduate students, theology professors, and Catholic journalists could be usefully set aside. Whatever relevance it has as a model for considering the present or projecting the future is also contained in Talcott Parsons' differentiation model, and this latter contains none of the evolutionary or value connotations which the secularization model contains. We would be much better advised if we were ready to agree with Emile Durkheim that on the basis of the present data and the theories currently available to us, there will "always be a religion." We could then turn our attention to an analysis of what is actually going on in religion at the present time and where it seems to be heading.

NOTES

[1] Though by his own admission he is not sure which particular Christian heresy he would be most at home in.

[2] A first cousin, perhaps, to Bellah's "Civil Religion," but Bellah has a great deal more respect for civil religion than Herberg does for the religion of Americanism.

[3] Talcott Parsons, "Christianity in Modern Industrial Society," in Edward A. Tiryakin (ed.), *Sociological Theories, Values, and Socio-cultural Change* (New York: Free Press, 1963).

[4] *Ibid.*

[5] Clifford Geertz, "Religion as a Cultural System," in Donald R. Cutler (ed.), *The Religious Situation* (Boston: Beacon Press, 1968), 643.

[6] Geertz, *op. cit.*, 668.

[7] *Ibid.,* 669.

[8] *Ibid.,* 677.

[9] The difference between the behavior of American Jews and American Gentiles (with the former moving up on measures of religious participation and down on measures of religious orthodoxy) is explained, I think, by the somewhat different tradition of the relationship between meaning and belonging in Judaism.

5 ★ ★ ★

The Future of Theology

Wherever divinity school faculty members gather these days, there is likely to arise a sympathetic discussion of the plight of Harvey Cox and William Hamilton, for these two "radical" theologians were the prophets of one of the shortest-lived theological fashions in recent memory. Cox's *The Secular City* contribution to the optimistic secularist fashion survived a little longer, but according to at least one theologian friend of mine, the "death of God" movement lasted from Selma to Watts.

The bright hopes of a secular millennium in which the radical theology found its origin were naive. The fervent religious enthusiasm of Selma was scarcely justification for believing that the Kingdom of God had come upon earth. Nor were the fires of Watts, Detroit, Newark, Chicago, etc., etc., necessarily signs that we could expect the Parousia on the morrow. The relevant point, however, according to my divinity school friend, is not that the secularist theologians were optimistic, but that they lost their secular optimism so soon. Harvey Cox has gone on to liturgy and eschatology, leaving the celebration of the secular city to others, and William Hamilton has grown silent. The lesson, according to my colleague, is that he who tries to be too relevant may not only be forced to change quickly, but he may also lose something valuable in the change.

Peter Berger is somewhat less charitable than my divinity school acquaintances.[1]

The relevancies they proclaim are, almost by definition, extremely vulnerable to changing fashions and thus of generally short duration. As a result, the theologian (or, of course, any other intellectual) who seeks to be and remain "with it," in terms of mass-communicated and mass-communicable relevance, is predestined to find himself authoritatively put down as irrelevant very soon. Those who consider themselves too sophisticated for mass culture take their cues on relevance and timeliness from an assortment of intellectual cliques, which have their own communications system, characterized by fashions that are more intolerant but hardly more durable than those of the mass media. In this country the maharajas of the world of true sophistication are mainly individuals whose baptism in secularity has been by total immersion. The theologian who wants to take his cues from this source is unlikely even to be recognized short of abject capitulation to the realities taken for granted in these particular circles—realities hardly conducive to the theological enterprise in any form. But even he who is ready for such capitulation should be cautioned. Intellectuals are notoriously haunted by boredom (they like to call this "alienation" nowadays). Our intellectual maharajas are no exception, if only because they mainly talk to each other. There is no telling what outlandish religiosity, even one dripping with savage supernaturalism, may yet arise in these groups, which will once more leave our theologian where he started, on the outside of the cocktail party, looking in.

But Berger also understands that behind the theological fads there lurks an honest human emotion—the search for meaningful commitment. Berger is not opposed to meaningful commitment, but he does not confuse it with theology.[2]

The self-liquidation of the theological enterprise is undertaken with an enthusiasm that verges on the bizarre, culminating in the reduction to absurdity of the "God-is-dead theology" and "Christian atheism." It is no wonder that even those clergy, younger theologians, and, with particular poignancy, theological students who are not simply eager to be "with it" in terms of the latest ideological fashions are afflicted with profound malaise in this situation. The question "What next?" may sometimes be the expression of an intellectual attitude geared to fads and publicity; but it may also be a genuine cry *de profundis*. In the American situation the option of political activity, made morally reasonable by the unspeakable mess of our domestic and international affairs, can serve as a welcome relief, a liberating "leap" from ambiguity to commitment. I do not for one moment wish to disparage this option, but it should be clear from even moderate reflection that the fundamental *cognitive* problem will not be solved in this manner.

The whole situation gets terribly complicated, because I am informed that it is now out of fashion even to criticize theological fashions. It is now unfashionable to mention the shift from neo-orthodoxy to neo-liberalism to neo-eschatology. In other words, it is not fashionable to mention fashions. But fashionable or not, the fashions are likely to continue, as theology scrambles around, sometimes desperately and sometimes pathetically looking for its proper place under the sun.

What is going on, of course, is dialectic between forces which, on the one hand, we might call "conservative," "orthodox," "fundamental," and on the other, "liberal," "progressive," and "modernistic." This is not a new dialogue in theology, and it is interesting to note that the University of Oxford at one time burned the collected works of St. Thomas Aquinas on the grounds that he was too modern (because he had attempted a "relevant" dialogue with the Arab Aristotelians). This dialectic has been accelerated in the last century and a half because of the perceived threat to religion and theology in modern times. Liberalism seems to have had the upper hand in the early part of the present century with the great Karl Barth tipping the scales in favor of orthodoxy in the second quarter of the century and Paul Tillich's Grand Compromise of an existentialist theology achieving popularity in the years after the Second World War. The rapid shift in fashions in the 1960's (from year to year one was never sure whom to quote—Barth, Tillich, Bonhoeffer, Altizer, or Moltmann) may well be explained by the fact that no intellectual genius of the ilk of Tillich or Barth has arrived to replace these prophetic figures.

Catholicism has managed to avoid the dialectic between the conservatives and progressives in theology by the rather simple expedient of freezing theology in the state it was in at the time of John of St. Thomas. But with the close of the Second World War, and more particularly with the Vatican Council, the theological freeze came to an end, and presumably Catholicism will be subjected to the dialectic once again, as it was in the years before the Reformation. However, the great theological names in Roman Catholicism at the present time—Küng, Rahner, and Teilhard de Chardin (who was a theologian, although he may have denied it) —are essentially middle-of-the-roaders, quite traditional in their conclusions but more or less progressive in their style and method.

My point in discussing the theological dialectic is to suggest that anyone who projected, say in 1910, the complete success of theological liberalism and in 1930 the complete success of neo-orthodoxy, or in the early 1960's the complete success of theological radicalism would have been quite wrong. He would have merely fastened himself to one pole of the theological dialectic and concluded that the dialectic was over. But it has never stopped in the past, and there seems very little reason to think that it will stop in the future. The nature of the theological enterprise seems to be that one tries simultaneously to honor and respect the traditions of the past and reinterpret these traditions in response to the demands of one's own situation. Apparently the dialogue between what is "received" and what is "perceived" is built into not merely the theological condition but the human condition. As Edward Duff has put it, we are all born either little Tories or little Whigs.

Therefore the first projection to be made about the future of theology is that the dialogue between theological Tories and theological Whigs will still be going on in the year 2000 and presumably in the year 3000. It would follow that orthodoxy or neo-orthodoxy are by no means doomed. Quite the contrary. The attempt of theological liberals to rewrite Christianity so that it will be acceptable to modern "science" has been conspicuously unsuccessful. The result of such efforts, as for example, Bishop Robinson's *Honest to God* approach, is frequently a watered-down version of Christianity which is unacceptable to most Christians and unconvincing to most scientists. At some point in the future it is not unlikely that this attempt to play marriage broker between religion and science will be abandoned by theologians, though it would doubtless be expecting too much to think that such a happy event will occur in the next hundred years. However, what does seem possible is that more scholarly approaches to both theology and the relationships between theology and other disciplines will gradually substitute for polemical controversy which attempts to refute either religion or theology.

It seems very likely that if the polarization between science and religion is ever to be resolved, it will be resolved only when dispassionate scholarship replaces proselytizing—on both sides.

I am inclined to believe that such a development will take place in the relationship between theology and the social sciences more quickly than it will between theology and the physical sciences, for the cosmology and the evolution with which men like Bishop Robinson are trying to dialogue has long since been abandoned by the biologists and physicists, and the work that these latter are presently engaged in is far too complex for any but the most sophisticated theologian to grasp. On the other hand, we social scientists are, despite the determination of some of our members to be as obscure as possible, still operating at a level of intellectualization that almost anyone can understand. Furthermore, even though I suspect that most of the senior faculty of the social science departments at many universities are hesitant agnostics, there is little tendency for them to engage in polemics against religion. Sociologists of religion, for example, are not those who are pushing the secularization hypothesis; if anyone is doing it, it is the theologians. Furthermore, the "unit ideas" with which many modern theologians are wrestling—person, community, relationship— are also ideas with which, if they were not introduced into contemporary consciousness by social science, the social scientists are at least quite familiar. Thus it seems safe to project that even if the age-old conflict between science and religion is not resolved in the social sciences in the next century, there will nonetheless be considerable interchange between theology and the social sciences.[3]

While it therefore seems likely that the ongoing dialectic between fundamentalist and modern, between liberal and orthodox, will continue in theology, there will still be considerable enrichment of theological enterprise because of the fruitful dialogue between this enterprise and social science—between now and the year 2000 (and beyond). At the present time, we have not progressed beyond the mere gathering of "raw material" for such dialogue. The relatively happy relationship that has existed between religion and psychiatry, for example, has taken place at a rather low level of generalization, with both sides frequently doing little more than exchanging happy sounds about human "growth potential." But I do not believe that the theologians have yet listened very seriously to what existentialist psychologists and other clinicians have said about the dynamics of personality growth and about the necessity for trust, openness, and affection in the growth process. It seems to me, as a nontheologian, that if they had listened closely to what was being said, they would have found much resonance in their own theological tradition, and we would have the beginnings of a much better developed theology of the human personality than we have now.

Nor, despite the vast literature on the subject, do the traditional religions seem to have coped very adequately with the tremendous breakthrough in understanding of human sexuality that Sigmund Freud made possible. Frequently, on the contrary, it seems that the only response theologians have made has been the attempt of certain divines to justify almost every form of sexual deviancy condemned in the past, including even some which, it seems to me, Sigmund Freud would have viewed with dismay.

Yet, given the pervasive sexual symbolism of the Judaeo-Christian scriptures in the Christian liturgy, one finds oneself wondering why there has not been much more original and creative theologizing about sexuality. The raw materials are there both in the religious tradition and in the work of the Freudians and neo-Freudians. But Puritanism still seems to be a hang-up, either because the theologians are unable to respond to the sexual symbolism within their own religion or because they feel the need to be punished for past Puritanism by justifying, if at all possible, adultery, fornication, homosexuality, and, if need be, sado-masochism and bestiality.

To project into the future a dramatic increase in theological concern with personality and sexuality is not too risky, even though only the raw material for such theologizing seems to be at hand. These two subjects are so much a part of the intellectual ferment in the contemporary world and so pervasive in the Judaeo-Christian tradition that it seems impossible for the most gifted theologians to be able to avoid them. I would be tempted to crawl out on a limb and say that in these two areas (or perhaps there is only one area) one might confidently expect the most important theological breakthroughs by the year 2000.

Perhaps sexuality and personality as subjects for theologizing are part of a more comprehensive element of intellectual concern which might be called "anthropology"—in the European sense of the word, meaning a philosophy of men. The social scientists have provided us with an immense amount of information about human life and human relationships. If theologians would cease being threatened, or alternatively, overjoyed by the relatively inefficient secularization model, they might be able to break through to a consideration of the implications for the understanding of man in the advances of the behavioral sciences. Curiously enough, it is the sociologist Peter Berger who, in my judgment, has done the most to point the way toward such a "theological anthropology."

In his *A Rumor of Angels,* Berger examines the human condition through the eye of a trained sociologist to unearth certain "signals of transcendence" which, I should think, should be very exciting to theologians. Analyzing play, humor, trust, passion for justice, and a desire to believe in order, Berger sees in the human condition not only "rumors of angels" but also aspects of the human condition which should be extremely stimulating to those whose profession it is to attempt to systematize man's "ultimate explanations."

It also seems not improbable that a generation of theologians will arise who understand that "community" is not always a good thing—that it is socially dangerous to make community an end in itself, that some communities can be oppressive and tyrannical, and finally, that communities without structures are a contradiction in terms. If the Theology of Man in years to come will necessarily involve a consideration of what the social scientists say about man's personality (and about sexuality), so the Theology of the Church or of the Christian Community will also have to consider what the social scientists have to say about the nature of human interaction in communities. It has often seemed to me, for example, that a good deal of the argument among Catholic theologians about the Papacy and the hierarchy could easily be resolved if the theologians would listen to the obvious sociological fact that any organization must have a leadership and a hierarchic structure of some sort.

A Theology of Man and Theology of Christian Community obviously overlap because man's personality develops in communities, and communities emerge out of the interaction of persons. Given the tremendous surge of interest (to be noted in a later chapter) in the small group fellowships within the Church, and given also the fact that these fellowships, sometimes intelligently and sometimes unintelligently, use the techniques of social psychology, it seems inevitable that theologians will have to face, in the not too distant future, the theoretical assumptions on which social psychology, particularly of the group dynamics variety, is based.

Within Roman Catholicism, one would suspect that the only barrier to theologizing about such matters is the lack of theologians trained in the behavioral science disciplines. Protestants have a head start in these areas, although the tendency of some Protestant theological experts on society and personality to become ethicians, clinicians, or social reformers may stand in the way of more sophisticated theological theorizing (which is not to say that the present author contemns ethics, clinical work, or social reform).

There is also every reason to believe that the theological

interest in death will continue. As Brian Wicker has put it, on the subject of death and the resurrection, Christianity and secular humanism must dialogue. The new popularity of eschatological theologians such as Jürgen Moltmann is closely linked to this renewed concern with the subject of death and resurrection. Furthermore, sophisticated developments in the theology of man, focusing as they must on the human quest for self-fulfillment and union, can hardly escape the question of death. Similarly, it is reasonable enough to expect that the increased interest in the nonrational described in the foregoing chapter may lead to a renewal of theologizing about the mystical and the contemplative. I would not want to go so far as to suggest that the increased interest and practice of witchcraft will lead to more theologizing about angels and demons, but at least the bland optimistic rationalism of some liberal theologians will have to cope with the problem of evil, quite possibly even personified evil, with some other response than the suggestion that eventually science is going to eliminate most irrationalities and most evil.

I am not competent to discuss the impact on future theologizing of linguistic philosophy, nor am I able to predict with any degree of confidence whether linguistic philosophy will continue to be the nearly "official" philosophy of American universities. It does not seem unlikely that theologians will continue to be concerned about language questions.

There are two final projections into the future that one might make: The ecumenical movement is apparently passing out of the "gee whiz" phase and entering into an era of serious confrontation, not only between the major traditions within Christianity but also between Christianity and non-Christian belief systems. This implies that theologians in the future will engage in serious scholarly examination of traditions as traditions, and devote rather less time to attempting to determine whether you and I really agree or disagree. One could expect, therefore, that American theology would increasingly be influenced by the thought of non-Western religious tradition, and presumably in a more sophisticated fashion than is made possible by reading a book or two on Zen Buddhism or spending a summer in Japan.

Finally, one can reasonably expect the continued persistence of what used to be called comparative religion and now has been renamed the history of religion. The work of Mircea Eliade, for example, has been tremendously important in influencing the thought of modern theologians, although the history of religion has been affected by the same amateurism that theologians have often shown in the face of psychology and sociology. One suspects that Professor Eliade is horrified by the use to which his students put his ideas—but no more horrified, one might note, than sociologists can be at the use to which theologians put their ideas.

In summary, it would appear on the basis of the present trends that the liberal-conservative dialectic will continue in the theology of the future and that attempts to end the conflict between science and religion by taking the mysteri-

ous and the sacred out of religion will be no more successful
in the future than they have been in the past. Theology,
nonetheless, is likely to enrich itself by making more sophisticated use of the behavioral sciences. We can expect that
the areas in which the theologians of the future will be
particularly concerned will be personality, sexuality, community, death, language, non-Western religious traditions,
and the history of religion. Attempts will continue to be
made, of course, to reconsider and reinterpret the concepts
of God—and in Christianity of Christ—in terminology that
will be more meaningful to the modern world. We can also
expect that contemplation of the nonrational will occupy
greater theological interest. Apologetic, controversial, and
polemic issues may recede somewhat, though one would be
unwise to venture a bet on their elimination. The theologians themselves will have to face the question of whether
the greater emphasis on man in the theology of the future
will indicate a lesser interest in God, but more theologizing
about man seems to be inevitable. In any event, the theologians will not lack interesting problems, nor, one imagines,
will they lack publishers with contracts for books about
these interesting problems.

NOTES

[1] Peter Berger, A *Rumor of Angels* (New York: Doubleday, 1969),
29-30.

[2] *Ibid.*, 14-15.

[3] In my experience, Protestant theologians are much more at home with, and much more tolerant of, sociology than are most Catholic theologians. The latter either reject social science categories completely (such as the Dutch theologian who affirms that it is impossible theologically to consider a priest a "professional") or insist on using social science terminology without any care to be precise in the meanings they attach to such terminology (the misuse of the word "community" is a classic example).

6 ★ ★ ★

The Liturgy of the Future

The late Monsignor Joseph Morrison, one of the founders of the vernacular movement in the American Catholic Church, used to tell about the day when one of his well-to-do Chicago North Shore parishioners appeared on the rectory doorstep with a gaitered visitor—a very High Church English canon. After being introduced, the visitor remarked that he and Monsignor Morrison had something very much in common, for he was the head of the Latin Society in the Church of England. Morrison and his followers won their battle (though, alas, he did not live to see the victory), and presumably the Latin High Churchmen have not yet given up their battle for Mass in Latin. But the confrontation between these two very dignified and very aristocratic rebels has always struck me as an extraordinarily intriguing symbol; man cannot live without ritual and he cannot make up his

mind whether to change it or not; he doesn't like it the way
it is and he doesn't like it when it's changed, either.

The question of whether ritual will persist into the future
is almost unnecessary. Edward Shils,[1] in describing ritual,
almost by definition indicates that its continuation is inevitable: "Ritual is a stereotyped, symbolically concentrated
expression of beliefs and sentiments regarding ultimate
things. It is a way of renewing contact with ultimate things,
of bringing more vividly to the mind through symbolic per-
formances certain centrally important processes and norms."
Shils[2] adds:

. . . the importance of ritual in any large society lies in its expression of an intended commitment to the serious element of
existence, to the vital powers and norms which it is thought
should guide the understanding and conduct of life.

. . . .

As long as the category of the "serious" remains in human life,
there will be a profound impulse to acknowledge and express an
appreciation of the "seriousness" which puts the individual into
contact with words and actions of symbolic import.

Shils, perhaps going further than most sociologists would,
argues that the sense of the serious is man's religious impulse, and is "given in the constitution of man in the same
way that cognitive powers are given or locomotive powers
are given."[3] Shils does not deny that this sense of the serious
is unevenly distributed and unevenly cultivated; some people
have it almost all the time, others have it intermittently, and
a few are "utterly opaque to the serious."

Shils leaves no doubt as to what he expects the future to be:[4]

To satisfy this universal need for contact with sacred values, for many persons the inheritance of religious beliefs with which our dominant rituals are associated will probably continue to serve. They have already shown much greater tenacity than nineteenth-century positivists and utilitarians assumed. The need for order, and for meaning in order, are too fundamental in man for the human race as a whole to allow itself to be bereft of the rich and elaborate scheme of metaphorical interpretation of existence which is made available by the great world religions. The spread of education and of scientific knowledge, as well as the improved level of material well-being, will not eradicate them unless those who have these religions in their charge lose their self-confidence because of the distrust the highly educated hold toward the inherited metaphors.

The significance of authority is not going to diminish either, nor will the vicissitudes which endanger human life and which infringe on the foundations of morally meaningful order. As long as the biological organism of man passes through stages resembling those now known to us, there will be transitions from one stage to the next; each successive stage will require some sort of consecration to mark its seriousness. Nor will the spirits embodied in nuclear weapons ever allow themselves to be put back into Pandora's box. Mankind will never be able to forget the fact that the means for its very large-scale and almost instantaneous destruction exist and will continue to exist. And with this will be attendant a sense of need to reaffirm the moral standards through which mankind might be protected from this monstrous danger.

There will be a need for ritual because there is a need to re-affirm contact with the stratum of the "serious" in human exist-ence. But the question is whether a new type of ritual which expresses the same persistent preoccupations in a new symbolic idiom will emerge. It is possible that the need for ritual will exist in varying degrees of intensity but that an acceptable ritual will not come into existence and become newly traditionalized, because, on the one hand, the system of beliefs that engendered the inherited ritual is no longer acceptable, and, on the other, the new beliefs about the "serious" will not find a widely ac-knowledged idiom or a custodianship intellectually, morally, and aesthetically capable of precipitating a new ritual.

I am not sure whether Professor Shils believes in God— I think I can remember that once in the classroom he re-marked that there "probably" was not a God—but like most other agnostic sociologists he cannot conceive of a situation in which there will be neither ritual nor religion. One won-ders if, at some date in the far distant future, a functional equivalent of Monsignor Morrison and the Anglican canon will not stand on the doorstep of a house in a well-to-do residential community and discuss once again the changing language of liturgy, for if it is sacred, then it must be in a sacred language; but if it is to be pertinent to man's sense of the serious, then it must be in the language which the serious understand. Or, to put the matter as Everett Hughes did, it is very helpful to confess one's sins in the language in which they were committed.

Liturgy, then, will continue certainly for the next cen-tury, and just as the great dialectic exists in theology be-tween orthodoxy and modernism, so liturgy will also have its own dialectic as represented by Monsignor Morrison and his Anglican counterpart—the dialectic between High Church and Low Church, between desire for elaborate and serious ceremonial and the equally powerful desire for simple, intelligible and "ordinary" ritual. Since liturgy deals with the sacred, it must be a very sacred event; but since it also deals with man, it must be a very human event. It is something very important, so it must be very solemn; but it is also something very intimate, and hence it must be playful and even comic. These two polarities not only contend with one another in ritual but sometimes coexist. The difficulty the Roman Catholic clergy used to experience in repressing their sense of the comic during the elaborate Byzantine court ritual of the solemn Mass need no longer be kept a deep dark secret, nor presumably do the Roman Catholics' Protestant brothers any longer feel the need to repress their feeling that much of the Low Church Protestant liturgy was incredibly drab and boring.

Curiously enough, in the present confused ecumenical condition, Catholics and Protestants seem to be passing in midstream, with the "High Church" strain in Protestantism gaining in vitality just as the "Low Church" strain in Catholicism is breaking out of the constrictions of rubrical legislation and establishing a simple (at times tasteful and at times tasteless) underground liturgy of its own. But just as it is a mistake in theology to project from the fads of the moment into a "secular" future, so it is a mistake to do the same thing in liturgy. Catholicism is no more fated to have a permanent Low Church liturgy than Protestantism is fated to have a permanent High Church liturgy. The tension between the sacred and the profane in ritual is every bit as much of a datum as Professor Shils would have us believe the sense of the serious is in man's constitution, particularly since the sense of the serious coexists with and overlaps with the sense of the comic.

But if the dialectic between the serious and the comic and the High Church and the Low Church is going to continue in the liturgy, what other developments can we expect to take place? I would like to suggest that one of the best places to look for hints as to the liturgy of the future is the world of psychedelia, where much of the authentic, yet bizarre "liturgical" innovation is going on.[5]

First of all, psychedelia is explicitly and consciously an attempt at the ecstatic, whether through drugs or music or a combination of the two. As one commentator on rock music puts it, rock can "move people's muscles, bodies, caught up and swaying and moving so that a phrase . . . can actually become your whole body, can sink into your soul on a more-than-cognitive level. Rock, because of the number of senses it can get to (on a dance floor, eyes, ears, nose, mouth and tactile) and the extent to which it can pervade those senses, is really the most advanced art form we have." And as Professor Goldman puts it:

Like the effect of LSD, that of rock is to spotlight [things] in a field of high concentration and merge them with the spectator in a union that is almost mystical.

The acid head or the rock devotee wishes to escape, tune out, to leave behind the prosaic, dull, "uptight" world of bourgeois society and to achieve union with higher forces as represented by throbbing rock beat with a marvelous clarity of insight furnished by an acid trip. Psychedelia enables rational industrial man and his children to pull out of themselves, to back away from and stand over against ordinary experience and judge it in the quality of new insight or from the perspective of new unity. Such have been the goals of ecstatics and mystics down through the ages, though they have sought their ecstasy much less consciously and in most cases much less artificially than does the psychedelic ecstatic.

Psychedelia is *primordial,* that is to say, prerational when not explicitly antirational. It seeks to put aside the hangups of organized society and its conventions in order to get in touch with the profound underlying natural forces in which we are all immersed, even though the conventions of society cause us to forget this immersion. Psychedelia strives desperately and highly consciously to be natural (which is probably, one might note, a self-defeating quest). The new hair styles for both black and white represent, if in a rather mild fashion in many instances, an attempt, however pathetic, to achieve naturalness.

Those who know about such things tell us that rock and roll music results from a marriage of black "blues and rhythm" music with the "gospel" tradition of black music. In our perspective this marriage was not an accident. "Blues and rhythm" are a superb manifestation of black soul— that is to say—the casual, primordial, sensual style which some blacks have (and which many blacks and many whites would like to have)—a style which is a ribald rejection of the industrial middle-class society which has first of all rejected the blacks. Gospel music, on the other hand, represents an enthusiasm, a vibrancy in religious devotion, which is also part of the black tradition. Putting the two together, one produces a combination of sensualism and near-hysterical enthusiasm which provides the hungup hyper-rationalized white man with two qualities of behavior—sensuality and enthusiasm—which are dysfunctional in his bureaucratized, formalized, computerized life.

The hippy communities, of course, are another manifestation of the highly conscious attempt to return to nature—an attempt which has been well described by Professor Philip Gleason as a new romanticism. Romantic it is, and unsuccessful it probably will be, but as a judgment on realistic secular society it is quite effective.

There are, of course, limits to how natural one can be. A friend of mine who is a medical resident of the University of California hospital (near the Haight-Ashbury district) tells me that when hippies show up in the emergency room of the hospital for treatment, they are usually to be found clutching the Blue Cross–Blue Shield cards.

Psychedelia is, or at least attempts to be, *contemplative.* By this I do not mean that it is quiet, for generally it is not, but I do mean that it tries to break through appearances and see *truth* "like it is." Professor DeMott comments, in the August 25, 1968, *New York Times Magazine:*

. . . . The truth "allowable only to the very great" which Professor Poirier heard in a Beatles' song is an explicit assertion of the arbitrariness of ego separations and of the desirability of soaring free from the mind-ridden world of subjects and objects. "I am within you and without you," these sirens call. "I am he as you are he as you are me and we are all together. . . ."

It must be confessed that this particular mystical insight is not terribly original and does not carry the mystical tradition much beyond John of the Cross or Miester Eckhart, to which the psychedelics will reply that while their insight is not new, they perceive truth as not merely on the cognitive level but in the deepest level of their personality. How deep that is, perhaps remains to be seen, but the significant point about the contemplative development in psychedelia is not that it is new, or not even that it is very meaningful, but simply that it *is*. Mysticism is alive and well and living in San Francisco.

Psychedelia is also *ceremonial*. By this I mean in the present context that it is given to the use of exotic and esoteric symbols—such exotic and esoteric things, that is, as beads and flowers, fancy garments, neck jewelry for men, turtle-necked shirts, Nehru coats, and other such costumes, uniforms, baubles, and trinkets. The Beatles in their nineteenth-century musical comedy clothes, the Merry Pranksters in their American Flag suits, the flower people with their neck amulets, and even the Hell's Angels in their black leather jackets are, in fact, wearing *vestments*. They have donned uniforms to set themselves off from, and over against, the Brooks Brothers gray flannel suit. I note in passing the supreme irony that precisely at the time when the Roman Church is under pressure to give up vestments and avoid ceremonies, the world of psychedelia is creating new vestments for its ceremonies, and that precisely at the time the Roman collar is becoming unfashionable, the turtle-necked sweater and the Nehru jackets have become fashionable. Finally, at precisely the time when bishops are under heavy pressure to yield up their beloved pectoral crosses, neck jewelry for men has become the rage. It's an awfully strange world.

The ceremonial vestments of psychedelia are, in part, a revolt against the dull, drab grayness of the bourgeois and rational-scientific world.

Psychedelia is *ritualistic*. By this I mean not that it has an elaborate system of rubrics which specify in great detail the protocol of behavior, but rather that it achieves its effects through the stylized repetition of sound and action which simultaneously releases the individual from old unions and immerses him in new unities. The rolling of the dervishes, the twisting of the Holy Rollers, the measured cadence of the Gregorian Chant, the repetitive dances of the black Africans and American Indians—are all ritualistic. But the ritual was not ritual for its own sake, as it used to be in the rubricized Roman liturgy, but rather ritual for the sake of producing psychological states in which the religious initiate was able to free himself from the controls and rigidities of ordinary life and "break through" (as the Doors put it) "to the other side." While most of the denizens of psychedelia would not think of their behavior as ritualistic, and would surely deny that the "Go-go" dance floor had anything to do with the religious ritualistic past, the similarity is unmistakable, and perhaps even a link can be traced through the black gospel music.

The psychedelic is *communitarian*—that is to say, it attempts to connect the relationships of everyday living with some kind of concrete and practical application of the insights of mystic union which it has perceived during its shamanistic experiences. Heavy emphasis is placed on being "natural," "out front," "honest," "authentic," and "spontaneous" in one's human relationships; but such honesty, authenticity, spontaneity, and frankness are often mere self-defeating pretexts for aggression and exploitation, and it is rather beside the point. Psychedelia is repulsed by the artificiality, the phoniness, and the dishonesty of the stylized relationships of bourgeois industrial secular society and tries to create communities of its own motivated by common faith and common love, in which true believers may relate to one another as authentic human beings. Hardly any small religious community in human history has failed to make the same claim. The only thing that makes psychedelia different is that it is equipped with the Freudian and Group Dynamics categories and insights which, while they do not necessarily facilitate one's relationships, at least provide one with the words by which one is enabled to *talk about* human relationships intensely. Nothing about Ken Kesey's Merry Pranksters was more religious than their frequently repeated insistence on being "out front" with one another. Perhaps without realizing it, they were merely striving to respond to the gospel injunction to say "aye, aye," or "nay, nay" to their brothers and sisters.

Finally, and I am sure it will come as no surprise to anyone, psychedelia is profoundly sexual, as are most religious phenomena. Sex and religion are the two most powerful nonrational forces of the human personality. That they should be linked, and even allied, in their battle to overthrow the tyranny of reason is surprising only to the highly Jansenized Christian who has lost sight of the sexual imagery in his own faith—the intercourse symbol of the candle and the water on Holy Saturday, for example, or the pervasive comparison of the Church to marriage in both the Old and the New Testaments.

A good deal of the sexual anarchy of psychedelia can be written off as plain old-fashioned lust, which operates in the square world, too, but in a more stylized and conventional fashion. However, in addition, psychedelia is dissatisfied with what it takes to be the narrowness, frustration, and joylessness of that relationship of convenience between the sexes called "upper-middle-class marriage," a relationship which keeps man and woman apart for most of their working day, and requires of each commitment in vast areas of concern and interest which are forbidden by very powerful taboos to the other partner (thus a woman should not be concerned with career, and a husband should not be concerned with childrearing, at least not very much). The psychedelics say, "You squares are hung up on sex; you talk about it, analyze it, worry over it, read books about it, strive mightily to achieve fulfillment with it, but you're too uptight about it to be able to enjoy it. All we do, man, is enjoy it."

On the philosophical level, Norman O. Brown seems to

be arguing for the same goal, and the popular novel *The Harrad Experiment* contends that some kind of relaxed sexual polymorphism is not only possible in the bounds of upper-middle-class society, but would make those who are trained for it far more effective in working within that society.

I have argued elsewhere that within the Christian tradition it is necessary to assert that sex must be joyous and playful and that all human relationships are profoundly sexual in origin. The sexual anarchy of the psychedelics or of *The Harrad Experiment*, for that matter, may not be an adequate response to these truths; but the sexual style of middle-class American society—even, or one might say especially, among its more enlightened and "liberated" segments—is neither playful nor joyous nor sustaining of a wide variety of healthy human relationships. Sex and faith, sex and mystical union, sex and the primordial forces of the world, sex and ritual—these relationships have been part of the implicit wisdom of most human religions. The failure of contemporary Western religions to remember this wisdom is one of the reasons for the reappearance of the wisdom in the world of psychedelics.

I should like to point out that the ecstatic, primordial, contemplative, ceremonial, ritualistic, communitarian, and sexual are words that can be predicative of almost any religious *liturgy* that the human race has observed. I am therefore contending not merely that psychedelia is religious, but that it is liturgical, and indeed a judgment upon us for our own past liturgical failures.

The world of psychedelia, then, emphasizes almost to

the point of caricature the mission of ritual to help man transcend the narrow, ordinary, and even drab routines of his everyday life. It is primordial, ecstatic, communal, nonrational, and sexual; it is, in the literal sense of the word, a form of tuning out and turning on. It has always been this, and man has always been, I'm rather inclined to think, aware that ritual was intended to be ecstatic. At the present time he is explicitly and consciously aware of it and may, for the first time, set about deliberately and systematically to create a liturgy that is ecstatic, or to put the matter more epigrammatically, to turn ritual into a trip.

In addition, then, to the polarities in ritual between the solemn and the comic, the elaborate and the simple, we can add the polarity between the Apollonian and Dionysian. It seems very likely that for the remainder of this century the dialectic between the serious and the comic and the High Church and the Low Church will continue more or less in a state of dynamic tension, but that the major development will be a dramatic resurgence of the Dionysian in the liturgy, the first signs of which, one supposes, are the guitars and the stomping feet of the Roman Catholic folk liturgy. Liturgy will then be used quite consciously to promote the release of nonrational and ecstatic forces in man—to take him out of himself, to open people up to one another, and to enrich and reinforce community ties in which a man finds himself. Liturgy will then turn to the popular arts (or perhaps one should say, return to the popular arts, because there has always been a close relationship between liturgy and art), and particularly to those forms of popular art which seem most ecstatic. It will become quite self-conscious about its own Dionysian character and very explicit about its own therapeutic intent. As a matter of fact, it would be an unwise projector of the future who did not face the possibility that—taking a leaf, so to speak, from the Peyote cult of the American Indians—at least some liturgists of the future will try to mix drugs with liturgy.[6]

Presumably at some point between now and the year 2000 or shortly thereafter, there will be signs of Apollonian reaction. The rational, the orderly, the sedate, and the respectable will begin to reassert themselves in religious ritual. But these forces have held sway for so long that they will very likely have to permit the Dionysian forces to have their day before a new balance is reached.

In addition to projecting more of the nonrational in the liturgy and the resultant outburst of liturgical experimentation, one could also readily project that this theological development described in the preceding chapter will have an impact on the future of liturgy. Thus the use of liturgy to create community, or at least to reinforce it, is likely to increase. Furthermore, the emerging synthesis between social psychology and theology with regard to the small group community is likely to produce a great deal more sophisticated use of liturgical technique in such communities—not always, one fears, in a non-manipulative fashion.

Theologizing about the dignity and the fulfillment of the human personality will also lead, one suspects, to an increased liturgical emphasis on self-fulfillment, self-development, and self-expression in liturgy which may come to mean that eventually everyone will have to play the guitar.

I also am inclined to suspect that we shall see ritualizing of sexuality. As stated before, the sexual elements in liturgy are so obvious that only the most puritanical can ignore them; but since puritanism has ruled supreme for several centuries, the sexual element in liturgy has been ignored, with the inevitable result that the ritual element in sex has also been ignored. The marriage ceremonial and an occasional renewal of the wedding vows are about all that remain of the once complex liturgical apparatus which, in the nature of religions, surrounded sexuality. I truly am not prepared to project what this ritualization of sex will involve, nor do I expect it to happen within the time limits of thirty to fifty years with which this volume is concerned. But given the "serious" nature of sex (Professor Shils' use of the word "serious"), it seems hard to avoid the conclusion that if both sexuality and liturgy become freed from the restraints the past has imposed upon them, it will be recognized that they have much in common.

It is curious that one can be more confident about the future of ritual than one could even be about the future of the traditional religious organizations, for organizations come and go, but ritual is a datum of the human condition. On the basis of the early chapters of this volume, we can assert that religion and indeed the present organized churches seem very likely to persist in at least their present strength into the next century. But in this chapter we are saying somewhat more about the future of ritual; we are looking forward, in fact, to an increase in the importance of ritual in human life, arguing that the psychedelic revolution is but the tip of the iceberg and that the ecstatic, the nonrational, the Dionysian are almost certain to increase dramatically in post-industrial society, if only because prosperity and technology make more time available for such behavior. One fears that Ben Franklin and John Wesley would be terribly disappointed. The industrial society which their frugal, controlled, disciplined ideals created has made it possible for their spiritual descendants to go back to orgies; not only, indeed, can they go back to orgies, but they can even do so in the name of mental health.

NOTES

[1] Edward Shils, "Ritual and Crisis," in Donald R. Cutler (ed.), *The Religious Situation* (Boston: Beacon Press, 1968), 735. Reprinted by permission of the Beacon Press, copyright © 1968 by Beacon Press.

[2] *Ibid.*, 746-47.

[3] *Ibid.*

[4] *Ibid.*, 747-48.

[5] I am reminded of a dialogue between two of the wittiest people I know—Mrs. Daniel Callahan and Professor Jaroslav Pelikan. Someone (Mr. Callahan, I believe) had remarked that if one wishes to know what the critical ideas in religion will be in twenty-five years, one need only look at the breakthrough of ideas in the secular world today. Mrs. Callahan then suggested that, similarly, if one wished to know what the liturgy of the future would be like, one need only look at the most important art forms today. "In that case," she

added brightly, "we can probably look forward to a liturgy of the absurd." "My dear," replied Mr. Pelikan, "that you have already."

[6] As the very name of the Dionysian tendency in liturgy indicates, the Peyote cultists were not the first ones to seek artificial stimulation to facilitate their ecstatic release.

7 ★ ★ ★

The Clergy of the Future

If one reviews the vast social science literature on the religious functionary, one is forced to conclude that man typically has been quite ambivalent about his clergy. The shaman, the witch doctor, the prophet, the seer, the diviner, the magician, the priest, have all been absolutely necessary. You really cannot have a religion without a functionary or a group of functionaries that play some or all of these roles. Religion not only deals with the Ultimate and the uninterpretable; it also deals with the powerful, for if something is ultimate or uninterpretable, it is certainly powerful. To cope with the powerful and the uninterpretable requires a certain amount of expertise and also a certain amount of specified personality characteristics. The average man is either unwilling or unable to acquire this training himself; he is afraid of the sacred or he doesn't have time for it, or it is not the sort of thing that a really male member of his tribe wants to do. Just the same, he needs the religious functionary, fears his power, respects him for his knowledge and perhaps for his courage, and he is rather ambivalent about the sacred; it's a good and necessary thing—we absolutely have to have it for human life—and yet it is a disturbing thing, threatening, at times unpredictable and at other times uncomfortably demanding. The religious functionary represents the sacred, and man is as disconcerted by the functionary as he is by that which the functionary represents.

Similarly, the holy man, it is to be presumed, has certain ambivalences with regard to his own role. He is conscious that he is a man apart, a man with special powers, privileges and prerogatives. He rather enjoys his holiness, the respect he is owed, and the power he possesses. Nevertheless the power is a burden, and a number of holy men have reacted to their vocation much the way the Prophet Jonah did—they try to get the hell out of Nineveh.

Being a man apart has its advantages and its disadvantages. One is respected but perhaps not exactly trusted. One is turned to in time of trouble, but not always welcome in time of merriment. One is expected to provide answers in situations where there are no readily available answers, but one's advice is not particularly welcome in other situations. One is viewed sometimes as a superman, but at other times as being something less than a man, and occasionally even as pertaining more to the world of women and children. One is supported because one is necessary, but supported grudgingly because one's supporters rather wish that one did not have to be supported. Indeed, one has certain powers and prerogatives that are never quite secure because it is an inconvenience to one's fellow tribesmen to concede these powers and prerogatives and an affront to the radicals in the tribe who think that one is a bit of a charlatan. One is assumed to be God's man and expected to live a life certainly apart from other men, yet if one fails to provide the particular form of revelation that the tribe expects from God, one will be in very deep trouble with the other members of the tribe.

The tribe, of course, can be a university religious foundation, a parish in the west of Ireland, a horde of Mongolian warriors, or the Senate and people of Rome—it makes little difference. If he goes too much in one direction or the other, he is certain to be criticized and, given the varying opinions and values of members of his tribe, he is almost certain, in the eyes of some, to have gone too far in one way or another.

Just as there is a dialectic in theology between the orthodox and the liberal, and in liturgy between the Low Church and the High Church, so there is among the clergy a dialectic between what we will call, for want of better terms, the monastic and the secular. The assumption of the former emphasis is that the clergyman should be a man apart, isolated from the world, living a life devoted particularly to things pertaining to God and the sacred, practicing great detachment, studying sacred writ, and devoting long hours to prayer and meditation. On the other hand, in the secular tradition, the cleric is expected to be a man of his people, understanding the problems of men, as the Epistle to the Hebrews remarks, because he has been taken from among men. Since the sacred cannot be separated from the profane, he is expected to be deeply involved in the problems of the profane, to be a warrior or a lord of the manor, a government leader, an artist, a musician, a scholar, a teacher, a family man, very much a member of his tribe in every way possible.

In the preceding chapters we suggested that the dialectic between polarities would continue for the rest of the century, save in the case of the Apollonian-Dionysian polarity in ritual. But there is no reason to think that in the immediate future there will be a resurgence of the monastic clergy. Monasticism is by no means dead in the Western world, as the resurgence of long hair, unwashed faces, vegetarian diets, and long periods of contemplation in the hippy communities and similar less far-out groups will attest, but monasticism among the clergy seems to be at very low ebb and shows no signs of being renewed.[1] Over the long haul it seems very likely that the monastic, otherworldly, clerical tradition will reassert itself, but at present there are almost no signs of such a development.

On the contrary, all the emphasis to be observed among the younger generation of the clergy is "incarnational." It is argued that the cleric must be a man among men, that he must be like his fellowmen if he is to understand their problems and be relevant to their needs. It is even argued, at least among Catholic theorists, that the clergyman is merely a man who happens to preside over the Eucharist or happens to fulfill certain community functions; in no other respect is he to be different from his fellowmen, nor is he assumed to be called to any greater degree of holiness than they.[2] Even the neighborhood parish, which by the monastic standards of the past was quite secular, is not nearly secular enough for the modern cleric. He must be "where the action is," which seems frequently to be in the inner city or in picket lines, or any other place where the most agonizing of social problems are to be found. If he happens to be a Roman Catholic, he cannot possibly be involved in the human condition, while living the partially monastic life of the celibate.[3] For only a married man can be sufficiently committed to the things of this world to be able to be a clergyman for people who live among the things of this world.

It is not the function of the sociologist as such to pass judgment on this sort of theorizing. He need only note that some of it seems to be based on theological assumptions which are themselves subject to a fashion change almost without notice. However, it also does seem to the sociological observer that the thrust for a more "involved," "committed," and "relevant" clergy transcends any theological fashion, for just as liturgy was too long constrained by a rigid Apollonian rationalism, so the clergy, and particularly the Roman Catholic clergy, were too long isolated from their people by the invisible but highly effective barriers of "clerical culture." It is therefore inevitable that the opposite tendency will exercise strong influence in the years to come.

It would seem safe to predict, on the basis of the present

evidence, that in the immediate future of religion the clerical function will increasingly be seen as a limited one. There
will be an increase in part-time clergy and limited-term
clergy. The former are those who will work at another occupation and serve as clergy in their spare time and on
weekends, while the latter are those who make a commitment to the clerical state for a given period of time, but
not for life. The part-time and limited-term clerics will not
necessarily contemn their function of being "God's man,"
and ministering and interpreting the sacred to their people,
but they will insist that this function does not exhaust their
personality and does not define the scope of their life and
interests.

One presumes that there will also be a much greater
plurality of ministries in the churches. Ministry to the local
congregation will no longer be seen as the only model, or
the only really acceptable model, of clerical behavior. Specialized "apostolates" among the poor, the rich, the educated, the uneducated, the young, the old, the central city,
the suburbs, the factory, the ghetto, the high-rise, the university and, for all we know, the nursery school[4] are already
widespread; given the instincts and values of the young
clergy, these apostolates are likely to become even more
widespread. It is an open question, of course, whether "specialized ministries" are more effective (whatever this means
from a religious viewpoint) than other ministries. Though
in the long run it may even be questioned whether they
are more humanly satisfying than the ministry to a local
congregation, in the short run, they are different and more

exciting and liberate one from the routine and the paper-work and the small talk and narrowness of the local con-greation. The proportion of religious functionaries, there-fore, in local congregations is likely to decrease, although it is altogether possible that the development of part-time and limited-term ministries will lead to a substantial in-crease in the number of clerical personnel available, but the direction of movement may be different. Instead of clergy-men moving out into worldly positions, we may witness the opposite phenomenon of men in other and "more worldly" professions moving into the clergy.

It also seems very likely that, given the feminist move-ment, the number of women who are considered to be clergy will increase, although there will be great resistance to accepting them as equally clerical with men. The Roman Catholic Church is in a rather peculiar position in this respect from the point of view of functional sociology. It has for a long time had far more female "clergy" than male, since the religious sisters play an obviously clerical role and are obviously intended to be "holy women." However, they have also been—not unexpectedly, perhaps—second-class clergy, in that they were denied the central powers of rule and worship. In practice, many of them did rule in con-vents and colleges and hospitals, with more power and more effectiveness than many male clergy. Nevertheless, even though it is now conceded that the deaconesses of the early Church were actually considered to be in "sacred orders," Catholic women have been denied access to the priesthood and the episcopacy.

It seems almost certain to the present prognosticator that pressures from women for access to these positions in the clergy will increase between now and the year 2000. How successful they will be remains to be seen. The prognosticator is forced to observe that over the very long run the pressure for equality for women in the clergy is likely to overcome even the most unassailable of theological arguments.

None of the projections made thus far in this chapter are original with the present writer, although his prediction of the eventual renewal of the monastic is not frequently heard at present. But it should be emphasized that the increase of part-time clergy, limited-term clergy, special apostolate clergy, and even female clergy does not indicate the disappearance of the full-time local congregation clergy. On the contrary, given the fact that the overwhelming majority of the rank-and-file members of American religions want, and seem to be willing to pay, a full-time local clergyman, one necessarily projects into the future that this will continue to be the most common and typical manifestation of the clerical role. As we will discuss in the next chapter when we consider the structure of the churches of the future, the relationship between this local clergyman and his congregation may change substantially. It is also very likely that he will have much more specialized training and will be hired by his parish (or assigned to his parish) because his special skills in counseling or youth work or community organizing are felt to be particularly relevant to the needs of the congregation. This professional competence will also presumably give him greater freedom and independence vis-à-vis his congregation—which he will insist on, in any event.

But despite his new skills and his new independence—and presumably his higher salary—the local clergyman will still be primarily concerned with being a minister of the sacred to his people in a fashion not so very different, essentially, from that practiced by all his predecessors in the role of holy man. Much may well be changed in the role of the clergy of the future, but some things will change very little; in particular, his function as an intermediary between the sacred and the profane, between the everyday and the transcendent, between the ordinary and the mysterious, does not seem likely to change very much at all.

Not only does modern man need affection and reassurance in his interpersonal relationships, but now, courtesy of Psychology 101 and other such marks of civilization, he knows he needs it, and his search for expressiveness in interpersonal relations becomes even more persistent and insistent because it has now become quite explicit and conscious.

Dragastin shrewdly observes that in this respect the priest is much like the psychiatrist—both are expected to play a reassuring, affective, and loving role. It is easy enough to dismiss a psychiatrist as a hired friend (the words are used in the pejorative sense), but it is nonetheless the reassurance, trust, and affectionate environment which friendship creates that the psychiatrist is supposed to provide, to enable his client to release the positive and healthy forces within his personality. It is much more difficult to specify quite precisely how the clergyman is to play his affective role, but he is still expected to play it, certainly by his "clients" and increasingly by himself.

A shortcut way out of the problem is to train the clergyman as a clinician so that he can engage in what is called "pastoral counseling." There is no reason why a priest or a minister or a rabbi, or any other holy man, cannot be trained as a therapist and play the therapeutic role, but in such cases it is difficult to distinguish between what is precisely psychiatric and what is precisely religious.

However, it does not seem likely that all clergymen are either willing or able to become licensed therapists or even that it would be a good idea if the two roles were permanently identified, for there is much healing that is done in ordinary human relationships—much reassurance, much affection, much encouragement that can be communicated in situations where formal therapy is neither necessary nor appropriate. To say that the clergyman should be a specialist in relationships, or even, to put the matter somewhat more lyrically, to say that his specialty should be love, is simply to indicate that he is to continue his traditional role of providing reassurance.

I do not believe that the ideas expressed in the foregoing paragraphs have become quite so explicit or formal either in the clergyman's role conception of himself or in the opposite role expectations of his people; nor have the ecclesiastical training institutions yet set themselves to produce the kind of warm, available, open, and trusting personalities that would be required to play such a role.[5] In addition, it is quite easy to confuse this expressive role of the clergyman with the "morale officer" function of the military chaplain (at least as it is judged by some commanding officers), and the hail-fellow-well-met style which is so painfully present in many clerics. In the meaning that the word would have for psychology or sociology, the expressive person must be far more than that. In a highly rationalized, formalized, technological society, expressive personalities are at a premium. If the present debate over the role of clergymen is ever settled, settlement will involve strong emphasis on its expressive nature.

We are therefore projecting into the future, and perhaps the not very distant future, increased emphasis on the recruitment and training of clergymen who are skilled in the expressive and affective modality of behavior. It seems very likely, in fact, that this will be a far more important development than the emergence of part-time or limited-service clergy, or even specialized apostolates, for this development will tell the clergyman, full-time or part-time, limited or permanent, generalist or specialist, what he is supposed to do and who he is supposed to be. The theological developments that we are projecting concerning personality, sexuality, and community, and a new liturgical emphasis on the nonrational, will also, we suspect, confirm and reinforce the development of the expressive clergyman.

One could be momentarily sidetracked by the somewhat appalling thought that the clergyman described in this chapter would somehow be a combination of a guru and a tealeaf reader. But if one changed the word slightly and said merely that he would be a combination of a saint and a wise man, one would possibly be saying the same thing and would be on much safer ground.

If this modification of the clerical role develops rapidly enough in the next several decades, one could also legitimately expect a reversal in the decline of vocations which apparently affects all religious denominations. The clerical life has lost its appeal for young people because it is perceived as so rigid, so bogged down with unimportant minutiae, so trivial in its impact on society, and so underpaid. Many of those who would otherwise be inclined by their personality and background toward the ministry or the priesthood seek refuge in academia or in social work or political reform movements, possibly because their need for affective activity is more challenged in these occupations, though they may soon discover that the affective is severely limited in these contexts too. But if the ministry can be presented as an occupation which in fact is merely an institutionalized niche for expressive and affectionate behavior, then one suspects that in an age of hyper-personalism the ministry will not want for recruits.

Some religionists will be inclined to view this development with dismay, arguing that the clergyman is essentially a prophet, bearing witness to God's prophetic judgment on a sinful people, or at least spreading, in a charismatic way, the teaching of the gospel. The sociologist is in no position to argue with such a value judgment, though he is obliged to point out that the expressive dimension of the holy man's behavior has always been present, sometimes more so and sometimes less, in the clerical role, be it monastic or secular. Whether being a "professional" lover is appropriate or not for a cleric, the sociologist cannot himself determine. However, if he has read the gospels, he at least remembers the phrase, "By this all men shall know that you are my disciples, that you have love for one another."

NOTES

[1] There was a great growth in the Trappist community in the United States during the Second World War, but this development had apparently ended well before the Vatican Council.

[2] This sort of theologizing, of course, must contend with the overwhelming burden of history to the contrary and the completely overwhelming burden of sociological and anthropological evidence that such a clergy will not satisfy a people.

[3] Father Joseph Fichter, in one of the classic put-ons of our time, has even written that for Catholic bishops to be as "relevant" as they ought to be, they should be *obliged* to marry.

[4] The present writer was once upbraided by a parishioner for not doing something for nursery school children.

[5] For such, it would seem is the nature of the modern "holy" man, and perhaps, indeed, of any truly holy man.

8 ★ ★ ★

The Future of the Churches

In theology we noted a polarity between fundamentalism and modernism; in liturgy, between Low Church and High Church and between Dionysian and Apollonian; in clergy, between the monastic and the secular. A somewhat similar polarity can be observed in religious organizations, at least in the Judaeo-Christian traditions, where religious organizations as such exist in a far more developed fashion than in any of the non-Western churches. We shall call this a tension or dialectic between church and sect, but it should be carefully noted at the very beginning of this chapter that by our use of the terms "church" and "sect" we do not intend the same sense as the words have in the long and tedious sociological literature on the subject; we do not mean them as distinct kinds of organizations. Most of the groups described in the literature as sects are not sects in

our sense of the word at all, but rather, small denominations.

By "sect," we mean, rather, the tendency with a large
religious body to form small, personal, intimate religious
communities of fellowship. Occasionally these fellowships
may break away and form new organizations, and in fact
most of the churches and denominations that have emerged
in the Christian tradition have been formed in this way.
But they represent only a very small minority of the sect
groupings that have been formed within Christianity. Most
sects do not break away from the parent body but are content to have their own intimate community within the
framework of the larger organization.

On the other hand, by "church" we mean the tendency
within a religious organization to evolve a formalized, hier-
archical, and juridic social structure with elaborate speciali-
zation of roles and institutionalization of behavior. No such
"church" is ever so elaborate or so juridic or so formalized
that it is unable to tolerate sects within its framework. So
every religious organization of any size contains within it
both church and sect manifestations, although at different
times in its development the emphasis may be on one or
the other dimension. The ability of an ecclesiastical structure to tolerate within its boundaries large numbers of
diverse communitarian groups is a strong guarantee
against schisms.

Schisms have occurred in Christianity precisely at that
time when the church dimension and the sect dimension
were not able to coexist with each other inside the same

organization. One need only compare Catholicism in the thirteenth century with Catholicism in the sixteenth century to see the effect of the loss of the sect dimension. It is very unlikely that the Renaissance Roman Church would have been any more able to cope with the Franciscans than it was with the Lutherans; and it is also at least possible that Luther and his followers would not have been forced out of the Church of the thirteenth century (or have chosen to leave, depending on one's interpretation of history).

Those believers who prefer the sect polarity within religion will generally justify themselves in terms of trying to recapture the simplicity, the intimacy, the spontaneity, and the informality of the founder and his group of followers, whereas those whose thrust is toward the hierarchic and the organizational will argue that they are trying to obey the founder's injunction to spread the religious faith to the ends of the earth, and that any religion that attempts to be universal will necessarily have to have some kind of formal hierarchic structure.

The sect members will contend that the formalized structure becomes sterile, rigid, autocratic, and impersonal, whereas the church supporters will respond by saying that sect is narrow, particularistic, self-centered, and frequently self-deceiving. Both are right.

At present, however, there is a certain romanticism about the communitarian as opposed to the institutional. Popular versions of sociology, going beyond the nostalgia for *gemeinschaft* society to be found in many of the greats of the sociological tradition, see institutions as the root of all evil; spontaneity, intimacy, informality are not only extraordinarily important values in human relationships, but the only values. At a more sophisticated level, the writings of Professor Thomas O'Dea have described at considerable length the diminution of religious fervor with the elaboration of religious organization.

But as valuable as Professor O'Dea's writings are, they by no means present the whole story; as I have noted elsewhere, the religious fervor of the followers of Jesus of Nazareth was not, at least in the initial instance, all that pure or authentic. Furthermore, if it should happen that the institutionalization in Christianity through the centuries has produced any more than twelve authentic Christians at the present time, it would, quantitatively at least, represent a net gain over the apostolic community. Institutionalization surely presents problems, but it is also inevitable in the human condition because it is the only way man knows to cope with large numbers of people and with a complex division of labor. Finally, at the present state of our knowledge of social organizations, it need no longer be said that institutionalization inevitably leads to a decline of spontaneity and intimacy among the members of the institution. While all the mysteries have not yet been solved, the sociological study of large organizations has at least proceeded far enough to be able to assert not merely that large institutions can sustain small intimate groups within their boundaries, but even that the maintenance of these groups is positively conducive to—indeed, imperative for—the health of the large organization.

Since the religious organization that is healthy has room within its boundaries for both church and sect, the church must facilitate healthy growth of the sects, particularly by preventing them from becoming too gnostic and self-centered, and the sects must promote the healthy development of the church, particularly by preventing it from becoming too juridic and stratified. However, this is a theoretical position that has not yet won wide popular support. At present in North Atlantic Christianity, there can be no doubt that the sect phenomenon is undergoing a powerful revival.

Among the most enthusiastic supporters of the so-called underground church there is the assumption that, much like the Marxist state, "institutional Christianity" is going to wither away and what will emerge will be a new "institutionalist community." They find support for this idea in the sociological writings of certain theologians who also see the institutional structures of Christianity as moribund and look forward eagerly to the emergence of a "religionless Christianity," by which they mean Christianity unencumbered by the religious institutions formed in the past.

Most of this is sheer romanticism. Ecclesiastical institutions are about as likely to wither away as is the Marxist state. The sectaries in the underground church have made the mistake of thinking that they and their friends are Christianity, whereas in fact the overwhelming majority of those who profess allegiance to the Christian denomination are not in underground communities and are not likely to join such communities. Penultimate, the witty columnist of *The Christian Century* (a magazine not generally known for its wit) has observed that the underground church has

come above ground and institutionless Christianity is rapidly developing its own set of institutions. From reports
about the above-ground meeting of the underground at
Boston College a year ago, it is not a very efficient kind of
institution, though it tends to be a rather rigid one.

Penultimate tells me that he was deluged with nasty
letters when he suggested that the institutionalist communities were already developing institutions of their own. But
Penultimate's problem is that he knows a little bit more
about human society than do the underground sectarists—
he understands that every community, even if composed
of two persons, quickly establishes routinized patterns of
behavior, some of which even become normative—and that,
fellows and girls, is what institutions are.

In the preceding paragraphs I have perhaps been somewhat too harsh on the emergent communitarian groups
within Christianity. Although no hard data are available,
I have the very strong impression that many, if not most,
such groups are not attempting to create a "religionless
Christianity" or institutionless communities (and some of
them even realize that such goals would be a contradiction
in terms). They are merely trying to establish within the
ecclesiastical structures new religious groupings that corre-
spond to what they perceive to be their own religious needs
and interests. However, such groups are not the ones that
get the headlines. The main intent of the previous paragraphs is to warn that it would be exceedingly unwise to
project into the future the demise of religious institutions.
What is much more likely to happen is that the various

underground communities will become institutionalized themselves, and new sect-like phenomena will appear in the decades to come.

Therefore we do not predict for the future of religion the decline of religious institutions. In the short run—that is to say, the next thirty to fifty years—the communitarian dimension is likely to receive more emphasis than it has in the last fifty to one hundred years. The theological concern over personalism, Low Church liturgy, and expressive clergy will all create a climate in which informal and intimate religious movements will flourish—much, one suspects, to the dismay of some institutional bureaucrats. But the bureaucrats will not lose their jobs.

Nor does it seem likely that religious denominationalism will vanish from the scene, despite the growing enthusiasm over ecumenism. For denominationalism is not merely a matter of doctrinal difference, and perhaps not even primarily a matter of doctrinal difference. Region and social class, and above all, ethnicity, are so intertwined with religious denominationalism that the denominational society will come apart only on that improbable day when social class, region, and ethnicity cease to be important variables which define themselves. Some "mainline" Protestant denominations—upper-middle-class, Anglo-Saxon, and North Eastern and Middle Western may possibly merge, but the Evangelicals, Baptists, Lutherans, and Roman Catholics, to say nothing of many smaller religious groupings, are too different from the mainline WASP groups for a merger to be very probable in the foreseeable future. A Southern Bap-

tist and a New England Episcopalian are not likely to feel
very much at home with each other, nor for that matter
will the liberal Methodists and the Missouri Synod Lutherans be much at ease with each other. Because of the
profound importance of the American social structure of
religious denominationalism, it seems likely that at least
for the remainder of this century, American ecumenism
will continue to be a denominational ecumenism, with
progress, such as it is, occurring within a complex of a con-
tinuance of the various traditions. Inner communion, joint
worship, social cooperation, endless theological dialogue,
and more tolerance for mixed marriages will characterize
the relationship of the elite in the various denominational
traditions. But it must be remembered that ecumenism
tends to be an elite phenomenon and the rank-and-file
memberships of the denominations are less likely, one suspects, to be enthused about such threats to their social
identity.

Within Roman Catholicism, various ethnic "denominations" may also engage in somewhat more dialogue with
one another, but it would be unwise to assume that these
denominations will disappear. On the contrary, with the
new conscious interest in ethnicity currently appearing in
American society, ethnic denominationalism within Roman
Catholicism may take a new lease on life.

If the Protestant denominations and the Catholic "denominations" are not likely to go out of existence, one
would be even less inclined to predict the merger of Christianity and Judaism, an idea so patently absurd on the face

of it that it hardly merits consideration. One would like to project an increase in Jewish-Christian cooperation, but data recently made available on the growth of anti-Catholic feeling among Jews makes one hesitate to offer such a projection.

Despite all these qualifications, however, inter-religious and inter-denominational dialogue and cooperation will surely increase in the future and become more realistic and more sophisticated by the end of the present century.

In an early chapter we mentioned that American religion was extremely pluralistic; not only are there many religious denominations, but within the denominations there are many competing forces. On the basis of the present situation, there is no reason to project the triumph of some of these forces over others; the churches, for example, will continue to be suspicious of their mushrooming bureaucratic structures (Paul Harrison, in his famous book *Authority in the Free Church Tradition*, discusses this problem with a great deal of insight). Yet, given the complexity of the society in which the religious denominations must operate, the bureaucracies will continue to increase and hopefully will grow somewhat more efficient. At the same time, the demands for increased autonomy for local congregations may well prove to be irresistible and the picture will be made even more complicated by the fact that local clergymen will also insist on their own independence vis-à-vis the congregation that hires them. The elites within the churches will continue to be critical of the social and religious conservatism of the masses, while the masses in their turn will be critical of the religious and political radicalism of the elites. Furthermore, the academicians, scholars, and "free" professionals within the churches will be highly suspicious of the institutional bureaucrats who, they may argue, are more interested in preserving their own careers than in stirring up the churches to prophecy. (The academicians having tenure don't have to worry about preserving their own careers.) Those elements within the church which are concerned with social relevance will continue to insist on direct action confrontation with those "establishment" powers who insist on maintaining what is defined as an unjust status quo. On the other hand, the much quieter and much less visible contemplative and mystical elements within the churches may rise up to protest against all the fervent and, to them, manic activity.

The strains and dilemmas, then, that face the organizational structures are not likely to dissipate in the future, and are likely indeed to grow more intense. One projects, therefore, that over the course of time religious institutions will become more sophisticated and more flexible. The leadership will understand that, given instantaneous communication and much better-educated membership, institutional bonds must be loosened somewhat if the churches are not going to be completely disrupted. They will also realize that some sort of formal (or more likely informal) "rules of the game" will have to be established within the denominations in order to provide a context for the many dialogues, debates, controversies, and confrontations that will continue to rage. Such a development would not be

new; the medieval Church was able to be much more tolerant of diversity within its structure than any of the denominational organizations which emerged at the time of
the Renaissance. One could project this tolerance for diversity within denominations as being caused not by virtue on
the part of denominational leaderships, but simply by the
increased awareness that the only alternative to organizational tolerance is civil war. Some denominations may learn
this quicker than others.

I do not feel qualified to project the future of relationships between ethics and religion, though I do think that
the ethical systems will be partly influenced by a dialogue
between theology and social science. I am not persuaded
that ethical systems will disappear, to be replaced by a complete situationist approach, but I do think that there will
be much more emphasis on the individual agent making his
own moral decisions in the context in which he finds himself. Furthermore, morality will, I suspect, stress more of the
whole orientation of a person's life than individual actions.
Finally, one somewhat hesitantly predicts the gradual demise of puritanism as the churches slowly integrate Freudian
insights into their thinking.

There is a certain undramatic quality about the projections of this chapter, as well as those in the previous chapters. We do not believe that the institutional church is
going to vanish from the scene, nor do we believe that religious denominations will be eliminated by ecumenical
mergers; nor do we see any decline in the internal confrontations now occurring in most religious denominations.

All we are projecting is greater sophistication; that religious organizations will be more tolerant of other denominations, more tolerant of a diversity of emphases within themselves, more tolerant of sect-like communities within their boundaries, and finally, more tolerant of the individual ethical agent in the situation in which he finds himself. We do not think that religious schools, religious journals, and religious organizations are going to disappear, though there may be some occasional retrenchment in their size and diversity. Quite the contrary. We are inclined to suspect that religious bureaucracies will become larger, more elaborate, hopefully more sophisticated, and more inclined to rely on social research to provide them with the information necessary for decision-making.

But the projection of greater tolerance and organizational sophistication—which really means virtually the same thing —in the future is, we think, not an unimportant or minor prediction. As a matter of fact, in its own way it is probably a more startling prediction than would be a prediction of the end of organized religion. If the present organized religions should disappear, they would simply be replaced by new religions which themselves would shortly become organized. But to predict organizational tolerance and sophistication is to suggest, we think, that democracy will ultimately win its battle with authoritarianism among the clergies.

Talcott Parsons is quite correct when he says that the Reformation strongly reinforced the principle of individual autonomy within the Western religious tradition, a principle which may have been latent in medieval Catholicism and at times perhaps not so latent, but which certainly came into its own at the time of the Reformation. However, neither Professor Parsons nor anyone else would argue that the Protestant sects or denominations were democratic in the sense that American society is democratic—that is to say, capable of tolerating and even promoting diversity, freedom, and spontaneity within a context of agreement as to what were the "rules of the game." Perhaps only the Episcopal Church has beeen able to achieve such a power for diversity in the democratic context, but in the United States, at least, Episcopalianism is both a small and a well-educated denomination. I am suggesting that by the end of this century, most other religious denominations will have begun to recognize that in a large, complex society pluralism, individual decision-making, collegial governance, tolerance for diversity, protection of fundamental rights with due process provisions, and tolerance for controversy are absolutely essential for any large corporate organization that is to survive with some degree of health. I am therefore predicting that in the years to come the churches will become more democratic in this broad sense of the word—not so much out of conviction as out of necessity. The implicit voluntaryism contained both in the Reformation and in the American democratic style (and vigorously defended by the American Catholic theorists of the nineteenth century) will come pretty close to having its final organizational effect on the religious denominations. This may very well be the most important historical development in religious organizations since the Reformation.

9 ★ ★ ★

The Future of Religion

I have the sneaking suspicion that this rather small volume will make me more enemies than anything I have ever written, for I am sure many readers will find this an infuriating book. Virtually all the expectations for the future of religion held by many devout Americans—both devout religionists and devout agnostics—are judged by this book to be highly improbable. Yet the social scientist finds himself thinking that most revolutionary expectations are highly improbable.

It is extremely instructive to compare that genera of science fiction which deals with mechanical wonders to that much more fascinating genera which may be called social science fiction. The famous TV program *Star Trek* is a model example of the latter, for despite all the wonderful gimmicks that the *Star Trek* Enterprise and its crew are equipped with, both they and the "aliens" they encounter in their journey through the quadrants face the same very human behavioral problems that we face today and our ancestors faced before us. Human society does improve, man does become somewhat more skillful in his relationships, but not very much, and progress is relatively slow. Therefore, to project into the next thirty to fifty years a religious situation that is not greatly different from the present one is the only course open to someone who believes that moral and social growth in the human race can only accelerate somewhat over its past rate. The acceleration may even be very impressive compared to the past, and yet the behavior patterns, the social structures, the human relationships of the beginning of the twenty-first century are not likely to be too different from those of the middle of the twentieth century. Therefore, much that is expected to happen to religion will not happen.

1. Religion will not lose its adherents. In the United States this means that membership, church attendance, and doctrinal orthodoxy will persist at the levels reported in the 1952-1965 surveys. In countries such as England where organizational participation and church attendance levels are much lower, this means minimally that levels are likely to fall no lower than they are, and even as Professor Martin suggests, they may begin to rise slightly.

2. Nor is religion likely to lose its "influence." It will still provide at least a substantial component of the ultimate interpretive scheme or meaning system with the overwhelming majority of the population. It will still have indirect

impact on society through the religiously influenced ethical decisions of its members, and it will also have direct influence over society both because it provides part of the underpinning for general social consensus and because in certain critical situations the direct confrontation between religion and social problems contributes to the amelioration of these problems.

3. The sacred is not being replaced by the secular. Scientific rationalism will not generate a new faith. It will not provide satisfactory alternatives to those modes of coping with problems of interpretability currently popular with the overwhelming majority of the population. The transcendent may no longer be coterminous with all human activity, but the "really real" will still persist where the core problems of interpretability are faced. On the contrary, in fact, the popularity of the current revolt against scientific rationalism suggests that new and deviant forms of the sacred will emerge.

4. Full-time parochial clergy may diminish in relative proportion to part-time specialized or limited-term clergy, but the full-time clergy working with the local congregations will continue to be the majority of religious functionaries.

5. Simple, dignified, Low-Church Apollonian ritual will not replace all other forms of liturgy. Rather, on the contrary, Dionysian and ecstatic ritual may be at least as common as the Low-Church liturgy of the underground.

6. Religious institutions will no more wither away than will the Marxist state. On the contrary, they will become

more elaborate and more sophisticated and more dependent on academic experts than they are at the present time.

7. Neither will denominations cease to be characteristic of the Western religious scene. Whatever ecumenism is likely to exist at the end of the present century and the beginning of the next century will, in all probability, continue to be denominational ecumenism.

8. Doctrinal orthodoxy has not breathed its last, and there probably lurks in divinity schools even now some *fin de siècle* Karl Barth ready to rise up and bear prophetic witness for orthodox traditions.

9. The local congregations will not perish. They may become smaller and more diversified, but the tendency for man to worship in the community where he lives with his wife and family and where he sleeps at night will not be eliminated—not, at least, as long as there are suburbs.

10. The crusade for social and secular relevance will not either sweep away the passivity of the religious masses or drive the masses out of the churches. Neither will the this-worldly religious concerns currently so popular eliminate the otherworldly residue which survives even in American religion. On the contrary, it is possible, perhaps toward the end of the present century, that the otherworldly and the monastic will undergo a notable resurgence in American religion. The monastic element within deviant social movements such as the hippies might even lead us to expect that this resurgence could occur much sooner.

Yet when one asserts that religion at the end of this century and the beginning of the next century will not be so very different in many important respects from what religion is now, one is not necessarily taking a conservative position unless it is decreed that anyone who denies the predictions of the self-defined liberals is *ipso facto* a conservative. There will be a number of very dramatic changes in North Atlantic and American religion in the next three to five decades. But these trends toward change receive somewhat less publicity than those revolutions that, according to this book, will not occur. This does not diminish the importance of those changes that will occur.

1. There will be a tremendous increase in the dialogue between religion and the social sciences, with both religion and the social sciences learning something in the process.

2. Social science will realize that religion plays a pervasively important role in human behavior, and no group of social scientists gathering together in the year 2000 to prepare a symposium on the year 2050 will assume that man's ultimate interpretive schemes are not worth considering.

3. Religion, and theology in particular, will be increasingly concerned about the interpretability of man and the human condition; those signals of transcendence that Peter Berger so ably describes point the way, it seems to me, to a much more intensive investigation of the meaning of man's life and death and new life by religion, with the aid of the categories of thought and the insight of the behavioral sciences.

4. There will be much more emphasis in religion on personality development being equivalent to religious develop-

ment, and on the central role of sexuality in this developmental process. Religion will not be equated with psychiatry; indeed, on the contrary, the tendency to make this equation will decline. But the role of man's ultimate interpretive scheme in guiding and defining his personal and sexual development will be much more thoroughly explored and much more comprehensively taught than it is at present.

5. For both theological and organizational reasons, religion will be much more concerned about small, intimate, fellowship congregations and will use the insights of social psychology to facilitate the religious and personal development of the members of the intimate friendship religious groups.

6. The next thirty years will see a consolidation of democratic and tolerant organizational theories and practices in most American religious denominations. Religion will be much better able to cope at the end of the century than it is at the present time with internal diversity.

7. There will also be considerably more sympathetic understanding of the wisdom of alternative religious traditions (both Christian and non-Christian) and also of those who profess these alternative traditions. Religion, therefore, will be able to tolerate not only more internal diversity but also more external diversity, and indeed we can begin to profit from these two kinds of diversities, or at least to realize that we can profit from them.

8. There will be a further strengthening, both in theory and in practice, of the responsibility of the individual as the ultimate religious and ethical agent in the context of

the circumstances in which he finds himself and of his personal relationships with those around him. The individual agent will not be seen as a lonely protestant, other-directed man making decisions entirely by himself, however; he will be seen, rather, as a responsible agent within an historical and existential community.

9. There will be substantially more emphasis in religion on the nonrational than there is today—both the ecstatic and Dionysian nonrational and also the reflective and the contemplative and mystical nonrational. One suspects that there will also be a further decline of puritanism, as part of which one may even begin to see the verification of Marshall McLuhan's prediction that sexuality will be much "cooler" (that is to say, better integrated with the rest of life) than it is at present.

10. It will be much clearer at the end of the century than it is at the present time that the clergyman's role function as "God's man" in contemporary society implies a considerable development of his skills as an expressive and affectionate leader—a man who generates authentic personal warmth, trust, and reassurance.

If all of these projections of change are pondered carefully, it would seem that they do represent very important religious developments—developments which will make religion at the end of the twentieth century something very, very different from what it was at the beginning of the twentieth century. It may even seem, in fact, that they are more meaningful, more exciting, and more "revolutionary" than the popular and almost mystical predictions of a re-

ligionless, secular, and institutionless Christianity. Whether
or not they are more exciting is open to debate, but what I
think is not open to debate, at least on the basis of present
sociological theorizing and data collecting, is that the second list of ten projections are reasonably likely to occur, and
the first set of ten are most unlikely to occur.

Will this religion of the future have more or less influence
than the religion of the present? Will it have more or less
members? Will it have more or less impact on the world
of ideas? Will it be more this-worldly or more otherworldly? To a considerable extent, the answers to these
questions depend on how one defines one's terms. But to
hazard some guesses, religion will have about the same
proportion of members as it has at present. It will surely
not have less influence on society than it does now, and it
may even have more impact on the world of ideas, since the
NORC data cited earlier suggest that a greater number of
young intellectuals are more religious than were their
predecessors.[1] It probably will be simultaneously more this-
worldly and more otherworldly, as we finally begin to understand that the sacred and the secular and the this-worldly
and the otherworldly are not necessarily contradictions, and
that indeed they have coexisted down through the whole
history of religion, particularly through the history of American religion.

What we are predicting, then, is that in the next thirty
to fifty—even a hundred—years we will not witness the
rapid, or even the gradual evolution, but rather the slow
evolution of religion. Of course it is possible that the whole

process of human history has been so shaken in the last half century that the projection of trends in the future, on the basis of the past and the present, is no longer valid. It may be that one can no longer assert that just as religion has evolved into the present, so it will continue to evolve into the future, perhaps at an accelerated rate. Furthermore, even though religion has outlived all those who prophesied its doom in the past, it may be that the human condition has changed so much that this time the prophets of doom are correct.

But the assertion that gradual evolution is being replaced by revolutionary doom must be made on the basis of poetic insight or metaphysical abstraction, or, quite possibly, revelation. Nothing in the data or the theories of behavioral science enables the sociologist to cope adequately with propositions made on the basis of data from poetry, metaphysics, or access to the plans of the Deity. All he can reply to such arguments is to observe that we will just have to wait and see—and if there happened to be a bookmaker present, he could add that the prophetic revolutionary might put his money where his mouth is.

NOTES

[1] As we noted before, this may simply be the result of the appearance of large numbers of Roman Catholics on the American scene for the first time.